A Cure for Humanity
by
A. L. Haringrey

A Cure for Humanity

By A. L Haringrey

Published by Gurt Dog Press

All rights reserved. No part of this book may be used or reproduced in any manner without written permission of the publisher, except for the purpose of reviews.

Editing by Nem Rowan

Proof-reading by Jordan Ray

Cover design by Tommie Glenn

Allura font by Rob Leuschke

This book is a work of fiction and all names, characters, and incidents are fictional or used fictitiously. Any resemblance to actual people or events is coincidental.

Copyright © 2021 A. L. Haringrey

Digital ISBN 978-91-986729-1-6

Print ISBN 978-91-986729-2-3

To Sophie

A Cure for Humanity

A. L. Haringrey

Chapter 1

Gyldan Crawford was the first to admit that he was quite privileged. As the personal assistant of one of the world's richest men, his pay cheque was nothing to be sniffed at. This was just as well, given his housemates had a much harder time getting employed than he did. He didn't mind being the one who paid for the majority of the rent and bills, of course. After all, Gyldan was lucky.

He had been born a human.

His housemates were not so lucky in that regard.

So, Gyldan could hardly hold it against them. Employment didn't come easily to vampires and werewolves in this society.

Other perks of being the personal assistant of one Albion Saint-Richter, CEO of Caladrius and major shareholder of more companies than Gyldan could remember, included VIP invites to some of the most exclusive parties in the world. It also included a free pass to jump to the front of any queue (via the power of the words, "*I know Albion Saint-Richter*").

Yes, being in Albion's employ ensured many privileges for Gyldan.

His own office was not one of those privileges.

Because he spent so much time running after Albion in his penthouse-sized office, somewhere along the line it had been agreed that Gyldan did not require much office space of his own. Thus, his own office in Caladrius HQ was something akin to a rather swanky storage cupboard—all sleek lines and clean cuts, but he could still touch all four walls if he held his arms out and spun in a circle. There was just enough room for a small table, a chair, and a personal computer. Papers were stuck to every available space on the walls, door, and ceiling.

Then again, there *was* a perk to having such a tiny office: no visitors. Everyone knew that visiting Gyldan in his office was a fool's errand, and so, no one did.

That made secret missions to smuggle a disguised vampire and werewolf into Caladrius headquarters much easier to orchestrate.

"Griffin, are you in position?" Gyldan asked, adjusting his headset and hunching over his laptop. With a few clicks, he had access to several cameras all around Caladrius headquarters, including those just outside the main entrance. Another perk of being the personal assistant to Albion Saint-Richter—Gyldan's company login had more privileges than most of the office staff did.

Still, Gyldan's heart hammered in his chest, and he tried to steady it with some deep breathing as he searched for any sign of the undercover vampire.

"Yup, yup, want me to wave?" Griffin responded in his usual gravelly tone. The ragged-looking vampire sauntered into view of one of the outside cameras. A rough smattering of stubble shaded his jaw, and tufts of long grey hair peeked out from under a wide-brimmed hat.

Gyldan's whole household had come together to try and clean Griffin up, and yet somehow, the vampire still looked bedraggled. The only part of his outfit that looked remotely fancy was the set of opaque glasses covering his eyes—Griffin could sport these glasses and pass as a blind human journalist, which was the only reason he had been chosen for this important role. That, and the fact that Griffin *was* legitimately blind.

"I bet Caelan could wave too," Griffin added cheekily, beckoning his 'guide dog' over. "Here boy!"

A rather large, auburn-furred dog plodded along at Griffin's side, a thick leather collar wrapped around its neck. Gyldan had to admit, Caelan had done a fantastic job of controlling his shapeshifting. It must have taken some practice to condense the raw power of a werewolf's controlled form down to the size of a dog. But his Caladrius-branded silver collar looked suspicious. They had tried to disguise it to look like a slightly chunky leather collar, but Gyldan wasn't convinced it was enough.

I'm overthinking it, Gyldan told himself, trying instead to focus on dialling in the rest of their team. *It looks fine. Big collar for a big dog.*

"Don't wave, I can see you," Gyldan hissed. He kept stealing glances at the door, his mind conjuring images of someone bursting in to point an accusatory finger. But, at least logically, Gyldan was somewhat assured that he was safe here. "And don't talk to Caelan like that... it's weird."

He opened more windows on the now-cramped laptop screen in front of him, dialling the other two members of their ragtag team.

"I'm kiddin', relax..." Griffin chuckled, then nodded down to the wolf. "Sorry, Caelan."

Caelan growled loud enough for Griffin's hidden microphone to pick up on it.

"He says '*fuck you, ya blind old coot*'," another voice chimed in, followed by a throaty laugh. In the top left corner of

Gyldan's screen, the fourth member of their team appeared with a wicked grin and a silver collar glinting around her skinny throat. "Yo! Werewolf translator at your service! How's it goin', nerd?"

Gyldan jumped and hammered at his keyboard, dropping the volume in paranoia despite wearing a headset.

"Keep it down, Seraph!" he pleaded.

"Oh, sorry…" Seraph's face fell, and she raked a hand over the short crop of white-blonde hair that already stuck out in all directions. She was one of the two werewolves Gyldan lived with, and right now, she was the only one who could understand what Caelan was saying while he was in his wolf form. "Hey, is Rukshana on the line yet?"

Gyldan glanced at the black box dialling out to their final teammate, but only his translucent reflection on the glossy screen greeted him—grey eyes sparking with mild panic and black hair a little more awry than usual from his agitated fiddling.

"Nah… she's not home with you yet?"

"Probably on her way back from her appointment," Seraph said, though a hint of nervousness threaded into her voice. The werewolf was hyper-protective of everyone she cared about, so it was only natural that she worried so much for her vampire girlfriend. "I'll text her. Yo, we can probably start this without her though, right? She explained the plan pretty thoroughly before…"

"Don't see why not," Griffin agreed. "Rukshana's probably just looking for a coffee shop nearby. Kinda sunny out here. Wouldn't blame her. "

The vampire shuffled closer to the building, slipping under the shade to avoid the prickly heat of the sun. Gyldan knew there would be no harm beyond a bad sunburn if he asked Griffin to wait out in the sun any longer, but waiting also meant dragging out the risk of being caught.

"All right, so I've managed to book you a meeting with Albion himself," Gyldan whispered into his headset, pulling up the CEO's digital diary for the day.

"A blind journalist and his guide dog... how many of us have tried to crack Caladrius' security and *this* is the play that worked?" Griffin mused to himself, adjusting his glasses and speaking into his sleeve.

Finally, the video call to their remaining teammate connected on Gyldan's screen.

"It hasn't worked yet," Rukshana pointed out by means of greeting, her usually velvet tone more like rough wool today. The female vampire looked annoyed, though Gyldan could tell it wasn't because they had started their daring heist on Caladrius without her.

Rukshana was wearing the latest Caladrius-issued ruby eye-guard, the bolts around her eye sockets sporting fresh polish. Sometimes, Gyldan thought the modern method of repressing a vampire's abilities was more barbaric than the old way.

Seraph leant forward, as though doing so would bring her closer to Rukshana.

"Hey, how'd it go? Did they sort out the headaches?"

"Yes. I'd outgrown my eye-guard. Needed it replaced," Rukshana sighed, rubbing at her temples and taking a sip from a coffee cup. Judging from the eclectic array of artwork and fairy lights on the wall of reclaimed wood behind her, the vampire had chosen a quiet, quirky coffee shop to hide in. "Now I have an entirely new sort of headache."

"Could be worse," Griffin pointed out, still loitering by the doors of the office. "Let me tell you about the headache *I* got back when they dealt with our kind the old way..."

"Let's not!" Gyldan interjected. An old vampire regaling the horror story of having his eyes surgically removed would definitely ruin the disguise. "You're pretending to be human, remember?"

"God, I'm just praying they don't look too closely at Caelan," Rukshana said, pursing her lips. "You can tell that's a trap-collar, can't you? I knew I should have wrapped the leather under the silver band too..."

"And set off the sensor? Y'did what you could," Seraphina replied, leaning back and putting her feet up on a table off-camera. "You can't see the silver unless you get *really* close. And no one's gonna get close to that mutt, look at him. Clearly, he bites."

Gyldan heard Caelan growling before Griffin began to walk up the steps with great care, doing a good job of 'relying' on Caelan to guide him.

"You still mad, Seraph?" Griffin asked around a small smile.

"There was nothing wrong with my transformation! I totally could have been a guide dog for ya!" Seraph complained, rocking back in her chair and looking away from the monitor.

"Yes, if guide dogs were the size of horses," Rukshana noted, stirring her coffee idly and smirking. "You didn't practise as much as Caelan did."

"You're meant to be on my side, Rukshana!"

"Oh, you sweet thing."

"Guys, no domestics on the shared line!" Gyldan spoke up, breaking off their squabble and focusing the group back to the matter at hand. "This *cannot* go wrong. You guys can get away, but if I'm caught up in this..."

His throat went dry just thinking about it, all words fleeing his tongue in fear of the hypothetical rage of Albion. He had never seen the CEO lose his cool before, and that only made the prospect more terrifying to consider.

"Wouldn't want to lose your job at the ol' oppression factory, would ya?" Seraph teased, hooking a finger under one of the iron bands of her trap-collar and giving it a shake towards the monitor. Though he knew she was only messing with him, it hit Gyldan hard with a pang of guilt. Working for Caladrius, the company that created the silver trap-collars for werewolves and ruby-lensed eye-guards for vampires, was both a blessing and a curse when one was friends with both vampires and werewolves.

Decades ago, there had been no need for such contraptions. Then, the mutations began—children were born who couldn't stomach normal food but displayed greater feats of strength and agility when sated with blood. They came into the world with feathered stumps on their backs and crimson eyes that could hypnotise other species. Others, while being able to eat as humans did, could shapeshift into beasts that walked on four legs. But when the full moon shone, they had no choice in the uncontrollable rage that consumed them.

As the years went on, these mutations evolved at a staggering pace. Now, around thirty per cent of the world's population were registered as *Homo lupus* or *Homo sanguinis*: names that the media couldn't make a sensational headline of as easily as *werewolf* or *vampire*. Of course, everyone's minds flocked towards the stories and films written by humans about mythical beings. Every single story of vampires and werewolves promised humanity one thing: that these species would dominate, and humans would lose their throne. They would be the weaker species, the cattle. A swift defeat would come to them.

It did not.

As always, humans adapted. They created tools. They changed the world around them. They caged the threat. They survived.

They were very good at that.

Gyldan pushed the sense of associated guilt aside and busied himself with watching Griffin and Caelan move through to the lobby. He flicked through the CCTV cameras, nervously observing the vampire and werewolf wandering through the stark, monochromatic headquarters of Caladrius. Like the rest of the building, the headquarters' lobby was so clinical and clean that it bordered on suspicious. Everything was polished to a bright white shine, with accents of striking ebony that gave the vast room the appearance that it had been carved from marble. A black strip of carpet ran from the glass doors at the front of the lobby all the way up the stairs to the reception desk, presenting the receptionist like a deity to be worshiped within a grand temple.

Gyldan had no doubt that the receptionist, Alexis, thrived on that.

As Griffin walked through the lobby, his hidden microphone picked up snippets of the proud infomercials playing on the huge 4K screens tiling the walls around him, infomercials Gyldan had heard so many times that he could recite the scripts by heart.

"*Make sure your bundle of joy is a bundle of safety too,*" a warm-toned lady beamed from behind a two-foot smile as Griffin walked by another set of screens. "*Ask your doctor about Caladrius' new and improved humanity test—now effective from just twelve weeks!*"

"Don't. Say. Anything," Gyldan warned Griffin, spotting the vampire's twitching throat muscle a mile off. "Not here."

"That is abhorrent though," Rukshana chimed in, nose wrinkling. "I bet someone out there has aborted their child after finding out it has the *Homo lupus* or *Homo sanguinis* gene..."

"*It is your responsibility to stay indoors during a full moon,*" another advert patronised, earning a grumble from Caelan. "*No one wants to end the life of a werewolf. Please—help us to keep everyone safe. Stay moon-aware. Download our moon phase tracker app today!*"

"Yeah, they *say* that." Seraph nodded, agreeing with whatever Caelan had said. "But just last month, my aunt's cousin was out during a waning moon, and someone reported him for being out during a full moon! Nearly had the officials kicking down his door to click his silver."

Clicking silver was a euphemism that severely dampened the complex kit that was the silver trap-collar. Gyldan was sure

Seraph only referred to it that way to spare his feelings—after all, it was his boss that had designed the weapon.

Werewolves called the process of activating a trap-collar *clicking silver* because of how the wide, suspended ring of silver would click down into the gap between the two iron bands that sat snugly around a werewolf's throat. There was no escape from the silver death trap should a police officer, judge, or high-ranking government official choose to activate the trap-collar.

"That'll all be a thing of the past once we get hold of those release codes," Rukshana said, fiddling with a long lock of dark hair that had gotten tangled in a bolt on her eye-guard. "In a few hours' time, the world will be free."

"You should have just done a runner when they took your old eye-guard off." Seraph smirked. "This woulda been so much easier. Could you imagine? You coulda just sprouted your wings, flown up to Albion's office window, and thralled him. Commanded the bastard to give you the codes, ha!"

Rukshana gave the camera a withering look.

"I doubt being able to control one person would save me from the hail of bullets that would ensue if I had tried that," the vampire pointed out, finishing her drink and setting her cup back down. "Besides, I don't want to go down in history as the vampire who caused humans to look for ways to clip our wings after all."

Vampires had a secondary skill that was, oddly, void of much human concern. They had wings that could grow on command or shed away like a lizard's tail when no longer needed. Sure, there were a few rules on airspace and flying that vampires had to abide by, but for one reason or another, it was relatively unchecked by humans. Gyldan had always assumed it was some sense of awe, some old instinct and belief in angels that meant humans didn't mind seeing a vampire in flight much. Some of the more verbal werewolf support groups often used this fact as a way to assert that werewolves were far more oppressed than vampires.

"C'mon team, focus," Griffin huffed, settling himself down on a black leather sofa in the waiting area near reception. He removed his hat and gave his shaggy mop of grey hair a tussle.

"Remember when we were worried that Caelan would raise suspicions?" Rukshana commented, head tilting to the side. "We really ought to have put more effort into Griff's... well, *everything*."

Griffin didn't respond, no doubt realising how busy the lobby was getting and that he couldn't afford to be caught talking to himself. Still, Gyldan noticed a muscle in his stubbled jaw twitch.

"I mean, he could have at least *shaved*," Rukshana said.

"Meetin' the CEO of Caladrius, lookin' like a tramp." Seraph snorted.

"And that is not the shirt I ironed for you."

"To be fair, he is actually blind."

"*Shh!*" Gyldan tried to get everyone to focus again as a woman walked across the monitor towards Griffin. "Griff! That's Alexis. She's the receptionist, and she's... actually really nice. Be nice."

Gyldan's chair creaked as he found himself edging closer to the monitor, trying to make out what was being said between the pair after Alexis greeted them. She only glanced once at Caelan, looking a little fearful, before beckoning Griffin to follow her out of frame. Gyldan let out a sigh of relief, his chest feeling a fraction less tight as he did so.

"All right, she should take you to the top floor, floor twenty-four. If she doesn't... tell me, 'cause that means something's up," Gyldan explained in a hurry, shuffling his seat and pushing one side of his headphones so he could free up an ear and listen out to the door. His office-cupboard was on the same floor as Albion's office, so he expected to hear the undercover vampire and his dog as they walked by. Indeed, after a few moments, Gyldan could hear the click-clack of Alexis' heels across the polished marble floors, followed by a pit-pat of paws, and then the shuffle of Griffin's feet passing by his door.

A sharp *bang!* slammed against the door to Gyldan's office.

Gyldan yelped, every muscle in his body tensing up as he jolted out of his seat. Over his skewed headset, he could hear Griffin chuckling to himself.

"God... *dammit*, Griffin!" Gyldan spluttered, realising the man had only knocked on the door as he had walked by.

"Visiting ya at work, son," the vampire muttered around a smile Gyldan could hear. "So proud." Griffin then raised his voice to address the receptionist. "Oh, sorry, don't mind me! Tripped over my own feet, haha!"

"Shut up and focus!" Gyldan despaired, and Caelan growled in agreement over Griff's microphone. "Thank you, Caelan!" he added, exasperated.

In the background, Seraph was doubled over laughing, and even Rukshana was making a veiled attempt to cover her snickering. Huffing to himself, Gyldan scooted the single step back to his computer, tapping away until his monitor view switched to a camera in Albion's office.

Gyldan watched as the receptionist and Griffin cut into view from the bottom of the camera, two bright figures painted stark against the dazzling facets of the CEO's colourless office. With the left wall lined with white shelves sporting numerous crystal-cut awards and trophies, and the other three walls formed from towering windows, stepping into Albion's office was like entering the cold inner domain of a diamond. The pressure for perfection that he and his office demanded cast wordless judgement upon a visitor as an uninvited imperfection. Despite working so closely with Albion, not even Gyldan was exempt from this silent verdict.

His heart pulled a little as he spotted the CEO at his glass desk, though Gyldan tried to push that nagging sense of shame away.

Albion Saint-Richter was sitting with all the airs of a king within the diamond office's realm, his sharp green eyes tracking Griffin so keenly that they robbed his perpetual smile of any sincerity. With his thick silver hair swept effortlessly back while clinging to the last few dark brown strands that peppered it, Albion was very much the only person in the room that looked like he belonged in the office—the only person who looked comfortable within it. Here sat the king of the civilised world, oblivious to the betrayal stirring at his right hand.

Gyldan shook his head, knocking black locks of hair in front of his eyes. This was for the greater good. Sure, Albion was nice to *him*, giving him all these opportunities and, well... more. But still, Gyldan wasn't an idiot. Albion was not a nice guy, and he was the direct cause of suffering for two entire species.

If Gyldan could help, he *had* to help.

Clearing his throat, he swallowed and stammered as he watched Albion get to his feet and offer a hand to shake. Griffin made a display of searching for said hand before shaking it.

"All right... the release codes are in Albion's office. If you can get hold of them, I can access the registered collars and eye-guards on Caladrius' network. I'll shut off the sensors on the collars and the UV light emitters on the guards. Then, it's up to you guys to get 'em removed," Gyldan explained, glancing across at Seraph and Rukshana on their monitors in turn. They had fallen silent, no doubt watching Griffin confronting their shared enemy.

Again, Gyldan's heartstrings plucked tight with guilt. "There's a safe. Caelan, probably best if you go looking—behind the velvet sofa on the right-hand side, loose panel in the wall. Really hard to spot, but I spilt a glass of wine over there last week, maybe you can still sniff that out?"

"Why were you drinkin' wine in the CEO's office?" Seraph asked, a pale eyebrow arching. Gyldan couldn't help it. His whole face prickled with embarrassment.

"O-Oh, er, big, er, big business deal. Went well. Albion likes to splash the cash for that kinda stuff." Gyldan's hand reached up to mess with the hair on the back of his head. "PA perk?"

Blue eyes narrowed at him, but Seraph didn't press the matter. Instead, she fell back in her chair and shrugged.

"Ah-right. Good move spilling the wine though," she admitted, tapping the side of her nose. "Could still smell that if you spilt it a month ago."

"That's why she gets so annoyed when you spill milk everywhere when making cups of tea, Gyldan," Rukshana interjected with a soft smile.

"Yo, it *stinks for months*. You guys don't have to worry about it, but me and Caelan? It *sticks around*. Honestly, never seen a guy make tea like Gyldan does, fricking noodles for arms wiggling all over, *oooohhh can't keep this whole entire milk bottle steady!*" Seraph made a great show of imitating Gyldan's act of making tea, flailing her arms around. In response, his lips pursed tight, but he could hardly refute the claim.

"Well, make it yourself next time," he replied, turning his attention back to Albion and Griffin. He could see Caelan slinking away, sniffing at the floor. Albion glanced at the dog, and he lingered just a moment too long on Caelan's collar, but Griffin waved a hand to steal the CEO's attention.

"Ah, he's just curious. New place. Mappin' it out for me." Griffin's voice was distant and distorted due to the placement of his microphone, but Gyldan could still follow the conversation. "I can call him back if it bothers you too much."

Albion eyed Caelan as he went pottering about the room, dutifully sniffing at the potted plants and artful statues that decorated the lavish office, doing nothing more suspicious than any dog would. Then, his critical gaze rested back on Griffin. But before Gyldan could figure out exactly what had caught the CEO's suspicion, the man shrugged.

"Not to worry." Albion's deep timbre was even quieter over his headset than Griffin's, yet it still managed to make Gyldan's heart flutter. "Please, take a seat. I am happy to keep Caladrius transparent to the media, of course, but you understand I'm a busy man. I have several meetings today."

"That he won't even go to," Gyldan muttered to himself. Albion had a brilliant mind, but a very easily distracted one. Meetings were not his forte, unless one measured the success of a meeting by disgruntled, stood-up businesspersons left scowling and complaining to Albion's PA at his boss's no-show. Albion did not suffer fools, and sadly, he viewed many as such.

"Gotcha," Griff agreed, finding his seat and sitting down. Albion sat himself down too, resting an ankle over his knee and lounging back with effortless grace. The two of them displayed an almost comical representation of the two ends of the spectrum of elegance, with Albion's tailored navy suit, shaved face, and perfectly styled silver hair making Griffin's stubbled chin, oversized shirt, and tangled mop stand out all the more.

Gyldan watched as Caelan began to drift closer towards the hidden safe.

"The code is 1-4-0-3-2-7-0-3," he relayed over the line.

"So... thought we could start with Caladrius' views on the recent scandal regarding the Daedalus employee murders? I mean, y'gotta know what folks are saying...?" Griffin said, having set his phone on the desk between the two of them to record their conversation. Albion's emerald eyes flicked down at the device, his whole body remaining otherwise frozen, then snapped his gaze back up to Griffin. His lips shifted into something of a smirk, but Gyldan could tell the man was already at the end of his patience.

And the interview had only just begun.

"Caladrius regrets the turmoil Daedalus is going through. A rival company makes for healthy competition, and it goes without saying that we at Caladrius would never condone such actions. I... *we*... certainly don't need to stoop to *murder* to stay ahead of the game. It's awful, and Caladrius will cooperate in every way to help bring the monster to justice," Albion replied, his voice almost smooth but betrayed by a hint of annoyance.

"Ah-huh," Griffin responded, threading his fingers together on his lap. "Still, you can see why people are looking at Caladrius? After all, even if the conspiracy theories aren't true... the media's sayin' the victims look like they were attacked by a rogue werewolf or vampire. Caladrius promises to keep humanity safe with its products. Are you willing to admit the trap-collar and eye-guard system maybe ain't working out?"

Though he could not see it on the camera, Gyldan knew damn well that tell-tale muscle in Albion's jaw would be quivering with irritation at that veiled insult. He tried to swallow, but his throat was far too dry to cooperate.

"In a perfect world, vampires and werewolves would never harm humans, and we would be able to take them at their word. But we do not live in a perfect world. In rare cases, a non-human will evade our system and choose to harm others." Every one of Albion's words was weighed down by a low rumble of impatience. "Caladrius' products keep the majority of these species safe to be around. It is a difficult but necessary step that someone had to be bold enough to take. Just look at what happened when the Eye Surgery Act was abolished in 1993— fourteen years of living in fear of non-humans and their power! We can do a great many things to help society function, but we cannot change a vampire or werewolf's natural moral compass. That is not Caladrius' responsibility. I believe the non-human community ought to look at its own responsibilities instead of its constant complaints of being hard done to. We cannot make them be good people."

Gyldan's face slapped down into his hands. Albion had absolutely no tact, and the strain in Griffin's voice was palpable as he spoke again:

"Your products ensure vampires and werewolves are *good people?*"

"Evidently, when given the choice, it is clear they would hurt people without a deterrent." Albion held his hands out in a loose shrug.

"...Gotcha," Griffin said stiffly. "So... Albion Saint-Richter admits the recent murder spree is likely a vampire or werewolf that isn't on Caladrius' network?"

"Most likely."

"Nothing to do with you guys?"

"No. Daedalus has my pity. But then again, it always *did*."

Gyldan let his head fall through his palms and slam into the desk. The PR they'd have to pull after this if Griff sold this story...

Wait, Gyldan reminded himself, *Griff isn't actually a journo*.

"...Sure. Caladrius is doing a great job," Griff said around a pained smile. "Daedalus talks a big game, but they haven't yet produced any real contender to the trap-collar or eye-guard. But, Mr Saint-Richter, more and more people are questioning the ethical implications of these devices. Once upon a time, vampires had their eyes taken out. A cruel practice, right? Then we moved on to the eye-guards. Do you think there could be further improvements? What new technology is Caladrius working on to help improve vampire and werewolf lives?"

Albion raised an eyebrow, but then, he let both feet hit the floor as he rested his elbows on his thighs. A finger coiled around his chin, and he watched Griffin for a moment before replying:

"Well, that would be filed under 'company secrets'. I can't tell you much about that side of things. But... how about a sneak peek at something else? I *have* been working on something that I believe will be a benefit to many."

Albion got to his feet, and off to the side of the monitor, Gyldan watched Caelan jump back from where he had been sniffing around the back of the sofa.

"Dammit, he's not got the safe yet?" Gyldan said, irritated at Caelan's tardiness.

Albion was helping Griffin up from his chair now, and he guided the blind man across the room. "Do you need to call your guide dog?" he asked lightly.

Gyldan had to admit that he was curious. What new technology could he want to show a journalist? He racked his brains, filing through every new idea and prototype Caladrius was working on right now, watching as Albion led Griffin to a side door in his office. The door, Gyldan knew, led to a small bedroom adjacent to Albion's office, for nights when the CEO worked too late to drive home and simply flopped on the bed there instead. Usually still in his suit.

Wait, why's he... leading Griff to his bedroom? Gyldan wondered, a slight tinge of jealousy blossoming like mould over his mind. *Is he flirting with—?*

Then, he spotted it. A clunky metal structure was clipped around the door frame, preventing it from closing properly. It was embellished with a rainbow of exposed wires in a classically Albion method of disarray.

—Oh no.

"Griff, do not go through that door!" Gyldan had to catch himself before yelling, needing every fibre of his being to keep his voice down. "Find a way out! He's rigged a prototype on the door... *fuck!* I didn't think it was anywhere near done...!"

"What are you talking about?" Rukshana demanded, perking up as urgency electrified the air. "Gyl? What is that thing?"

"It's a-a-a scanner thing. He was talking about it the other day, like, *literally* the other day!" Gyldan babbled, leaping to his feet and pacing as much as the confined quarters and headset wire would allow, hands raking through fistfuls of black hair. "He never works this fast! How the hell did he get a prototype made up already?"

"A scanner? For what? Gyl?" Seraph brought Gyldan's attention back to the matter at hand. "You're not seriously saying..."

"Y-yeah, that... that thing, if it works, detects whether a person is a human, vampire, or werewolf. H-he wanted to install 'em through Caladrius, getting paranoid about stuff, a-a-and y'know, big money-spinner for other businesses and stuff..."

"What, the frigging collars aren't sign enough?"

"Y-yeah but it's like Al said! Not everyone is on the system. Some of you guys get under the radar, he's been all hooked up on that recently."

"...*Al?*"

"Oh my god, I just work for him, okay?" Gyldan snapped, arms flapping up in despair and his voice rising a little more than it ought to. "Listen, Griff, make an excuse, get out of there! Do not step through that door!"

On his screen, Gyldan could see Rukshana pulling out her phone and putting it to her ear. On cue, Griffin paused on his screen, holding up a finger to Albion.

"Oh! E-excuse me one moment, it's my daughter..."

"Of course." Albion smiled, though it brought as much comfort as the smile of a shark.

Griffin put the phone to his ear, ducking away from the CEO a little.

"Hey sweetheart... I-I'm in the middle of an interview right now, can it wa—what? Calm down, I can't hear a word you're saying..." Griffin said, though when Gyldan looked at Rukshana, the vampire was the picture of calm.

"Tell him I'm crying. My boyfriend works for Daedalus and he's gone missing. I'm hysterical because of the murders. You better come pick me up, I'm scared." Rukshana invented the story with ease, looking at her now-empty coffee cup. "Bring the dog, he can protect us, right?"

"Clark? Oh, honey, I'm sure he's just runnin' late is all. Daedalus always ran the boy ragged. N-no, you're worrying over noth—no, he won't have been—no, I know what the news is saying, I work for 'em—okay, but just 'cause he's late doesn't mean he's been attacked too." Griff gave an admirable display of holding the phone away for a moment and giving Albion a shrugging gesture that said wordlessly: *daughters, eh?* "What? Aw, no, don't get mad at me, I'm not—no I'm not dismissing ya worries, I just think it's not very likely that... no-no don't cry, Emilia. No, I... listen, I'll come pick you up, okay? Yeah, yeah, me 'n' Parker will come getcha, nothing'll fight Parker, right? Okay... yeah, yeah, you stay there, I'll be ten minutes. All right. See you soon."

Griff tapped the screen of his phone once, pocketed it, then turned to Albion. "I'm so sorry about that, Mr Saint-Richter. Listen, this has been a great opp, loads to write on, but I gotta go pick up my daughter. She's got herself all in a tizzy about the murders... can't blame her, her boyfriend's a Daedalus guy, they've been freaking out about it... here, Parker!" The vampire patted the side of his leg and Caelan trotted obediently over.

"Of course; I understand. Well, why don't we wrap up here and one of my drivers can take you to your daughter?" Albion smiled, eyes twinkling. "A ten-minute walk means she can't be too far away. A two-minute drive frees up plenty of time for you to get your exclusive article. A never-before-seen piece of Caladrius technology—I am sure your boss will be over the moon with your success."

He knows, Gyldan thought, his skin crinkling with a clammy frost. *Something's tipped him off. He knows.*

"Er, I mean...not sure she'd be happy with me rocking up in a Caladrius car..."

"Oh?" Albion feigned confusion with a tilt of his head and a frown pulling across his brow. "She doesn't work for Daedalus, does she? I am sure she won't tell her boyfriend you've been driving with the enemy. We have plenty of unmarked cars if you prefer, though." The CEO chuckled and put a hand on Griffin's shoulder, but Griffin did not move to walk with him. "Come! I assure you, it is no trouble."

The silence stretched for what felt like years, and Gyldan dreaded the moment it would break. He could hear his breath in his chest, heaving and falling. What could he do? Go in there? Make an excuse? Yes, but what? He had to get Griff and Caelan out of there, but fear rooted him to the spot and addled his mind.

He couldn't think. He couldn't think. He couldn't *think*.

"Gyl, *do* something!" Seraph yelled over the connection.

Too late. The hesitation on everyone's behalf had turned Albion's suspicion into confirmation. In one fluid movement, he pressed the panic button near the door frame and pulled a gun from under his jacket, training it on Griffin. The vampire slowly raised his hands up as security personnel poured into the room.

"This? This is precisely why I continue my work," Albion snapped, tapping the prototype door scanner behind him with the heel of his shoe. "How the hell did a vampire get into my office?" He glowered at the guards that were circling Griffin, and he jerked his head towards Caelan. "Check the collar. How did that collar escape everyone else's notice? I employ you to use your *eyes* as well as your trigger fingers!"

Immediately, four guards rushed towards Caelan to inspect the collar. The dog whimpered, getting up on its hind legs and morphing rapidly into a human form. Auburn fur receded into a mop of hair framing a pale face, the iron bands of his collar sliding and adjusting to fit his now slimmer neck.

"W-w-wait! It's me!" Caelan yelped, turning to Albion like he was his last hope in the world. "Mr-Mr Saint-Richter, sir, it's me, Caelan? Listen, there's a traitor in your company, I can—"

Shhhhtick!

Caelan's words burnt from his throat as the silver ring of his collar clamped around his neck. The flesh scorched and the man wailed, hands clawing frantically at the device as his skin blistered and bubbled, staining red and blossoming out across his neck and face. The whites of his eyes, wide and fearful, surged crimson and then, with one awful, gargling gasp, Caelan fell to the ground. Just behind where the werewolf had been standing, a guard was holding out a small handheld device, thumb over a flat, circular button, trembling from head to foot. Albion let one hand clap down to his thigh in exasperation.

"For the love of... I said *check* the collar. You're lucky that wasn't a human informant you just killed or there would be a bloody court case," Albion growled without grief, rolling his eyes then looking towards Griffin in disgust. "Grab the vampire at least. He could be useful. And try not to kill him, for God's sake."

Gyldan could only watch as Griffin hunched, ready to make a valiant effort to escape the onslaught of guards. They dove at him as Albion holstered his gun again—punches swung, yells tore out, and Griffin almost disappeared in the small crowd of security. One punch knocked the glasses from his face and sent him sprawling across the floor.

Caelan... Caelan's ...dead. Gyldan's stunned thoughts finally caught up. *Caelan was... giving information... to Albion? How did I not know...?*

Griffin scrambled to his feet, eyes shut, sniffing the air. He rounded on the advancing group again, though Gyldan could only watch, helpless, numb, and horrified.

Caelan's dead.

Gyldan was acutely aware of Rukshana and Seraph's voices yelling over the headset, pleading for Griffin to get out, to fight, giving him directions as guards lunged at him.

Strangely, the group of guards broke formation for a moment—one guard stepped completely to the side, limbs limp like a puppet, perhaps in fear of fighting a vampire. Griffin didn't need a second chance. He grabbed the guard's gun and fled from the room, leaving Gyldan's monitor view. He heard Griffin's feet stamping by outside of his office not long after.

"Oi! These windows. Bulletproof?" Griff's voice crackled over the comms then, and Gyldan knew he was addressing him. A name would be dangerous. 'Oi' would do.

"Y-yeah. Yeah, don't... don't try shooting them..." Gyldan stammered, blinking and swallowing to try and restarted his stunned self.

"Right... front door it is, wings after. See you back home. Rukshana, get back home. And Gyl... ya might wanna slip out when you can. Think your boss is gonna be in a bad mood for the rest of the day."

At that moment, Gyldan's phone buzzed in his pocket, making him jump. As each camera went offline on his screen, Gyldan shut his computer down and took off his headset before looking at his phone screen. He paused for a second before answering.

"H-hey, what's—"

"Where are you, Gyl?" Albion's voice cut him off, taut with concern and annoyance in equal measure.

"I er... just doing some paperwork at the café round the corner." Gyldan slipped out of his office and slunk down the corridor to jab at the elevator button. "Why, you need me to come into the office?"

"No—I'll find you," Albion replied as Gyldan dashed into the lift and mashed the ground floor button, knowing his boss was only at the other end of the corridor in his office, pulling on his coat by the sounds over the phone. "We have a problem."

Chapter 2

  Gyldan hurried down the street, weaving between people and trying to make it look like he hadn't sweated several years off his lifespan for the last hour. He attempted to smooth down his hair and almost elbowed a man in the process, forcing a bleated apology to his right. He then tried to straighten his shirt collar and his tie, and definitely elbowed a werewolf on his left, bringing a more urgent apology to his lips.

  As he half-ran down the street, he crossed Rukshana going the other way. She only nodded at him, a gaze of steel catching Gyldan from behind her crimson visor—he had some explaining to do later. That was fine. *That* he could deal with. A pissed off Albion? Less fun than a vampire-led inquisition.

  Gyldan skidded into the café and, for once, was blessed with a queueless counter. He offered the stunned waitress a breathless smile and a sharp nod, hoping the motion would somehow lessen the inelegant manner in which he had crashed into her establishment. After collecting what was left of his dignity, Gyldan ordered a latte, then stood at the side of the semi-clean counter to wait.

He started absently drumming his fingers, glancing around the small room and offering silent thanks to whatever deity might exist that there was no one sitting in the mismatched collection of wooden chairs. With nothing to entertain his fretful mind in the café other than several framed pictures that were more dust than artwork at this point, Gyldan took to watching each person passing by the window with more than a little fear that one of them would be a handsomely dressed blur of silver hair heading right for him before his alibi was in place. Eventually, the waitress cleared her throat and handed Gyldan his latte with decidedly more force than was needed, slopping milk down onto the countertop.

"Oh... thanks. *Oh!* N-no, I wasn't... the finger-drumming wasn't... you..." Gyldan tried to explain, realising the entire scenario had made him look like a prime example of an utter dick. "Just er... someone... never mind, thanks!"

He picked up his coffee and scurried over to a corner table. He then dropped down on a chair and proceeded to drink as much of the scorching liquid as he could in an effort to make it look like he'd been there a while. It occurred to him somewhere between moving from first-degree burns to second-degree burns in his throat that he could have made life a lot easier by ordering an iced latte.

"...Crap," Gyldan mumbled to himself, setting the now-half-finished coffee down on the table.

A jingle sounded through the small coffee shop and the man gave a start. He looked over to the door in time to see Albion striding in. Everyone responded as they should: Gyldan's heart leapt into his throat. The waitress promptly dropped the coffee she had been pouring. Albion's ego beamed.

The older man looked around the room for a moment, spotted Gyldan, and headed over. Usually, the man would smile to see him, but no such sun broke through the stormy expression on Albion's face today. Gyldan did his best to look convincingly confused, acting like he had no idea why Albion would be upset.

"Hey, er... everything... good?" he asked. Was that casual? Too casual? Suspicious? Gyldan wished he could shut his brain up at times like these.

"Perfect, yes. Wonderful," Albion said, sitting himself down opposite his personal assistant. Easily gorgeous, Albion's lips always bore the ghost of a curl at the corners that let everyone know that he was well aware of his good looks. "Everything was going swimmingly until a *vampire* managed to break into my office."

"What? A vampire? How? I-I mean, are you okay?" Gyldan asked, performing a well-timed splutter of his coffee.

"I'm fine, it was *one* vampire." Albion brushed off Gyldan's concerns. "But that is, frankly, one vampire too many. We need to talk about the scanner, immediately. It needs to be fast-tracked. Did I tell you I finished a prototype?"

"You did not," came Gyldan's rather clipped response, and he set his coffee mug down with a slightly aggressive tap against the table.

No. No, you did not, Gyldan's brain hissed, annoyed at the other man. Albion blinked, looking confused and combing his fingers through his hair. In the last few years that Gyldan had known the other man, the colour had rapidly bled from Albion's hair. The man was prematurely grey at this point, but Gyldan knew Albion was in deep denial about that, hence his one nervous habit of raking a hand through his hair when he was caught out.

"Oh? I could have sworn I... well, it hardly matters. The prototype is running. Didn't get a chance to test it though..."

Gyldan froze, his coffee halfway to his lips again. He peered over the rim at Albion, who was making no effort to hide his distaste for the aged décor around them.

"You... haven't tested it?" Gyldan repeated back to him, his heart having long since fallen from his throat and now attempting to burrow into his stomach. Albion chuckled.

"Of course not. Vampires and werewolves aren't *supposed* to just stroll in off the street. I suppose today was a blessing in disguise, in some ways." Albion arched his eyebrows and gave a sidewards nod. "Still, I'll get it tested properly. Fast-track this one, Gyl. I want Caladrius' finest to make sure that it looks sleek, cool, and functional. It doesn't exactly look store-ready at this point; you know what I'm like when I work... Does this place do mochas?"

Albion got to his feet and strode over to the counter, leaving Gyldan to process what the other man had just said. The prototype hadn't been tested. It might not have gone off if Griffin had stepped through it. He could have played it off as a glitch if only he'd *known*.

All that panic. All that fallout. But then again, they wouldn't have found out Caelan was a traitor without all that. *Silver linings*, Gyldan supposed as he stared blankly at the faded green wallpaper, sipping his coffee and wrestling back the unaddressed chaos that Calean's betrayal demanded he process.

A few moments later, Albion returned with his drink, the well-worn coffee mug looking laughably out of place in the manicured hand of Caladrius' CEO. Gyldan rested his cup against his bottom lip again, frozen in thought and grief for his fallen friend. Traitor. Whatever the memory of Caelan was to him now...

"Do you suppose they would serve blood coffees to humans here? They're on the menu. I wonder if anyone's tried? ...Gyldan? Gyldan, are you all right?" The older man clicked his fingers in front of Gyldan's face, making him blink.

"Wha—oh, yeah. Just er... you know, thinking that I shoulda been there." Gyldan set his coffee down again, looking and feeling genuinely guilty even though he'd orchestrated the attack. "Can't believe you got attacked by a vampire in your own office. Where were the guards?" He knew exactly where the guards were. They were where their botched schedules told them to be, courtesy of one Gyldan Crawford.

"Most likely they were deploying all of their shared braincells towards remembering how to breathe," Albion drawled, straightening his jacket. "But the vampire? Quite unusual. He didn't have an eye-guard. Older fellow, probably from the surgery generation. Still, they all get the chance to sign up for eye-guard registration later in life with no questions asked. You have to wonder about these people who choose not to have a collar or guard. I mean, they *want* to be a threat to society at that point, really. We can only do so much... they have to meet us halfway or this isn't going to work out for all of us."

"Mmmm..."

Gyldan sipped on his cooling latte then, if only to avoid having to speak further. He hated discussing this with Albion. One, it was work-talk. Two, it was a subject in which Gyldan was pulled both ways. Sure, he understood the need to protect humanity. Hell, he'd be lying if he said he wasn't nervous about vampires and werewolves. If a war broke out in earnest, humans wouldn't win if it was a matchup of strength or speed. Their strength was in their technology, their minds, their ability to create. Where a vampire and werewolf's power came from within, a human's came from everything around them that they could manipulate and use to their advantage. If it hadn't been for the thousands of years humanity had had to establish complete control of the planet, Gyldan wasn't sure they would have adapted so quickly.

But then again, he hated how vampires and werewolves were treated. Everything had been imperfectly fair before the introduction of the eye-guards and trap-collars. Indeed, there had been a thousand ways in which the world of yesterday could have been improved. But it was damn sight better than the perfectly cruel world of today.

In an ideal world, everyone would be able to trust everyone else. Gyldan knew this was a ridiculous wish though. The problem wasn't one or two species... it was the capacity for selfishness and evil in all beings. There would always be someone who wanted more than others. Or someone who was just bored.

He couldn't help but look at Albion. His perfect frustration. The man sipped at his mocha, pulled a face, then set the mug back down.

"Hmph. Slumming it doesn't suit me after all. Back to mine?" An instruction wrapped around an offer, Gyldan knew if he said no it would hurt the man, but he would let him go home all the same. Albion was a jerk, but there were still flecks of goodness left in his heart. Gyldan believed he could coax them out, and what a day it would be if he could.

The most powerful man in the world... a good man. What a dream.

"Sure," Gyldan replied. In truth, Albion's place sounded more appealing anyway.

After all, the vampire-led inquisition was waiting for him back home.

※ ※ ※

Albion's home was the sort of home where one had to wonder how it was kept so spotless. It spanned such a huge area that Gyldan was pretty sure an entire cleaning company existed just to cater to his home. Still, he would have thought it was a twenty-four seven job to keep the building tidy, yet he had never once seen a cleaning person wandering around the place.

Calling its grand pillars of ivory white and sprawling grounds of plush grass a mere mansion was a bit of an understatement, but it was the closest Gyldan could get to an accurate description without resorting to Grecian temples. Even the living room, which he was currently settled in as he waited for Albion to return from the kitchen, was bigger than the entire ground floor of his own home. Carved in the man's silken taste for monochrome, the only splash of colour in the room came from the large family photograph on the wall next to the television screen. Printed across a luxurious stretched canvas, it was an image that Gyldan had a strange sense of respect for—a snapshot of Albion's fractured family.

A younger Albion smiled out from the photograph, radiating with pride for the people around him. To his right, a gorgeous woman with glossy brown locks that waved past her shoulders was leaning forward to hug a sulking girl sitting on her knee. The little girl, who could not have been more than one year old at the time, had inherited her mother's hair and her father's eyes. To the girl's left, held securely in Albion's arms, was a slightly older boy who was doing his utmost to out-smile his father, all crooked baby teeth and scrunched-shut eyes for the effort of it. It was sorrowing to think that, at the moment this photo had been taken, the boy had had no idea what a legacy he would create.

For Albion's son was a well-known and respected part of the company. Every Caladrius employee knew his name, and the annual fundraiser for the boy was always one of the biggest events they hosted. In truth, Caladrius usually broke even between the lavish spending on the event compared to the actual donations they received. It was bad business. But no one could tell Albion not to throw his dead son this thinly veiled birthday party each year.

After all, Caladrius Saint-Richter was the reason the company that bore his name existed.

Gyldan broke away from the picture before he could get lost any further in its sadness. He cleared his throat, partly to get Albion's attention, partly to dislodge the lump forming there.

"There's something really wrong about ordering a grease-covered pizza to a place like this," Gyldan pondered out loud, dragging a slice of pizza from the open box on a coffee table that had no doubt cost more than an entire year's rent at his house. He sat himself down on the sofa and added: "It just feels wrong."

"You don't have to eat it. Yanatha loves cold pizza, she'll save you from yourself." Albion emerged from the kitchen he had not used once in the time Gyldan had known him, save for collecting beers as he had done now. He plopped down on the sofa next to Gyldan and handed him one of the bottles, green eyes glittering with mischief. It was in moments like this that the man made it so easy for Gyldan to forget how awful he could be, how skewed his view of the world was.

"Is Yanatha home?" Gyldan glanced out towards the hall, as though Albion's daughter would walk by with burning ears.

"She's in her room. As always," Albion huffed, taking a swig of his beer then wincing. "You know, she says I'm too overprotective, but then she never leaves her room. Except when she's visiting Freya..."

Upon hearing that name, Gyldan found his attention back on the family portrait again, gazing up at the beautiful woman in the photograph. Many things had died with Caladrius Saint-Richter... including his parents' marriage. The name 'Freya' was something of a taboo with Albion, and Gyldan didn't dare press the matter yet.

The older man continued: "I'm begging her to go outside. It can't be good for her. I suppose I was something of a hermit at nineteen too, but I was working."

"Maybe she's nervous," Gyldan offered, leaning across the man to pick up the TV remote from his arm of the chair.

"About what? I hire the best security guards for her. She's got nothing to worry about."

Gyldan flicked the TV on and, as if to confirm his point, the first thing that beamed across the ridiculously sized screen was a news story—a specialist analysis of the recent spate of murders, all of which seemed to target Daedalus employees.

"That? Maybe?"

"*Pssh*, please. No daughter of mine is working for Daedalus. She couldn't be further from this lunatic's target list."

"But this guy seems to think it's a werewolf," Gyldan said, pointing at the screen with the neck of his beer. "See? Claw marks, that's more like a werewolf."

"That's because he's a *fool*," Albion said slowly, leaning into Gyldan with his shoulder to knock him slightly. "It can't possibly be a werewolf. The victims have bite marks, and it is clearly lucid enough to target people. It's obviously a vampire."

"What makes you so certain?"

Albion regarded him with a withering look that did nothing to conceal his rude concern for Gyldan's intellect.

"Because werewolves lose their minds under a full moon. These attacks aren't only happening during a full moon. Unless you are suggesting this is a werewolf in its controlled form, but they go about on four legs then, not two. The height of this beast would suggest it walks on two legs. I am sure it is just a feral, unregistered vampire. Most likely, it's never been within society before. Let its nails grow too long and embraced the 'wild man' look." He smirked and chuckled to himself.

Gyldan chose not to argue. For one, he wasn't wholly convinced of this expert's analysis of the situation himself. But he wasn't sure Albion had the right of it either. From what gruesome information the media had lapped up and sent out to panic the masses, the victims were ripped to pieces. That didn't fit most vampires' abilities. But, his boss was also right—werewolves, under the full moon, weren't able to tell friend from foe, let alone make a targeted attack. Not that Gyldan had seen much of a moon-form werewolf, even living with Seraph and Caelan. There were laws and regulations for werewolves regarding the full moon, and if they were caught out, authorities were allowed to collar on sight.

To *kill* on sight.

It was only natural that they had taken great pains to ensure a full moon could never creep up on them, and they spent their time indoors with all the curtains drawn during such nights.

"I bet it was that cretin who got into my office today," Albion piped up suddenly, taking a thoughtful swig of his beer. Gyldan almost choked on his own drink.

"W-what?"

"Maybe he's moving on up in the world," Albion continued, ignorant of the other man's shock. "Maybe he's grown tired of Daedalus targets, and now he's aiming higher. Aimed a little *too* high and went straight for me."

"N-nah, I don't... he didn't seem like he'd... lived in the wild..." Gyldan countered, becoming very fixated with the label on his beer, peeling the edge a little under his fingertips. To his left, Albion shifted, sitting up a little straighter.

"Do you think so?"

"Mmm."

"From what you saw?"

"I—" Gyldan's voice abandoned him as Albion's accusation and suspicions latched around his windpipe.

Crap.

He scrambled to recover, his shoulders tensing, throat constricting: "N-no, from what you *said*. You said before he didn't have an eye-guard. An older vampire who went through the first eye process. The surgery would have been noted in medical records. This specialist said whoever's behind these attacks isn't showing up on any vampire or werewolf records."

After a brief pause, Albion settled back down, the leather of the sofa creaking a little as his back pressed into it.

"All right," was the man's only response, and it both relaxed and terrified Gyldan. The less Albion spoke, the more worrisome it was.

For a while, the two men watched the news in silence. Gyldan allowed himself to settle against Albion, leaning ever so slightly into him and asking a silent question—*we good?* Peering up at the man, he could see the CEO's valiant attempts to maintain a rigid and stoic expression. Then, his lip quivered up, cracking into a smirk, though his attention remained fixed on the TV screen.

"Are you hitting on me, tiger?"

Gyldan rolled his eyes. Though Albion was ten years older than he was, Gyldan often felt like the more mature of the two of them.

"Yes. It's taken *this* long and *this* many nights together for me to work up the courage to hit on you," he drawled. Then again, their being together was such a closely guarded secret that Gyldan could forgive Albion for being shocked to hear about it.

It had not been part of the plan when Rukshana suggested years ago that Gyldan's promotion at work was "the perfect chance" to get close to Albion and make a real change from the inside. Well, he had gotten close. Too close.

It turned out that, under all the bravado and ruthlessness, Albion was Gyldan's type. Gyldan had spent the first few months of their secretive meetings and stolen make-out sessions in company closets, assured in the fact that this was just another way to achieve his group's goal much quicker. His brain agreed. His heart had not, and it had rather rudely ruined Gyldan's plans by falling for Albion. He often wondered if this had slowed down their plan to steal the release codes, and more than once, it had left Gyldan with yet another sleepless night riddled with guilt. At the end of the day, he knew he was betraying both his friends and Albion, in one way or another.

"I was beginning to wonder," his perhaps-boyfriend wondered aloud. "So unprofessional of you. As my PA. Verbal warning. Tut-tut."

Still, Albion moved to loop his arm around Gyldan's shoulders, letting him burrow himself more snugly into the warmth and comfort of the older man's side.

"You're one to talk," Gyldan mumbled, drawing in a deep breath as he did so. Despite all the problems in Albion's orbit, Gyldan couldn't help but yearn for that scent of amber and earth.

It just never failed to settle his heart. "Gonna flag it with HR tomorrow. Boss is making eyes at me."

"God, I'm going to miss you, you were a *great* PA..." Albion teased, flicking Gyldan's ear.

"Eh, well, I heard Daedalus has a few vacancies." Gyldan met his teasing with some newfound confidence he'd not known he possessed until this comfortable moment. He was immediately jostled by Albion laughing, his chest rising and falling so sharply that he knocked Gyldan from his comfy position.

"Oh, please... even without the murders, Daedalus has got a year or two left. Deep down, Carpenter knows it. *Urgh*, speak of the jester..."

Albion let his head fall back against the sofa, a hand resting across his eyes for dramatic flair. Gyldan turned his attention to the TV screen, noting that the news anchor had moved on from interviewing the specialist to interviewing the CEO of Daedalus, Walter Carpenter.

Gyldan had only met with Walter Carpenter once before, but he hadn't changed much. The man looked like an overgrown weasel wearing a suit, hands wringing, nose twitching. His pale eyes pierced the news anchor in place with a look that accused her of being against him already.

"We're joined now by Daedalus CEO, Walter Carpenter. Walter, thank you so much for joining us." The dutiful news presenter flashed him a smile. It was not returned.

Albion gave a loud and grumbling sigh, getting to his feet and picking up the empty pizza boxes and beer bottles before heading into the kitchen.

"Shout me when Walter's crawled off my TV screen." The man grinned as he left the room, then called back: "Oh, are you wanting to stay the night? I don't like the idea of you walking home this late with a killer around, and the drivers are off-duty..."

"Ah, yeah, if that's okay?" Gyldan called back, tilting his head over his shoulder a little but keeping his eyes fixed on the

TV screen. Albion might be happy to dismiss his competition, but Gyldan liked to know what they were up to.

"—viously, whoever this *cretin* is, he is trying to scare us." Walter's creaking voice attempted to muster some gusto, but it only made him sound flustered. "With Daedalus' cure just on the horizon, it's natural that some less-upstanding members of the Lupus and Sanguinis community may want to stall us."

"But, correct me if I'm wrong, Walter—Daedalus has missed the last two promised deadlines for its proposed cure. Why would this be the killer's motive?" the news presenter asked. From the kitchen, Albion gave an audible snort of laughter.

On the TV screen, Walter bristled and tugged at the lapels of his jacket.

"Well, I don't think—"

Gyldan's attention was once again taken from the TV screen, this time by the sound of his phone rumbling across the coffee table, demanding to be acknowledged.

"Is that mine?" Albion called. Gyldan leant forward, grabbing his phone from next to Albion's.

"Nah, mine. Housemate's probably locked out or something," he quickly lied, opening the message. It was from Seraph, and despite everything, the little icon of the pixie-haired blonde sticking her tongue out made Gyldan smile.

You still stuck in your office, dude? Need me to come in there swinging?

Settling back in his seat and tucking his legs under him, Gyldan typed back:

No, I'm fine. Lying low at a friend's just in case. Griff ok?

Three dots danced on the screen, and a reply came soon after:

He's good. What about the cameras in the hall though? They'll have seen you leave at the same time as shit hitting the fan. Just say the word and claws can be swinging.

Gyldan huffed a laugh, shaking his head a little. He was pretty sure Seraph was just upset that she'd missed out on a fight today.

I dealt with the cameras. All pointing away from my office. No worries. No claws, please. See you tomorrow.

Once again, three dots bounced up and down before a response arrived:

Nerd.

Smiling, Gyldan leant over to put his phone back on the table. Just as he did so, Albion's phone buzzed to life. He hadn't really meant to look, and yet, Gyldan couldn't help but notice a few words jump out from the message preview:

Cure test... progress... still not...

He was struck with a primal urge to grab the phone and tear open the message, but he managed to calm himself enough to sit back in his seat. Still, his blood ran cold.

A cure? From Caladrius?

Daedalus had been mocked for years by the media for its ambitious and, frankly, ridiculous quest. The only reason they had stuck so rigidly to their daft claim was *because* Caladrius wasn't even attempting it. It was an ethical nightmare, a scientific conundrum, and simply ludicrous. It was so far away from realistic that Albion hadn't even entertained the idea of looking into it himself.

Or so Gyldan had believed.

In the background, he was numbly aware of an advert playing on TV—"*If you suspect someone of being in the thrall of a vampire, remember: F.A.N.G. Face, Answer, Name, Gone... firstly, face. Is their expression blank or slow to—*"

"A-Al?" Gyldan's voice squeaked a little.

"If they've locked themselves out, tell them to go to a hotel and give me the details—I'll pay for it. I'm not having you wandering home at this hour for your idiot housemate," Albion said, arriving back in the living room with two fresh beers.

"Wha—oh, n-no, it wasn't... she's fine. Listen, do you think er... Walter sounds really sure of himself. About a cure," Gyldan said, trying to avoid showing any suspicion. "Do you think it's plausible?"

"You're not worried about a little competition, are you?" Albion hooked his arm around Gyldan and pulled him in for a one-armed hug. "Don't worry. He's crazy. It's genetic, not a virus or disease. Walter hasn't got a hope in hell of untangling this mutation. Daedalus isn't, and never will be, a threat to Caladrius."

Gyldan looked at his untouched beer, a coldness still wriggling in his chest, then considered Albion's beautiful face that was inches from his own. His perfect frustration.

Daedalus wasn't the threat that would follow Gyldan into the early hours of the morning, wringing his brain with worry.

Chapter 3

  He had only intended to stay for one night. But the problem with Gyldan was that once he started worrying, time ran away from him. He could lose hours to rumination, and even more hours trying to hide the fact that he was wrapped up in his own head. Luckily, Albion was not the sort to notice another's plight, nor to question why someone would want to spend longer in his company. So, when one evening rolled into two, not a single question was raised.

  At least, not by his boyfriend.

  "If your phone goes off one more time, I'm going to have Jeeves throw it from the third floor," the older man complained as the familiar buzzing of Gyldan's phone reverberated through the wooden bedside table. Between his grumbling and the phone's vibration, Gyldan was half-asleep, stirring from the tangle of silk covers with a deep inhalation. He was rudely jostled awake by Albion's arm landing across his lower face as the CEO tried to paw across Gyldan in search of the offending phone. "Who is it? I'm going to... get them fired from wherever they work..."

Gyldan sat up, peeling Albion's arm off his face as he did so and picked up his phone.

"You don't even *have* a butler," Gyldan noted, his brain catching up to his ears much too late. "Or a third floor."

"*Meergh*... I'll... get some..." his disgruntled lover mumbled, brows furrowing even though he hadn't bothered to open his eyes yet. A soft chuckle huffed from Gyldan's nostrils and he patted Albion's upper arm once, then turned his attention to his phone.

One missed call from Rukshana. One voicemail from Rukshana. Fifteen messages from Seraph. Two messages from Griff that both started with: "Seraphina asked me to message you—".

Steeling himself, Gyldan opted to open one of Seraph's messages.

Yo, we're getting worried! What's happening? You ok?

One of the calmer ones, then. Gyldan tapped out a reply:

Sorry, phone died, didn't have a charger with me, just bought one. Heading home now once I've charged a bit. See you soon.

No three dots danced for him this time—no doubt the werewolf was still asleep. Seraph wasn't much of a morning person, but her girlfriend would have been up at the crack of dawn. With that in mind, he swiped across his screen and sent a quick message to Rukshana:

Messaged Seraph. Sorry, things got hectic. I'll be back this morning. Need anything?

This time, three dots began to jump across the screen quickly.

Understandable. It all could have gone better. Could have gone worse too. Can you pick up some steak for Seraph on your way back, please?

Gyldan allowed himself to wince a little. Steak? Seraph must have spent the night foaming at the mouth about his silence. Steak was an expensive apology suggestion.

That bad, huh? Ah man, I'm sorry. Seriously. I just didn't want anyone following me home from work. Steak it is.

He scooted out of bed and crept across the overly plush carpet on his quest to find fresh clothes from the walk-in wardrobe at the end of Albion's room. Another one of Gyldan's favourite perks as Albion's personal assistant was having his wardrobe taken care of for him. He was the sort of person who yearned to look fashionable, and yet, once the rent, food, and bills for four people were taken care of, his wallet was left wanting. It had only taken a few months on the job before Albion had finally cracked and, unable to take Gyldan's best attempts at budget high fashion anymore, had hired him a personal shopper. Thus, anything he took out of his wardrobe, either at home or from the stash of clothes he kept at Albion's house, always suited him perfectly.

Gyldan didn't risk turning the light on in the walk-in wardrobe lest he wake Albion up. Plus, it was depressing to see clearly under the bright light that the man's wardrobe was twice the size of Gyldan's bedroom.

Squinting through the gloom, he picked out a pair of dark wash jeans and an open-buttoned shirt over a snug black tee. He quickly changed, then headed back into the bedroom on light feet. Gyldan felt a little more casual than he might have liked, but at least he knew he looked good. After a quick check in the mirror to sort out his hair, he crept over to Albion's side of the king-sized bed and pressed a light kiss on his temple.

A grunting "*Meeergh...*" was the only response he received for his gentle display of affection.

"Gotta go, work stuff. My boss is a dick and will fire me if I don't get some paperwork pushed soon," Gyldan whispered.

"M'going to… punch your boss in the face…" Albion muttered back, and Gyldan could only choke back a laugh at the idea of the man punching himself in the face.

"Thanks, appreciate it," he said instead around the restrained laugh. "Later!"

Half-jogging down the stairs and into the hallway, Gyldan lurched to a halt as he noticed a young woman sitting at the breakfast bar in the kitchen through the archway to his left. Her rich brown hair was scraped up in a messy bun to keep it from dipping into her breakfast, and familiar green eyes caught him from a less-familiar face. She nodded upwards in greeting, or more accurately, acknowledgement of his presence.

"Gyl."

"Morning, Yanatha." Gyldan shuffled over to lean in the archway, feeling uncomfortable at the fact he'd just barrelled out of her father's bedroom. Though he and Albion had been together for months now, Gyldan had only crossed Yanatha a handful of times, with little more than pleasantries exchanged. It didn't appear as though she objected to Gyldan—worse, she just did not seem to register him at all. Yanatha had her own life, and for all the world, it did not involve her father much. She appeared perfectly content with that.

"Dad said if you left before he got up to tell you to take the spare activator," Yanatha mumbled, going back to her cereal. "On the counter by the door."

Stumbling a thanks to the woman, Gyldan darted to the door if only to avoid the cloud of palpable awkwardness that was lumbering towards him the longer they attempted to interact. Just as she'd said, a silver device on a small keychain lay on the counter. It was smooth, no bigger than Gyldan's palm, and housed two flat, circular buttons that raised mere millimetres from its surface in a slick display of design work. Once more, his stomach coiled up in knots as his brain coldly reminded him of the purpose of those buttons.

One for vampires. One for werewolves. Range: one metre.

If he didn't take it, Albion would be suspicious. But on the other hand, having a device sitting in his pocket that could kill his friends didn't make him feel much better. Gyldan hesitated, then picked up the device, the keychain entwined between trembling fingers. He had already resolved to take it and destroy it. Albion need never know.

Swallowing against the dry lump forming in his throat, Gyldan hurried out of the front door. Squinting against the sun and bracing against the bright morning chill, Gyldan shrugged on his jacket and stuffed his hands into his pockets, setting off down the gravel driveway at a trot.

Albion's mansion wasn't far from the city, and it was a walk that the personal assistant had done time and time again. His feet knew the route without much thought, which unfortunately left Gyldan a good twenty minutes trying to ignore his brain's attempts to bombard him with questions.

They're going to be so mad at you.
You should have gone home sooner.
What about poor Griff?
What about the bloody message?

It kept coming back to that brief glimpse he'd caught on Albion's phone a few nights before. He hadn't been able to see the full message, of course, but what he had seen of the notification refused to leave his head.

Cure test... progress... still not...

The man was so wrapped up in debating different ways to sleuth out information regarding these secretive tests at Caladrius that he didn't notice he was at risk of walking right into someone. Their hands shot out and grabbed his upper arms, startling him out of his thoughts. Almost on instinct, Gyldan went for the activator in his pocket, halted only by a stab of guilt for doing so. He felt even worse when he realised who it was he'd almost walked into—the grinning face of Griffin dragged Gyldan from his anxious thoughts.

"I thought you might walk this way eventually," the old man said around his smile, without a hint of accusation. There was something comforting about seeing Griff in his usual clothes again instead of his journalist disguise—a baggy, long-sleeved shirt that might once have been white but was now unashamedly beige was rolled up to the elbows, and a simple pair of jeans matched up shoddily with the royal purple silk that Griff liked to wrap around his missing eyes. On more than one occasion, Seraph had teased the vampire that his silk wraps were more expensive than the rest of his wardrobe put together.

"Griff! Are you okay? How did you—?"

"Hmmm, I'm fine. A few bruises, but healing quickly, as we do," Griffin hummed, absently scratching at his exposed forearm. An angry red rash was prickling over the vampire's skin as they spoke, and it wasn't long before he caved and took hold of Gyldan's shoulders, steering them both into a shaded part of the street. "*Yeesh*, but it'll take longer if I'm sitting here cooking in the sun. What doesn't kill us gives us blisters, son." His nostrils flared and he added: "You smell tired. Coffee?"

"...*Smell*... tired?" Gyldan gave a cautious sniff to his armpit. "You can... smell tiredness?"

Vampires and werewolves had slightly sharper senses than humans, but Gyldan had always thought it was the wolves that had keener noses. Vampires had keener eyesight. Unless... had all of Griff's senses increased when he was blinded?

Griff patted the younger man once on his back, giving the impression that he knew what the other was thinking.

"Yeah. It smells like stale beer, junk food, and sweat. Ya friend doesn't have a shower at his place? You always walk back this way when you stay a night at your friend's house."

Oh.

"Oh erm... well, you know... it's always weird asking, don't you think? In someone else's house?" Gyldan babbled, letting Griff steer him into a café whilst being horribly aware of his own apparent musk. It wasn't until Griffin had found them a table and sat the young man down in a rickety steel chair that he realised they weren't in a café at all.

The air was candied with thick clouds of vanilla and sugar, and a sharp scent of coffee tried in vain to be noticed among the din of syrups and sweetness. Gyldan looked around at the bright pink-and-white room and then plucked a creased menu from its stand and flipped it over.

He didn't have the heart to tell the blind vampire that he'd walked them into an ice cream parlour and not a café. They still sold coffee though. He could mask the mistake easily enough.

"Sit down, I'll get them. Least I can do after disappearing on you guys," Gyldan smiled, getting to his feet and helping Griff find his seat. "What do you fancy?"

"Ah, thanks, kid! Glucose Glory sundae, please," the vampire replied, grinning up at Gyldan.

Gyldan cycled through being surprised, unsurprised, and impressed that the blind vampire *had* known this wasn't a café the whole time. He should have guessed—the old man had a sweet tooth so great that it threatened to rot his fangs. A vampire's diet was limited, but if it could be carried in the blood, it was fair game to the species. Luckily for Griff, this included copious amounts of sugar.

Smirking to himself, Gyldan clapped a hand on Griffin's shoulder and gave him a playful shake.

"'*Let's go get a coffee*', huh?" he said, imitating Griffin's gruff voice.

"For you, son, not for me," the old vampire replied, matter-of-factly. "You're the one that smells like a kebab shop on a Saturday night."

Gyldan's mouth twisted with a bleak smile that didn't even reach his nose, let alone the rest of his face.

"Thanks, Griff."

On that emboldening note, he moved over to the glass counter housing a colourful display of ice-cream to order the old man a sundae and a particularly strong coffee for himself. He made a concerted effort to angle himself downwind from the shop assistant, lest she catch a whiff of *eau de junk food*.

As the lady set about fixing his order, Gyldan turned to lean against the candy-pink counter and watched the small TV that mumbled away on the wall.

"*If you suspect someone of being in the thrall of a vampire, remember: F.A.N.G. Face, Answer, Name, Gone. Firstly, the face. Is their expression blank or slow to change?*" The sombre-sounding man droned through the TV screen as two actors hammed their way through a pretend thralling. "*Then, their answers—does your loved one trail off when asked a question? Ask them their name—do they struggle to recall it quickly? Finally, gone—have they gone out for long periods of time without telling you where they are going?*"

"I swear this advert's been on repeat the last few days," the shop assistant noted as she slid Gyldan's order over to him. Adorned with red sweets and a tiny parasol, the sundae was almost as well-dressed as Gyldan was. "You heard about the murders, right? It's all 'cause of that."

Gyldan frowned as he picked up the mug and sundae glass, but he didn't return to his seat immediately.

"'Cause they think it's a vampire?"

"Nah—some scientist on the news this morning reckons the markings don't match up with a werewolf or a vampire. Said people have been forgetting there's another possible culprit." The lady smirked, sitting on the little titbit of information for a moment longer. Gyldan only got a moment to stew on the conundrum before she leant in to stage-whisper: "They think it's a *human*. Under an illegal vampire's thrall!" She moved back then, shaking her head and giving a small *harumph* of distaste to herself. "Crazy world, I tell ya. Revoking the housing laws for werewolves after the collars came in was a mistake. Shouldn't have got rid of it—shoulda added the vampires to it too, ban the lot of them from living in cities. It's not *safe*, is it?"

Gyldan gave the woman a weak smile before heading back over to where Griffin was sitting.

"It wasn't a bloody human," the old man chuckled, making no effort to hide that he'd eavesdropped. "Even if some unregistered vampire thralled a human, we can't make people do the impossible."

He scooted his sundae glass closer, drew out the long, thin spoon buried within its frozen sweetness, and then popped it in his mouth, the metal clicking against his fangs. After a moment, he pulled the spoon back out and added an afterthought: "Unless a vamp told a human to file his teeth down to fangs and *then* attack people. But then the claw marks don't add up..."

Griff's voice wandered off as he muttered away to himself, leaving Gyldan to sip his coffee and wonder if the other man had forgotten he was there. Griffin wasn't senile by any stretch of the imagination. He'd simply lived in a world that had been built against him for too long. It had jaded him, stripped the shine from his soul. Yet, Gyldan adored how the vampire refused to let it have the last of him. He still smiled through the tired lines etched into his face. He still trusted people despite knowing the sting of betrayal all too well. He still loved with all his heart, and that had been a lifeline for Gyldan, Rukshana, and Seraph.

"How're you feeling anyway, Griff? Y'know, after..." Gyldan motioned to the side a little, motioning at days gone by. He stopped as he realised the vampire wouldn't see the gesture anyway, and an embarrassed blush prickled across his face. Meanwhile, Griffin hummed low in his throat, then waved one hand once, twice to the side.

"I told you, I told Seraphina, I told Rukshana, I'm *fine*," he said. "But for what you're really asking, I'm not mad at you for not coming home right away. It made sense. After what Caelan said, they'll be looking at everyone in Caladrius now. You were right to lay low—"

The old man's faith in Gyldan only made his guilt treble in size and threaten to suffocate him. Here he was, absolving him of any wrongdoing, not knowing that Gyl hadn't just been laying low, but had been lying with the enemy they—

"—even if your choice in men is fucking awful."

Gyldan's breath got stuck somewhere between his chest and his nose, causing him to choke on his spit. The only balm against this raw shock to the system was Griffin's crackling, barking laugh.

"H-how did—what do you mean, *my taste in men?*" Gyldan hissed, leaning over the table and shooting a panicked look towards the waitress in case she showed any signs of overhearing. If she had heard, she was doing a very good job of being engrossed in wiping down a coffee mug. Gyldan's suspicious mind latched on to that and assured him she had definitely overheard, and he would need to overthink that later.

Griffin drew forward to meet him, sniffing once.

"He wears too much cologne. Could smell it all over his office, son," he said, though he didn't sound angry or disappointed. It didn't stop Gyldan from feeling utterly wretched.

"I... I'm sorry, Griff. I would have told you guys, but... it wasn't meant to—"

Griff stopped him, holding up a hand against his barrage of apologies.

"Don't worry about it, Gyl. I trust you. If nothing else, it could be useful," he said, then lowered his voice to a hushed tone. "Those release codes are still in his safe. We need you to broadcast the code when we get it, so we can't risk you getting caught lifting 'em yourself. But he trusts you now. You can distract him for us next time. You'd rather that than us having to fight him, right? I mean... Albion ain't the enemy. Not really."

"He's... not?" Though he was confused, Griffin's words had lightened the load on his heart. The vampire nodded.

"Sure. He's just giving people what they want. What they asked for."

"So, what... people are the problem for you?" Gyldan raised an eyebrow. Griff leant back in his seat and shrugged.

"...Aren't they for you too?"

A silence settled over the men as Gyldan considered Griffin's words of wisdom. He had a point—after all, hadn't he been thinking the same thing? That there would always be someone who wanted more? Someone who would give the people what they wanted in exchange for fame and fortune? If not Albion, it would have been someone else. Yes, he was a problem... but he was just the figurehead of a deeper problem, a face and a name to put against an immaterial sickness simmering in the underbelly of the world.

Griff dropped his spoon into the now-empty sundae glass, metal chiming on glass. He wiped the edges of his mouth with a napkin, then tucked that into the glass too. "Probably shouldn't tell the girls just yet though. They aren't ready to make an enemy of the world yet. Good thing too. That's too much bitterness for anyone. Albion's face is punchable enough for now."

Gyldan couldn't be annoyed at that. He couldn't expect them to see what he saw in Albion. Lust was blind, but love? Love just sighed and nodded, seeing every flaw in stark contrast against a backdrop of everything good in a person. When it came to Albion, sometimes it was difficult to see that colourful backdrop at all.

Getting to his feet, Gyldan left a few coins as a tip before taking Griff by the elbow and helping him up too. The two men made their way out of the ice cream parlour and along the bustling street once more.

After a while, Griff leant into him and said under his breath: "Still... Albion's going to be a bit of a problem for me, son. He saw my face after all. I'm a wanted man now."

Gyldan chuckled.

"You sound pretty proud about that, old man."

"Hmm-mmm, maybe," Griff cooed, waggling his head from side to side with a smirk blooming across his lips. "But still, if Caladrius announces what happened at their offices, I'm... I'm gonna have to disappear for a while. To keep you and the girls safe." The smirk had disappeared, and Gyldan heard Griffin's heart break within his words. He gave him a reassuring squeeze across the shoulders.

"Nah, don't worry about all that. There's been nothing on the news about it, right? Because the company can't afford to look weak. It can't afford to let its enemies know its security can be breached. Albion won't tell anyone what happened, he's too proud. He'd be a laughing stock if the media found out that a vampire got all the way up to his private offices," he explained. "So, no disappearing on us. Okay?"

Griffin looked thoughtful for a moment before an unsure hum curled from his throat.

"*Hmmm*, if you say so. But if he does... I can trust Seraphina to look after you lot."

The two men continued down the road and turned a corner, heading away from the busy centre and out towards the quieter edges of the city. Their home was atop a small hill that was just steep enough to rob Gyl of his breath by the time he got to the top. At the foot of the hill, the two men passed a church and its humble grounds, a few gravestones piercing up from the earth. It was only when they walked by the stone wall separating the path from the cemetery that Gyldan realised he'd missed his usual Sunday trip.

"Ah crap..." he said under his breath, but Griff's sharp ears caught it all the same.

"What's that?"

"Oh, nothing, just... didn't visit my parents yesterday," Gyldan admitted. His ability to let people down, alive or dead, was unmatched.

"Ah." Griff nodded in understanding. "Rukshana went for you. Popped some flowers down. She's a good lass."

Griffin's words slowed Gyldan's pace. His jaw dropped in awe, his heart swelling with gratitude. He had thought Rukshana and Seraph would be mad at him for his disappearing act, and yet, they still looked out for him like this.

"...*Shit!*" Gyldan yelped, suddenly remembering. "Steak! Rukshana wanted me to—oh, goddammit, the *one* thing she asked. Griff, I gotta head back to the shops and pick up some steak for Seraph. You wanna come with me, or...?"

"I'll be fine, it's all uphill from here," Griff assured him, unlinking his arm from Gyl. "Go on, I don't wanna deal with a grumpy werewolf all night any more than you do!"

"I'll not be long!" Gyldan promised him, before darting off back down the road, heading to the nearest shop.

There was no shortage of options in the city, with several franchises all vying for custom. The first shop he passed proudly displayed a message in the window that declared they didn't serve vampires or werewolves, so Gyldan walked by on principle. It added an extra five minutes to his walk, and an extra sense of decency overall.

Finding another store, Gyldan popped in and headed over to the small display of meat in the refrigeration unit. He decided that his apology needed to be sirloin-steak level rather than a mere rib-eye, so he picked up a few packets of the wrapped, raw cuts. On his way to the counter, Gyldan paused at the cabinet displaying candied blood clots. He couldn't help but wrinkle his nose up—someone in the vampire community could make a killing by starting up a good marketing company. There had to be a better way to brand blood-based food products. Either way, he picked up a few packets of the candied blood too and headed to the counter.

The portly shop keeper looked at him, then his neck, then his pile of meat and blood purchases. Maybe it was a bit odd for someone without an eye-guard or silver collar to buy sugar-coated clots, but Gyldan didn't see the need to explain himself. He gave the shop keeper nothing but a forced smile, then paid for his goods.

Gathering up his purchases, Gyldan headed outside again, carrying the items under one arm and shoving his hands in his pockets. He found his mind wandering to the sign in the first shop he had passed and, as though it would prove any sort of point, he elected to walk a slightly different route home to avoid it altogether.

Not long into his rerouted walk, Gyldan spotted a small gathering of people, the noise swelling through the air as he approached. Crossing by an alleyway, a large cordon had been set up in an arc around its entrance, forcing disgruntled pedestrians to either walk around or pause and crane their necks to see what was going on. Gyldan fell into the latter category. He slowed his pace and tried to catch a glimpse of whatever it was that had caused the commotion. He could see a few police officers—a fight, perhaps?—and a white material on the floor.

He couldn't help the audible gasp as he realised what was being covered on the floor, with officers scurrying to conceal the scene from the growing amount of prying eyes. Whoever had been killed here had met their fate recently.

His pulse quickening along with his footsteps, Gyldan was consumed with the desire to get home, to get safe, to get away. He tore down the street as fast as he could without breaking into a run, dipping into a different alleyway to cut his route down as much as possible.

Between trying to ignore what he'd just seen and trying to focus on getting home, Gyldan almost missed the gleaming eyes watching him from the shadows of the alleyway.

Almost.

His legs locked. His jaw clenched, demanding that he didn't scream in terror. His arms went slack, sending packets of food tumbling to the floor. For all the world, Gyldan could do nothing but stare back at the four eyes glinting in the gloom. Crimson in colour, save for a starburst of green around the irises, Gyldan only realised that all four eyes belonged to one being when each one blinked in unison.

Then, they rose. Even if his jaw hadn't locked, Gyldan knew he would not be able to scream, his mouth and throat drying as he tilted his head to follow the creature.

Vampire. Vampire. Wild vampire, his mind stammered. *Run. Gyldan. Get out of there.*

He couldn't move.

But *it* could.

In a blur of staggering speed for a creature its size, the being howled and started forward. A scream scraped from Gyldan's dry throat then and he lurched backwards, arms up to shield himself, falling back onto the ground and landing among several rubbish bags. He yelped, he blubbed, he made a frantic scramble to the wall to try and get out of the way. His hands tore at his pockets, yanking out the activator Albion had left for him. He smashed at the buttons once, twice, three times, again and again.

It wasn't until he realised he could still hear his own breath, shaking and whimpering, that Gyldan stopped his frenzied hammering of the activator's button. He uncurled a little, casting a frantic look up and down the alleyway.

No dead vampire. No dead werewolf. No monster at all. He was alone, quivering against the stone wall, thumb slowly jabbing at the activator one more time.

All at once, every limb in his body went limp as an audible exhalation of relief spilt from Gyldan's lips. Once he had regained his breath and mind somewhat, he looked down at the activator resting in his loose grip.

At that moment, Gyldan realised he was one of them. The chasm between him and his friends yawned ever wider as he realised that, in that moment of fear, he would have killed a vampire or werewolf without hesitation. He was one of the people Griffin had spoken about in the ice cream parlour—the ones that demanded weapons be made against every little thing they felt personally threatened by. The call of humanity that Albion had answered.

Chapter 4

  The days that followed the encounter in the alleyway churned together, becoming a thick and dredging heaviness that weighed on Gyldan's conscience. He found he could not yet speak to Griffin, Seraph, or Rukshana about the creature he'd seen on the way home that day. He knew he should. But his tongue remained shackled out of shame and out of confusion over what exactly the monster in the alleyway was.

  The creature had lunged at him. It had been near the murder scene and had charged at him. Was he a bad person for pressing the activator? For being prepared to defend himself? Gyldan couldn't answer those questions, but he also couldn't give them a voice either.

  "Hey? Earth to Gyl?" Seraph's voice chimed in.

  Gyldan blinked, his eyes stinging in response. Everything surged back into focus—the colourful lights, the rumbling of crowds, the electronic blips of machines around him. The local arcade, *The Blue Rocket*, was something of a refuge, as it was one of the few places that allowed humans, vampires, and werewolves in as customers.

Seraph was sitting on top of a blue and white crane machine to Gyldan's right, while Rukshana was paying a pocketful of coins into the next crane machine along, engrossed in her quest to win a soft toy white wolf that was more fluffy than ferocious. There was a palpable tension between the two women, one that had lingered ever since their attempted heist of Caladrius. Whatever Seraph had said, Gyldan assumed she was trying to make Rukshana feel better, but he'd missed it entirely.

"S-sorry?" Gyldan asked, assuming he'd missed something.

"About Caelan?" Seraph prompted him, her eyebrows raised a little. She shook her head when it became clear Gyldan had no idea what she was referring to and repeated: "Do you think he was a traitor the whole time?"

He was glad to have something else to ponder over, but the topic of their late friend was not an enjoyable alternative. Still, Gyldan pursed his lips in thought and crossed his arms.

"I don't think so. I mean, why wait so long to tell Albion about the traitor in the company? Caelan could have told him back when he and I first met."

"I guess… well, that's good. A scumbag at the end, rather than a scumbag to the end," the werewolf declared, though Gyldan suspected her brazen dismissal of Caelan was her way of attempting to warm the frosty aura Rukshana was clad in. Seraph and Caelan had been close, and Gyldan hadn't had a moment to really speak to Seraph about how she felt. The werewolf had been so focused on trying to coax Rukshana from her icy silence—no doubt half to help her, and half to avoid confronting her own feelings on the matter. "We'll stick it on his gravestone."

Somewhere behind Gyldan, a grumbling voice replied: "And I'll be sticking something on your gravestone if you don't stop sitting on my damn crane machines, woman!"

Gyldan leant back and looked over his shoulder. Behind him at the prizes counter stood a male werewolf with shoulders broad enough to carry the burdens of everyone in the room. With arms like tree trunks, he hunched across the counter, as though the waist-high furniture was any sort of insurmountable blockade between him and Seraph. Crystal blue eyes were framed by a mess of platinum white hair that looked like it had been wrangled into a ponytail several days ago. Indeed, the owner of the arcade cut an imposing enough figure that Gyldan was often the only human who dared visit, let alone head to the counter with prize tickets to exchange.

Seraph bristled, curling her lip and baring her sharpened teeth at the other werewolf as a low growl rumbled in her chest.

"How about you come over here and make me, Orion?" Seraph snapped back in a tone far more aggressive than was strictly needed. Then, she smiled, relaxed in a split-second, and added: "Nah, I'm just messing with you, I'll get down. You're good."

The blonde pushed herself off the top of the crane machine, landing on her feet next to Rukshana and Gyldan. However, the motion jostled the machine and, with a shaking sigh from her nostrils, Rukshana watched as a soft toy slipped from the claw's grip and tumbled back into the pile of prizes below.

"Why do I bring you anywhere?" she asked, tilting her head to scowl at a sheepish Seraph. It was the most Gyldan had heard her speak since they'd arrived at the arcade. He had his suspicions about why Rukshana had reacted so badly to Caelan's treachery. Other than Seraph, Rukshana's history with werewolves had not been a pleasant one. Gyldan dared not ask for the details, but Seraph had mentioned on more than one occasion that it had been a surprise to everyone when Rukshana had asked Seraph, a werewolf, out on a date. It was clear that Caelan's betrayal had wounded Rukshana's pride more than anyone else's, and her stoic silence had been why the trio had dragged themselves out of the house and down to the arcade in the first place.

"'Cause I'm cute? Engaging conversation? 'Cause otherwise you'd be stuck with Gyldan and he's been about as much fun as licking the display counter at a jewellers?" the werewolf offered, jerking a thumb over her shoulder at the human.

He couldn't even be mad. She was right. He hadn't exactly been very sociable lately, and he hadn't made much effort to explain why to either of the women. Rukshana's silent gaze confirmed her agreement, but she nodded towards the crane machine.

"I really wanted that..." she muttered, glancing over at Seraphina. "Will you try for me, please? I was so close last time, and you knocked it..."

The werewolf didn't need telling twice. She switched places with her girlfriend and started shoving coins into the machine in order to win her the object of her affections. Rukshana smiled, then turned to Gyldan and asked in a low voice:

"Let's talk."

The vampire guided Gyldan away from the crane machines, heading over to the small bar area Orion had set up near the prize counter in some vain hope of getting Seraph to sit somewhere normal, like a chair. As the pair sat down, Gyldan let out a long sigh, resolved and relieved that he would finally try to talk to someone about his woes. If Rukshana was coming out of her shell a little, it was only fair for him to respond in kind.

"It's... man, where do I start...?"

A quick process of elimination in his head told him precisely where to start. After all, Gyl had agreed with Griffin that his relationship with Albion should be kept quiet for now. There was nothing to be gained from discussing that with Rukshana here, other than creating another problem to wrestle with later.

"I think... I'm not sure yet, it's just a rumour, but... discussions about a cure seem to be ramping up," Gyldan settled on, unable to look at Rukshana. The vampire's brow wrinkled ever so slightly.

"A cure? I had heard of Daedalus promising it countless times, but such a thing is ridiculous. It is also nothing new," Rukshana noted, her voice level. "You never seemed worried about it before."

"Yeah, well..." Gyldan could feel that chasm between him and his friends again. He didn't want to give it a voice, but he couldn't keep hiding everything from them. Besides, Gyldan had found himself wondering during his frequent fretting sessions regarding the message he'd seen on Albion's phone—was a cure the easier way? If anyone could make it, it would be Caladrius. Plus, if it worked, it could change everything. Vampires and werewolves... being human. They wouldn't need the guards and collars. They would be treated better. All they had to do was change everything about themselves.

Gyldan immediately disregarded the idea. The cure was an awful plan. "Well, it *wasn't* something to worry about with Daedalus, but... other companies..."

"I see." Rukshana cut him off, her voice calm but for a sharp edge that clipped her tone. It was unusual for her to get ruffled by anything, but Gyldan would have been more surprised if this conversation hadn't upset her. After all, they were essentially discussing the idea of a cure for her existence. The thought made every word trip out of Gyldan's mouth, a verbal tip-toe across broken glass.

"Y-yeah. It's probably because of the murders lately," the man said, attempting to give some sense of reason behind his species' need to control everything. "People are panicking... blaming... I don't think it'll happen. I don't think it *can* happen."

"The scanners your boss is creating. They are to heighten security while they attempt this cure?" Rukshana asked. There was no hiding it from her then. She knew it was Caladrius that had become interested in Daedalus' pipe dream.

Gyldan looked up at her, then bowed his in shame for being associated with this madness at all. There was no sense of blame in her piercing gaze, yet it crippled him all the same. Unintentional, he knew that—Rukshana's stern look could pierce through concrete without meaning to.

"Makes sense... I guess they're worried this killer will run out of Daedalus employees and might come for Caladrius next, too."

Rukshana shifted in her seat, but even peeking out from under his bowed head, Gyldan couldn't quite read her face. He could see thoughts swirling in her silence, thoughts which took a moment to find a voice.

Finally, she inhaled to speak, but was cut off by a bundle of energy chucking itself down on the seat next to her.

"Hey-hey, look who's the best! It's me! I won it, so you can't be mad at me anymore!" Seraph declared, pushing a fluffy toy into Rukshana's chest. The vampire took the white wolf plush and gave it a look over, turning it this way and that way in her hands. Then, at last, a true smile ghosted across her lips.

"Perfect. Thank you, Seraph," she said, leaning over and dusting a light kiss on the werewolf's cheek. Seraph beamed, and whatever unspoken tension that had built between them since Caelan's death began to disperse.

Rukshana placed the toy down on the table and turned her attention back to Gyldan. "As I was saying—this killer is a concern for our kind too. Your kind believes it to be a vampire or werewolf. We're taking so many steps back because of this creature..."

Hearing Rukshana speak of the killer like this brought a thousand questions to mind. All of them had one answer: the memory of those four eyes, crimson shot through with emerald, gleaming through the dark of the alleyway. Gyldan couldn't even be sure that it was a wild vampire at all. But in his panic, his mind had leapt to the nearest possible answer available to him.

The man pinched the bridge of his nose in irritation, knowing that the motion would raise questions from the girls.

"It... I don't even know if it *was* vampire, to be honest..."

Gyldan lifted his head and, sure enough, two quizzical faces were trained on him, demanding an explanation. Inhaling deeply, the man set about trying to explain what had happened that day. He glossed over the crime scene he had walked past, more for himself than to spare them the details. He stumbled over an explanation of what he had seen leering at him in the darkened side street. Then, he hesitated.

"I mean, it had red eyes, but... I don't know. It all happened so fast. I thought it was going to kill me. It ran right at me, it was huge, snarling, I—some Caladrius employees, we have... I only got one the other day, never wanted one before. I was just going to break it but... I..."

He couldn't do it. He couldn't say it out loud. So, instead, Gyldan took the activator from his pocket and set it on the table between them. Seraph flinched back, watching the device in clear fear that it could go off any second. Rukshana, however, just looked at it.

"You thought it was a vampire?" she asked, still watching the activator warily.

"At the time, yeah. I was scared, I didn't think, you know, about the eye thing..."

"And you attempted to use that? To kill it before it could kill you?"

"...Yeah."

A painful moment curdled the air between them until Seraph spoke up:

"Wait, you've been beatin' yourself up over that?" She snorted, an incredulous expression dancing over her sharp features. "Dude! It was trying to *kill you?* Don't feel bad. If a human tried to kill me, I'd defend myself too."

"But… I just *assumed* it was," Gyldan admitted, picking up the activator and replacing it in his pocket, taking care not to press the buttons. "I mean… it might not have been trying to kill me, and I literally went for the kill-switch."

"You had walked by a murder scene, and a creature jumped at you," Rukshana said. "Coming to the conclusion that it meant you harm was hardly a leap of logic. I don't think it was wrong to attempt to defend yourself if you felt your life was threatened. While we appreciate you are a rarity among humans for treating us as equals, it would be foolish to think there are no bad vampires or werewolves. There are plenty of bad people out there who would hurt you, Gyl. Whether they are human or not has no bearing on their kindness, or lack of it. That being said…"

A grimace pulled across her face then, and her attention darted to Gyldan's pocket. "If you could get rid of that thing, I would appreciate it. It does make me nervous to think it would be in the house. What if it malfunctions?"

Seraph paled, pushing back into her seat as far as she could.

"Mal… fu… those things can *malfunction?* Oh, yeah, erm, can you like, hoy that thing right into the sea for us?"

Seeing the two of them cower for its existence brought Gyldan's mind back to the issue of a cure. Maybe it wasn't his place to disregard the idea after all. It would mean an end to the eye-guards and the silver collars, and all the fear that went along with that. It would mean they could be free—free to pursue normal lives, get jobs, and just… live. Perhaps it wasn't his place to make that call after all.

"I'll get rid of it," Gyldan assured them both. "But listen… hypothetically, if Caladrius were testing an alternative, something that would make the eye-guards and collars obsolete… would you buy into it?"

Seraph and Rukshana looked at each other, exchanging wordless questions between themselves. Rukshana, who clearly didn't connect this question to their previous discussion, asked precariously: "Potentially. What would it entail?"

Gyldan glanced around to see who was in earshot. Orion was busy serving a pair of excited vampire teens who were bundling piles of tickets across the counter. Someone was sitting behind him at the next table, but other than that, no one was nearby. He gave one last cautious look to the person behind him, then lowered his tone.

"Y'know, from before," he muttered. Still, the fact Rukshana hadn't equated the cure with a means to be free of her eye-guard ought to have been a telling red flag to Gyldan. "If... there *was* a cure. Y'know... making werewolves and vampires human? It would mean the end of the eye-guards and silver collars, right? Not being scared of activators anymore. Maybe it's not totally a bad thing?"

The effect was immediate. Both the werewolf and vampire looked more insulted and offended than when Gyldan had admitted to using the activator to defend himself. Gyldan's chest tightened in panic, his eyes widened, and he sat back in his seat to distance himself from his hushed words.

"A *cure?* We're not a *disease*, Gyldan," Seraph growled, alight with anger. "What kind of logic is that? Tigers can kill humans too; what, you're gonna turn tigers into humans and call 'em *cured?*"

"N-no, that's not—"

"—What you meant? Well, what *did* you mean, huh?" The werewolf cut him off, folding her arms across her chest and slamming her back into her seat, face twisted into an expression of disgust. "Making everyone the same would be better? All right, well, why don't *you* guys become werewolves or vampires? Hmm? What if it was like the stories and-and-and a werewolf or vampire bite could turn humans into one of us? Would you do it? Would you *cure* you being human by turning into a werewolf or vampire?"

Rukshana moved then, setting a delicate hand across Seraph's elbow. The vampire looked at Gyldan, then to her girlfriend.

"He wasn't thinking of that. He wasn't looking any further than our guards and collars. He was only thinking of our freedom... weren't you?" she offered, turning to face him again. Gyldan swallowed and looked down at his hands.

Any debate of the cure being a good thing had been dashed from his mind in Seraph's fury—how could he have been so blind to the obvious? The cure was just another way to repress those who weren't human. A final oppression by taking away their very identity. Their existence. Turning them into something the rest of the world approved of for no other reason than it matched what they saw in the mirror.

"N-no... I'm sorry. I just... I hate seeing you guys in those things. I thought... if there was a way... no you're right. That was totally thoughtless of me. I really didn't think of it that way."

Deep down, he couldn't answer Seraph's question about curing his *humanity* with quite as much confidence as she had answered his. If he could choose to not be human... would he? There had been a time when Gyldan would have leapt at the chance to be a werewolf or vampire. After all, every little brother wanted to be just like their big brother...

Sterlyn... Gyldan thought to himself. *Would a cure have changed—no.* Gyldan caught himself, then pushed the memories back into the box he kept locked in the corner of his mind. Now wasn't the time to think about his brother. After all, he'd not really spoken to Rukshana and Seraph about his family any more than Rukshana had explained her distrust of werewolves beyond Seraph.

A noise brought Gyldan back to focus. Behind him, their table-neighbour piped up without warning:

"You're all the problem," the stranger said bitterly. Gyldan, Rukshana, and Seraph all exchanged confused looks, unsure as to whether the person was addressing them or not. In the end, the blonde werewolf leant forward a little across the table to ask:

"You talkin' to us, chic?"

"Yes. I said you're all the problem," the woman repeated, turning around to scowl at them. Gyldan's heart skipped a beat as he realised who it was. Frozen jade eyes pierced from a pale face, accusing them all of stupidity with a single look. Yanatha looked at Gyldan, then tilted her head to face Seraph in full. "We need to think of the many, not the few. The strength of a werewolf or vampire, in the wrong hands, could be awful. People are being *killed* because of it. This power means one person can kill so many, so quickly... if there were a cure that meant we would all be equal, *I* would take it."

Yanatha stood up then, scooping up her bag and picking up her drink. She gave one last look at Gyldan, and for all the world he wanted to make an excuse, to say something that would cover his ass. One word to her father about Gyldan's friend circle and everything would unravel. Two words about the potential company secrets he'd been discussing and... well, Gyldan would unravel.

"Y-Yanatha, I, er... this..." Gyldan stammered, gesturing with an open palm to Rukshana and Seraph. Yanatha shrugged.

"You said *hypothetically*," she said silkily. "Besides... it's not like they work for a competitor, right?"

She gave a soft chuckle then and made no effort to hide her judgemental inspection trailing up across Seraph's collar and Rukshana's eye-guard. It was no secret that companies seldom hired werewolves or vampires beyond manual labour jobs. Gyldan found his blood boiling for the woman's mockery of his friends. But before he could say anything, Yanatha was gone, sauntering out of the arcade. Gyldan let his head fall into his hands.

"Oh my *god*, can I get a bloody *break?*" he pleaded to no one.

"Well, she seemed nice," Seraph said, smiling after Yanatha. "If you like snobby bitches. Work friend?"

"Worse," Gyldan admitted. "She's my boss's daughter."

Chapter 5

  If Yanatha had decided to tell her father about Gyldan's clandestine meeting, Albion either didn't care or wasn't showing he cared. He didn't act any different, save for a few messages complaining about how his chronic migraines had flared up yet again. The casual note of their conversation was comforting, at least.

  Everything was normal enough, and as the weeks passed by, Gyldan managed to set that particular worry aside. Perhaps Yanatha had meant what she said. Perhaps she really didn't think much of catching Gyldan speaking to werewolves and vampires. Or perhaps she simply didn't care that much about her father's company.

  In fact, not only did Albion fail to mention any suspicion of Gyldan's friend circle, but he also didn't speak of any tests at Caladrius regarding the pursuit of a cure. Though Gyldan had attempted to steer the conversation towards that route numerous times at work, his boyfriend had dismissed every effort. It was starting to get to the point that the man was questioning what he had even seen on Albion's phone. After all, it had been the briefest of glances—he may have misread the message preview, he told himself.

Right now, everything was one big question for Gyldan. Even the memory of the creature that attacked him was beginning to crumble between his fingers. He had reported the incident to the police, but on reflection, he didn't have much information to give. A big shadow with four red eyes had leapt at him and disappeared. Still, it had given the authorities a different avenue to explore—two vampires working together was the only logical explanation for what Gyldan had seen. Gyldan had readily accepted that theory, as naming the monster made it seem less nightmarish.

Even if a whisper in his heart remained unconvinced.

Sighing, Gyldan attempted to refocus on the task at hand. Tonight was a big night for Caladrius, and he could not afford to look like he'd gotten ready while half-distracted by overthinking.

He stared at himself in the wardrobe door mirror. Dressed in his best tuxedo, the pressed black suit was everything Gyldan wanted to be. Smart, suave, and effortless. It was made all the more stark by the contrasting mess of his bedroom. Behind him, an old oak desk was burdened with several discarded projects, abandoned by either Gyldan's lack of time or lack of confidence. Tucked up against the wall, his bed was a mess of navy sheets balled up from that morning and his discarded clothes. Even the mirror was speckled with dirt, and the whole affair gave Gyldan the sensation of wearing a costume rather than an outfit. He was an actor, trying to convince the world of his worth, but he was standing before an audience of half-finished projects on his desk that knew better.

Smart, suave, and effortless. Yet he had already failed to fasten his tie several times.

Gyldan undid the tangled knot of white silk at his collar and muttered curse words at himself under his breath.

He made to start again when a knock at the door stilled his hands. Letting the tie drape around his neck for now, Gyldan turned away from the mirror to open the door to his room. Standing on the landing, looking decidedly more casual than Gyldan, was Seraph. The werewolf shifted from one foot to the other, her hands in the back pockets of her blue denim jeans. She kept her head down as she spoke.

"Yooo," Seraph drawled, scratching the back of her head and still avoiding looking up at Gyldan. "Listen, erm... this fundraiser tonight. All you Caladrius employees are gonna be... in a hall or something? Mingling?"

The question struck Gyldan as peculiar, but he answered warily, "Yeah... why? What's up, Seraph?"

The blonde readjusted her stance yet again, glanced down the hallway, then finally looked up at Gyldan.

"Can I, er..." She gestured into his room with her hand, and the man jumped a little and stood aside to let her in.

"Oh, yeah, yeah! Sorry."

Seraph gave one last look down the corridor, and Gyldan could see a flicker of guilt tightening the muscles in her jaw. But then she shuffled into his room and sat herself down on the edge of his bed as Gyldan shut the door. She was holding her right arm with her left hand at the elbow, and her shoulders were hunched up.

"Seraph, what is it?" Gyldan asked gently, his voice softening now that privacy shielded them. It wasn't like Seraph to look so cornered.

She frowned, staring at one particular floorboard before her eyebrows slanted upwards in pained sadness.

"It's... the fundraiser tonight, right?" she asked again, her voice low. "You'll be at work?"

"Y-yeah?" Gyldan replied, sitting himself down on the old computer chair at his desk. "You didn't get this worried about it last year though. I'll be fine."

The werewolf shook her head.

"I know that. I mean... all the important people, they'll be busy drinking champagne and bigging each other up, right? S-so... I was wondering... look, I know he was a dick in the end, but..."

Seraph's voice caught in her throat, and her head snapped to the side as she growled at herself in irritation. Gyldan realised she was referring to Caelan—as Seraph's fellow werewolf, Caelan's death left Seraph as the only werewolf in the house. But surely that fact alone was not why his death had hurt her quite so much. It had wounded them all in one way or another, but Gyldan suspected Seraph's anguish came from her own heartbreak mixed with how different her grief was from Rukshana's. After all, Rukshana had avoided discussing Caelan's betrayal at all and reverted to icy silence at his name being mentioned. It was her right, her grief. But clearly it had left Seraph's own pain to fester unaddressed.

"What can I do to help?" Gyldan coaxed Seraph to speak again. He wanted to help her and Rukshana to deal with this, and right now, only Seraph seemed open to that offer.

"I... I wanna know what they did. Did... *with* him. I mean, I want to know that he was at least... buried or something? I-I know he doesn't deserve it... *our*... well... look, I know I shouldn't give a shit!" Seraph finally snapped, lip curling and eyes ablaze. "He betrayed us! But dammit, he was our friend at some point, and I'm not gonna let him being a traitor make *me* less of a friend! I'm not gonna do wrong by him just 'cause he stabbed us in the back! I'm gonna be better than he deserves just to *spite* him, all right! So I wanna know Caladrius hasn't just chucked his body in a dumpster or something! I wanna make sure he's at rest, Gyl. Even if it's more than he deserves."

Her fury scalded the air around them, and it was all Gyldan could do to let the pressure of it have its moment around them, unchecked and unleashed. It wasn't until the crackling anger of her words fizzled away that he spoke again.

"Don't worry. I'm sure they at least buried him, Seraph. But I'll find out for you, okay?"

He offered her a small smile. After a moment, she gave him half of one in return.

"Thanks, nerd."

* * *

No matter how many black-tie events Gyldan attended, he never felt quite like he belonged at them. Caught in a lilting wave of the upper classes, the tittering shrill of unfelt laughter responding to droll jokes coiling around him—it was the world Gyldan wished he was good enough to be a part of, and yet, was almost glad he wasn't.

Wandering around the glowing ivory hall, the young man was more drunk from bedazzlement than drink. The grand chandelier above scattered crystal-torn light across the bright walls, dancing over the high-brow attendees swirling below. Champagne flowed, lights glanced from glasses and jewels and shimmering gowns, and music thrummed across the air, ensuring every inch of the room was occupied with sight, taste, or sound. Every year, the fundraiser grew more spectacular, and every year, Gyldan worried that this was a sign of Albion's grief getting worse rather than healing.

Before Gyldan could be swallowed up by the spectacle of it all, a stabilising voice cut through the articulated madness.

"Oh! Gyldan! When did you sneak in? Come here—you remember Walter, don't you?"

Gyldan was pulled to Albion's side, the smell of amber and earth reaching his nose before Albion's gleaming smile registered in his vision. Absently, Gyldan set his half-finished champagne glass down on a passing server's tray and tried his best not to think about how incredible Albion looked in his tailored tuxedo. This was all disorientating enough without alcohol and feelings thrown into the mix.

"Mr Carpenter," Gyldan said, facing the older man with as much collectedness as he could muster. "How are you? Are you enjoying the evening?"

The camera had not been kind to Walter Carpenter, Gyldan noticed now. Or perhaps the man's twitching nature on television in the weeks prior had simply been nerves. Either way, the man looked far more regal now, though he still fell far short of Albion in terms of cutting an imposing figure. That only made Daedalus' CEO all the more worrisome for Gyldan. Albion was intelligent, but he could convince people to follow him from sheer silken words alone. Gyldan wouldn't have been surprised if it turned out the majority of shareholders didn't realise Albion had actually created most of Caladrius' products himself, rather than employing someone else to do it. In the business world, the ability to charm was often valued over true intelligence. Walter lacked much of the former, which meant he was smart enough to make up for that fact—or he was shrewd enough to manipulate people without relying on an award-winning smile.

Either option made Gyldan uncomfortable with the man being in Caladrius' headquarters, but he knew well that this was Albion's idea of a dare. Inviting the enemy into his territory just to remind them that he wasn't afraid. That he had no concerns over their abilities and had every faith in his own. His company secrets were safe, Albion said with this wordless gesture, whether Walter was a country away or a centimetre away from them. It could only be so long before Albion's arrogance backfired.

Walter offered Gyldan what was a smile only by textbook definition.

"Caladrius always puts on a show," he offered the man by means of a snapping reply before facing Albion again. "Albion, why have you—?"

Albion placed a hand on Gyldan's lower back, coaxing him to stand in front of Walter and stepping out of the way himself. Gyldan realised too late that the man was tagging out of an awkward situation.

"Wait, no, no, no!" Gyldan protested, but Albion merely flashed his pearly whites at him.

"I must mingle with the other guests. Look after our guest of honour for me, darling," Albion pretended to request, then he left before Gyldan could respond. The younger man scowled at the back of his boyfriend's head as he disappeared among the crowd. Turning back to Walter, Gyldan gave a nervous laugh.

"He, er... he's a busy guy."

Walter was already halfway through rolling his eyes. He plucked a glass of champagne from a passing tray and did not deign to look at Gyldan as he spoke.

"Oh, run along," Walter huffed, taking a sip of his champagne and glancing around the room. "Unless Caladrius grants its *assistants* the authority to engage in collaborative projects, I hardly think we have much to discuss. Tell your superior this conversation *will* continue. All he's doing is making it take longer than it needs to."

With that, the CEO of Daedalus scurried off with his upturned nose in the air, leaving Gyldan to brood on his words.

A collaborative project, he thought, casting a sidewards look to Albion. *Does he mean the cure?*

Albion had been right—Daedalus must be sinking if Walter himself had requested they work together instead of against each other. With all their promises of finding a cure, Walter had reached out for Albion's help in that endeavour. Gyldan wouldn't have worried over the fact Albion had clearly brushed Walter's request away—prior to a few weeks ago, Gyldan had no reason to think that Caladrius was pursuing the same lunacy as Daedalus. But now, Gyldan found himself recalling the fractured glimpse of the message he'd spotted on Albion's phone a few weeks prior.

Maybe Albion had rejected Walter's collaborative offer simply because he had no need to accept it. He didn't need Daedalus' help.

"Dammit..." Gyldan hissed to himself. He needed to find some answers—but if the company was working on a cure, it would be down in the laboratories. He didn't have clearance to go there, and even if he wanted to sneak in, his key-card wouldn't unlock the door.

Gyldan scanned the room, looking over to where Albion was laughing with a group of well-to-do guests.

Hadn't he saved him from Walter? Didn't his *wonderful* boyfriend owe him big time for that?

Emboldened by this and the anxious need for answers boiling over, Gyldan swiftly made his way over to Albion.

"S-Sir?" he said, a mode of address he used in public. It still felt odd to call someone 'sir' when one had seen said person waste an entire Sunday sitting on the couch in his pants.

Albion at least had the good graces to look at Gyldan with a mild reflection of guilt flickering over his expression.

"You escaped! Ah, but I am sorry about all that. Walter can be, er... well, Walter. Did he talk your ear off?" Albion asked, wrapping an arm around Gyldan's shoulder and pulling him close. Clearly, the man had already indulged in one too many glasses of champagne—the action raised more than a few eyebrows from those he'd been talking to.

"No, he's wandered off... listen, I, er... c-could I borrow your key-card please, sir?"

Albion's perpetual feline smirk faltered for once, and he blinked slowly.

"What? Why would you need it? You have your own."

"I left it in my work coat..." Gyldan said sheepishly, tugging on the hem of his tuxedo jacket. "But I need to pick my laptop up from my office before I go tonight."

The older man paused, and it seemed like he might question Gyldan's real motive, suspicion deepening the fine lines of his face. But then, the man took his arm from Gyldan's shoulders and ferreted in the back pocket of his trousers to find his key-card.

"Hmm, well... just this once," he slurred, handing Gyldan his key-card at the command of the drunken blush staining his cheeks pink. Albion then cast a look at the people he'd been talking to before his assistant had arrived. He placed a finger over his lips and hissed, "*Shhh!*" at his observant company. They responded with appropriate, tittering laughter.

"Thanks, I'll be right back!" Gyldan smiled, then dashed away with Albion's key-card in hand. He weaved through the crowd once more, heading through the doors out of the main hall and into the long corridors of Caladrius' headquarters.

A blissful wave of silence swept over Gyldan as soon as the door closed at his back. He gave himself but a moment to inhale and steady himself, enjoying the brief respite of calm that had appeared between the crowded room behind him and the concerns that needed addressing ahead of him. All too soon, it was gone—he had to move before his courage could abandon him and send him scampering back to Albion to hand his key-card back.

Gyldan darted down the corridor, the white walls gloomed to grey by the dim lights of an office building after hours. Despite being away from prying eyes, he attempted to find a gait between a civilised walk and a panicked run. The corridors and offices were deserted save for a few overtime employees who hadn't climbed the ranks enough to be invited to the fundraiser. They were disgruntled, discarded, and disinterested as a result. None of them would question where the CEO's personal assistant was going. None of them were paid or felt valued enough to care.

This was Gyldan's best chance to do some digging. To find out once and for all if his fears were founded, and if the company he worked for was truly heading down such an ethical nightmare of a path.

So the man crept through the halls, heading to the laboratories on the fifteenth floor that he'd never had a chance to explore before. If the cure was being tested anywhere, it would be here. As he reached the door, Gyldan couldn't help but look over his shoulder to check that all was clear. He then swiped Albion's card over the lock and slipped into the lab.

Gyldan crept through the ill-lit room. The vials and glass cabinets that lined the walls watched the man, and each step accused him of a gross betrayal to Albion. He tried to shake the thought from his mind with logic—it had to be done. If Caladrius were going to go as far as to call vampires and werewolves patients that needed to be cured, then he couldn't stand by and let that happen. First, he had to confirm it. Then, he was sure he could find the strength to confront Albion, to drag out the flashes of a good man that he saw within him to really look at what he was doing.

Still, Gyldan's bravery did not extend so far as to turn on the light. His heart threatened to break his ribs for the pounding anxiety that rattled him, that demanded he stop and run away. If it weren't for the mantra rattling in his head, Gyldan may have submitted to that fear.

He skulked through the room, regarding the documents pinned across the walls of the research office with curiosity. Upon closer inspection, Gyldan realised that many of them were news article print-outs. Most of them were dated between 1993, the year the Eye Surgery Act was abolished, and 2007, the year Albion's eye-guards and trap-collars had become a legal requirement. A large number of stories pinned to the wall detailed the tragedy of Caladrius Saint-Richter's murder—killed by non-human activists, right in front of his family.

Gyldan walked along the length of the display, his stomach churning as he beheld the collage of fear that papered the room. This was a war declaration against the majority, written with the bloodshed caused by a minority. A masterpiece of terror painted with a limited palette. Anyone who looked at this would assume the fourteen years of relative freedom for non-humans had been a bloodbath against humans. But Gyldan knew this was selective history at its finest, fuelled by human panic. There wasn't a single mention of the blood spilt by humans against non-humans, of course. By this false account, humans had never lifted a violent hand against non-humans.

Absently, Gyldan let his fingers curl under one of the newspaper clippings as he scanned the headline and story. A vampire who had run for mayor in London back in 1994, only for it to be discovered she had thralled the Prime Minister. The Job Restriction Act had come into play swiftly after that scandal, limiting the career prospects of non-humans in one legal swoop. It was the first of many restrictions that paved the way to the eye-guards and trap-collars.

Gyldan let the paper slip from his hands and stepped back from the twisted tapestry. The stories were displayed like motivational posters, no doubt to alleviate any concerns the lab staff might have about the ethical nature of a cure.

Look what they have done, the cherry-picked news shouted from the walls. *They attacked us. We are right to defend ourselves.*

And yet, to Gyldan's surprise, other print-outs on the wall were not detailing attacks on humans. One clipping in particular caught his eye: a tiny snippet of a story, given a fraction of the word count Albion's family tragedy had been, reporting a werewolf attack on a local vampire group. All dead, save for one young woman who had managed to fight back and survive the night.

Gyldan's hand brushed against the paper before his brain caught up. The blurry photo of a dark-haired vampire dashing away from a prying photographer...

"Rukshana...?" Gyldan whispered to himself.

The silence shattered in an instant then, a crash off to Gyldan's right making him start and almost yelp in shock. Without thinking, Gyldan ripped the pinned story about Rukshana from the wall and stuffed it in his pocket, then turned to peer out into the gloom.

"H-hello?" he called out. "Just... just doing a security... sweep...?"

Gyldan was certain that precisely no one in the field of security would announce themselves that way, and his face twisted into an expression of self-scorn.

"Oh! Oh, I *do* apologise!" came a curt and refined tone that Gyldan did not recognise. "I fear I have rather misguided myself in an attempt to return to tonight's celebrations!"

Who the hell talks like—?

Gyldan's thoughts slammed to a halt by the sudden appearance of a broadly smiling visage and empty eye sockets inches from his face.

"Gah!" Gyldan stumbled backwards. The vampire newcomer, however, did not move. He remained as he was, standing inches from where Gyldan had been, bent slightly at the hip and smiling.

"Apologies once more!" the vampire called out, turning his head this way and that, sniffing the air. He then turned his face directly at Gyldan, his hollow eye sockets somehow finding him with pinpoint accuracy. "Lovely cologne, dear heart. You *must* tell me where you purchased it. A topic of conversation for our way back to the festivities?"

The strange man offered an arm to Gyldan then. Gyldan paused to let this assault of a personality sink into his senses. The vampire's lack of eyes meant he had to be at least Gyldan's age, though he looked a little older. Deep scars fractured the upper part of his porcelain face, culminating in the disfigurement of his lost eyes. Unlike Griffin, this vampire elected not to hide his empty eye sockets with cloth wraps or opaque glasses, giving him the appearance of wearing a splintered mask. He wore a suit of black velvet, the shoulders decorated with a gaudy display of multi-coloured gemstones, as though he were expecting to partake in a masquerade rather than a black-tie event. The only thing about him that seemed to fit the dress code of the evening was his blond hair, which was swept back and cropped short at the sides.

"How did you... get in here?" Gyldan asked, taking the man's arm out of habit from helping Griffin so many times. The vampire's fanged smile drew wider, and he curled his arm in tight to bring Gyldan close to his side. He seemed harmless, however, and the stranger folded his other hand on top of his linked hand neatly.

"I rather overestimated my ability to sniff out the gentlemen's toilets," the vampire admitted. "I've never had a problem before. Your company must keep a spotless loo, dear heart. Not a whiff! But my pride forbade me from returning to the hall to ask for help and lo, here I am."

"But... the door only opens with a key-card," Gyldan said, glancing at said door.

"Oh yes," the vampire said gravely, and he bobbed his head. He then tilted his head to the side. "But a door is not the only entry to a room."

Frowning, Gyldan looked up, down, at the walls—then spotted an open window.

"Y-you climbed in? Through the window?"

The vampire nodded.

"Mm-hmm! I smelt something funny wafting from this direction, thought I might have been onto a winner in my quest for the lavatory. So, I popped my wings out for a moment and flew around the outside. I couldn't open the door, you see," he added, as if to suggest leaping out of the fifteenth floor of a building and flying around to an open window to enter a locked room were a reasonable step of logic. "But, alas, it was a cadaver.

You understand the average gentlemen's bathroom and a rotting corpse smell similar at the best of times."

A... corpse...?

"In here? A c-corpse?" Gyldan's throat dried in an instant.

"Oh! Not a murder, dear heart, bless you, no! No need to call your fellow security team!" The vampire laughed, patting Gyldan's arm lightly in a display of reassurance. "I mean your test subjects! In here. The *specimens*."

Gyldan's skin went clammy, a sickly sweat seeping into his clothes.

"For the cure..." he realised. He wanted to look around some more; he wanted to confirm the awful, sinking feeling in his stomach—was Caelan held in this very room, a test subject for this cure?—but he couldn't afford to raise further suspicion. The vampire on his arm hummed happily.

"Ah, you know of it? Between you and me, it's all rather *hush-hush*. Albion, bless him, he wants to keep it a secret. Announce it the day of its release, such a showman! But, when one donates quite as heavily as I do to the Caladrius Fundraiser Event, one is privy to where one's money is going. Isn't it exciting though? A cure? And not a moment too soon, I should think!"

Limbs limp and numb, Gyldan began to walk forward, guiding the blind vampire out of the room and back towards the event hall.

It's true.
A cure.
He's working on a cure.
Caelan's body... could be...

"Aren't... Why would you donate to this?" Gyldan asked without thinking. He knew well that there were pockets of vampires and werewolves who agreed with measures such as the eye-guards and silver collars. Usually, they were the older generation. Still, holding on to some odd argument of *how it's always been* when it came to advocating their own oppression was one thing. Supporting the idea that their existence was a disease to be cured? Gyldan couldn't get his head around why a vampire would agree to that.

"Because it's exactly what we need!" the vampire exclaimed, his voice marked with shock at Gyldan's confusion. "Why, humans are killed by the rather unsavoury members of my kind, and by werewolves. And then we risk miserable deaths from those newfangled collars and eye-guards, although I confess to being a tad jealous of that in comparison to my own situation, haha! But no, no. Certainly, a cure is the best course of action. Logical, really. It solves so many problems! No need for collars or eye-guards, no more tragedies like Albion's poor little boy..."

The pair reached the door to the event hall with Gyldan lost in his thoughts. Curing the vampires and werewolves would solve those problems? Was that really true? Was it really worth turning everyone into a human?

"Why would anyone *want* to be human?" Gyldan asked.

"Why would—?" The vampire's question broke away into laughter, doubling him over at the waist as he unlinked his arm from Gyldan's own. "Oh, *why* indeed! Oh, very good, yes! Ahahaha! Who would want to be human, oh! Oh, exactly, exactly! Ah, well, thank you, my good fellow! Ah! How rude, I didn't give you my name," the man prattled, his speech darting around as though his thoughts escaped him. "Luca de Varis owes his gratitude to... whom?"

"Ah, Gyldan." Gyldan decided it wasn't necessary to come up with a false name for this flighty gentleman. Besides, his mind was still digesting Luca's outburst of mirth over the idea of wanting to be human.

Luca offered him a low bow before opening the door to the hall and heading back in. The event's frivolity poured out for a second, before silencing as the door shut once again.

Gyldan stared after Luca. He had laughed away the idea of questioning the want to be human. As though it were no question at all.

Who would want to sit at the top of society? That was what Gyldan had essentially asked the vampire who had had his eyes scooped out for daring to exist. Who would want to live in a world that didn't hate them?

He realised then why Luca had laughed so hard. Why he had thought Gyldan was joking with him.

Never in his life had Gyldan been quite so aware of how lucky he was.

Sterlyn, Gyldan thought of his wayward brother once again, the memories seeping from that locked box in the corner of his mind. Of his werewolf brother that he'd spent his childhood in envy of, and his early adulthood in disgust of. *Did you wish you were human like me too?*

Chapter 6

  Gyldan had been tempted to return to the laboratory. His head was sickened with worry, a pressure building between his temples that dripped down to his throat as he teetered on the edge of panic. Luca had mentioned the foul smell had lured him to the labs, the smell of death. Prying further would have raised more questions than Gyldan could take right now, but he had to know—he had to know if it was Caelan.

  However it had ended, the werewolf had been their friend in the past. If nothing else, Gyldan owed the memory of Caelan a more dignified end than to be prodded and poked in some experiment at Caladrius. Even if it was nothing less than what Caelan deserved for selling them out.

  Still, his absence would be noted, and though he had only just met the man, Gyldan wasn't convinced Luca wouldn't be in the events hall right now regaling the tale of the nice young man who helped him find his way back. Plus, while Albion had been somewhat tipsy when Gyldan had left with his key-card, he was by no means inebriated. No doubt he was beginning to wonder why it was taking his personal assistant so long to get back from his office.

Gyldan inhaled, then promptly forgot how many beats he was meant to count to in order to lower his anxiety. Air rushed out in an irritated sigh rather than a calming breath. He shook his head then made his way back into the hall.

As soon as he opened the door, the light and noise of the room spilt out into the quiet corridor and pulled him back in. Within moments, he was skirting around the room again, twisting and snaking through the crowd to reach Albion. Upon reaching his side, his boyfriend's forest-green eyes were already narrowing in suspicion.

Damn, was the only word that echoed in Gyldan's head as he gingerly placed the key-card back into Albion's outstretched hand.

"It wasn't in there," Gyldan replied to the unspoken question on Albion's face, noting that his line of sight had shifted to Gyldan's otherwise empty hands. "Must be in my work bag at home, forgot to check. Sorry…"

"And it took you that long?" Albion said, his voice worryingly flat. Every alarm bell sounded in Gyldan's head, and every nerve fired to assure him it was indeed *very* much a time to grovel. He'd never quite gotten past the sensation that the bond between them was very much on Albion's whim—if he crossed him even once, he would leave Gyldan. For reasons he wasn't ready to confront, the idea terrified Gyldan.

"Well, I ran into a vampire on the way back. Older-gen, he couldn't find the hall," Gyldan explained, a nervous hand already raking through his dark locks. "So, I helped him out."

For a moment, Albion didn't reply. Instead, he pocketed the key-card and took a sharp breath, craning his neck to look around at the crowded room. Then, his arm shot out and grabbed Gyldan by the elbow. Before he could demand an answer, the older man forced him through the crowd and out of the room. He was marched into the foyer and out the front doors of the building, the cold night air shocking his skin.

"Albion, what the hell?" Gyldan demanded, wrenching free of his grip now that all facades could be safely left at the door. He glowered up at the taller man, though his bravery fizzled somewhat under Albion's stern expression. Somehow, Gyldan already knew. He knew that Albion knew—they *both* knew where Gyldan had really been.

The truth was confirmed in Gyldan's mind long before his partner pulled his phone from his pocket. Albion didn't look away from Gyldan, nor did he even tap the screen of his phone to bring it to life. Its presence was enough to make Gyldan's fears a reality.

"Do you think I am so stupid?" Albion finally spoke, his head twitching in what might have been half a nod. "It didn't occur to you that I would track my own damn key-card?"

Gyldan tried to swallow against the growing lump in his throat.

"I-I was... heard... a..." The lies dribbled away from Gyldan's lips, his voice tapering to a squeak. In a micro-movement that the other man almost missed, Albion shifted from a stoic wall of anger to shattered pain.

"I didn't think it could be you," he admitted, the perpetual curling of his lips only making his expression all the more pained. "When someone tells you there is a traitor in your company, you know you have to consider those closest to you. And yet, knowing this... I couldn't bring myself to consider you. I didn't think I was foolish enough to be blinded by a pretty face and a few compliments. I'm Albion Saint-*fucking*-Richter!" Albion's frustration boiled over his calm façade with an unexpected yell, resulting in the sudden and violent twisting of his body as he threw his phone out across the street and into the road. Gyldan could only tense his shoulders, trying to hunch away from the man's outburst without moving.

It wasn't meant to hurt. It had always been the plan that Gyldan would get close to Albion, use his job to weasel in and get information. To help people. He was doing this for good reasons. But it wasn't meant to hurt in the end.

"I... I'm sorry, Al." Gyldan heard his voice before his brain had even attempted to formulate a response. "I—"

A way out.

The realisation hit him so hard that Gyldan struggled to keep his face neutral.

He didn't have to admit to knowing Caelan was Albion's informant. He didn't have to admit *when* the betrayal occurred. Only that one had.

Taking a shaking breath, Gyldan turned to his boyfriend, tearful.

"I got a little tipsy, and I... I wanted to see the labs. It was stupid, I-I shouldn't have gone down there. But I swear, I didn't see anything. I mean... not other than your informant, obviously..."

At this, Albion's eyes narrowed.

"What?"

"The vampire. Luca?" Gyldan spun his lie from a truth. "He was in the lab too, went back into the hall before I did. I didn't realise he'd spoken to you... but I swear, I don't know why he'd call me a traitor. I didn't see anything in the lab, I got too scared! I was in there for like, two seconds before he showed up."

Albion kept Gyldan under his scrutiny for a moment longer than was comfortable. For a second, he was sure his plan had failed. But then, a half-smirk crept across Albion's mouth and he looked out across the street where his now-shattered phone was.

"...Luca. You think Luca de Varis was my informant?"

"He's the only person I saw," Gyldan replied, his voice threaded with faux confusion. "I didn't think your phone would track your key-card... and I didn't think Luca would accuse me of anything! But I *swear*, I was only in there for a second, Albion. I was just curious. What, you think I'm selling company secrets? I wouldn't do that to you! I... I just got curious! It was a stupid mistake a-and I'm so sorry."

Another long pause wound between the two men, and eventually, the weight of it lowered Albion's shoulders. The man even had the grace to laugh to himself.

"You think I'm talking about Luca..."

"Huh?"

"Luca was not my informant, tiger. Though why the hell he was snooping around the labs is a worry..." Albion pinched the bridge of his nose and shook his head. Gyldan knew he was trying to remain composed, but his pet name sneaking back into the conversation told the man he'd gotten away with this. "It isn't you... thank God. If it were you... well, I don't know what I'd do." Albion straightened up, letting his arms jerk into a loose shrug before his hands slapped down to his sides wearily. "I'm... I'm sorry, Gyldan. I'm sorry I doubted you."

The proud man's admission only made Gyldan's heart hurt more for his deception.

"I-it's okay. I get it. Y'know, you've... you've gotta be wary of everyone. It sucks, and I wish you could relax but... I get why you can't," Gyldan replied, meaning every word for once. "Maybe I can help? What did your informant say? Can we go ask him for more details?"

Albion shook his head, ferreting in his pocket for a moment and producing a box of cigarettes.

"No. That's the bloody problem. The informant who alerted me is dead now. It was... well, a mess, really. I had a thousand questions for him—like why the hell he was with a vampire who had gotten into my office. I suspect he had heard of the attempt to break in and had befriended the vampire to keep a close eye on him for me. Perhaps the state of the collar was meant to be a warning to me... ah, I don't know. He'd only been on the payroll a few days, so it's difficult to judge," Albion complained.

Gyldan had to focus on keeping his expression neutral despite the emotional flooring he was taking here. Caelan hadn't betrayed them from the start? It had been recent to the heist? It explained why the werewolf had tried to introduce himself so rapidly before the collar was activated. Gyldan couldn't help but wonder if Caelan's yelp that there was a traitor in the company was just a thoughtless attempt to stall itchy trigger-fingers, knowing his face wouldn't be recognised by the security team. Or maybe Caelan really was going to drop them in it right there. His thousand questions would remain unanswered alongside Albion's own.

Trying to still his shaking breath, Gyldan did his best impression of someone who didn't care much. It didn't come naturally.

"That sucks... but it's not the end. We'll find out who it is. Together," he offered, taking hold of one of Albion's hands in both of his. The man looked down at their joined hands, then looked at Gyldan with a smirk.

"Well, isn't this romantic?"

"Shut up..."

＊＊＊

They had had little inclination to return to the night's merriment, with all their energy scattered out onto the street. After Albion had confronted the frustration of not being able to phone his chauffeur, ("Why did you let me fling my phone?"), the two men bundled into a cab, with the CEO looking distinctly uncomfortable at the less suave mode of transport. Indeed, the cab driver kept gawking so much into the rear-view mirror at the celebrity in his back seat that Gyldan began to feel uncomfortable too.

He leant in towards Albion, noticing the man glancing down at him as he moved.

"So... you tagged me on Walter," Gyldan muttered under his breath, checking the cab driver to see if he showed any signs of having heard him. He had thought of a perfect way to ask Albion about what he was really searching for in the lab, without admitting to a single misdemeanour. "He didn't wanna talk to me much, but... Al, what did he mean about collaborating on a cure?" Albion visibly flinched, casting an uneasy glower to the driver himself then looking at Gyldan, teeth clenched.

"*Shh!* God... Do I have no secrets anymore?" the man hissed, wrapping an arm around Gyldan's shoulders. "Look, just... don't worry about it. I'm not working with that idiot. You'll be pleased to know that I rejected his proposal."

Gyldan nestled in closer, the sharp scent of alcohol clinging to Albion's clothes. Maybe it had loosened his tongue too.

"Yeah, that's what he said too. Mentioned *Caladrius* was working on a cu—"

Albion's hand clamped over Gyldan's mouth then, robbing him of the rest of his utterance.

"*J*e*sus Christ, Gyl!*" Albion said in a harsh whisper. After a moment, he let go of the man's face and settled back. "Goddammit... yes, all right, this isn't how I wanted you to find out, but... we're working on a—" Albion looked at the driver again, "—*competing product.*"

Gyldan swallowed against the lump in his throat that seemed to have taken up permanent residence of late. Then the message he'd seen on Albion's phone had been true. There *was* a cure in the works.

"You think that's the way forward?"

"You don't agree?" the man countered quickly, but Gyldan noted he didn't sound annoyed.

"I... don't," Gyldan admitted, surprising himself with his honesty. "I don't think it's right to give everyone the, er... *competing product*. Maybe not everyone wants *that*."

"Hmmm," Albion mused, a noise of half-agreement. "You're quite right. Not everyone should receive it. Few of their kind deserve such forgiveness. Yet, I am striving for them all the same."

Gyldan pulled his bottom lip between his teeth, chewing on it to bite back a retort. He hated it when Albion spoke of the other two species like that. Every time he did, it was like the man was personally shattering Gyldan's belief that Albion could be convinced out of his prejudice someday. That Gyldan could be the man to do that.

"So why make it?" he asked tentatively.

"Because something more needs to be done. I understand your concerns, of course. It isn't like a collar or eye-guard—it is a life-changing solution. I would never force such a thing on anyone, regardless of my own feelings towards non-humans," Albion explained, one hand toying with the black locks just above Gyldan's ear. "So, it'll be a choice. They can stay as they are, or they can choose to be like us."

"Oh," Gyldan chirped, his heart feeling fuller. That wasn't so bad then. A choice was a start, at least. He could work with that, prise open that glimmer of understanding and maybe start to talk about getting rid of the eye-guards and silver collars. Maybe he could—

"And obviously, the people who choose *not* to use it will be arrested." Albion concluded with a small shrug, turning his attention to the street whizzing by the window.

Gyldan's heart crumbled. A crushing pulse of disappointment seared through his limbs, jerking him up and away from Albion's side so suddenly that the older man's attention immediately snapped back from the window to Gyldan.

Albion had the audacity to look affronted, snapping a sharp demand of "What?" towards him.

"*Arrested?*" Gyldan repeated, gawking at the other man, mulling over Albion's face to see if insanity had any visual cues. "On what grounds?"

Albion's eyebrows knotted together. He stared at Gyldan as though the other had just suggested he swallow live scorpions.

"The very concerning grounds of *choosing* to remain a threat to humans," he scoffed, having apparently made his peace with the cab driver overhearing this conversation now. "Look, when they're born, I'll grant you, they don't have a choice. They didn't choose to be born a vampire or a werewolf. Isn't that what you're always nagging at me about?"

"I don't *nag*, Albion, it's the truth!"

"And I'm agreeing with you! They can't be held accountable when they're born, that's preposterous. The eyeguards and collars were always a necessary evil until we could create something better, but I loathe that they must be used from birth. That is precisely why I have looked into alternative measures. When they're adults, they *know* what the problem is, the *threat* they create in society. If they choose to ignore that, ignore the new solution offered to them—then they're happy to remain the problem," Albion argued. "They're happy to put lives at risk, Gyldan. That choice makes them bad people!"

"For wanting to be who they are?" Gyldan's voice rose as his blood sparked under his skin. Bravery had nothing to do with it. He wasn't going to sit here and listen to Albion dictate that being a *good person* was only possible if you were a certain species. He couldn't accept that that was how the man truly felt, that perhaps the image he'd built of Albion in his mind was far better than the reality.

Everything felt cold, but colder yet was Gyldan's voice as he spoke to the driver, still staring at Albion in sheer disbelief: "Pull over."

Albion's right eye spasmed in irritation, confusion evident on his perfect face. Everything about it only served to strengthen Gyldan's resolve as he repeated: "Pull over!"

The driver muttered a curse under his breath, but he did as he was told. Without listening to Albion's weary protest, Gyldan got out of the cab and stormed down the road, stuffing his hands into his jacket pockets. He didn't even know if he was walking in the right direction for home. He almost hoped he wasn't. Right now, all Gyldan wanted was to feel like he was getting away from it all, his feet pounding the pavement, driving him away from all of the confusion and chaos of his life, the incessant plate-spinning he'd performed for months.

"Gyl? Gyldan, don't be so over-dramatic! *Gyldan!* Get *back* here!" Albion's voice roared behind him, but Gyldan bit down on his bottom lip and refused to let himself turn around. He continued to storm down the quiet street, wondering if he could walk fast enough to leave behind the painful realisation that Albion hadn't even bothered to chase after him.

Of course not. That's it. It's done, Gyldan thought to himself, turning the street corner as angry tears prickled and made the street signs swim in his vision. *He doesn't care what I think unless I agree with him. Jesus... was it worth ruining everyone else's life over though?*

His muddled mind lumbered into every other problem a break-up with Albion would create. He was sure he'd lose his job, for one. No job meant no money. No money meant no home. Griffin, Rukshana, Seraph, all out on the street. But he couldn't just stay quiet. He couldn't.

As he approached the end of the street, Gyldan sniffed, cleared his throat, and rubbed his tears away with his sleeve. This was stupid. He needed to know where he was going. He had to pull himself together and get himself home. He pulled his phone out, texting Seraph to ask if she knew where their house was from the street he was on.

It wasn't until his own feet had stopped that Gyldan realised the sound of footsteps had not. His heart fluttered a little in spite of his leftover irritation—Albion had chased him after all.

"Impressed you're not gasping for breath, old ma—"

Turning around to greet who he thought was his boyfriend, Gyldan's words retreated in fear of what he saw.

Four crimson eyes, pupils framed with a starburst of emerald, leered down upon him. Under the stark beam of the streetlight above, Gyldan was spared none of this creature's horror. An almost-human face snarled at him, a lipless mouth riddled with too many fangs, ears slashed upward into sharp points. A cacophony of broken bones grew outwards from its brow, forming a macabre crown of antlers and horns. Its skin was cast in a dull, stony grey, and a dark, ragged mane tangled out from its skull and down behind its broad shoulders, out of Gyldan's line of sight. Talons mangled its hands and feet, and a pair of wings twitched and trembled at its back, dragging like a torn cape behind it.

For one, blessed moment, neither Gyldan nor the monster moved.

Then, Gyldan couldn't help but move. His whole body shook, every ounce of his being knowing, *screaming* that this *thing* would kill him in an instant. He had no idea what it was, he couldn't string a thought together enough to even question that right now. All he could think of was to run.

His instincts kicked in at the exact moment the creature's did. A low growl tore from deep within its chest like a rising storm and then it struck out, claws and fangs slamming into the very spot Gyldan had only just managed to scurry away from. There was no precision in its movements, no accuracy or thought to refine its strike into a single, calculated move. It was raw, it was feral, and it was scrambling towards Gyldan in a flurry of bloodlust and teeth.

"*Ah!* No, please, I don't—oh god!" Gyldan babbled, fighting with his fear-frozen limbs to move.

The monster offered him nothing but a bellow of anger. It paused only to rock back on its haunches, ready to pounce at him again. But suddenly, the creature was cut from Gyldan's sight.

In a rainfall of feathers, someone had landed in front of Gyldan, standing between him and the beast. Copper wings stretched and shivered in the evening air—a vampire, eyes covered with a binding of silk. A merciful rush of air pulled back into Gyldan's lungs as he beheld his saviour. Seraph must have sent him looking...

"Griff?"

"Time t'go!" Griffin greeted him, turning to grab Gyldan. But the monster was not about to let Griffin take its prey—it struck out once more, slamming a furious limb into Griffin's side and swiping him out of the way.

"Griff!"

The vampire grunted as he crashed against the floor, rolling to get back on his feet swiftly. The beast rounded on Griffin, cutting Gyldan off from him. It gave this apparent contender to its meal a threatening growl.

"What the hell're you, huh?" Griffin asked, and to Gyldan's horror, fear trembled through the older man's voice. Slowly, so as to avoid startling the creature into action, Griffin raised a hand up to the silk wraps around his eyes. "Ain't a vampire, that's for sure... lucky me..."

Griffin tugged the silk wraps from his face. Gyldan's mouth dropped at what he saw as the silk fell away from Griffin's face. There was no mess of scars knotting over his eyelids. Instead, when the vampire opened his eyes, it was not to reveal hollow sockets at all. A pair of perfectly intact crimson eyes pierced out, locking the monster in its thrall.

"*You're leaving*," Griffin hissed at the monster. Gyldan slowly shuffled further away from the beast, which had come to a halt at the vampire's persuasion-infused words.

Its lips curled in a disobeying grumble.

"*Leave!*" Griffin demanded. The creature did not, and yet, it appeared to be fighting with itself. Muscles rippled across its grey hide, but it did not strike at Griffin or Gyldan. It remained where it was, grunting growls and whines splintering from its clenched maw.

Griffin only frowned, then beckoned to Gyldan with one hand.

"It doesn't wanna leave, son. But if there's a part of it that wants to stop—I can use that. Get ready to run, I don't know how long this thing'll thrall for!"

Gyldan could only nod, his mouth long-since too dry to form words.

"*Stay*," the vampire demanded. In response, the monster twitched and staggered down into something that resembled an obedient crouch. Gyldan didn't need telling twice—he bolted from his spot behind the creature and towards Griffin. The older man caught hold of him by the upper arms to stop him tumbling forward as he reached him. Then, the two made their escape, tearing down the street, not daring to pause even to exchange words.

They could only ignore the howl that resonated into the night sky behind them, the monster already breaking free from Griffin's thrall.

Chapter 7

  Skidding around yet another corner, Gyldan could only let Griffin pull him along and trust that the vampire would find their way home. He didn't have the breath to ask Griffin why the hell he had hidden his eyes from them, what on God's good earth the creature behind them was, or why his side was aching and damp.

  His lungs burnt as he dragged in air, the muscles in his legs stiffening and screaming with every frantic step as he tried to keep up with Griffin. The streets blurred around him, and with all his attention spent on remaining on his feet, Gyldan couldn't begin to tell where he was in the city. It wasn't until they were tearing up the front path to the house that the man even clocked that they were home.

  Griff's free hand pounded on the front door. The feathers at the base of his wings fell away as the limbs rotted, dropping from his shoulder blades and landing on the concrete behind him. The bloodied stumps under his torn shirt were already healing by the time Gyldan's groggy gaze drew up from the fallen wings to Griffin's back again.

"*Seraph! Rukshana!*"

Gyldan slumped on his side against the wall by the door, chest heaving, absently coiling an arm around his torso as he cast a desperate look back the way they had come, seeking out any hint that the demon was hunting them down.

"Wha... wha' th'..." Gyldan spluttered as the chains of the door rattled next to him. It opened to reveal Rukshana, her stunned expression darting between Griff and Gyldan in turn. Her nose twitched.

"Come, come," she beckoned, stepping aside. Griffin took Gyldan by the shoulder and helped him in. It was only now that they had slowed down that the man realised he was leaving a steady trail of blood behind him. In front of him, Seraph skidded down the hall to greet them, socks sliding on the wooden floor. Her shock was rather less restrained than Rukshana's—she openly gawked at Griffin.

"*Woah!* Eyes! What? Gyl? Oh shit, *Gyl!*" She jumped forward to help Griffin guide the man into their small living room.

Seeing the comforts of home through his blurring vision took some of the edge off Gyldan's panic. Familiarity pierced through the haze of his shock, anchoring him once more. The ancient TV in the corner was blasting a mix of colours at him, though Gyldan couldn't make out what was on the screen. The iron fireplace swirled past him on his left as Seraph and Griffin guided him to the worn-out sofa, his fumbling steps almost crashing shins-firsts into the coffee table in the middle of the small room.

The old couch creaked as Gyl settled on its well-worn springs. He'd been meaning to replace some of the 'old faithfuls' around the house, but even with his handsome pay cheque, after covering every household expense, there wasn't much left for interior decoration.

"Oh... hey Seraph..." Gyldan mumbled too late, a clammy cold creeping over his skin and replacing the burning jolt of adrenaline from minutes before. Everything ground to a halt around him, while everything violently restarted within him. Pain seared at his side, neglected until now. He drew a sluggish look down at where his hand was clutching at his torso, noting for the first time that the shirt was torn to ribbons and deep red gleamed between his fingers.

He hadn't been as agile as he had hoped then. Those ragged talons must have caught him as he had scrambled away from the creature after all.

"Griff, m' bleedin'..." Gyldan mumbled, lifting his hand up to show him. The dim lights were growing brighter at the edges of his vision, and he couldn't tell if Seraph had lifted her hand from his shoulder or if he just couldn't feel her anymore. The world grew muddy, tiresome, and confusing, yet it was all a much more appealing sensation than the fear, pain, and heartbreak he had felt that night.

He held onto consciousness for one more moment, wondering if letting himself fall into that quiet embrace would be selfish. Then, for one blissful second, Gyldan did not care.

* * *

Gyldan did not want to wake up. He spent a little while with his eyes shut, acutely aware that he was likely doing a terrible job of feigning sleep. But opening his eyes meant facing the fallout of the memories his mind was vomiting up. Of that monster. Of Griffin's eyes. Of Albion.

A sigh preceded the man begrudgingly opening his eyes against the dull daylight that stained the walls of his bedroom. He couldn't tell if it was day breaking or waning that cast the amber glow across the faded jade paint, so he had no idea how long he had been out for. And yet, Gyldan did as he ever did when waking. He turned his head on the pillow and pawed at the side table for his mobile.

Fingers curling around the device, the man brought the too-bright screen to his face. Wincing one eye shut, he tried to read the notifications stacked up on his screen.

Not one was from Albion.

It stung, and he knew he shouldn't try to balm that wound by typing a message himself. Yet, like muscle memory, Gyldan's thumbs tapped and swiped the extended message thread with Albion open.

I know we left on a bad note, but I

Gyldan paused, thumbs hovering over the screen. He deleted the message, retyped it, deleted it, then tried again.

Hey.

He smashed the send button then let his arm flop back on the bed, the phone still nestled in his hand. Everything ached, but the epicentre hummed from his side. Tentatively, Gyldan peered down at himself, lifting the blankets up a bit. Swathes of bandages greeted him, and he didn't have the heart to risk peeking underneath them.

He looked at his phone again, even though it hadn't vibrated and he knew damn well Albion hadn't messaged him back yet. Though he scolded himself, Gyldan typed another message.

I know you're pissed off at me, but I really need to talk to you. Something happened last—

Again, Gyldan paused. He swiped his thumb downwards, noting the date, then went back to his message:

—Something happened last night.

Gyldan sent the message, then set his phone down on the side table, as if having it out of his grip would change how often he checked for a new notification. He took a moment longer to collect himself before attempting to swing his legs over the side to drag himself out of his bedroom. He only had to place a small amount weight on his legs before realising this was a bad idea.

The sharp cold of the wooden floor seared through his feet and up his shins, and Gyldan decided to abandon the idea then and there. Instead, he curled back into the safety of the blanket burrito.

The man remained there for a few seconds before twisting, shooting an arm out and grabbing his phone to bring it into his lair with him. The bright glow illuminated Gyldan's face, making him squint as he jabbed at the screen again, the cold glass dampening with condensation from his breath under the thick quilt.

Gyldan brought up his messages to Albion—they hadn't even been read yet. Scowling, he tapped a message to Seraph instead.

Yo, I'm awake. Feeling a bit sore. Is Griff ok?

This message was read a mere second after he had sent it. He didn't receive a reply in the form of a message back, however. The reply came via crashing footsteps reverberating up the stairs. His door slammed open, and before he could look up from his cocoon, Gyldan was bounced bodily up and down as an overly concerned werewolf jumped onto his bed.

"Gyl! Oh my God, are you okay? Do you need anything? Can you speak?" Seraph blurted out, dazzled with distress. She peered into Gyldan's line of sight, arching over his blanket burrito. It occurred to him that Seraph had never seen him injured like this before. In fact, she'd likely never seen a human injured at all, save for the occasional drunken stumble on Gyldan's behalf.

"I can speak..." Gyldan said, muffled by his quilt. "Sore... not dead."

"You need water? Food? Extra pillow?"

"...Actually, a glass of water would be—"

Seraphina was gone in a blur of blonde and limbs, yelling down the hall to her girlfriend that their "precious human son" needed "water, stat!"

Gyldan snuggled down into his blankets, casting a quick look to his phone again before doing so. After a moment, a much calmer pressure weighed down on the edge of the bed, the sound of a glass clinking against the side table.

"Are you all right?" Rukshana's velvet tones coaxed Gyldan out from his nest. He rolled onto his back, looking up at the woman. Her dark hair was worn loose, reaching her waist and impossibly glossy in the faded sunlight bleeding into the room. Behind the cruel visor screwed into the bones of her eye sockets, Rukshana's gaze was soft, though her face was taut with concern.

Gyldan uncoiled himself from his warm entrapping and sat up on the bed, picking up the glass of water. After a few grateful sips to wet his throat, he replied.

"Not really. I mean, yeah, I'm fine... all things considered... but..."

Rukshana nodded as he trailed off.

"You've had quite the encounter. And we've all had quite the shock. Did you know?"

Gyldan frowned.

"Know what?"

"About Griffin."

In just two words, Rukshana's presence no longer felt warm. Instead, all Gyldan could see were shields long discarded, yet longer-since forged, start to rise. Unspoken between them was the name of their former friend who had betrayed them and an awful question.

Gyldan sat up straighter.

"No. No, Rukshana, I know it looks bad. But Griff must have had a good reason for keeping that from us. Hell... I mean, if it meant dodging getting his eyes scooped out, I'd hide 'em too!"

Rukshana's face did not soften.

"But how did he—"

Her question was cut short by a knock at the door—Seraphina, looking infinitely calmer than when she had left the room, peered in.

"I know you said I had to go calm down, but Griff says we should change Gyl's bandages if he's up," Seraph said to Rukshana, holding up a handful of clean bandage rolls and gauze. "But if you wanna gossip about his big reveal, I'm down for that too."

The werewolf came into the room, closing the door behind her with a delicate touch, then moving over to the bedside. She knelt down, poking Gyl on the arm to get him to shuffle closer. He did as he was silently told, lifting his arms so Seraph could start to unwind the old bandages. He watched as she reached around his torso, nose wrinkling as she came into close proximity with Gyldan.

"Dude, in the nicest way... you need a shower," she said, bundling up the old bandages and starting to peel the gauze away.

"Oh... wow, thanks Seraph," Gyldan mumbled, tilting his head down to try and sniff-test his armpit without being too obvious.

"Hey look, man, a friend tells you not to worry. A real friend tells you to take a shower." Seraph smirked, then gestured to the wound at Gyldan's side. It looked vicious to him, but from Seraph and Rukshana's expressions, it wasn't too serious. Two jagged, diagonal lines clipped from just under his armpit and down beneath his pectoral, each around four inches long. Given the size of the creature's talons, Gyldan assumed he'd been caught by the very tips of them. Steri-Strips were lined across the wounds, keeping them closed.

"You were very lucky." Rukshana leant in closer, inspecting the wounds. With a feather-light touch, her fingertips rested on either side of the cuts. "If Griffin had not told me what you encountered, I would have said these wounds were caused by a werewolf. The cuts are identical to a wolf's claws..."

Her words brought the creature to the front of Gyldan's memory—it certainly hadn't been a werewolf, though it had attacked like one crazed by the moon. Greyish skin, eyes like a vampire, claws like a werewolf, and a crown of broken bones at its temples...

"You should be okay to shower. The wounds are not very deep," Rukshana continued, rising from the bed and heading to the door. "I can see if we have a waterproof dressing in the first aid kit if you would feel more comfortable with it covered though?"

"I-I'll be fine, thanks," Gyldan said, making another effort to get to his feet now he was more awake and settled. Seraph straightened up too, leaving the clean bandages and gauze behind as she followed after Rukshana.

"Knock on my door when you're done, nerd, and I'll put the clean stuff on."

The girls left Gyldan alone. With one last check of his phone, the man got up and plodded after them, heading to the bathroom. Pulling the light cord, most of the spotlights above flickered to life, the cold blue tiles biting underfoot. He locked the door, then set about awkwardly twisting himself into the shower without agitating his wound too much. Still, once the shower head spluttered to life overhead and the temperature settled to something between icy dust and molten magma, Gyldan was treated to utter bliss. The warm water sloughed several layers of grime off his skin—the smell of the crowded events hall, the knotted muscles of his argument with Albion, the anxious sweat that clung to him as he ran from the monster.

That thing... is that what's been killing the Daedalus employees? Why'd it go for me then? Gyldan thought, letting his head fall back as the shower rained over his forehead. *Didn't seem like the type to pause and confirm before killing, though.*

He began to gingerly wash around the wound, patting the area for fear of tearing the Steri-Strips off, especially when he was so distracted.

Albion must be pretty pissed... Is it really over? God—why do I even care? I mean, other than the job and the money... and the rent... That should be bothering me more. Why isn't it?

Gyldan ignored the answer that his heart offered. He didn't have the energy to confront that yet, let alone to process it. Instead, Gyldan finished up his shower and smoothed his dripping hair away from his face. He wrapped a towel around his waist and headed back to his room, doing everything he could to avoid looking at his phone.

He looked at his phone, of course.

Clucking his tongue in frustration of the lack of reply from Albion, the man busied himself with drying off and shrugging some grey lounge pants on. He wrapped himself in a dark green bathrobe and then went across the hall to knock on Seraph's bedroom door. She opened it before he could finish three knocks.

"Hey!" she chirped, then inhaled. "Ah yeah, way better. Is that cinnamon?"

"Errr..."

"Think it is. Anywho, let's go get you mummified and keep them innards in tight." Seraph smiled, hopping out and heading across the hall to Gyldan's room. "Sit down please, sir. I wasn't allowed to go to medical school, so I need you to be as still as possible."

Gyldan couldn't help but chuckle at Seraph. Her energy couldn't be described as a light in his life—it was more a flare of pure fire. Dazzling, bright, and sometimes a little misguided. But she always had every intention of warming everyone around her. It was at moments like this that he was thankful for that.

He crossed the hall to his room again, only to be stopped by someone else walking up the stairs. Griffin lumbered up the steps, lacking his usual silk wraps on his face. He gave a small nod to Gyldan as he passed him, then he turned to Gyldan's room. Leaning in the doorframe, the vampire jerked his head over his shoulder to motion Seraph to leave.

"I'll do that, kid. You go talk to Rukshana. She's still furious at me, and you know I was never very good at talking her down," Griffin said with a sad smile. Seraph looked at him, then to Gyldan. The flame had petered out from her aura, the tension of everyone's suspicions of the older vampire thickening in the air. Still, the werewolf obeyed, leaving the room with a passing glimpse at Gyldan.

Griffin beckoned him to sit down on the edge of the bed. The man did as he was told, and for a while, the two were silent as Griffin set about applying clean bandages to Gyldan's torso. Gyldan didn't know what to say. Would it be rude to ask about his eyes? Why he'd kept it from them? He wasn't at all convinced by Rukshana's apparent judgement that Griffin might be a traitor too. After all, he'd unveiled his secret to save Gyldan.

For want of something better to do, Gyldan looked around the room, then found his attention being pulled towards his phone on the bedside table. To his right, Griffin snorted.

"Boyfriend trouble?" he asked, guiding the roll of bandage over Gyldan's back. Gyldan's face burnt with embarrassment. He wasn't sure he was ready to discuss his relationship woes with Griffin.

"S-something like that."

"Ya tell him about last night?"

"Told him something happened, and that I needed to talk. Caladrius is the only company with the technology to even attempt to figure out what that creature is. If that's the thing that's been killing Daedalus employees—"

"—Then it might have crawled outta Caladrius' labs," Griffin interrupted gruffly. Gyldan swallowed.

"It... could have. I don't know, biology isn't really our selling point. But maybe if I describe this thing to Albion, he'll know how to track it down and get it off the streets. I mean, whatever it is... it attacked me and you. It could kill anyone, human, vampire, or werewolf."

Griffin nodded, still busy with Gyldan's bandages.

"Eh, you're right on that part. But he's not got back to you yet, I take it?"

Gyldan's heart hit his knees.

"N-no... no, he, erm... he hasn't. Kinda had a bit of a row last night," he admitted. His arms were starting to ache from holding them up so long, and he was thankful to see Griffin knotting the bandage in place and leaning back, allowing him to finally bring his arms down. "Did Seraph or Rukshana tell you about... the rumour I heard?"

"'Bout the cure?" Griffin rocked back to sit on the floor, crossing his legs and holding them at the ankles. "Yeah, Seraph mentioned something about it when you guys came home from the arcade the other day. You find something?"

"Worse—Albion *admitted* it. That's our big secret project right now. He's not gonna make it mandatory."

"Oh, how kind of him."

"Yeah, but... he's gonna pull some strings and have people who don't opt-in *arrested*."

"...Oh, how *kind* of him."

Gyldan couldn't help but feel guilty by association. He hated discussing this side of Albion with people, but then, it was the side that Albion chose to show most people. It was starting to dawn on Gyldan that maybe that little sliver of goodness within the man might not be worth saving after all.

Griffin sighed, resting his elbows against his legs as he leant forward.

"Look... a little bit of fatherly advice? Am I allowed to do that?"

Gyldan gave him a little half-smile.

"Sure."

"Albion makes his money outta oppressing people," Griffin said. "It's no secret that he isn't a great guy. I mean, hell, he let you walk home even with the recent killings. I only got there 'cause you'd messaged Seraph and we all know you're crap at following directions. I was just gonna walk y'home, son!"

Gyldan shifted in his seat, turning away from Griffin.

"Sorry about that..." he muttered.

"That's not my point," the vampire said, shaking his head. "What I'm saying is, the fact you got attacked after Albion let you walk home? Let his pride get in the way of looking out for you just 'cause you dared to disagree with him? That might serve as a wake-up call."

Gyldan frowned, turning back to Griffin then.

"For who?"

Griffin shrugged.

"That depends on his reaction."

∗ ∗ ∗

Griffin had left Gyldan alone for a few hours after tending to his wounds, and the man had wasted them lying on his bed, alternately dozing and checking his phone. Every time he checked, the result was the same—Albion hadn't even looked at the messages, leaving Griffin's observation ringing in Gyldan's mind.

He knows something happened, but he'd rather be mad about an argument, Gyldan thought to himself for the seventh time, trying to rile himself up with enough anger to cut the other man from his life. This was his wake-up call, Gyldan knew. This *should* be his wake-up call.

And yet, when he finally decided to scuttle downstairs in search of food later that night, his body clock in shambles, Gyldan still pocketed his phone in case Albion messaged him.

Heading to the living room, Gyldan gave a small wave to its occupants as greeting. Seraph was sitting on the discoloured carpet in front of the TV in the corner, playing a games console Gyldan had bought with his bonus a few months ago. A decision had been made that day between buying a new sofa and buying a console; a decision not everyone had been happy with. She looked up from the screen and beamed at him.

"Hey, dude! Feeling more like yourself?"

"Yeah, I always feel like my lung might slip out," Gyldan replied, slowly lowering himself to the battered sofa next to Rukshana. Seraph rolled her eyes.

"Such a drama queen. You venturing down for food? Griff's gone to pick something up. Gave him your usual order. 'Cause I'm a top-quality friend," Seraph said, her attention being dragged back to her game.

"Pizza?"

Seraph shook her head.

"Thai."

Gyldan heard Rukshana huff, exhaling through her nose. Thai food was Rukshana's usual choice—she was a fiend for a dish called *zhūxiěgāo*, or as Gyldan had later learnt, pig's blood cake. Clearly, Griffin was still trying to smooth things over with the other vampire.

"You okay?" he asked, leaning back in his seat. Rukshana wore the look of royalty in the midst of treason, and yet, there was a weariness to her face that hinted she did not wish to remain angered at Griffin.

"He has promised to explain everything over food," Rukshana replied, her shoulders relaxing a little. "But how do we know it won't be more lies?"

"I'm sure he had a good reason for not telling us, Rukshana. This isn't like with Caelan," Gyldan said, addressing the elephant in the room so bluntly that Seraph dropped her controller. It thudded on the floor, and the two women pinned Gyldan to his seat with a shared look. "What? It isn't! Griff saved my life. If he was a traitor like Caelan, why would he do that? Why would he reveal his secret to me and make his life more complicated?"

Rukshana's lips pursed, but there were thoughts whizzing across her face as her stance drooped even further.

"...I want to believe you. I suppose... I'm a little more on edge about these things than you two are. I am not sure it is a good thing, but I don't really know any other way."

Seraph turned and lay on her front on the floor, propping her chin in her hands. "Babe, you've already made *loads* of progress. No one's saying you have to forgive and forget everything that ever happens to you! Think about it! A few years ago, what Caelan did would make you hate all werewolves again."

Gyldan recalled the newspaper clipping he'd stolen from the lab's collection of documents regarding werewolf and vampire attacks around the world. A wolf attack on a vampire group, and one young woman who had survived... the photo of Rukshana. He hadn't had a chance to read it, but he didn't feel the need to pry anymore—what had happened that night had obviously left deep scars on her, and she was still healing. Rukshana was bringing down the walls she'd built all those years ago. Gyldan didn't want to be the one to bring them back up again by asking her to relive that night.

Seraph continued: "To be honest, I was kinda scared you would go back to that mindset. But yeah, okay, the whole thing with Caelan has made you a little on edge about werewolves again, and now Griffin's got you worried about trusting *anyone*, but... you're still here. You didn't run away. You didn't, y'know... hate me?"

"I could never..."

"Exactly!" Seraph smiled. "Even though I'm a werewolf too! You've come a long way. Don't feel bad if something makes you stop on the road and catch your breath for a moment, okay?"

The vampire smiled back, looking embarrassed as she did so.

"He had better have a bloody good reason for lying to us. Or I'll take his eyes out myself," she said. From the look Seraph gave Gyldan, neither one of them was sure if Rukshana was joking.

Chapter 8

While Griffin spent the next few days trying to repair the fractured sense of normality within the group, Gyldan attempted to do the same with Albion. He still wasn't sure if they were really over, and the man's utter silence served as an answer that Gyldan didn't want to accept yet. Sure, he'd been angry that night. Beyond angry. The stubbornness of Albion was matched only by Gyldan's frustration. He understood the man's anger over the loss of his son, but Gyldan doubted whether Albion would have looked into a way to turn everyone into vampires or werewolves if his son had been killed by a human. But, they had much bigger problems to contend with right now.

There was a monster roaming the streets.

For the umpteenth time that day, Gyldan checked his phone. For the umpteenth time that day, he was greeted with nothing. Gyldan had thought that ringing in sick to work would have piqued some of Albion's curiosity—his personal assistant had never had a day off sick in his entire tenure at Caladrius.

Stuffing his phone into his pocket, Gyldan was about to make his way to the living room when he paused at the top of the stairs. He looked around then scuttled into the bathroom, locking the door behind him. There, Gyldan faced the circular mirror on the windowsill that was surrounded by a rainbow of lotions and potions mostly belonging to Rukshana. It wasn't the first time he'd been possessed to double- and triple-check his reflection. Gyldan craned towards the mirror, pulling his lip up to examine his teeth.

Nothing but normal, blunt human teeth greeted him.

Straightening up, Gyldan had to laugh at himself. All those old vampire and werewolf stories, written long before the species leapt from fiction to fact, had left a ghost of worry in Gyldan's mind. Countless conspiracy theories floated about online, and with a few days of bed rest and phone-scrolling, Gyldan had read one too many of them. Many of the conspiracies he'd read were rooted in the myths of these fictional books. Vampires could turn into bats, they claimed. Men could become werewolves by drinking water out of a wolf's pawprint, they fretted. Naturally, one of the most prevalent concerns was that vampires and werewolves could 'turn' a human with a bite or scratch. That somehow their entire species was just an infection that needed a human host.

It didn't make sense, of course. Neither werewolves nor vampires were human at all. Weary scientists had explained this over and over again—these two species were evolutionary branches, and not an infection to be passed via tooth or claw. Vampires could no more turn a human than a lion could turn a cat by biting it.

Then again, the creature that had attacked Gyldan had been neither of those species. It was different, and bearing its wounds left the man with the awful sensation of being a laboratory rat.

Trudging out of the bathroom, Gyldan made his way down to the living room to fling himself bodily onto the couch. He had his pick of things to mope about.

Not being at work didn't suit him, for one. He was bored. He was restless. And his side hurt.

Before Gyldan could commit to a good sulking, Seraph's head popped out from the doorway leading to the kitchen.

"Well, ain't that a grumpy face!" She smiled, flashing sharp teeth. "What's up, man?"

"Thought it would have healed by now... or at least enough for me to go to work." Gyldan shifted in his seat to try and get comfortable.

"Dude, it's been like, three days. Humans are kinda squishy," the werewolf commented with a sage nod. "But you guys bounce back from anything. Just be patient."

"Rukshana out?" Gyldan called after Seraph as she dipped back into the kitchen again.

"Yeah, her and Griff went for a walk. Or a fly. I don't know. But at least they're talking again," Seraph replied. After a while, she wandered through from the kitchen to the living room. She was carrying a two-litre drink bottle under one arm, two glasses precariously in her hand, and a bag of tortilla chips in the other. Between her teeth, she was holding a packet of sweets. She chucked herself onto the sofa next to Gyldan, setting the glasses down on the table and dropping the bags of food between them. "Y'know, I always feel sorry for those two not being able to digest anything other than blood-stuff. Really missing out."

Gyldan smiled back, letting the werewolf pour out two drinks for them both before he spoke again.

"So, what did you think about the other night? Griff's... story?"

Seraph shrugged.

"I believed him. And wasn't really surprised," she admitted, opening the bag of tortilla chips. "What about you?"

Gyldan recalled the explanation Griff had given that night after he had returned with way more takeaway food than four people could eat. There was no doubt that the man felt bad about not telling them about his eyes. And his explanation had been quite simple—he'd been born on the streets. There was no doctor to whisk him away from his mother to perform the cruel surgery, as was the norm back then. So, for a long time, Griff had lived underground, off the radar, and was spared the brutality. He'd rather glossed over the details of how or why he'd come back to the surface. The older vampire simply stated that he had grown tired of living in the shadows, so he had covered his eyes like a city-dweller and lived among them instead.

Simple. Neither Seraph nor Gyldan had had further questions. Rukshana had.

"Griff's Griff," Gyldan replied, helping himself to a handful of snacks. "I believe him. And I trust him. If he was a bad guy, he'd have left me there with that monster, told you I was dead when he got there, and never have to tell you he wasn't blind. But he didn't. He risked you guys hating him to save me. The least I can do is trust him."

Seraph nodded along.

"No, I know, I totally get it. He's not exactly gained anything for keeping it hidden from us. Not like Caelan keeping his little side-hustle from us, I mean, I can see why he kept *that* schtum. Kinda wondering why Griff didn't just tell us but... y'know."

The pair sat in silence for a while, with Seraph's words reminding Gyldan of what Albion had told him. Caelan was only recently on the payroll, according to his boss. Had the werewolf just gotten frustrated with their slow progress?

"I... couldn't find him at Caladrius, by the way. Snuck down to the labs but... no clear sign. Worse, Albion caught me," Gyldan said, reaching for his glass. Seraph inhaled through her teeth.

"*Yeeeesh*, sorry, dude, didn't mean to get you in trouble with your boss."

Gyldan shook his head.

"Don't worry about it. I didn't find anything, but... I'm not convinced his body isn't somewhere in the labs. I'll keep looking. You were right—Caelan was a true friend, once. Albion said he hadn't been in contact long."

Beside him, Seraph heaved a sigh, her expression falling as she looked across the room.

"...Goddammit, Caelan..." she muttered, more to herself than to Gyldan. The pain was covered in a flash with a smile. "Thanks for checking though, dude, appreciate it. Least we can rest easy knowing he wasn't a total ass-kisser the whole time we knew him."

Their conversation was brought to an end by Gyldan's phone buzzing across the table. The man lunged forward, wincing as his side told him off for exerting too much energy all at once. That same energy dissipated once he saw the message wasn't from Albion. Still, a message from the company's receptionist was odd. It wasn't that Gyldan didn't get along with Alexis, it was just unusual to hear from her. Plus, he was surprised she'd managed to keep her job after the whole vampire-in-the-CEO's-office fiasco. He'd have to ask her about that particular escape later.

Hi Gyldan, hope you're feeling better. Just a friendly head's up: people are talking.

Gyldan's cheeks burnt, and he turned away from Seraph to text back.

Hi Alexis. Still a bit sore. Can't believe I managed to hurt myself so badly just from walking home. What are people talking about?

It wasn't long before he got a reply that made him choke on his own spit.

You and Albion, both off at the same time? And who breaks a rib falling over on the way home? No one's buying it, Gyl.

People were talking. Then they already suspected. Gyldan had thought they had covered it up so well! But then, why was Albion off too? His brain tried to sort out this whirlwind of concerns into an orderly fashion.

He bristled at Alexis' accusation of lying. Okay, so he hadn't *fallen over*, but he had gotten injured on the way home. That much was true. To prove it, Gyldan yanked up one side of his shirt and took a photo of the bandages, sending it to the receptionist.

I did! Look, I'm bandaged up, at my house... Seriously, people think Albion and I are together? Just 'cause I'm his PA? That's so stupid. Still, he might've told me he was ringing in sick too. What's up?

As he waited for her to reply, Gyldan checked his messages to Albion. Still no response. Not even read. Alexis' reply popped up shortly after.

His daughter rang up, said he wasn't well. He's been getting loads of migraines lately, maybe one just really kicked his ass today. Ah well. Thought there was gossip. Hope you feel better soon.

Between his days-long frustration of having no response from Albion, along with a new concern that the man was unwell, Gyldan was losing his grip on being at all level-headed. He got to his feet, earning him a look from Seraph as he went to go get his shoes from the wooden rack in the narrow hallway.

"Yo, where you going? What's happened?" she asked, shifting forward in her seat as though she meant to pounce on him. "Hey-hey, Shana will *kill* me if I let you wander off on your own when you're hurt. I'll come with you! Wherever you're suddenly jetting off to…"

Hopping on one foot to try and shove his foot into already-laced trainers, Gyldan shot a hand out to steady himself against the wall while also trying to look over his shoulder.

"N-no, no, no need. Just going to check on a friend, they just messaged to say they aren't well. Gonna see if they need anything."

But Seraph was already on her feet, heading to the shoe pile that might once have been a shoe rack.

"I'll walk you over then."

"This friend isn't—"

Gyldan was cut off by the front door opening next to him. He managed to shove his shoes on and straightened up to see a perplexed-looking Griffin and Rukshana. The dishevelled older vampire nodded at Gyldan and Seraph in turn, then a sloppy smile spread over his stubbled face.

"Did you miss us, son? We weren't gone that long, I didn't think..." he said, rubbing a hand through the tangled matt of overlong grey hair on his head.

"*Too* long," Rukshana said, starting to take her shoes off. She was shaking her head as she did so, and fixed Griffin with a look. "I am glad the underground community recognised you, Griffin."

"Told you you can trust me!" Griffin grinned. "I just didn't wanna risk getting you guys in trouble, knowing a vampire who'd dodged the system and all. It was easier to pretend I hadn't, and safer for you to believe that too."

"Not that..." Rukshana admitted, moving into the living room. "They seemed a little... unhinged. I was glad they greeted you so warmly..."

At this, Griffin frowned, safe from being caught by the other vampire now that she'd moved rooms.

"Well, you'd be a little unsteady too if you'd lived in a sewer all your life," the older vampire mumbled. Then, without warning, he clapped a hand on Gyldan's shoulder. "Bored? I don't blame you. Come help your favourite old bastard with something."

"B-but I—" Gyldan looked at the front door over Griffin's shoulder, but promptly gave up. Even if he did make it outside, he couldn't talk Seraph out of being his chaperone. And walking with her to Albion's house would raise far too many questions on both sides. He sighed, nostrils flaring, then yanked his shoes off. "All right... what is it?"

Griffin tapped the side of his nose with one finger, then pointed upwards.

"Just need a little Caladrius expertise, as it were. C'mon. I got what I need, but you're the guy to figure out how to use it."

He gave Gyldan a light push on the shoulder, coaxing him first up the stairs and towards Gyldan's bedroom. He'd kind of hoped he wouldn't—after all, Gyldan was pretty sick of the sight of those four walls during his bed rest.

With the gait of a stroppy teenager, Gyldan dragged himself into his bedroom, glaring daggers at the walls in question, before facing the vampire. Meanwhile, Griffin closed the door behind them, then reached into his tattered jacket's inner pocket, producing a tied-up plastic bag. Gyldan frowned, tilting his head to the side to try and make out the package a little better. He needn't have bothered. The vampire fumbled with the knot for a few seconds, then poured out its contents onto Gyldan's overfull desk.

He nearly threw up his heart at the sight of it.

A cherry-red tinted lens, a number of wires and UV light components, several large bolts, and a patented Caladrius eye-guard fitter clattered out across the tabletop.

"My mate Corin managed to scavenge one of these up pretty quick. It's amazing what people throw away, you know! Loads of these knocking around from refits," Griffin chirped, his lips still curled into a smile. "So, is this somethin' you know how to fix on? Be honest, son—as much as I trust you, if you don't know, I'll figure something else out."

"Griff..." Gyldan fell back into the office chair next to the table. Griffin's request had made his whole world lurch like a ship in a storm, causing everything to veer off-balance beneath him. With knots in his stomach that threatened to bring up what little he'd snacked on earlier, Gyldan spluttered out: "Why? Can't you just... pretend you're blind again? You don't think we'd ever tell anyone, do you?"

Griffin chuckled, toying with one of the bolts on the desk.

"Nah, I'm sure you wouldn't. That's partly what's bothering me. You lot would keep that secret regardless of what happened. I hope it never comes to that, but knowing there's an unregistered vampire skulking about? That's a crime, and I ain't making criminals of ya."

"...Griffin, we tried to pull off a heist on the biggest tech company in the world."

The older vampire scowled at Gyldan, tarnishing his noble act.

"That's different. We all agreed to the risk. This?" He gestured to his eyes. "You guys didn't agree to this. I need to... start being more responsible."

Gyldan almost laughed, though it wasn't born of mockery. While Griffin was undoubtedly the father of the group, he was the sort of father-type with a heart of gold and the tact of a scrubbing brush. He would patch a person up after they fell over, but only because they did so after doing something he had told them was a great idea. A good man, yes. But responsible?

Gyldan shook his head, then rested his forehead in his hands.

"Griff, I-I can't. I mean, I don't know how to, for one. I'm just a PA. And even if I did know how, I still wouldn't. Think about it—that eye-guard is deregistered now. It'd be as bad if you got caught wearing it than if you didn't have one at all."

Griffin stopped messing with the pile of bolts on the table, staring intently at them instead.

"Maybe. But when I first came up here, if I was caught, the only person I was risking was me. If I get caught now... I shoulda done this years ago, kid. I should have done this when I first met you guys. If I get carted off, you guys'll get caught up in it all too."

Gyldan stood up, paced over to Griffin, and began to gather up all the pieces of the eye-guard from the desk. He put them back in the bag, tied the top, and pushed it into the vampire's chest.

"We're already caught up in this. We always were." Gyldan smiled. "Besides, you've dodged the system for how many years already? No sense worrying about it now."

Griffin looked down at the bag, lifting one arm up to take it off Gyldan. His lips pursed and he seemed like he wanted to object. He narrowed one eye at Gyldan.

"What if this old coot goes looking down back alleys for someone to screw this to his face anyway?" Griffin asked, shaking the bag of bolts and metal between them. Gyldan laughed.

"Then I look forward to watching Rukshana treat you for septicaemia while tearing you a new one for being the *opposite* of responsible," Gyldan said around a smile before his expression rapidly dropped and he added: "Please don't go asking down back alleys for someone to screw your face."

The vampire's expression turned sour then, his nose crinkling as he turned away a little.

"Don't talk to your elders like that," he countered, heading for the door with a ghost of a smirk playing on his lips.

Griffin skulked out of the room, and Gyldan was content that he wouldn't try anything foolish for now at least. As admirable as his intentions had been, he didn't like the idea of Griffin wearing that awful device. After all, if they couldn't free one vampire from the current system, what chance did they have to free them all?

His phone buzzed in his pocket then, snapping Gyldan from his thoughts. It vibrated twice more before he'd even torn it from his pocket and tapped on the screen. As much as he loathed to admit it, Gyldan's heart leapt to see who it was from: three messages in a row stacked up on his screen.

I'm sorry. I just woke up. I have been sick since Saturday morning.
Something happened? After you ran off?
Are you at the office?

Part of him wanted to set his phone down and wait an hour or two, to let the man stew for a bit as Gyldan had. But he lasted all of thirty seconds before typing back.

What's up? And yes, after our argument. I got attacked. No, I'm not at the office. I'm off too.

This time, there was no long pause between Gyldan's message and Albion's response. Not long after it had been read, Gyldan's phone burst with an incoming call that he answered far too quickly.

"Hello?"

"Gyldan, what the hell is going on? What do you mean *attacked?* Are you okay? Are the police aware of this?" Albion's voice would have exploded from the speaker had he not sounded quite so exhausted. The clattering in the background suggested the man was only just getting out of bed. "Do you know who it was? Why didn't you call me?"

"We were arguing, and I was pissed off at you!" Gyldan reminded him with a hiss, closing the door to his room and pacing the floor. "But..."

The man sighed, running a hand over his hair. He calmed himself a little before continuing. "...I'm fine. Just a little bruised. And no, the police aren't on it—"

"Why not? I will call them then. Whoever did this to you—"

"Albion, don't! Let me finish! It... it wasn't a some*one*... I have no idea what it was. I didn't want to go to the police as I didn't think they'd be able to help. But... you might?"

The noise at the other end of the phone stopped, followed by a long sigh.

"I suppose I'll have to stop being annoyed at you for now then," Albion grumbled. "I'll send a driver to pick you up. We're working from home today."

Chapter 9

Getting to Albion's house was one thing. Getting out of the door to meet his driver while avoiding the heightened senses of two vampires and a werewolf was quite another. Gyldan hated lying to his friends, but in order to peel Seraph from his leg and assure her over-active sense of responsibility for his welfare, Gyldan had had no choice.

"I'm just nipping into the office for something," he had said. "I'll be fine. If it's late by the time I get out, I'll message one of you to come meet me and walk back home with me, okay?"

It was for their own good, he knew. And yet, the dishonesty dragged behind Gyldan as he trudged out the door and down the front path. He had given Albion the adjacent street as his address in order to protect his secret home life, and so, when he reached the sleek silver car waiting outside someone else's house, Albion's chauffeur raised a critical eyebrow.

"Hey, you, er... you got here before me!" Gyldan laughed to hide his nerves as he bundled himself into the back seat. He pointed out the window. "I was just... at the corner shop. Needed some gum."

Fuck, why did I say gum? Gyldan immediately thought as the chauffeur's other eyebrow rose to meet its twin.

"I'm sure you did, sir," the driver drawled.

"N-no, not like—we're working! That's all," Gyldan protested, shoving his hands into the front pocket of his hoodie. He wasn't even dressed for a date, and yet, between this and Alexis' texts that morning, he couldn't help but feel acutely aware that he was doing the worst job in the world at hiding his and Albion's relationship.

"Of course, sir."

With that, the car pulled away, leaving Gyldan to alternate between pretending to be on his phone and brooding over what was to come. After all, he and Albion had left matters on a sour note. Sure, it was nice that Albion had set his ego aside to check on Gyldan, but they were going to have to address their conflict tonight. Gyldan could feel it in his heart, but for the life of him, he had no idea what he would do.

Yes, you do, the unhelpful little voice in his head said. *You're going to ignore it. You're going to ignore the worst of him to cling to the best of him. Like you always do.*

It wasn't long before the vehicle grovelled towards the front of proud manor awaiting them. Gyldan tried to breathe his way out of a tight chest and rising anxiety as gravel crackled under the wheels of the car, heralding their arrival.

Getting out of the car, Gyldan paid the driver with a lifeless wave of thanks then half-jogged up the steps to the front door. He raised a hand to knock, though he was uncomfortable at the idea of hitting a door that looked more expensive than his entire life. It was just as well that he paused at all, however, as the elegantly carved oak swung open to reveal a man Gyldan did not recognise for an entire heartbeat. He gasped upon realising who had greeted him.

"—Al? Jesus, should you be up?" Gyldan blurted out, reaching for Albion's shoulder in an instinctive need to steady the other man. Albion was clinging to the doorframe, his eyes unfocused as he searched for Gyldan to fix him with a scowl. His hair was a tufted silver mess, and more than a few days of dark stubble shadowed his jaw. He had not even gotten dressed properly, sporting only a pair of slack grey joggers.

"I did feel a lot better sitting down, I'll admit," Albion muttered, dragging one hand down over his face and then pushing himself off the doorframe. He turned and padded into the room, bare feet slapping against the hardwood floor. A blithe gesture beckoned over Albion's shoulder for Gyldan to come in, and so the man followed his lead, shutting the door behind him.

"What... what happened?" Gyldan asked. He couldn't help but gawk at the other man's retreating form as they both headed into the living room. A strange, ruddy rash was blossoming over Albion's upper back, darkening at his shoulder blades like freshly healed skin.

His boyfriend chucked himself onto the pristine sofa with a heavy sigh, and Gyldan could only shuffle into the living room after him, studying Albion's face with concern.

"A reaction, I assume. Likely something from the fundraiser." Albion let his head fall back against the leather sofa and closed his eyes. Dark circles bruised under his eye sockets, made all the more evident against the striking monochrome colour-scheme of Albion's living room surrounding them. When Gyldan took an unsure seat next to the older man, he noticed the skin of his face seemed dry and lacklustre, flaking at his temples and across his forehead in sore, irritated patches.

"A reaction? Seriously?" Gyldan asked, running tentative fingertips over Albion's cheek. The other man snapped around and a frown brewed over his forehead. With a limp hand, Albion tried to swat Gyldan away and missed.

"If people would stop fussing over me, I would be much better!" Albion's pride forced the worn-out man to make display of sitting up and being absolutely fine. "Even Yanatha's been worrying after me. Can you imagine that? She cancelled on her mother so that she could keep checking in on me every other hour. You would think I was dying and she's making up for lost time."

"Don't say that," Gyldan said without much conviction. The strained relationship between Albion and his daughter was not a topic he wanted to stick his nose into, lest he fracture his own precarious connection with the man.

"Regardless, I didn't call you here to pity me," Albion continued, tilting his head to glance at Gyldan. He even managed to muster the strength to bring his trademark grin back, as though the sight of it would assure Gyldan that everything was fine despite the mess around it. "You said you were attacked the other night. Tell me everything. I will see it all set right."

Gyldan paused, wondering where to start. He wanted to discuss their argument first, to find out where they stood now. But he knew Albion well enough—he was already building a vendetta against this unknown assailant, and if Gyldan tried to switch topics now, Albion would just switch them right back.

"It's… a long story. And a weird one. Coffee?" Gyldan asked, placing his hands on his thighs and pushing himself to his feet. "'Cause I'm gonna need one to tell it. Latte?"

Albion reclined back, resting one hand on his leg and the other leisurely behind his head. He winced a little in thought.

"Black, please. I need to wake up a bit," he replied, face crumpling in pre-emptive regret of his bitter request.

*　*　*

A short time later, the men were back in the living room with the story of the unknown creature in full flow. Gyldan's coffee sat on the glass table, neglected upon its slate coaster and yet offering its unrequited support by its presence all the same. If nothing else, it gave Gyldan something to stare at as he avoided looking at Albion. They were sitting opposite each other, with Gyldan having elected to sit himself down on an armchair and leave the tired CEO slumped on the sofa across the room. In some strange way, it felt like Albion embodied all of his worries right now, and if he didn't look at him, he didn't have to confront them. Yet Gyldan's mind would flit between wanting to confront their personal matters and wanting to avoid them. It made for a distracting companion as he retold the story of the night he'd left Albion in the taxi and stormed away.

He had gotten to the stage where he needed to describe the creature. Albion, who had been utterly devoid of energy, seemed to scrape the last of it from some deep recess of his body. He had regained more of his focus as time went on, and he looked over at Gyldan properly, face rigid with concern.

"*Wings?* So, I was correct. It was a feral vampire?" Albion asked, brow knitting together in thought. "Doubtless there would be a few living off the radar, but to think they would be so bold..."

"N-no, not a vampire. Definitely not," Gyldan interjected, clasping his hands together to stop himself flapping gestures of frustration. "It had... horns, I think? Antlers? Just, loads of bones and stuff coming out of its head. And its skin... Al, it wasn't a vampire. I'm telling you, it wasn't."

"All right, all right, I believe you. Grey skin, horns, wings, claws..." Albion listed back to him, assuring Gyldan that he had been paying attention.

"And four eyes. Like, two right above," Gyldan explained, tapping his brow bone. "I've never seen anything like it."

"So... how did you manage to escape?" Albion asked.

"I... I ran," Gyldan lied. In hindsight, he realised he should have put together a more conceivable lie than this.

"You ran. From an unknown, non-human behemoth with wings?" Albion raised an eyebrow and took a loud slurp of his coffee, pinning Gyldan with a sceptical look over the rim of his mug. Clearly, the bitterness didn't agree with him though, and he screwed up his face and put the mug to the side again. "You *outran* this monstrosity?"

"C-confused it, I think," Gyldan said. It was strange to feel hurt that Albion would direct his lack of trust at him, especially when in this case he was quite right to. "Sorta... darted down alleyways, it didn't seem very... intelligent."

"Mmmm..." Albion did not look convinced. Gyldan sighed, letting his head drop to his hands for a moment. Then, he rubbed his face and straightened up to address his boyfriend far more directly than he felt comfortable with.

"Look, Al, seriously? I kinda—I just—I just needed a little bit of support. That's why you were the first person I messaged, even after everything that happened that night, even after our argument, I contacted *you*. 'C-cause I... I was scared, I was... a mess and hurt and... and..."

Gyldan gave a frustrated grunt, his heart hammering, aware that Albion was watching him as he unravelled. He had to look away as he finished with more than a snap of frustration: "...and you were the first person I thought of. The first person I wanted to tell me I was safe now. Even though I was—am—still so pissed off at you and your stubborn *cure* idea. I know we gotta go back to that, and I know we're still arguing, and I don't know if you're done with me or what, but... even if we are... even if you..."

The words spilt from his lips faster than his brain could keep up, tying him in verbal knots and leaving Gyldan equal parts terrified for his outburst and frustrated at not being able to smooth out his feelings enough to communicate. It was like he was performing some sad little show for Albion, and it only added to his fears that he was being deemed an idiot. His head fell back down into his hands, and every muscle in his body twisted up in frustration.

"...Gyl."

Gyldan looked up, watching as Albion got unsteadily to his feet. He wasn't looking at him, but he paced over to Gyldan and crouched down in front of him. He brought Gyldan's hand away from his face, keeping it nestled in a firm grip. Albion watched their interlocked hands as he spoke:

"We can come back to that once you are in a better headspace. Yes, it is a pressing matter, but it isn't nearly as pressing as you being attacked, Gyldan. I can be frustrated at you and still care for you, you know. Disagreeing with you about one thing does not cancel out my feelings for you as a whole. I… I am sorry that I wasn't there for you. I was…" Albion got flustered then, lost for words as he shrugged and gestured vaguely with his other hand upstairs. "Well, I was ill. But I am here for you now. We will figure out what happened, what this creature is, and I will protect you from it. You have my word that no one else will be harmed by this monster under my watch. All right?"

"…Okay," Gyldan mumbled, remaining fascinated by their hands together.

"And once that is all sorted, we'll talk about the cure project. We will discuss whether or not it will make or break us. Agreed?"

"…Okay," Gyldan repeated, flicking his glance up to meet Albion's. It still stung, but part of him was soothed to know the other man would really swallow his ego enough to put him first. Albion was not a man to back down from an argument, and Gyldan supposed he still wasn't. But he was agreeing to postpone it, to act like it hadn't happened yet. To focus on the present threat first.

The best of you, Gyldan thought sadly.

Albion patted his hand on top of Gyldan's, then straightened up with a loud complaint.

"Then we have a plan. You first, us later," he repeated, pressing his hands against his lower back and arching it until it clicked, his face knotted. Then, Albion relaxed, running a hand across his chin again, disgust flashing over his face. "Or, perhaps a shave first… and a shower."

Gyldan allowed himself a small chuckle then, nodding at Albion.

"Yeah, the, er... scruffy-chic look is really hammering home that you're gonna be 40 next year. Is that grey in your beard?" He dared to tease him. Albion scowled down at Gyldan, though the whole expression was declawed by the man's dishevelled state.

"Oh, please—you're hitting the dreaded three-oh this year and let me tell you: it's *all* downhill from there," Albion grumbled, pointing at Gyldan's hair. "*That* is a perfect candidate for the old salt-and-pepper look."

Albion plodded from the room then, heading through the dividing archway between the living room and the hallway and starting his struggle up the stairs. Gyldan's hand made it halfway to his phone in his pocket, intending to message Griffin to ask that he make sure he would be the one to walk him home later. After all, Griff was one of the few people Gyldan didn't have to hide his relationship with Albion from anymore, though he still wasn't quite sure how happy either of them was about that fact. But Gyldan's hand flinched away and his head snapped up in shock as a dull crash punctured by a restrained grunt of pain burst from the hallway.

He darted up from his chair, slipping a little on the polished dark wood flooring in his mad dash to get to the hall. There he found Albion standing precariously on the stairs, one hand grasping the carved black bannister, the other coiled around his torso. He was bent slightly at the hip, shoulders hunched, head hanging limply with his chin resting on his collarbone.

"Al? What's wrong?" Gyldan climbed the stairs to reach the other man, putting a hand across Albion's upper back and trying to coax the limb-locked man to walk down the stairs with him. "Hey, hey... c'mon, let's get you... sitting down..." Gyldan spoke as they slowly moved, guiding Albion back down and sitting him on the lowest step. Albion did as he was instructed without a word of protest. A red flag if there ever was one.

The older man let his hand slip from the bannister as he sat down, wrapping it around his midriff to join the other. His face was screwed up in distress, a film of cold sweat glistening across his paling skin. Gyldan sat down next to him, leaning in and cupping Albion's jaw to make him lift his head up a bit.

"Albion? What's up? Talk to me!" Panic was seeping into Gyldan's voice, betraying how helpless he felt. Albion just pressed his head to the side, burrowing into Gyldan's palm. Then, his whole body convulsed, making the man lurch forward. A painful retch shook through him, both hands shooting up to clamp over his mouth.

Without a word needed, Albion threw himself to his feet and scampered from the hall, crashing through the door of the downstairs bathroom. Gyldan remained where he was for a few minutes, grimacing with empathy as he heard Albion cough and gag. He wasn't sure if he ought to follow him to comfort him, or if the act would grate on Albion's pride and sense of dignity.

After a brief inner tussle with this conundrum, Gyldan's concern eventually won out. He got to his feet, pacing down the hallway to peer into the bathroom.

Albion was sprawled on the floor with as many airs and graces as one could muster when hugging a toilet bowl. Gyldan inched in, stepping with great care around the tangled limbs of the stricken man, and crouched down next to him.

"That help?" he asked with a shy smile. Albion's unfocused stare found him with an echo of irritation pulling at his brow. It gave away after a moment though, and he closed his eyes and half-shrugged.

"Actually, yes..." he admitted, shifting to give Gyldan more room to join him on the cold, tiled floor. "We'll need a new catering staff, though... our current team are getting *fired* tomorrow..."

Gyldan huffed a sympathetic laugh, his smile a little stronger as Albion spoke. Colour was indeed creeping back into the other man's face, his once-clammy skin now broken with sweat as the fever relinquished its grip.

"Hope no one else got sick. They'll think it was company sabotage." Gyldan tried to lighten the mood, taking Albion by the shoulders and sitting him up. Once he was steady and away from the toilet, Gyldan hit the flusher and then brought Albion up to his feet. A tired sigh followed Albion as he stood up, but he already seemed much stronger than before.

"It *was*. The catering sabotaged Caladrius. Look at the state of me," Albion noted despondently, pouting as he caught his reflection in the bathroom mirror. "Urgh... I *must* shower. I can smell myself right now, and I am upset about it."

Albion made his way out of the bathroom, making a much bolder effort of the stairs this time. Gyldan trailed out after him, his mind wandering back to memories of the fundraiser. That had been a few days ago now—what could have been up with the food to make Albion so ill? Plus, Gyldan liked to think he had more than one finger on the pulse at Caladrius, even when he was off himself. He hadn't heard of any mass sick days in the aftermath of the event.

"Woah, hey, that's bad luck!" Albion's voice called, bringing Gyldan out of his thoughts. He looked up, watching as Yanatha crossed her father on the way down the stairs as he was going up. Albion scowled after her but stomped onwards for his much-needed shower.

Yanatha got to the bottom of stairs and pinned Gyldan with a disdainful look. He offered her a limp wave.

"Hi."

Yanatha did not return the greeting. She appeared distracted with her own thoughts, registering Gyldan for a mere second purely to scowl at him. Her long brown hair was all gathered up in a messy bun atop her head, and an old, baggy shirt drowned her. Her jeans were stained, and she was sporting odd socks—the uniform of someone who was working on a project with enough fervour to forgo personal hygiene for a few days.

"Dammit. Was he sick?" She pushed past Gyldan to look into the bathroom, one hand on the frame as she leant in through the doorway.

"Yeah, but he's okay," Gyldan assured her. It was somewhat heart-warming to see the usually cold woman so concerned for her father. "Everyone feels a bit better after a good puke, right?"

Yanatha flashed a look of contempt over her shoulder at him, as though he were being horrifically slow. Gyldan had zero idea what he had missed. In truth, her attitude towards him was starting to fray his nerves. Sure, she knew about his friends, but Yanatha had never really warmed to Gyldan in all his time with Albion. He wouldn't have cared, but the least she could do was return his civility.

He opened his mouth to kick that particular can of worms when Yanatha halted him with a single request:

"Please... tell me if anything else happens to him."

Her words were icy water over his just-sparked irritation, and it was all Gyldan could do to stare at her like an idiot, mouth still agape in preparation to give her a piece of his mind. Yanatha wouldn't meet his gaze, and despite her deadpan utterance, Gyldan could tell she was being sincere. It was rare and fragile, and he refused to be the one to shatter it. Sure, she usually treated him like an unwanted guest in the house, but Gyldan wasn't going to throw this unusual display of vulnerability back in her face.

"Oh... yeah, er... yeah, I mean, of course. He's gonna be okay, you know," he added, a hand reaching up to scratch the back of his head nervously. He wondered if Yanatha's concern was born of some old scars of fear following the loss of her brother. He could relate—after all, Gyldan himself often felt overly nervous for those he cared about, particularly after the loss of his parents and the disappearance of his brother, Sterlyn. This could be a common ground for him and Yanatha to finally bond over, Gyldan realised.

Perhaps his voice betrayed this, as once again, those scornful emerald eyes were upon Gyldan again.

"Good," Yanatha snapped. With that, she breezed past him and up the stairs, returning to her bedroom.

Gyldan blinked.

"...Good talk..." he muttered, letting his hand fall with a clap against his leg.

Chapter 10

After any great disturbance in his life, Gyldan was always keen to return to normality. There was a safety in routine, in averageness, in that state of life that almost risked being boring. The older he got, the more Gyldan treasured that place.

Yet, once that desired routine returned and pushed away the last ripples of whatever unusual event had upturned his life, Gyldan always found there was a strange sense of unrest that followed. An odd feeling that things *should not* simply return to normal.

It was within this peculiar cloud of restlessness that the man now found himself. Sitting in his tiny office, hands hovering over the keyboard of his laptop, the crushing silence only served to fray his nerves further. He eventually accepted that his ability to focus had been left at home that day, and he leant back in his chair with a loud sigh. An idle hand reached up to rest against the side of his torso where only his memory reminded him of the once-aching wound that had been there. Under his shirt, Gyldan knew nothing other than a dark pink patch of fresh scar tissue remained of the cut; an unwanted souvenir of his fateful encounter with the bizarre abomination weeks before.

He had wanted to pursue it further, but Gyldan had left that road for Albion to follow. Gyldan had to stay focused on what he *could* do—he had to remain committed to his friends and his beliefs. He would continue to search for a way to pull the reins of Caladrius away from oppressing non-human beings, to lead the example for others to follow suit. Gyldan was under no illusion that this ambition would be a painfully slow change, one that he might not even see the true end result of in his lifetime. All the more reason for him not to go galivanting off after monsters. Besides, what could he do against a monster? No, he had done all he could on that front, Gyldan told himself. He had told Albion, a man far better placed to track, capture, and prevent this new creature from harming anyone else.

But, if he had done all he could, why was it that he felt so *uneasy?*

Grumbling to himself, Gyldan pushed his wheeled chair away from his desk, reaching backwards in the same motion to grab his coat off the wall behind him. He got to his feet, shrugging the black denim on as he covered the two steps from his desk to the door within the tiny office. Heading out of the cramped room, he turned left, wandering down the too-quiet, too-clean corridors of Caladrius HQ. He paid blithe attention to linear patterns of light the mid-afternoon sun painted on the floor ahead of him as it cut in through the huge glass panels of the building's fanciful walls.

Reaching Albion's office at the end of the corridor, Gyldan paused. Nerves stayed his hand, that same uneasiness that had gripped him every day since their argument surging upwards again. Albion had promised they would return to their disagreement after the issue of his attack had been sorted, and the shadow still hung over them. Every smile needed a little more effort, and every word weighed heavier with the acknowledgement of what they were both ignoring for now.

Steeling himself for the next performance, Gyldan rapped twice on the door then swiped his card, peeking his head around the doorway. Opposite him and across the expansive office, Albion was sitting at the crystalline desk in the middle of the room, hunched over his keyboard. A pair of black-rimmed glasses were perched on his straight nose as he inspected the monitor to the right of him, and every so often, he would glance down to see what he was typing. Gyldan couldn't help but huff a light laugh at the sight—Albion had to be the only person in the entire company that couldn't touch-type.

Opening the door wider, Gyldan slipped into the room. He bent over a little to wave, that he might catch Albion's downward gaze. Two startled emerald eyes flicked up; the man had clearly missed the sound of Gyldan's knocking. The ever-present smirk on Albion's lips drew back into a true smile, and he yanked his glasses off, folding them and slipping them into the front pocket of his deep red shirt.

"Afternoon." Albion greeted him, casting a look to his wristwatch. "Lunch? No—already did that."

"What're you so engrossed in?" Gyldan asked, nodding at the computer as he made his way over to Albion. The older man stretched back, his spine giving an audible *pop!* around the same time as a sigh escaped his lips. He lifted his arms up high over his head for a moment, limbs shivering as he undid the knots in his muscles.

"Your cryptid sighting," Albion teased, relaxing and letting his arms fall. He rested his head back against his seat and glanced up at Gyldan. "It... actually makes sense."

Gyldan blinked, then stepped closer. He put one hand on the back of Albion's chair and craned down to look at the monitor. Albion's screen was a mess of windows, most of which displayed the various Daedalus employee murders of late. On a second monitor to the left, Albion had been typing notes and observations, alongside a document detailing everything Gyldan had observed of the new creature. There was even a crude sketch of the beast scanned into the document, and it wasn't far off what Gyldan had seen.

"It does? 'Cause it didn't *look* like it made a lot of sense," Gyldan said, recalling the nightmarish monster that had tracked him in that dark street. The healed wound in his side pulsed with a phantom ache, his body recalling the memory as sharply as his mind did.

"Not so much the creature itself," Albion admitted, crossing his arms across his chest. "I mean the fact it has appeared at the same time as these killings. Looking over these case files, you would struggle to fit them to one species. Too strong for a human, fangs too thin for a werewolf, claws too big for a vampire." Albion clicked through the windows, affording Gyldan the world's worst slideshow of gory crime scene photos that he really did not want to see. "But this?" He pointed at the sketch. "From what you have described, this would fit."

Gyldan frowned at the screen. Something stopped him from being wholly convinced—after all, the monster that had attacked him did not seem to have the mind enough to make a conscious decision on a target. Or, Gyldan realised, perhaps it was easier to think that it didn't.

Because if it *could* think, why did it pick *him* as a target? Had he simply been mistaken for a Daedalus employee on his way home from a fundraiser held by their competitor?

"Y'know, I came in here to offer a cheeky coffee run," Gyldan said, turning away from the monitor to fix Albion a wry expression. "If I didn't have the brainpower to focus on my actual job, I definitely don't have it for monster-hunting."

Albion's eyebrows slanted upwards, a mock expression of pain softening his seriousness and tugging at his bottom lip.

"And here I thought you were visiting me for me." Albion sighed dramatically. He propped an elbow onto the table, dropping his chin down onto the heel of his palm, and became half-interested in his screen again. In a few clicks, the windows were gone, replaced with a muted livestream of a news channel that the man had left open in the background of his research. Gyldan assumed Albion had been keeping a lookout for any other reports of attacks or murders, but there wasn't much going on in the world—the stream displayed a rather sour-looking news reporter out in the drizzle-speckled streets.

Gyldan straightened up, ignoring the small click his own back made, and patted the back of Albion's chair. He buttoned up his jacket, cursing his luck for missing the sunshine and now being condemned to a drizzly coffee run.

"Latte?"

"Mmm..." Albion replied, still engrossed in his work, fingers curled up against his bottom jaw. "Vanilla, please."

"All right, back in a—" Gyldan's foot shifted, but something on Albion's monitor made him pause. At the same time, Albion lifted his head up from his hand in an alert snap. The news reporter had moved to the side of the screen, allowing Daedalus' headquarters to come into a fuzzy focus through the spitting rain. A banner shot across the bottom overlay, splashing breaking news across the screen: Daedalus was hosting an unexpected live announcement.

"...The hell?" Albion muttered, clicking the unmute button to let them listen in.

"—sources appear to have been right, Chris," said the news reporter. "I'm getting word that Daedalus' CEO himself, Walter Carpenter, is going to be leading this special press conference. Early speculation is that Mr Carpenter intends to reveal a new product that could be the long-awaited competitor to rival company Caladrius' vampire and werewolf safety technology."

Gyldan chanced a look at Albion, half-expecting the man to scoff and ridicule Walter. Instead, the man shifted, resting both elbows on the desk and threading his fingers together. Green eyes pierced, unblinking, from over his steepled fingers, fixated on the screen, silently daring his rival to make a move worthy of his undivided attention.

"Others suggest that Daedalus may finally have made a noteworthy step in its long-promised attempts at a *cure* for the non-human mutations, though that would—oh! Oh, wait, it looks like"—the news reporter turned to look at the building, gracing the camera with a shot of the back of her cropped copper hair—"yes, it appears as though Mr Carpenter has exited the building. Let's tune in to this exciting announcement."

The camera cut to another stationed closer, bringing Walter's pinched face and drizzle-dampened hair to the screen. But that wasn't what made Albion bolt to his feet, hands crashing down onto the glass table, utterly ablaze with insult and betrayal. Standing next to Walter, her face as calm as undisturbed snow, was Yanatha Saint-Richter. Her composure revealed no hint of worry for her father's inevitable reaction, and Gyldan had no doubt as to why she was so relaxed—however Walter had twisted her into this situation, her father would respond twofold.

On the screen, Walter cleared his throat, fixing a non-existent issue with his tie.

"Good afternoon, ladies and gentlemen. Here at Daedalus, we understand that progress requires more than innovation. It requires communication. It requires collaboration. It requires a *united* effort. That's why, in our search for a cure, we have been reaching out to our fellow researchers from across many corporations. We have looked beyond personal profit and glory in order to deliver our society's much-needed next step. And we are proud to say that our call has been answered by one of Caladrius' own—"

"What the *hell* is he doing?" Albion grunted out through teeth clenched so tightly that Gyldan might have heard them squeak. His whole body was trembling with barely contained rage, muscles quaking in his neck and along his tightened jaw. Gyldan stepped back on impulse, for he had never seen the man's stoic composure shatter like this before. True, poaching one of

Caladrius' employees would have been reason enough for Albion to lash out. But Yanatha wasn't even on the payroll. Why Walter had thought to approach her, other than as a means to get back at Albion for rejecting his collaboration proposal, was beyond Gyldan. He hadn't pitched Walter as being petty enough nor stupid enough to poke a lion in the eye out of spite.

Albion's outburst had cut off the end of Walter's speech, and now, Yanatha stepped forward to take his place on the podium. She tucked a few stray strands of hair behind her ear, then let her gaze scan over the small crowd of journalists. Gyldan observed her with keen interest, and he could have sworn a brief ripple of disgust loosened Yanatha's listless expression for a second as she looked out across them all.

"Thank you, Mr Carpenter," Yanatha said. "And thank you for being so kind as to allow me to make the announcement. Ladies and gentlemen. The cure is in hand. And I—" Here, Yanatha's mask slipped just enough to send a message loud and clear to those who knew her. She gave a fearful glance back to Walter for just one moment before the walls came back down over her expression. "—I will be *v-volunteering* myself in the trial and testing stage."

The effect was immediate. The crowd swelled forward, a hundred arms and recording devices thrust out, a flood of questions assaulting Yanatha at all sides. The audio was a mess of noise, but Gyldan could pick out fragments of the hurried questioning:

"Are you admitting you are not *human*, Miss Saint-Richter?"

"Has your father hidden this from the world, Miss?"

"How soon will the cure be ready?"

Yanatha... isn't human? Gyldan's stunned brain caught up with the implication of the woman offering herself as a test subject for the cure. He turned to Albion, intending to press the matter further, to address the hypocrisy and unfairness of her not being subject to an eye-guard or silver collar, but stopped in his tracks.

Albion was coiled, an aura of repressed energy clinging to him, the air thickening with rage like a mantle around his hunched shoulders. His eyes were wide, pinned on the screen, hands pressing down into the desk until the knuckles were white. His lips peeled back into a savage snarl unbecoming of a human, let alone a gentleman of his stature.

Gyldan's heart slammed against his chest, demanding he run, every fibre under his skin picking up the primal warnings of danger that crackled in the air around him. He swallowed, bracing himself.

Albion was pissed, sure. But he would never hurt him.

"A-Al?"

Albion did not seem to hear him. His back arched upward, and a pained grunt snuck out from between his bared teeth as he let his head hang down, chin against his collarbone, finally breaking his furious focus away from the screen. He was still shaking, and now, heavy panting heaved his chest in and out, each breath shivering through ground teeth.

"...The *hell* is he *doing* to my daughter?" Albion's voice was no higher than a whisper, and yet, it was barely his own voice at all. A low growl rumbled through his words like the threat of thunder in the distance. Gyldan's feet dragged him back a step without conscious thought, and he dared not speak as Albion snarled again. "Who does... he think... he *is?*"

The last word punctured the air as a howl, surging from Albion's lungs as the man's spine suddenly snapped inward, his body arching backwards in a violent lurch. His arms folded under him, elbows slamming against the desk as his knees buckled. Gyldan couldn't move, despite every base instinct screaming at him to flee. He wanted to run. He wanted to drop down to Albion's side, to help him, to find out what the hell was happening. He could do neither, his heart choked in fear's squeezing grip.

The tremors reverberating through Albion's body got worse, pulling his limbs from his own control as he spasmed. He dragged himself upright, to at least kneel rather than remain in a crumpled heap on the floor. Grunts of pain and fury pulled from his throat as he shifted his position, shaking arms wrapping around his torso. Albion managed to remain upright for only a moment before he keeled forward with a sharp gasp of agony.

Gyldan tried to speak, but whatever courage he had was deftly robbed from his throat as he watched Albion cough and splutter, blood and teeth splattering onto the glacial-white carpet in front of his kneeling form.

What... the hell? Gyldan's dumbstruck mind managed to ask, his dizzy focus flitting from Albion to the crimson and ivory mess he had just spat out.

Run. Get away, his body demanded, his legs aching from the tension of his coiled muscles, ready to burst into a sprint in the opposite direction. *Run.*

A gargled inhale sounded from Albion, one arm unwrapping from his body to slam into the floor to try to steady himself. His nailbeds were bruised deep purple and maroon as the nails themselves began to lift and peel away, something thick and dark pushing up from the flesh to replace them.

Gyldan's skin flushed cold, his senses growing muddy, vision wavering, sound pinpointing to nothing but Albion's pained breathing.

YOU WILL DIE. RUN, his mind wailed at him, the silent sound shattering the shackles of disbelief that had rooted Gyldan to the spot. His whole body burst into action, freed from fear and thrown straight into panic. He turned, bolting from the room in an inelegant flailing of limbs. He tore the door open, slamming it behind him, breaths audible and ragged as he fumbled with his key-card to lock it.

Somewhere behind the now-locked door, an inhuman scream of anguish and anger shook the walls of the building. Gyldan backed away from the door, unable to avoid the sounds of bones snapping, flesh tearing, and Albion's voice turning from a stream of whimpering to a guttural growl.

"Oh my God... oh my God..." Gyldan's lips fluttered into a mantra, stammering with each shaking exhale, trying to calm himself. What did he do? What could he do? What... had just happened?

His first thought was that Albion was a werewolf. If he had believed this for even a moment, it might have served to settle Gyldan a bit—after all, he had seen Seraph change into her controlled form outside of a full moon a hundred times. And yet, not once had it been as brutal as what he had just witnessed. Her body simply *shifted*, muscles growing, skin stretching, teeth sharpening, fur growing. Her whole body seemed to *know* where it needed to be. She had never mentioned that shifting to a wolf hurt, save for full-moon transformations, which she had once described as being "too quick, too strong, and too hungry".

His second thought was that Albion couldn't be a vampire. Vampires didn't transform as far from a human appearance as werewolves did, and the wings they could grow and shed on command did not appear to cause them any discomfort. Plus, Gyldan had been to enough dinners with Albion to know that he could eat.

His third thought was the grey-skinned beast that had lumbered from the shadows that night, ebony claws catching the flesh of Gyldan's side, eyes an emerald starburst upon a crimson field, a crown of twisted bones erupting from its brow...

Gyldan could not stop staring at the office door, the room behind it unsettlingly quiet. The door stared back at him, squaring off with the petrified human, assuring him nothing would change if he didn't open this door and check.

Tentatively, the man stepped forward, a hand outstretched enough to press the tips of his fingers to the door handle, easing his shaking somewhat.

He couldn't leave him in there. Whatever he was now. He had to know. He had to know, and he had to tell someone. He had to know. Someone... had to know what to do...

He dragged his key-card centimetre by centimetre through the reader, praying against logic that the slower movement would make the door unlock any quieter. Then, Gyldan softly turned the door handle, letting the door open just enough for him to peer through.

Through the vertical sliver he had afforded himself, Gyldan could make out the corner of Albion's desk. He shuffled to the left, changing his view—and immediately yearned for his ignorance of seconds ago.

A grey-skinned hand was on the desk, and black claws screeched and cracked across the glass surface. The creature pressed its weight down, pulling itself up to its full, staggering height. A dark matt of hair scrambled past its shoulders, getting lost among the torn and tattered wings that hung limp down its back and out of sight behind the desk. The creature had not noticed Gyldan at the door, and in profile, the crown of bones upon its brow was all the more regal and terrible to behold. Some of the horns glistened with blood from their painful emergence from under Albion's skin, catching the light like war-gilded blades.

A lipless mouth full of fangs parted just enough to allow its rumbling growl to crackle louder, and it turned to look down at the desk and monitors. Gyldan immediately threw himself to the side, praying he was out of sight even if the monster looked at the parted door. He clapped a hand over his mouth, silencing his panting panic.

Albion... Albion was...? Gyldan's mind stumbled through the truth, flashes of memories from the creature's previous attack assaulting him, demanding to be acknowledged. *It was... no... no, it couldn't be... why would... he...?*

Footsteps sounded, though even as Gyldan screwed his eyes shut against the fear of the beast coming towards him, the sound grew weaker. A hinge creaked, and wind soared through the room and whistled through the slightly opened door at Gyldan's side, rushing by his arm and ruffling his coat.

Then... silence.

Gyldan tried to stand firm, telling himself he had three more seconds of cowering before he would *turn* and *look* through the door again.

Three... two... one...

He counted himself down, then he twisted against every rational thought of survival in his head to look through the door again.

The monster was gone, which, to Gyldan's surprise, actually made him feel worse than when it was there. Knowing the object of his nightmares was *somewhere* turned out to be infinitely more stomach-curdling than knowing it was *there*.

At least then, he had known which direction to run in.

Gyldan pulled the door open an inch further, checking as much of the room as he could. He opened it a little more, and a little more, until he spotted it—a window open behind Albion's desk. A horrible design, the huge panels opened like small doors, and Albion had often joked that they were big enough to open out for "those days when painting the concrete seems more appealing than a board meeting".

Gyldan walked towards it, a numb sense of entrancement pressing down on his whole body. The truth was standing in front of him, and while Gyldan could hear it, he could not accept it. He could not accept that the beast that had attacked him that night had been someone he cared for, let alone... someone he loved.

Gyldan paused and checked over his shoulder at the last thing he had spotted the monster—spotted *Albion*—looking at. Anything to distract himself.

The news continued to stream, the Daedalus press conference coming to an end with Walter's grinning, self-satisfied face plastered on the screen, fielding questions from the crowd as Yanatha stood behind him. She was studying the crowd again, only now, her eyes darted this way and that, as though she was searching for something in particular.

Gyldan turned around fully, spotting something that chilled him to his core. He paced towards the desk, a hand finding its smooth surface to prop his numb body up with. He tried to ignore the rough, splintered cracks in the glass under his hand, reminding him of the brutish creature that had been standing there just moments before.

Gyldan leant closer to the screen, brow furrowing.

Yanatha was *smiling*.

Chapter 11

Just when he thought there was no more room in his head for another tornado of problems, life proved Gyldan wrong.

The stiff heels of his dress shoes clattered across the smooth flooring of Caladrius headquarters' corridors, threatening to send him skidding across to the elevators at the end of the hall. When he got there, Gyldan began slamming his hand against the button, his other hand ferreting in his pocket for his phone.

Who could help him? Who could know? Which lie had he put where? The sound of plates shattering filled Gyldan's mind as his barely balanced triple life began to bleed and meld together. Caladrius employee. Non-human ally. Albion's lover.

Yet the fear of those delicately spinning dishes crashing to the ground, undoing years of careful work and calculated moves, sounded like an orchestra compared to the howl of the monster Albion had transformed into.

The doors to the lift opened and Gyldan bolted inside, slapping the ground floor button with one hand and calling Seraph with the other.

Hiding his relationship was the last of his worries right now.

"Yo, you want a bodyguard?" Seraph's voice greeted him, punctuated by crunching sounds. "Lemme finish this and I'll ride over to pick you up."

"Seraph, I need you to come get me," Gyldan blurted out, watching the floor counter tick down above the lift doors. "The- the creature. I know where h—where it is. We gotta go stop it before it hurts someone."

A rustling sound was followed by Seraph's suddenly serious voice.

"Front doors. I'll bring the bike."

Gyldan pocketed the phone, lunging out of the lift doors the moment they began to crack open. He burst out of the front gates of Caladrius headquarters, bouncing up onto the balls of his feet impatiently as he waited for Seraph to arrive.

"C'mon, c'mon..." he hissed under his breath, scanning out across the road to try and spot the woman.

After a few minutes, Gyldan caught sight of her. The werewolf pulled to a screeching halt at the front of the office on an old Suzuki SV650 motorbike, a particularly fond birthday present from Gyldan years ago. No doubt she had accrued a few speeding tickets in order to get to him so quickly.

She chucked a helmet at him as he hurried over, leathers creaking, and he flailed about to catch it before it hit the ground.

"Shana and Griff are flyin'," Seraph said as Gyldan struggled his way onto the back of the bike, looping his arms tightly around her waist. "Where is this bad boy?"

"Daedalus headquarters, it's on Curlshank Road. Drive towards the Blue Rocket arcade, I'll direct you," Gyldan spluttered. "Shit, it's probably already there..."

The werewolf looked over her shoulder.

"Can you get me outta a couple more speeding tickets?" she asked, flashing a sharp-toothed grin.

"I might know a guy who can pay them off for you?"

"Sick."

Seraph's wrist twisted, and the engine roared to life between them. With a screeching of tires and a few startled looks from passers-by, the pair hurtled down the road.

* * *

He hadn't needed to direct Seraphina after all. The screams cut through Gyldan's ears as they drew closer to the competitor's base of operations, so he could only imagine that Seraph's heightened senses had picked up the blood-chilling sounds long ago.

Gyldan leapt off the bike before the werewolf hit the brakes properly, fumbling under his chin to ditch the helmet and running into the screaming wave of people heading the opposite direction.

A flurry of suits and panicked faces beat against Gyldan like a storm, yet he kept pressing forward, arching his head up towards the imposing tower of Daedalus headquarters, trying to catch a glimpse of Albion.

Bodies shoved against him, knocking him back, almost toppling him—somewhere behind him, Seraph called out, struggling against the fleeing crowd too.

The sea of people finally thinned enough for Gyldan to find Albion. When he did, Gyldan couldn't stop himself—strength and energy bled from every limb. His knees quaked then gave way, and Gyldan collapsed to the ground in horror. He could not escape from the nightmarish scene painted before him.

The grey-skinned abomination stood atop the conference platform, a crowd of carnage and blood gathered around it like faithful servants beholding a momentous day. Four ruby-and-emerald eyes glowered down in triumph over the suited, headless body of Walter Carpenter, who was lying upon a bed of crimson silk stretching slowly out across the concrete.

In its twisted hand, the beast's claws gripped the man's relinquished head.

Albion... you can't have, Gyldan pleaded in the shellshocked silence of his mind. *You wouldn't...*

He didn't notice himself being hauled to his feet, and only realised he had been when Griffin's stubbled face blocked out his view of the chaos in front of him, eyes wrapped in violet silk once more.

"You can't be here. Seraph, get him home," Griff grunted, nodding over Gyldan's shoulder to the werewolf.

Gyldan heard himself slur out a protest:

"...Nnnno ...no, I gotta... Yanatha. Where's Yanatha?"

He shoved at Griffin, though he didn't knock the vampire away so much as he forced himself to stagger out to the side of the older man. Gyldan started forward, making a fretful check for the beast as though knowing where it was would diminish his fear of it.

He wouldn't... not her... not Yanatha... oh god, Al, please tell me you didn't...

Then, he caught sight of her. Relentlessly calm and unwavering, the young woman was standing behind the creature her father had become, looking no more surprised at Albion's appearance than she did at Gyldan's arrival. She noticed Gyldan's approach, and once more, she offered that same, hollow smile upon her otherwise blank expression.

It stopped Gyldan in his tracks, and his limbs began to quiver. The same impossible thought struck through his whirling mind as it had the moment he had noticed her smile on the monitor.

She knows, his numb inner voice observed. *She knows that's Albion.*

Then, the creature stirred. It dropped Walter's head like a played-out toy, a quiet grumble rumbling from its chest. The head thumped into the ground, rolling along until its own lifeless body became a barrier to stop its journey.

Gyldan wanted to call out, as if some power in Albion's name would bring him to his senses. But somewhere along the line, Gyldan had picked up that particular plate and set it spinning once more—he couldn't. If Seraph and Rukshana heard...

Albion lumbered around, turning his wing-draped back to Gyldan, the tattered skin of the limp limbs scraping the floor behind him.

"No..." Gyldan stumbled forward again, watching as the monster raised claw-bladed hands towards its daughter. "Al, *don't!*"

His yell was enough to bring the beast to pause. Its ragged head whipped around, fixing Gyldan with blazing eyes, expression coiled tight in unbridled rage.

It leered back then let loose a deafening wail, every layer of sound grating against Gyldan's ears as the air itself resisted the creature's unnatural cry.

Daedalus. Walter. Me. He's killing whatever makes him angry, Gyldan's fear-addled brain managed to deduce.

He couldn't let Albion's feelings of betrayal see Yanatha torn to bloody pieces. He couldn't watch an innocent woman be killed.

He had to help.

Whatever the cost.

Albion began to turn his hulking form away again, forcing a desperate and thoughtless cry of dread from Gyldan. The panicked energy that had been building in his legs was finally put to use, but not to carry him away from the threat. Gyldan ran towards Albion to a chorus of shouts from Seraph, Griff, and Rukshana.

Once again, the beast moved its attention to Gyldan. Gyldan's throat constricted, his entire body fighting against the stupidity of what he was about to do, every survival instinct scrambling to shut him down.

He tried to look past Albion's warped gaze by fixing his attention on Yanatha, and he made a beeline for her. Gyldan did his best to look angered even as terror strangled his movements, to give every sense that he was charging at Albion's daughter with the intent to harm her. He allowed himself only a brief, flicked glance to the monster, half-praying it wouldn't take the bait. For a moment, Gyldan wondered if the creature even cared, or if it was merely curious at this squeaking, noisy human darting up to it.

Then, sheer wrath erupted across Albion's form. Fury rippled through his towering body, razor teeth parting to unleash a bone-rattling roar, wings lifting and arching out in a shivering display of ebony. Muscles surged in his arms and legs as he prepared to strike at this new perceived competitor to his prey.

Gyldan barely registered Albion crashing forward, smashing the podium out of the way to make a beeline for his new target.

His bravery spent, Gyldan did not even spare a moment to call to his friends for help. He skidded on the spot in his desperation to turn and flee, hands hitting the ground to try and propel himself up into a sprint. He bolted as fast as he could, uncaring of the direction other than to lead the monster away from Yanatha, to stop Albion's heart from breaking should he harm her.

The cacophony of sounds behind him served only to keep Gyldan running, ignoring the rising burning in his chest with each shortening breath he hauled in. Feet pounded concrete, talons scraped stone, sirens shrieked, and the shouts of strangers and yells of his friends swirled around him. Wingbeats sounded above him, and a golden-white blur streaked by his side—Seraph was shifting into her wolf form, overtaking Gyldan with ease. As she ran, her body grew longer and broader. Her limbs strengthened, the hair on the back of her head growing into silver-gold fur, and Gyldan heard Rukshana's voice above him yelling out for Seraphina to stop.

By the time Gyldan caught up to Seraph, her transformation was complete. She was standing on all fours, her blue eyes piercing from a lupine face, calm without the moon's light to stir them to bloodlust. She stepped forward, claws scraping concrete, ready to strike as she snarled at the monster chasing Gyldan.

Gyldan slowed only as he passed the wolf, turning to look over his shoulder in time to see Albion slam into Seraph full-force.

"*Seraph!* Get it away from here!" Griffin's voice called out from somewhere above Gyldan. The vampire dropped down in front of him soon after, blocking his view of the monster and the wolf locked in battle. "We need to go. *Now*."

"But—" Gyldan began to protest, trying to move past Griffin towards Seraph, not that he had any idea what he could do to help. Still, he did not feel comfortable at all with leaving the woman to deal with his mess, especially when it meant Seraph was putting herself in danger. Though most people had run screaming, plenty remained crowded in the street to watch this strange battle unfold, and more worryingly, police officers were swarming nervously around them. Any one of them could have an activator, and one fearful trigger finger, one unchallenged prejudice, and Seraph's collar would deliver a fatal brand of silver to her throat.

Griffin's chestnut wing shot out to shield him from getting past. He grabbed Gyldan by the upper arm, yanking him away and fixing him with a stern expression, the silk around his eyes creasing as his brow furrowed.

"Seraph can run a helluva lot faster than me, and a damn sight faster than you," the vampire said, starting to drag him away. He looked up then, calling out above: "Rukshana! We gotta go!"

"I'm not leaving her behind!" Rukshana's voice replied, drawing a grunt of frustration from Griffin.

"For Christ's sake, do you both think I'm gonna leave her behind? Get moving!" Griffin retorted, looking over his shoulder at the entangled beasts—Albion was tearing chunks of silvery-gold fur from Seraph's legs, and the wolf's jaws were clamped around the abomination's shoulder. It scarcely phased the monster, and Gyldan's heart dropped as he watched the battle rapidly tilt in Albion's favour. "She'll be right behind us. *Seraph! Drunk tank! Go!*"

Gyldan and Seraph found each other for a single, shining moment, and he could have sworn her lip curled up in a smirk around a mouthful of Albion's shoulder. Then, she leapt away from the monster, delivering a slashing parting shot across his face. The beast howled, staggering back and then rounding its full attention on Seraph. The wolf turned tail, hunching down and bolting down the street. The creature, all but ignoring Gyldan as a target for now, tore after her.

Gyldan watched in horror, realising Griffin's plan. The *drunk tank* was what they called their garden shed. Reinforced with shackles, steel lining, and a number of Caladrius-borrowed goods, it was where Rukshana would bundle Seraph off to on the rare instance she was caught out under a full moon. The idea that it could hold a moon-crazed werewolf staggered Gyldan, and the idea it would hold whatever creature Albion had turned into seemed ludicrous.

"Griff—" Gyldan started but was forcefully hurried to a side street, away from the crowds and officials.

"*Move*," the vampire snapped, the last of his patience evidently long since spent. Gyldan could only do as he was told, praying to any power listening that Seraph was faster than Albion too as Griffin bundled him away.

Heading home seemed utterly ridiculous to Gyldan. Had the world not just swayed underfoot, knocking everything they thought they knew off-balance? Had every false hierarchy humans cherished not been blown to smithereens in a public display of violence and fear?

If Seraph hadn't staggered out from the side gate leading to the back garden of their home as they arrived, Gyldan might have snapped and demanded Griffin explain what his plan was.

"Seraph! Holy shit, sit down." Gyldan put a hand out on instinct. In truth, he had no idea what to do. His hand hovered over her arm, torn and bloodied as it was, unsure of how to help. The werewolf managed a tired but thankful smile for him.

"Coulda been worse. Luckily for me, dude wore himself out when we got to the garden and collapsed... Rukshana's locking him in the drunk tank now," Seraph said, shuffling by him and wincing. "*Ow*."

"You shouldn't have tried to fight that thing, Seraphina," Griffin added, though his features couldn't hold much of the annoyance from his tone, softened as they were by concern. "I told you to run once you got its attention."

The woman limped to the front step of their house, closing her eyes against the older man's blunt logic. Her cheeks puffed out as she exhaled a shaking breath, her wounded body slowly lowering until she was seated. Then, Seraph opened one eye, leaning to the side towards Gyldan with a small smile.

"Ya welcome, nerd," she said and gave him a nod. "Saved your life. Hold the applause."

This was all she could manage, however, before a grimace of pain pulled her back in on herself. Gyldan made to move, pulling his keys from his back pocket and tossing them to a startled Griffin.

"Get her inside. Call a doctor—I'll cover the charge."

He could already see the protest forming on Griffin's tongue as the vampire's head cocked to the side.

"You're not paying our guest a visit, Gyl," Griffin said. "I'm banking on it calming down. It's attacked *you* twice already. If it fires up again and the tank doesn't hold, we're screwed. I already tried thralling that thing once before—it was like trying to wrangle several werewolves, I can't do it!"

Another voice, as even-keeled as a frozen lake, cut above their squabbling.

"You don't have to worry."

Rukshana appeared from the around the side gate too, though she was looking back over her shoulder, no doubt at the outbuilding the beast had been left in. She turned to the trio at the front of the house, face a touch paler than usual.

Shit, Gyldan realised.

"Our friend has worn himself out. He's returned to his usual state," the vampire reported, regarding them each in turn. Her look lingered longer on her girlfriend, worry dancing over her sharp features. "I... I think you may wish to see this."

"W-wait!" Gyldan stammered, stepping forward. "I-it came from Caladrius, right? I saw it leave the building, so I guess he's one of ours. Maybe I should...?"

He levelled the desperate plea at Griffin, hoping he understood. From the momentary shock that shattered his calm aura, Gyldan knew he did. The older vampire cleared his throat, jangling Gyldan's keys and reaching over Seraph to unlock the front door behind her.

"Gyl's right. If this guy's from Caladrius, he'll freak out if he wakes up to a werewolf and a coupla vampires looming over him. Might set him off again. Let's get Seraph seen to while the guy's sleeping it off. Gyl, go get your *colleague* some clothes."

"But Griffin, it's—" Rukshana started to say, but the older vampire cut her off.

"It can wait. Seraphina can't. Those wounds need looking at."

Mouthing a silent word of thanks he realised Griffin wouldn't be able to see, Gyldan moved to help Rukshana lift Seraph gingerly to her feet and walk her inside. Once the werewolf was settled comfortably on the sofa and had threatened to bite him if he kept fussing her, Gyldan dashed up the stairs two at a time to his room, leaving Rukshana behind to bandage Seraph's injuries.

"Okay, *okay, okay, okay*, clothes, er…" Gyldan muttered to himself, falling on a cupboard door and throwing it open. He pulled at the clothes hanging in there, trying to find something that would fit the taller man. "Er… right…"

The man continued to mumble to himself, yanking a shirt out here, a pair of trousers there, discarding any unsuitable items behind him onto the navy bedsheets or the mottled wood floor. Eventually, Gyldan settled on a pair of wash-loosened joggers and a blue hoodie that he had 'borrowed' off Albion anyway, so at least one of the garments would fit him properly.

Scooping them over one arm, Gyldan ran from the room, crashing down the stairs with all the elegance of a child on Christmas morning, and burst out through the front door into the cold night air again. He darted around the corner of the house, knocked the side gate open with his shoulder, and walked through into the small garden.

Gyldan almost yelled out in frustration when he saw the door to the shed was ajar—sure, Albion was shackled in there, but leaving the door open set off all of Gyldan's nerves, as though it would provide any sort of extra shielding to the fearsome creature if it awoke again. Then, catching sight of a figure in the evening gloom standing in the doorframe, Gyldan realised why.

"Oh no… no, no, no…" he stammered to himself, jogging across the garden to reach the door. He pulled it back, revealing a haggard-looking, half-bandaged Seraphina, an irritated-looking Rukshana, and a brow-beaten Griffin. Not one of them looked at him—everyone was watching the bruised and unconscious man lying on the small floor-space of the now-cramped shed.

"Will you sit still for me to bandage you now, Seraph?" Rukshana asked, "He isn't going anywhere."

"Dude…" Seraph said, inspecting the fallen man. "That's… that's Albion Saint-Richter? *The* Albion Saint-Richter? Same dude we broke into the—"

Griffin's hand darted out to cover Seraph's mouth, his other hand laying a single finger over his own lips.

Meanwhile, Rukshana's nose wrinkled up and she turned away from the man. She jerked her head from Gyldan to Albion, stepping aside to let him past with the bundle of clothing.

"I thought I'd stopped believing in karma," she commented as Gyldan squeezed by them, crouching down in front of Albion and dropping the bundle of clothes on the floor. "But perhaps she does have a sense of humour after all."

Dressing Albion was an awkward and cumbersome affair. Taking a small key from Griffin, Gyldan unfastened the shackle on Albion's left ankle and pulled the trouser leg up over it. He then re-secured the restraint, ignoring the pain in his chest that twinged as he did so. He did the same on the other leg, then repeated the one-at-a-time process on the cuffs on his boyfriend's wrists as he wrangled the limp man into the hoodie, holding Albion's feverish form in a clumsy cradle. It fit him better than the joggers did, which stopped far too high above the ankles, but it was better than nothing. At least he wouldn't freeze to death.

Gyldan zipped up the hoodie, being careful not to brush too much against Albion's bruised and battered skin. The man looked disastrous and not only for having gone a round with a werewolf—deep indigo stains under his eyes marred against too-pale skin, and once again, the skin on his forehead burnt raw and red.

Before Gyldan could set the man back down, Albion stirred and moaned. Gyldan froze, watching in horror as Albion awoke, sluggish and unfocused. Green eyes sparkled with fever, rolling in his skull in search of something to focus on for a second before landing on Gyldan.

Oh, thank god... Gyldan allowed himself to relax a little, glad that the man had not spotted the band of non-humans behind him. That was not a conversation he was ready to wriggle his way out of yet.

A sloppy smile drew across Albion's pale and tired face, a slow blink doing nothing to clear away the disorientation etched all over him.

"Hello, tiger..." Albion slurred out, shifting to sit up straighter.

Gyldan's whole body froze at the pet-name, several prayers stampeding through his head that the three people behind him might've missed that remark despite their heightened senses.

"...The *fuck* did he just call you?" Seraph demanded, shattering all of Gyldan's hopes.

"He, er... he calls everyone that?" Gyldan offered lamely, turning his head to the side but finding himself unable to face anyone. Then, a hand snaked up against his jawline, turning his face back to Albion. The man was shaking his head, a rolling, bumbling action absent of any of the CEO's usual grace and poise.

"No, I *don't*..." He chuckled. Then, a light frown creased his brow, a tiny flicker of focus breaking through the fading mist of confusion. "Wait... who're y'talking... to?"

Albion shifted again, pushing away from him while Gyldan tried to keep him cradled close and shield his view of Seraph, Griffin, and Rukshana.

"No, no, wait, Al! You're not—!"

It was too late. Albion shoved away from Gyldan with a pained grunt, palms slamming onto the hard ground to his right. Albion staggered to his feet, unbalanced, and he fell against the wall for support. Leaning heavily on it, head bowed, Albion took a few deep breaths. He then lifted his gaze to look out from under his brow at Seraph, Griffin, and Rukshana.

Emerald eyes darted between the three of them, settling on Griffin, recognition strengthening his glower.

"*You...?*" Albion half-snarled and half-questioned in a single word, the whites of his eyes beginning to stain crimson.

Perhaps Albion would have had more to say to his old office intruder had a violent tremble not seized his body.

Chapter 12

Such a small motion, and yet, the effect was astounding. Seraphina shoved in front of Rukshana, her entire body taut with protective fury and her lips peeling back to reveal a warning of canines towards Albion; Griffin sidestepped in front of the werewolf, squaring off against the CEO. Gyldan lunged to his feet, grabbing Albion by the shoulders and forcing himself into his line of sight, blocking Albion's dark glower from reaching Griffin. Albion's shoulders not only quaked under Gyldan's palms but began to swell, muscles pushing against the material of his hoodie.

"Al. Listen to me," Gyldan begged. "I know you're pissed, but—"

"*Pissed?*" Albion cut him off with a growl-laced shout, a sharp twitch of the head bringing his undivided attention to Gyldan. "That *vampire* broke into my office and you—you're... you—!"

Words fell beyond Albion's reach as his rising anger bested what small fragment of composure he had left. He gave a sharp inhalation, back hunching up, spine pressing against the tightening hoodie.

Gyldan wanted to step back. He wanted to run away. He couldn't face this monster again and live; surely his luck must have run out by now. Behind him, Griffin's voice served a grave warning:

"Gyl, you gotta calm him down, or—"

"Y-yeah, on it, I don't wanna die either!" Gyldan snapped back, turning his head a little over his shoulder but keeping Albion in his sight. No doubt Griff could probably thrall Albion in this state, but adding that fuel to the man's fury would just defer the current problem until later—he would snap out of the thrall twice as furious as before.

"No," Griffin interjected. "Not you. *Him*. Whatever's happening... it's not natural. His body isn't built for it. Look at the state of him, Gyl. He can't go through it again so soon. You gotta calm him down."

"Nah, let him." Seraph's voice joined the fray, filled with venom and unrestrained disgust. "Let him tear himself apart, the prejudiced *asshole!*"

A bubbling rumble rose from Albion's chest at that, though it was clear that Griffin was right. Blood seeped over the older man's lips, framing his bared teeth, yet none of them had been replaced by the rows of dreadful fangs the monster sported. The whites of his eyes were dotted with bursts of crimson, but nothing close to the abyssal look of the beast that had chased them from Daedalus' headquarters. The man's struggle with this rage-induced transformation was apparent, his exhausted and battered body unwilling, or indeed, unable, to find the energy to complete the violent change.

Desperation fuelling him, Gyldan grabbed Albion's head and forced him to look up at him, his hands cupping either side of his face.

"Albion. Please... if you don't calm down, I... I don't think you can come back from this." Gyldan's voice became strained by tears threatening to fall. Albion fixed him with such a look of pain, such a look of heartbreak that it was all Gyldan could do to not look away.

"You... *you're* the... traitor..." Albion mewled, the tiny sound almost lost beneath the rumbling growls of his throat. "*You're* the traitor... Caelan was..."

"He was right. Yeah. He was trying to tell you about... about *me*," Gyldan confessed, the words burning up his gullet and embittering his tongue. The weight of his secret clawed down from his shoulders to his chest. "Caelan was... a friend of mine. These guys are my friends, Albion. But that doesn't mean I don't wanna help you. It wasn't... it wasn't meant to happen like this—"

Albion doubled over then, a rasp of pain bringing him to his knees. Gyldan followed suit, crouching down in front of the ailing man.

"You... know what they did." Albion's shaking words struck Gyldan like an accusation. He lifted his head, eyes flashing under a lowered brow, and repeated: "You *know* what they did. What *their kind* did to my son..."

"Yeah. Yeah I do," Gyldan admitted. Yet a long-buried frustration began to unfurl within him, harshening the edges of his words. "And I'm sorry about it, Albion. But you can't blame an entire species for it. These guys didn't kill your son. The werewolves and vampires out on the streets, just trying to survive, they didn't kill your son—"

"*Blame?* What I am doing is an act of *forgiveness!* You... you don't understand it at all!"

"Don't I?" Gyldan finally snapped, the pressure of everything in this tiny room finally breaking through the chains around his own, stifled pain. "Why'd you think I joined Caladrius in the first place, Al? My parents were *killed* by a werewolf. Yeah! And I'm still friends with a werewolf, because I get that she doesn't carry the weight of every crime her kind commits! God,

Albion, how many humans have *other humans* killed, what, do we have to be responsible for that? How many humans have killed werewolves and vampires? Me and you, are we guilty of something just because a human did it? That's ridiculous and *you know it!*"

His outburst flooded the room, rinsing away the tension for one, blissful moment. Then, all too soon, it was over, leaving Gyldan to sit with his emotional skin torn clean off in front of everyone he had betrayed in some way or another.

Albion was staring up at him, conflict stirring over his face, sclera slowly clearing of those crimson blooms. He no longer looked angry, but he hardly looked sympathetic towards Gyldan either. If anything, Albion just looked shocked for the other man's sudden explosion.

"I... you never... told me..." came his meek response, seemingly stunned to some form of calm by the other man's outburst.

Before Gyldan could reply, someone stormed out behind him, the door of the shed bouncing against the walls as it was slammed open.

"*Seraph!* Wait!" Rukshana's voice sounded, and Gyldan turned in time to see the vampire leaving the tank too. Griffin didn't go after them. His face was unreadable, a thousand emotions flickering across his face too quickly for Gyldan to read.

"...Outside if ya need me," the older vampire gruffed, turning and heading out himself to leave Gyldan and a shellshocked Albion in the cramped room.

Calling the other man calm might have been a stretch, but Gyldan noted that Albion had stopped trembling. He was far more alert now and anger didn't radiate off him so much as exhaustion.

"So... what occurred between us." Albion lifted a hand and waggled a finger between Gyldan and himself. "This was... a means to an end, I assume?"

His tone was bitter, and the threat of anger hummed beneath his words.

"No," Gyldan admitted, shifting to sit down on the floor properly. He crossed his legs, holding his ankles and letting his shoulders slump. Suddenly, the idea of Albion transforming and ripping him apart did not seem so bad anymore. It couldn't be worse than sitting in his own emotional word vomit in front of everyone. "No, that part was... *real*. They, er... they didn't know. Guess they kinda do now... squabbling like an old married couple and all..."

"Real enough that you would help a vampire get into my office to try and murder me?"

Albion's fingers brushed across the floor, curling up into a fist that he pressed into the ground. Gyldan found it easier to watch that hand, lightly shaking though it was, than to confront Albion face-to-face. His heart still felt numb to fear, a strange and blissful state he was not quite ready to let go of.

"We weren't trying to kill you, Albion," Gyldan explained, listening to his own voice become worn-down and deadpan. "We were trying to get the release codes. For the collars and eye-guards. We wanted to send 'em out so everyone could take them off without triggering the removal sensors."

"Oh, marvellous. So, you were just undermining my entire life's work instead of killing me. How romantic of you."

"Al, for the love of God..."

Gyldan knew exactly how this would all look in Albion's mind. As much as he tried to look past it, it was undeniable—Albion did not view vampires and werewolves as anything close to equals. The idea of trusting them not to kill people out of the goodness of their hearts was ludicrous to him, even though he trusted every person he passed on the street to do just that.

It was not an argument Gyldan could get into right now though, not when Albion could end the debate by quite literally chewing his head off.

"No, you don't get to act like the victim here, Gyl!" Albion retorted, irritation seeping back into his words. "You're not the one who has been accosted and abducted by monsters here!"

"I—"

Gyldan's brain shut down. His numbness clicked to alertness in a single heartbeat, followed by a swift punch of confusion.

What...?

He blinked, frowned, and looked at Albion incredulously.

"What did you say?"

Albion flopped back, sitting down on the floor and dragging his legs into a curl. He winced and pulled at the collar of his hoodie, inspecting the bruises on his skin.

"I heard your *unkempt* friend threatening me. That I *could not go through it again?* I shouldn't be surprised at such arrogance after an unfair fight," Albion barked, sending a glare cross to the door and raising his voice to Griffin. "I'm not giving them anything, Gyl, and when the authorities find me, I'm not defending you from this either."

"You—wait, you think this is... no, no, this isn't—we're not *abducting* you, Albion!" Gyldan stammered, his brain catching up with what the man was saying. "No, we didn't... we didn't knock you out, Al, that was—" Gyldan hesitated. Though he suspected Albion would lock up on him, he asked: "You don't remember any of it? Daedalus headquarters, none of that?"

Albion's own narrowed look met Gyldan's, suspicion swimming in his emerald eyes. "What are you talking about?"

"Th-the whole thing! Outside Daedalus! You—" Gyldan stopped, his stomach roiling sick with the realisation. He couldn't tell Albion what he had done to Walter. Not right now. Instead, he opted for a different tactic: "Al, what is the last thing you remember?"

"Go to hell, Gyl, I'm not playing your game."

"Albion, *please!* This is really important! You think we beat the crap out of you and abducted you, but what do you actually remember?"

Albion's face screwed up, though he only resisted for a second before his memories forced him to speak.

"I... was in my office," he said, expression clouding as he moved away from the present and focused on his thoughts. "We were watching Walter on the news... then I felt sick. Most likely down to your little friends hitting me in the back of the head and dragging me here."

"No, I... I didn't. I can tell you what happened—I swear, Al, we didn't hurt you. You have to believe me."

Albion's focus returned with whip-like ferocity, hitting Gyldan with such an expression of disbelief that it stung.

"Believe you?" Albion scoffed, a bitter sadness tempering his words. "That's the last thing I have to do anymore."

***

A short while later, a defeated Gyldan trudged back to the house. He had not only failed to convince Albion that he had not been abducted in some covert non-human attack on Caladrius, but he had failed to find it in him to tell Albion the whole truth. The phrase would have been simple enough to say.

You're the monster you've been hunting, Albion.

But everything that came after it—the blood on his hands, the clear blanks in his memory, his self-appointed identity as protector of the human species—that was too much for Gyldan to throw on Albion in good conscience. Not right now. Not when the man seemed so fragile and vulnerable. Albion had passed out from exhaustion during their talk, his pride making his lips form soundless words even as his eyelids fluttered closed.

Tomorrow, Gyldan thought to himself, heading into the house and attempting to ignore the sickening feeling brewing in his stomach. *I'll tell him tomorrow when he's had time to rest.*

It was a small deflection of responsibility, but Gyldan felt he had earned it. After all, he was well aware that he was walking away from one argument and straight into another.

As if on cue, the loud hum of a raised voice muffled through floors and walls greeted Gyldan upon entering the house. He paused, looking up and ever-so-slowly closing the door behind him, hoping to keep the noise down.

He crept through the house, crossing through to the hall and starting to tip-toe up the stairs. With each step, the voices grew clearer: Rukshana and Seraphina were arguing. Gyldan knew the sound ought to make him feel guilty, but in truth, guilt never quite left his chest enough these days to really return at times like these. It had taken up as permanent a residence there as his heart, pulsing away alongside it with a shared sense of duty.

"We're not *leaving*. Look at you! You need to rest."

"I'm *fine*. We're *going*."

"Seraph, stop this—"

"Why aren't you *mad* about this?"

"I *am!* But being angry doesn't mean abandoning all *reason!* We cannot simply gallivant off into the night. Where would we go, hmm? You're wounded."

"And we might be bloody worse if we don't go. First Caelan, now Gyl... *God*, seriously, *Gyl?* I can't—I don't..."

Seraphina's voice tapered away, followed by a squeak of bedsprings. Gyldan froze on the stairs, one foot hovering awkwardly over the next step. Being counted alongside Caelan did not hurt so much as it solidified the truth that had dragged behind Gyldan all this time: that he had betrayed his friends. It did not matter to what end, or whether or not he had still fought for their cause. At the end of the day, Gyldan loved a man who would see them subdued.

"Listen to me. And listen to me without interrupting. You are angry, you are tired, and you are hurt. Any one of these things would mean you aren't thinking straight. Now... I want you to hear what I am about to say," Rukshana's voice drew low, a calming wave across the fractured rocks of Seraph's outburst. "Gyldan's actions have hurt me too. But... I do not doubt him."

"*What?* But you of all pe—"

"*Seraphina.*"

"...Sorry..."

Gyldan could picture the stern look on Rukshana's face, and her declaration of trust gave him the strength to creep up another few steps, the conversation rolling down around him.

"It hurts to think he could love a man who has caused us such pain. But it hurts because we *know* Gyldan is not a bad person. It hurts because we *know* he still supports our cause. It hurts to think he could love the man who created this world because we know he would give anything to undo it."

"...Would he?"

Gyldan reached the top of the stairs and padded to Seraph's room. He held a hand out, wondering if he ought to go in. He supposed they both knew he was there, one way or another.

When he pushed the door ajar, he wasn't surprised to find Rukshana and Seraph already facing him. The women were both sitting on the edge of Seraph's unmade bed, a tangle of white bedsheets bunched up behind them. The werewolf was hunched over, her arms resting on her thighs.

"...Yeah," Gyldan answered the lingering question, his feet finding the threadbare brown carpet as he summoned the courage to enter Seraph's bedroom. "I-I would."

Seraph gave him a long, inscrutable stare, then huffed and turned away. Rukshana, however, beckoned him in with one curling finger, gesturing to the wooden desk-chair near the door, tucked under a tiny plastic table strewn with books, magazines, plates, and empty cups. He did as he was wordlessly told. The vampire let out a soft sigh, eyes trailing up and down Gyldan once over.

"Am I wrong to still trust you, Gyldan?" she asked, her tone frank, as though they were discussing a business deal. "You were presumably this close with Albion when we broke into his office. That says to me that you would not choose him over our goals, despite your clear feelings for him. But perhaps I am simply scared of what will happen if I can't trust you. It has taken me a long time to relearn the skill, you know."

"I know..." Gyldan mumbled, becoming fixated on his own hands. "And... I don't know what I can do or say to prove it: I want you guys to be free. I really do. I swear, everything I'm doing is with that in mind. I... I really didn't mean to get *that* close to Albion. But when it happened, I-I figured... if I backed away then I'd be picking my own comfort over yours. I'd be stopping myself from falling in love with the guy who's... well, *wrecked* your lives... but at the cost of our best chance to change that. But then, if I stayed... I'd fall deeper in love and... I guess I thought he might, too. And that he might love me enough to try and change. I wanted to tell you. I'm sorry."

Even as he spoke, Gyldan's shoulders curled further, shielding his face away from his friends.

"So... is he? Changing his mind, that is," Seraph asked, voice guarded and clipped, an olive branch stripped of leaves. Gyldan wouldn't cast it away though. He looked up, but Seraph didn't acknowledge the movement.

"...No," Gyldan admitted. "The night I got attacked by the monster—well, by *him*, I guess—we... we had an argument. I pressed him about that *cure* idea I'd heard about. And he admitted it was true. He admitted Caladrius was working on a way to change werewolves and vampires into humans. Said it would be a choice but... that anyone who chose not to take it would be arrested. I tried to make him see sense, to see that you guys aren't something to be *cured*, that you're your own species and he just... he wouldn't see it that way. I... stormed off and..."

Gyldan waved out to the side with an open palm, then let his arm drop back down in defeat. "Yeah. I realised I couldn't change his mind. I might see the best of him but... then there's this one awful thing he won't change. Not even for me. I thought he might come around to my side of things if he loved me back, open himself up to a new way of thinking, realise his old mindset was wrong. I realised that night that I couldn't sway him, so... it basically ended."

Gyldan's chest pulsed with a dull chill at admitting that out loud. Despite their awkward pantomime born of a mutual agreement to ignore their argument until the beast was dealt with, somewhere deep down, Gyldan knew it was over. How could it not be? He had tried everything to prise out the best of Albion, to hope that it would override the bad and make him become the better man Gyldan thought he saw. But the stubborn man refused to let go of his grief, refused to see the truth of his actions: that he was making two whole species stand trial and take unjust responsibility for the actions of a few criminals among them.

"What does 'basically ended' mean?" Seraph pressed him further, arching an eyebrow at him and finally turning to meet his gaze.

"We've been working together to try and track down the monster that attacked me," Gyldan explained and was relieved when a tiny nod of understanding twitched Seraph's head. "We agreed to put aside our argument until that was done. I needed his help, and he needed to know what I saw that night. If we didn't work together, more people might've..."

"Yeah okay," Seraph grumbled, waving a hand at Gyldan. "Logical. Very grown-up of you both."

What was left unspoken still managed to linger in Gyldan's ears: his apology had been heard, but not yet received. It hung in the air between them, ignored and yet wholly unavoidable. Before long, its presence became too much for Gyldan to bear.

Without a word, he rose from his seat and left the room. What more could he say? A few weeks ago, Gyldan would have fought with a passion to defend the belief that Albion was a good man, a good man who could be made to see the error of his ways. But the feeling had disintegrated within Gyldan's heart the night Albion had admitted his plans for the so-called cure. It was difficult to fight Albion's corner when Gyldan no longer felt that he could be dragged away from his hatred.

He was halfway down the stairs when footsteps behind him brought him to pause. Sullenly, Gyldan glanced back— Rukshana was behind him, padding her way down the first few steps, fingers trailing the bannister on her left.

"I'm sorry..." Gyldan muttered. He wasn't surprised by Seraph's reaction, nor was Gyldan upset because of that. He agreed with her anger, and that made it all the more difficult to process. Still, he had to admit, Rukshana's calm response to it all had shocked him. It had only been a few months since Caelan's betrayal had almost reignited the vampire's difficulty in trusting others. Seraph had made little effort to hide her concern that the event would act as confirmation to Rukshana that she was wrong to start trusting again. This worry had been one of the many factors that had kept Gyldan from telling them just how close he'd gotten to Albion. And yet, now that the secret had spilt, it was Rukshana who was surprisingly accepting of it.

"I know," she replied, shifting her weight and leaning against the bannister, an elegant arm draped on the side. She regarded him with a flicker of sympathy from behind the ruby lens covering her face, but he dared not ask why she had chosen sympathy instead of rage. "I am not thrilled at the idea, and much less that you kept it from us. But... I must confess to feeling slightly responsible. Getting you close to Albion to make getting the codes easier was my suggestion. We only ever see the face he presents to the world. I suppose it never occurred to me that he has a more appealing face for people he cares about."

Gyldan's heart trembled as Rukshana's words hit home too precisely, too painfully.

"He... does. *Did*. I'm not sure anymore," he confessed, letting his head dip away from looking Rukshana in the eye. "I thought there was something there. I thought I could—"

A hand dropped down on his shoulder, the lightest of touches offering the grandest of reassurances.

"Seraph is resting, and Griffin will be standing guard over Albion," Rukshana said. "Why don't you and I go and get a drink somewhere? I believe you may have needed one several days ago, and we need to discuss how we will move on from here. As a family."

Chapter 13

The Star and Hammer was not Gyldan's first choice of watering hole. It wasn't his second or third choice either. However, the run-down establishment did have a few perks. One, the bartender was a terrifying, stern-faced old vampire who somehow managed to glare daggers at everyone despite having had her eyes removed long ago. This meant it was one of the few bars in the city that allowed both human and non-humans drinkers in while also having an unusually low number of fights break out.

Two, the bartender was a terrifying, stern-faced old vampire who somehow managed to glare daggers at everyone despite having had her eyes removed long ago by *Caladrius*. This meant Caladrius employees did not drink there, so Gyldan and Rukshana would not be overheard.

Still, rules were rules. Gyldan waited at the door of the bar, having been waved through by the broad-shouldered bouncer that blocked the way. Said bouncer resumed her position as Rukshana approached, pulling out a handheld device from the pocket of her quilted jacket. The bouncer was not the bar's employee, of course, and the freedom of *The Star and Hammer* was a double-edged sword—allowing everyone in made for the perfect trap to catch unregistered non-humans.

With a swift, jerking nod upwards, the bouncer indicated to Rukshana's eye-guard. Rukshana stepped forward, closing her eyes as the handheld's red laser traced over her eye-guard. A shrill blip and a small screen lit up to confirm whether or not she was a registered vampire.

The bouncer's lips pursed, examining the tiny screen on the gadget for a second. Gyldan's jaw tensed as he prepared to step forward if need be—it wasn't unheard of for guards to turn non-humans away from places they were allowed into simply because of a bad day or a sudden power trip. But after a beat, the bouncer stepped aside and waved Rukshana through.

"Sorry. Forgot me glasses and these screens are flippin' tiny…" the bouncer noted gruffly, shaking the device in her hand. "Have a good one."

The pair headed inside, and in place of a warm welcome, they were greeted by a waft of smoke and the sharp scent of spilt beer mixed with sweating patrons who had been there all day and night. Dark grey stone walls bent from the grime-crusted floor to the low ceiling, and with a good clean, the place might have looked chic and rustic. Alas, the stones had not seen soap and water for some time, and the thick shielding of smoke and dirt robbed the place of any charm it had once had. The only aspect of the pub that might have been noted as endearing by a lenient reviewer was the bar itself. It rose up from the centre of the room as an island oasis for the lost and drifting souls of the city, the mahogany top and polished taps the only parts of the alehouse that were spotless. Behind the curved bar was a grand pillar of stone that supported the roof and embraced numerous bottles of spirits, wines, and aged blood.

The place wasn't exactly huge, and while Gyldan appreciated the bartender being so open about letting everyone in, he did wish she wasn't quite so blasé about people smoking in the building. That said, the bartender struck him as the type who might not have left the building herself in decades. There was a very real chance she didn't know smoking indoors had been banned long ago.

"What are you drinking?" Gyldan asked Rukshana, heading to the bar and squeezing in between two hunched-over werewolves. Rukshana bristled with nerves at the people either side of Gyldan with more than a flicker of worry tightening her face. But it passed quickly, and she found her voice for Gyldan.

"Swan," she replied, glancing at the row of taps. One eyebrow arched. "If they have it. If not, any bird source will suffice."

"Cool, er... grab a table and I'll find you." Gyldan smiled, impressing himself with the scraped-up energy he had found to do so. Rukshana glided away to another corner of the room as he turned around to face the bar properly. It wasn't long before the long, wizened face of the bartender cut into view. Her face was pinched at every angle, skin stippled with a mix of wrinkles and scars over the upper part of her face. White hair threaded with strands of black was tied up in a bundle atop her head, and she was drowning in once-bright shawls of faux-silk.

Her nostrils quivered once, her lips upturning as she sniffed.

"Human here," she said, rapping her knuckles on the bar in front of Gyldan. "Whatcha drinking?"

"Oh, erm... one Jack and coke please, and one swan blood."

"Double on the Jack?"

Gyldan's mouth moved before his brain did.

"Yes, please."

The bartender nodded, a flicker of a smile soothing her face.

"Aye, you smell like a bad day," she said, pulling two glasses out from under the bar. Gyldan grimaced and turned his head down to sniff at his armpits. He was developing something of a conscience about being sniffed out like this.

"I do? What does a bad day smell like?" he wondered aloud.

"Like salty tears and taut muscles, boy," the bartender answered him sagely. "Who caused it? Human? Vampire? Werewolf?"

She slid his first drink across to him, dropping a straw into the mild fizz. Gyldan closed his hand around the chilled glass, but he didn't take a sip yet.

"...Does that matter?" he asked, a mixture of exhaustion and irritation bringing him to the end of his nerves on that matter. He knew he shouldn't have, but it still felt as though the skin was torn from his body, all filters and masks removed, leaving Gyldan with a strange courage at his disposal. A reckless courage forged from defeat; he was braver now that he was stripped of his shield.

His words brought the bartender to pause. The two werewolves either side of him stirred, but Gyldan didn't look up. He continued: "Does it?"

"...No. No, it does not." The bartender smirked, and Gyldan found himself lifting his head and thinking what a terrible tragedy it was that the sparkle in her words would never dance in her eyes. He was sure it would look like mischief and wisdom all at once. "Doesn't matter one bit if the person who caused ya bad day is a wolf, bat, or bloke. They're an asshole all the same."

Gyldan snorted a hollow laugh, taking the second glass of deep crimson from the woman.

"Thanks."

He went to find his companion then, watching the drinks in his hands as he concentrated on not spilling them. Gyldan didn't mind too much if a dribble of cola stickied his hand up, but he didn't much care for spilling blood down the back of his hand as he wobbled a drink over to the table. Sure, he was accustomed to seeing Rukshana and Griffin drink the stuff, but Gyldan would never be okay with cleaning the glasses afterwards.

Setting the drinks down, Gyldan eased his tired body into the booth to sit next to the vampire. Now that he had stopped, every limb throbbed to remind him how overtired he was, and what an excruciating day he had endured.

But, through it all, one feeling blistered through the aches and pains. A feeling of unrepentant gratitude towards Rukshana, his unpredicted saviour and supporter through his one, grand mistake.

He turned his head to look at her, resting it against the back of the booth.

"I really thought you'd be the first person to kick off about me and him," Gyldan said.

"I might have been." Rukshana's reply was frank, and she laced her fingers around her drink, nails clicking against the glass. "Had I not felt so responsible. I don't think I can be angry at you for falling in love. People can't help their hearts—we love the most confusing people."

"Did you think that about you and Seraph?"

Gyldan's boldness clearly alarmed Rukshana, as she looked at him with unveiled surprise.

"Y-yes. I suppose. No... I *know*. I hated werewolves when I first met Seraphina. I was quite miffed when I realised I was falling in love with her." The vampire took a slow sip of her drink. She set the glass back down, arching an eyebrow at Gyldan. "But no matter how angry I was, I couldn't stop it. My heart wanted her, even though my soul loathed her kind. Love seldom makes sense, and it makes even less sense to the person falling. But... I don't think you ever hated Albion."

"Hate's... a strong word," Gyldan countered. "I didn't really have reason to hate him. I didn't *like* him, that's for sure. He was the figurehead causing you guys so much grief. I was pretty shocked when my smiles stopped being faked. It was infuriating. Why can't he be that nice to everyone? Seriously, he's... he's smart, he's kind, he's a good person when he wants to be. Just this one *massive* topic I can't change his mind on. If he'd just step back and *look* at everything properly instead of fixating on this, I don't know, revenge? I guess?"

Gyldan took a long gulp of his drink, hoping the burning liquid would steel his nerves. "I just... I'm not ignoring what he's done, Rukshana. I'm really not. It's all I bloody think about. It's all I bloody argue with him about. How easy would this have been if I could convince him to change his mind about your kind? Everyone freed, eye-guards and collars gone, and a multi-billionaire supporting humans and non-humans. Albion has that desire to protect people, Rukshana. I just needed to get him to want to protect *everyone*. I can see the good in him, and... I hoped I could save him."

The more he spoke about it, the more real it all seemed—that it was over, the rift between him and Albion having grown too great, too insurmountable. So, when Rukshana spoke, words that might have once burnt Gyldan's heart only seemed painfully obvious now:

"It's difficult to save a man who doesn't realise he's drowning," the vampire mused, drawing one long finger around the rim of her glass as she thought. "People like him think revenge keeps them warm in a cold world—they don't see that the warmth is coming from people burning around them."

Gyldan let his eyes close, blocking out the world for a blissful moment. For so long, he had worked himself to bones and dust in his endeavour to prove to everyone around him that he was good enough. To fight against that voice in his head that told him he was far from good enough for Albion. How strange that now he should question if he had it all upside down. Maybe he was good enough all along. Maybe it was Albion who wasn't good enough for him. Albion knew that his stubbornness was a mountain Gyldan sought to conquer for his sake. Yet Albion had chosen to keep climbing higher and higher instead of meeting Gyldan halfway down.

For the first time in his life, a crystal-clear thought cut through the swirl of confusion and pain in Gyldan's head.

I deserve more than that.

True, he still loved the man. That feeling would not be so easily removed. But Gyldan was no longer helpless to that fact. If Albion wanted to be better, then Gyldan would support him. But he was done being the only one trying to save him from those dark waters when Albion seemed quite content to keep diving beneath the surface to seek his misguided vengeance.

"Did you want revenge?" Gyldan asked, opening his eyes and considering Rukshana. "On werewolves...'cause of what a few assholes among them did?"

Rukshana sat up straighter, the grip on her glass tightening as it hovered before her parted lips. She stayed frozen, captured in her discomfort like an elegant painting, then slowly lowered her hand to put the glass back down without drinking from it. Fixated on the sanguine liquid, she shrugged.

"I suppose I did, for a while. I suppose... I was a little like Albion in that regard." The vampire's nose wrinkled in disgust. "I hated them. The whole species. A handful of their kind killed my family, and I wanted justice. I felt as though every werewolf was responsible—I wanted them to do something to make it right, to take responsibility for the actions of those evil people. But what could they do? Deep down, I knew it was not their burden to bear. It was not their crime to pay for. Quietly, I was questioning if what I called justice was not just rage. After all, there are evil humans and evil vampires too—we do not expect to take the blame for their actions either. But... I couldn't help it. It's still... *difficult.* When I close my eyes, it is wolves' teeth rending flesh from bone that I see. Wolves' claws ripping my loved ones apart. I know it is irrational to place the blame on all werewolves. I always knew it. But it's hard to make the heart listen to the head.

My dreams are plagued by the sight of those wolves tearing my life asunder."

Rukshana drew in a deep breath, the exhalation unwinding her body into a small slump as she folded her hands on the table. "I suppose this is why I can sympathise with your questionable choices. After all, Seraph saved me. Changed my view. Made me see that those flames of hatred weren't keeping me warm but consuming me. She made that inner question ring louder. But—that's where the similarities end, Gyldan."

She turned to face Gyldan then, her expression steady. "I'm not convinced Albion has ever questioned himself. I do not think he has ever doubted whether his path is right or not. To him, *these*"—she tapped a nail against her eye-guard—"are to protect mankind. He can't even see that he's still looking for revenge for the work of a few bad vampires and werewolves who have long since paid for their crimes. He's never questioned his hatred."

Questioning hatred... Gyldan mused to himself. The idea didn't bring Albion to mind. Despite everything, a person quite unconnected to Gyldan's current plight sprang forward from his memories yet again: his lost brother, Sterlyn.

A strange common ground sprawled out before Gyldan, connecting him, Albion, and Rukshana with the hazy memory of Gyldan's older sibling at its centre. How long had Gyldan spent idolising Sterlyn? For so long, Gyldan had wished he were as strong as his brother, as fast, as cool. That his older brother had been born a werewolf seemed painfully unfair to a young Gyldan.

Of course, that all changed when their parents died. It had to, Gyldan supposed, given Sterlyn had been the one to kill them.

Joining Caladrius to work towards protecting everyone had been the next logical move for Gyldan, but it had never occurred to him until now that his actions may have been fuelled by the same sort of hatred and desire for *someone* to pay for his tragedy as Albion and Rukshana. That he was seeking retribution as a salve for his wounds.

Just as Rukshana had met Seraph, Gyldan had met Griffin. Before he knew it, he had ended up friends with the older vampire and his rag-tag family. Gyldan had embraced that, knowing deep down that what his brother had done did not put blood on the hands of his whole species. Gyldan hadn't noticed it at the time, but it was clear to him now: they had saved him. They had made that silent doubt in his own hatred grow louder. They had shone a spotlight on the real injustice at work: Caladrius.

Is that it? Albion... can't be saved? Tears of insult started to well up. Gyldan sniffed sharply, sitting up and shaking his head to rid himself of those tears before they could fall.

"Do you think Seraph will forgive me?" he asked.

"Forgive *you?*" Rukshana cocked her head to the side. "Gyldan... Seraph is angry at you, yes, but she is also your friend. In fact, from what she said to me, I daresay she's more upset at herself."

Gyldan frowned, reaching for his drink.

"What? Why?"

"Because she feels ashamed." Rukshana's voice wavered with sorrow, and Gyldan was certain he saw tears glittering behind the red lens. "After she stormed out, she was shouting about how it seemed like werewolves really were the awful ones. Caelan betrayed us, werewolves killed my family, and then you saying a werewolf killed your parents. Seraph feels everyone must hate her or think she would do something awful."

"What, no!" Gyldan yelped with half a mind to get to his feet and dash back home to set the record straight. "What, no, no, no, that's not—does she really think that? Jesus, it's just... coincidence. I know plenty of people who have had loved ones hurt by vampires. And I know more people who have had loved ones hurt by humans! I know you guys for a start! God, when did we start keeping a tally of whose species has the most criminals in it?"

Rukshana let out a hollow laugh, an empty sound save for a hint of bitterness.

"Calm down," she warned, flicking a look over Gyldan's shoulder. "I'm not sure who will be more annoyed at you, but I'm quite certain some elitist will be wanting words with you if you speak like that too loudly. Even in here."

"*Urgh...*" Gyldan complained. He grabbed his drink and threw his head back, downing the rest of it in three large gulps. "I can't... *ahh...*" He cleared his throat of the burn before continuing: "Listen... I'm... I gotta go clear my head. Gonna take a walk now I'm sure I'm not gonna get jumped by the beast that turned out to be my *boyfriend*. Thank you for, er... well, for everything. For understanding. For... I dunno, did-did you forgive me?"

Rukshana gave a wry smile, bringing her drink to her lips and shooting him a sideward glance.

"I suppose. But your taste in men is truly unforgivable, Gyldan. You ought to have said, I know a lovely vampire bachelor or three who could have helped your heart."

"...I'll keep that in mind," Gyldan said, getting to his feet. "You okay getting home?"

"Are you?" Rukshana scrutinised his glass, sniffing once. "A double is bold for you."

"Shut up..."

Shaking his head and trying to hide the relief on his face that Rukshana had forgiven him, Gyldan left the bar slightly lighter in the head and the heart.

Everything still seemed like a colossal mess, but somehow, it did not look like an impossible mess anymore. Not if he still had one friend at his side. Two, he thought to himself as he walked down the darkened street towards the foot of the hill that led to their house. Griffin already knew about Albion weeks ago.

Gyldan crossed the road, and instead of walking up the hill, he headed over to the other side and towards the small chapel and graveyard that lay at its foot. It had been far too long since he had visited, so it was with some relief that the man opened the small iron gate to let himself in, feeling as though he was finally doing something both productive and good.

He made his way through the dotted gravestones, winding the path to his parents' plots. The route was as familiar to him as walking home. The action was so automatic, so ingrained in Gyldan's being, that he could name each person who rested beneath the earth as he walked by without looking at the headstones. After all, they were the old family friends that kept his parents company.

Indeed, Gyldan knew the graveyard like the back of his hand, which was why whenever anything unusual happened, it stood out starkly.

So it was that a certain blond-haired vampire standing a few rows away from Gyldan caught his attention as he arrived in front of his parents' graves. Gyldan peered through the gloom, recognising the man as the one he had bumped into back at the fundraiser. *Luca*, Gyldan recalled the man's name.

Luca was not dressed quite as flamboyantly as the charity night, but his attire could not be called subtle. A black leather jacket decorated in steel studs over his shoulders all but smothered the bright yellow shirt the man wore beneath. From one ear lobe, a delicate fluff of a feather hung on a chain, and even in the dark of the night, gemstones glimmered across Luca's fingers. The vampire was talking to someone, though Gyldan could not make out who, blocked as they were from his view by the vampire.

They had not spotted Gyldan. His gut churned with discomfort, telling him to keep it that way. It was clear these two were not in the graveyard to pay their respects. So, Gyldan did not pause at his parents' gravestones. Instead, he continued walking until a larger tomb built for a figurehead of the city shielded him from the duo, as though he were simply visiting a grave further along. There, Gyldan stopped, leaning against the grey stone wall and peering out. From this angle, he could make out Luca's face and the back of his companion. Gyldan didn't recognise the other person, though even with the dark of night hampering his vision, he could make out Caladrius' company colours on the person's jacket. They were handing over a silver briefcase to Luca.

Hands like skittering pale spiders reached out to take the offered briefcase from the other, and Luca's scarred, thin face split into a wide Cheshire cat grin.

"You said *you* made it?" The companion sounded distrusting, head tilting at Luca. "No one at Caladrius is gonna miss it?"

"Oh yes, this is *my* handiwork, dear heart," Luca assured the other, clicking opening the locks of the briefcase and lifting the lid. His nostrils flared, and he sniffed the box. Apparently satisfied, the vampire snapped the box shut, leaving Gyldan to a fretful check whether or not he was downwind from Luca's sharp nose. "For my little sister, no less!"

Luca let the briefcase swing down in one hand to his side, gesturing to his right with his other hand at a grave decorated with freshly placed white lilies. This made his friend uncomfortable, shifting from one foot to the other as they asked:

"Oh, sorry... were you, er... close?"

"Good heavens, no," Luca replied, one barely visible eyebrow arching beneath the thick knot of scars that covered his upper face. "Couldn't *stand* the woman."

"But you wanted a memento?"

"The mask is the only good thing to come from her sorry existence," Luca explained, swinging his left hand to and fro, the weight of the briefcase carrying it higher with each swing. "Can't *believe* I went into the wrong lab at my only opportunity... you lot ought to do more than one fundraiser a year, you know, give a scallywag a sporting chance!"

A chill coiled around Gyldan with a sickly, thick grip—that night at the fundraiser, *he* had found Luca in the lab. The vampire had claimed to have been drawn there by the smell of *death*. Why he would concoct such an awful story to cover looking for a mere mask was beyond Gyldan.

"It wasn't easy to find," the other person said, folding their arms. "I expect compensation."

Luca's lips twitched, fracturing his smirk long enough to show a hint of disgust boiling beneath his cheerful demeanour. It was enough to make Gyldan's breath catch, and he wondered why the other person didn't bolt on the spot.

"And I am a vampire of my word! You will be compensated, dear *heart*." The last consonant of his utterance clicked harshly behind Luca's sharp teeth. "The mask of mirrors ought not sit gathering dust as a mere relic of Caladrius' legacy. Rest assured your *heroism* in rescuing it for me will be rewarded in due course."

A mask of mirrors? Gyldan thought, scouring his recollection for any time in his career at Caladrius when such an item was mentioned.

"Did it... y'know, *would* it have worked?" Luca's companion pried, nodding down at the briefcase.

Luca shrugged.

"In theory. I shan't bore you with the science and... *not-science* involved in its creation, but in layman's terms, the mask was designed to cage a particularly powerful vampire. It reflects emotional energy back upon the wearer. I'm rather proud of that little eureka moment of mine working out! In theory, it would work for a werewolf too," Luca explained, giving a small nod to the side as though the thought had just struck him. "Outdid myself, frankly. I suppose that's why Albion agreed to work with me in the first place. Well, that and my fortune and family name. Just like why *you* took an interest in me!"

The Caladrius employee looked down at the grass at their feet, as though the answers to the new questions lay there. It was as if his unknown co-worker were reading Gyldan's mind, as the other ventured further with a renewed curiosity of the item they had stolen for Luca:

"If Caladrius had such a device... why make the eye-guards and trap-collars? This mask sounds—"

Barbaric, Gyldan's inner voice interjected, but at the same time, he thought of Albion's anger shuddering through his body, teetering on the edge of transforming into a monster. He couldn't help but wonder if the answer to that problem had landed in his lap here in the strangest of ways.

"Well, because it wasn't very practical, for one," Luca cut the other off. "Could you imagine? Every non-human wandering around with a mirror covering their faces. It would be dreadful in summer, your lot would all go *blind*. I don't know how you'd cope with that appalling sense of smell you have."

The vampire moved then, pushing his free hand into his pocket and ruffling up his coat as he did so. He produced nothing more sinister than a mobile phone. Tapping on the screen a few times, he turned the device to his companion.

"Enough?"

"...Enough," the other confirmed, reaching out and tapping the screen too. The other looked to leave, but their feet faltered, head turning back to the briefcase. "What... what are you gonna do with it?"

Luca pocketed his phone again, flashing pearly white fangs at the other. "Don't you trust me?"

At this, the Caladrius employee walked away with a shake of their head and a dismissive wave over the shoulder.

"Of course not, vampire. Your money's just good enough."

Gyldan stayed put, keeping watch as the Caladrius employee left the graveyard. Once they were far enough away, Gyldan looked back at Luca. The vampire lifted the briefcase up to his chest, cradling it against him. In a flurry of white and black feathers, his wings unfurled from his back, a proud display befitting their magpie-like appearance. With that, Luca took off into the night sky.

Gyldan hesitated before slowly creeping out from behind the tomb.

A mask of mirrors... Some kind of prototype? Why would he want old tech? Gyldan wondered, not noticing his feet had brought him to the gravestone Luca had gestured to instead of going to his parents' resting place.

Gyldan refocused, coming out of his thoughts and looking down at the lily-strewn stone. He read the engraving to himself with a muttered whisper.

"*Penelope de Varis.* What's your brother up to, huh?"

Chapter 14

A stalemate festered between everyone in the house for the next few days. Gyldan had managed to talk his housemates into letting Albion stay indoors as opposed to the shed, though it had been a battle hard fought. Not that Albion acted very grateful either—with the doors locked and two hyper-attentive vampires watching him, the most affluent man in the world, who was used to doing what he wanted when he wanted, was indignantly placed under house arrest.

He hardly touched the food Gyldan brought up to his room, choosing instead to sulk like a scorned child.

Gyldan sat down on the office chair in his room, readying himself to ask for the umpteenth time:

"When were you going to tell me that you aren't human?"

Albion was standing by the window, hands clasped behind his back. Gyldan wouldn't have been surprised if he were debating climbing out and escaping, prevented only by his pride. A soft cluck of irritation prefaced a stiff reply:

"I *am* human."

"Okay well... what about the whole..." Gyldan gestured around his own head, mimicking horns with his fingers. "Transforming thing?"

Albion shot him a sour sideward glower.

"...So you keep telling me. I don't know anything about it."

Once more, the stalemate yawned between them. Gyldan might have been more annoyed if he didn't partly think Albion might be telling the truth. After all, the spate of murders through the city had only begun this year. If Albion had been born as a new species of non-human, unregistered and with unseen abilities, the problem of the goliath creature would have raised its head long before now.

Gyldan looked over his shoulder at the closed door behind him. Rukshana and Seraph were working in their room, studying what little they had gathered of Albion's violent alter-ego. Every so often, the sound of their door opening and footsteps shuffling over the carpeted stairs told Gyldan they were moving something down into the living, though he wasn't sure what.

He returned his focus to Albion. This line of questioning was getting Gyldan nowhere, and in truth, Albion's icy demeanour was starting to gnaw at the edges of his feelings for the man.

Gyldan leant back and laced his hands behind his head.

"All right, let's talk about something else then. What's the mask of mirrors?" he asked suddenly, taking some satisfaction at the visible jolt of shock that Albion couldn't catch before it cracked his stoic stance.

"Nothing." The word snapped out of Albion's mouth too fast, a knee-jerk reaction without thought. He turned away from the window and relented with a scowl. "God, how do you get into everything so easily?"

Gyldan looked up at the ceiling, feigning nonchalance.

"Just overheard. Was curious."

Albion's jaw shivered, muscles tightening. Gyldan expected he wouldn't answer. But the man rolled his eyes, something of a smirk tugging on his lips, as though he was quietly proud of the other man.

"It's a prototype. An old vampire family had a problem. A genetic variation that made some of them more powerful than usual. The government continued using the eye surgery method for this particular family as a safety measure, even after the practice was abolished—their variations were just too unpredictable. One of them in particular was a living nightmare," Albion explained, looking wistfully out of the window again.

Penelope de Varis, Gyldan inwardly gave the nightmare its name.

"They couldn't have removed her eyes if they tried," Albion continued. "Couldn't let her loose on the world either, so the girl was kept locked up in her room. Hardly ideal, so the family contacted me in the days before Caladrius. They asked me to work alongside one of their sons to create a device that would let Penelope out safely into the world. We worked together to design the mask, but it ran into problems. The girl died later that year anyway." Albion shrugged. "But, it gave me the basis for the eye-guards and silver collars. Within a few years, I brought an end to fourteen years of living in fear and solved the age-old question of how to make the wolves safe enough to come live among us instead of on the outskirts. It was a *good* thing."

Albion spat the word venomously at Gyldan's feet, the insult to his ego still worn on his tired face like scars. Gyldan didn't rise to it.

"Why didn't it work out?"

Albion's jaw tightened, and he rounded on Gyldan.

"Because, contrary to what you and your little friends think, I am not the villain here," the man growled, pointing an accusing finger at Gyldan. "The mask was a failure. So, I called the project off; I took the mask with me when I started Caladrius to try and make the technology useable *and* ethical. The mask turned its subjects into emotionless dolls. They could not use their powers, but they couldn't do much else either. I wouldn't wish that on my worst enemy, so I didn't *do* it to my worst enemy."

There it was again—a glimmer of good immediately snuffed out by the suffocating hatred Albion wouldn't let go of.

Gyldan resisted the urge to let that disappointment show too much.

"Your worst enemies are sitting in a jail cell somewhere, Albion. Not living out here," Gyldan said, even as Albion screwed his face up and turned his back to continue to brood.

"Oh, don't start that again! You think I'd be a better man to leave everyone else unprotected? If I can do something to protect them? Use your head, Gyl. You remember life after the Eye Surgery Act was abolished, before Caladrius shielded us. You know what happens."

Gyldan was about to retort when a knock at the door cut him off. Both men turned as Griffin's shaggy head poked in through the tiny amount he had opened the door. He was wearing his purple silk blindfold again, even though his eyes were no longer a secret to anyone in the house.

"Hey! House meeting, son. Rukshana's got news," Griffin said, tilting his blindfolded face and a fanged grin to Albion. "You, er... you wanna join in, dickhead?"

Albion's face flushed red, and Gyldan worried the man might explode into a ball of fangs and fury. But he took a deep breath in, exhaling and letting his whole frame shudder, then turned his head up and away from Griffin.

Gyldan got to his feet, heading over to Griffin and opening the door wider. He turned back to Albion for a moment, feeling like he ought to say something. Yet, for the first time, Gyldan found he didn't *want* to say anything.

He left the room, letting the door close behind him with a sharp click.

"He's not warming up t'me, is he?" Griffin said, a playful smirk dancing on his lips.

"I wouldn't take it personally," Gyldan replied as they headed downstairs toward the living room. "Griffin, can I ask you something?"

The old vampire paused midway down the stairs, turning and leaning his upper back on the wall.

"Course. What's up?"

"I was wondering... does the name *Penelope de Varis* mean anything to you? Saw the name in the graveyard when I visited my parents the other day, and I swear I've heard it somewhere before. It's boiling my brain trying to remember!" Gyldan partly lied.

Griffin lost his carefree aura, settling instead into a harder, sterner countenance.

"Of all the—Christ, yeah, of course I do. Every vampire knows the De Varises," the man said with all the distaste of recounting a traumatic memory. "Family of vampire prodigies. Like how you humans sometimes come out with one who can memorise everything or play all those fancy instruments before they learn to speak? We got that too. The De Varises are the most well-known though, got their abilities dialled up to eleven, the lucky sods. But Penelope? Hers was something else. Could put a whole city under her thrall if she wanted to. For the record, I tried thralling two humans once. Thought my head was gonna explode."

"But I saw her headstone in the graveyard," Gyldan pressed on as Griff started walking down the rest of the stairs. "How powerful could she be if she died?"

"Powerful enough that she lost control and it killed her," Griff said. "I don't know the details, but I heard she thralled a huge group and it slipped out of her control for a second. Thralling's all emotions, kid, your puppet's got no emotions

197

unless your own seep in. She musta got angry or scared and accidentally let that feeling go out to her thralls. They ripped her apart."

The vampire turned at the bottom of the stairs then and shoved a finger squarely into Gyldan's chest.

"Moral of the story—with great power comes—"

"Are you quoting *Spider-Man* at me?" Gyldan laughed. Griffin's cheeks prickled pink.

"...Look, just, if you ever run into a De Varis, make your excuses and go. Even with their abilities removed, they're a dangerous lot. Promise?"

"All right, yeah," Gyldan said, thinking of the smiling pantomime of a vampire that was Luca de Varis. He hadn't seemed so awful, though Gyldan wondered what his amplified ability had been before his eyes were taken out.

The two headed into the living room, which, to Gyldan's alarm, had had the furniture shoved back as far as possible. In the middle of the room, Rukshana was standing next to a flip-chart, a wooden pointer in hand resting against the palm of the other. Gyldan's spine twitched a little straighter at the sight of it.

"Caladrius would love you," Gyldan commented as he read the charts and clippings tacked to the walls around him. "Presentation skills on point."

"Sit down, gentlemen, this won't take long," Seraph crowed from the middle of the sofa, patting both empty spaces each side of her. "It's wild though. Like, tin-foil-hat wild."

Gyldan took a seat to Seraph's left. The werewolf had been the loudest to object to having Albion in the house, and of course, he couldn't hold it against her. The man was a tyrant against her kind. But, slowly and surely, she seemed to be forgiving Gyldan for his stupid heart.

"Thank you for that gold-star review of my work, Seraph," Rukshana drawled.

"Hey, wait, *our* work, I helped! You're just better at the explaining thing, babe!" Seraph objected, flopping back into the sofa and flapping one hand towards Rukshana. "You got this!"

"Anyway." Rukshana began tapping the stick against a print-out pinned to the board. The image was a still from the live feed of Daedalus' public announcement. An unlucky cameraman had hung around long enough to capture footage of the monster arriving, it seemed. "I've been pulling together what we know about Albion's transformations. For ease of explanation, I've elected to name the creature. I call it the Alkonost."

Seraph nudged Gyldan.

"That was my idea," she stage-whispered proudly. "Cause they sing pretty things and make people forget everything they know. Like how his pretty words made you forget he's an oppressive piece of shit!"

The forgiveness was slow-going.

Rukshana cleared her throat, the whispering having been noted.

"*That* and because I suspect the Alkonost was made in woeful error," the vampire continued, turning the page to show a zoomed-in version of the same print-out. This time, the focus was on the calm Yanatha. "See here. This? This is peculiar. The only reason why Ms Saint-Richter would be so calm would be if she knew the Alkonost would not harm her. How could she know this, about a species no one has encountered yet?"

Rukshana turned the page again. The next one was littered with prints of screenshots of various web pages.

"As the daughter of the wealthiest man in our country, Yanatha Saint-Richter has an impressive digital map to look through. It didn't take long for me to find that despite her youth, Ms Saint-Richter is quite the over-achiever. Accolades in biology, chemistry... coupled with—"

Rukshana flipped the chart page again, landing on a display that made Gyldan's heart sink: newspaper clippings depicting a tragic event.

"—the murder of her brother, Caladrius Saint-Richter. It is no secret that one of the motivators to Albion creating the collars and eye-guards was the death of his son at the hands of non-human extremists. But, presumably, his ultimate goal is to eventually 'cure' the world of what he sees as a threat. I propose that he and his daughter, with their combined knowledge, have set out to do just that," Rukshana said. "And, with the need for utmost secrecy, Albion has chosen to experiment on himself, causing the recent emergence of the Alkonost—a creature with facets of vampire, werewolf, and human biology. A failed experiment. As the only person who knew about this, Yanatha is the only person who would not be shocked by his appearance. Presumably, she knew she would be safe from the creature's wrath, given his emotional method of selecting targets."

Gyldan had already disagreed with Rukshana's analysis halfway through her speech, though he could see the logic. Rubbing a finger across his chin in thought, he shook his head, politely waiting for her to finish before he interjected.

"Possibly, to a point," Gyldan hedged a partial agreement. "But that's not Albion. He's way too proud of being human to risk changing that. He wouldn't experiment on himself."

A frown disturbed Rukshana's calm façade, and she let her hand drop to the side, the tip of her pointing stick tapping on the floor.

"Not even for his daughter? If she asked for her father to cure the world of a perceived threat…?"

"I think he'd do anything for Yanatha," Gyldan admitted. "But Albion would explore a thousand other paths before risking his pride. Besides, remember where Yanatha was that day—she was at the Daedalus public announcement. I was there when Albion saw the stream. He was shocked she was there, mortified even. If they were looking for a cure together, why would she ask Daedalus for help?"

This threw a spanner in the works, dragging out a long and heavy silence between the group. Rukshana turned back to her work, studying the various papers with her lips pursed tight.

"Good point," she conceded with disdain. "That does change things. Still, I believe Yanatha knew about her father's condition. But if they were working together on a cure... why go to Daedalus...?"

The vampire trailed off, turning her back on the group and stalking around the room, pausing every so often and muttering at a different paper on the wall. At Gyldan's side, Seraph sighed and threw her arms behind her head, sprawling out on the sofa.

"How is *that* a cure anyway?" the werewolf wondered aloud. She angled her head back as though looking for her answers on the ceiling. "The Alkonost, I mean. Even a werewolf caught out in the full moon causes less trouble than that thing."

"I don't believe the goal was to turn vampires and werewolves into that creature, Seraph," Rukshana replied over her shoulder, sounding distracted, her voice teetering on monotonous. "I think it was created to wipe us out."

"No, no, that's *not* Albion," Gyldan said, getting to his feet. He could already feel Seraph rolling her eyes, and he turned to face her and Griffin on the couch. "No, seriously, Albion is a colossal dick when it comes to non-humans. I get that. He's done terrible things to you guys. But no way would he advocate *genocide*. He just... he wouldn't go that far."

Seraph was looking at the floor, jaw set so tightly the muscles along her face shivered. Griffin looked away too, but he looked less uncomfortable than the werewolf.

Gyldan rounded on Rukshana, though her back was still turned to him.

"Rukshana, I'm telling you—Albion wouldn't do that."

"...It wouldn't be the first time he has surprised you with the depths of his hatred, Gyldan," the vampire responded smoothly, with a logic that grated on Gyldan's every nerve because of its accuracy. "You were angered by him telling you he was looking for a cure, and those that did not choose it would be arrested, were you not?"

"Exactly!" Gyldan turned between the three of them, knowing full well that he had no right to plead for their understanding when it came to Albion. He wasn't quite sure why he kept fighting for this man's soul—he had been so sure he had given up on it. "He said those that didn't choose the cure would be *arrested*. How does that make any sense if you're right about what the cure is?"

"Or, it went wrong, and he just rolled with the hand he was dealt," Seraph suggested.

"That still doesn't make sense—it went wrong *before* he told me about the cure," Gyldan interjected, feeling himself getting irritated. "The Alkonost killed a load of Daedalus employees before Albion even told me about the cure. I don't think he remembers turning into the thing anyway."

Suddenly, Rukshana grew ridged, her shoulders twitching higher, spine jolting up straighter. Everyone in the room noticed, with Griffin shifting forward in his seat and Seraph tentatively asking:

"Shana? What is it?"

"But *she* knows," Rukshana mumbled, heading back to the flip-chart and scowling at the print-out of Yanatha. "She clearly *knows*... it couldn't be possible..."

The vampire offered no explanation, nor any sign that she would explain her sudden burst of movement, concentration drawing deeper over her face. Gyldan shook his head, heading to the door.

"Listen, I'll go speak to Albion again. Maybe he can figure out why Yanatha didn't freak out."

He wanted to press the man more about the mask Luca had received in the graveyard anyway, and all this talk of additional questions was making his head spin. Still, Gyldan had to admit he was as curious as Rukshana about Yanatha's perpetual calm—other than knowing the creature wouldn't harm her, there was no clear reason to react so mildly at the sight of the Alkonost.

Gyldan opened the living room door and was startled by a sharp green scowl and a shock of tangled silver hair.

"*Jesus*, Albion... scared the hell outta me!" Gyldan stepped back, one hand on the door and the other over his chest. He did his best to ignore the unsettled aura that crawled into the room as Albion appeared, though he was sure Seraph growled in warning to the older man by the look Albion cast over Gyldan's shoulder towards the sofa.

"I'm not staying here like this," Albion announced, voice disturbing the silence like ripples on a lake's glassy surface. "I'm not a goddamn prisoner to a bunch of *freaks* and my *employee*. I need fresh clothes, I need to see my daughter, and I'm *leaving*."

"Oh wow, you hear that? *His employee*, Gyldan. Y'know, he sticks up for you, asshole," Seraph addressed the CEO, cutting in as Gyldan found his tongue numbed by the coldness of Albion's address. The werewolf got to her feet, one thumb hooked in the pocket of her jeans, a hip bucked to the side, pointing from Albion to Gyldan with her free hand. "You can call us what you like, old man, I've heard worse from better. But him? Spit in his face and I'll getcha some food—your own fucking teeth, how's that sound?"

"Seraph, it's fine," Gyldan half-muttered, half-grumbled, making to walk forward and push Albion back out into the hall before the bristling man could retort.

"No, it isn't, Gyl! It isn't fine! I'm sitting here, listening to you shield this douchebag, risking friendships to tell the people whose lives he's *ruined* that he's worth tryin' to save, and he can't even be nice to *you* anymore?" Seraph's voice deepened, rocked with a raw snarl no human tone could reach. Gyldan looked over, watching as her bright blonde crop began to sharpen and stand wilder than before, icy eyes flashing at Albion. "Look at him! *This*,"—she gestured wildly at Albion—"this is what *we* see, dude.

That's the real Albion, not whoever you're kissin' when he puts on a nicey-nicey act!"

"Enough..." Griffin interjected, a gentle hand reaching out from where he was sitting on the sofa to take hold of Seraph's forearm. "Gyl... let's compromise. Go shoppin', make the Princess feel comfy here."

The old vampire got to his feet then too, and for the first time, Gyldan noticed that he was standing straight, his usual hunched and weary form unfurling to bring an air of power and command to Griffin that both ill-suited him and yet fit him like a glove. It was uncanny to behold, making Gyldan want to run and smile at the same time.

Griffin turned to Albion, and a tremor of muscle twitches contorted Albion's furious expression.

"As for you... you might not like our kind. And in some ways, I get that. Losin' a son, demanding payment from us all... it ain't fair, but I get it. But you have to understand—that feelin'? That... *getting it?* That's *pity* I got for you there. Pity." Griffin spat the word as an insult in Albion's proud face. "I want you to know that. *Pity* kept me nice and polite with you. *Pity* is all that's letting me listen to Gyl and try to help you out here. But if you speak to my boy or my girls like that again under our roof?"

In a blurring display of agility, Griffin was between Gyl and Albion, somehow making the two inches in height he had on Albion seem like a towering difference as he loomed over the man.

"Speak to my family like that again, and you'll need a lot more than pity, *Al,*" Griffin warned, nose almost brushing against Albion's. The other man did not flinch away.

Then, just like that, the sickening, dark cloud that was pressing down on the room dispersed like the sun breaking through a storm, and Griffin turned on his heel to face Gyldan, a wide smile lighting up his stubbled face as he effortlessly stepped back into his usual bumbling self. Over the vampire's shoulder,

Albion's face crumpled in indignation at having Griffin turn his back on him.

"Errr...?" Gyldan managed to squeak out.

"While you're out with the Princess, could ya pick me up some Cherry Clots? Had a sugar craving all day!" Griffin beamed, clapping a hand on Gyldan's shoulder.

"Ah, s-s-sure?"

"Good lad! Rukshana! Let's get our heads together about this whole weird mess," Griffin declared, walking away from Gyldan and Albion and waving at the flip-chart. "The answer's there, we just ain't seeing it. Seraph, what do you think about heading back to the scene and giving it a sniff? Can't sniff photos, maybe we missed something."

Gyldan put a hand on Albion's chest as the man started forward after Griffin, pushing him back into the hall and closing the door to the living room behind them with a muttered, fatigued, "Don't... just don't..."

If Albion had not been visibly struggling with residual exhaustion himself, Gyldan knew he would have pushed past him to settle some score of his pride against Griffin. But instead, the man contented himself to attempt to burn the now-closed door between them with a cold stare.

Chapter 15

It wasn't long after they had left Gyldan's house that he realised Albion was not leading them to the centre of the city for any kind of shopping. The route to Albion's house was almost as familiar to Gyldan as his own walk home, and once upon a time, it had been as comforting too. But not today.

"Al, where are we going?" Gyldan broke the silent tension between them that had been building since Albion had stormed out of the house. "I thought you said you needed—"

"I overheard your vampire-friend's presentation," Albion cut him off, turning sharply down the next street and leaving Gyldan to jog after him. "She's wrong. Yanatha and I aren't working on anything together. You really think I'd let my daughter get involved in something as dangerous as non-human studies?"

"No, but..."

"...but your friend has a point."

The admittance sounded alien coming from Albion, and the gravity of it was enough to falter Gyldan's steps. Albion wasn't just admitting a vampire was right about something—he was finally and indirectly accepting the truth. That he was the Alkonost, the killer that had roamed the streets of late. It was equal parts a relief and agony to hear.

Catching up to Albion's side, Gyldan fell into pace with the man's determined power-walk.

"Yanatha knows you're the Alkonost," Gyldan said by means of confirmation. From the look on Albion's face, he didn't appreciate the new title.

"Clearly," he drawled, looking resolutely ahead. "Which means she's hiding something. She's smart, Gyl, really smart. If she knows who's done this to me, she's going to tell me. And I swear to God, if this is Daedalus' doing…"

Albion's voice petered away from restrained anger to a guttural growl, drowning the words that were meant to come after. The man shook his head violently, screwing his eyelids shut. "…God*dammit!*"

Soon, the luxurious, white-stoned mansion came into view. As the two men hurried up the gravel driveway, Gyldan couldn't help but notice the absence of Albion's usual security team.

"…Al?"

"I know," was the only confirmation Gyldan got that Albion had noticed too.

Albion hurried up the steps to the house, thrusting out his hand in a silent command for Gyldan's spare key. He only slowed down long enough to snatch it off him and unlock the front door. Then, Albion burst through and into the hall, leaving Gyldan to creep in after him and shut the door behind them.

"Yanatha?" Albion called, heading into the kitchen then back out into the hallway again. He grabbed the end of the bannister and called up the stairs. "*Yan?*"

Muttering under his breath, the older man darted up the stairs. Gyldan shuffled to the bottom step, glancing up and watching as Albion went to open a door on the right of the corridor. A dull thud told him the door was locked.

"Got a key?" Gyldan asked, immediately regretting it. Albion glared at him, backing away from the door.

"No, because I didn't even know it had a *fucking lock on it!*" Albion roared in frustration. He clenched his teeth and struck out with his leg, kicking the door with enough force to rattle it in its frame. "*Yanatha! What the hell are you playing at?*"

"Woah, woah, woah, Al, calm down!" Gyldan rushed up the stairs and pulled Albion away by the shoulder, turning him from the door in the process. He had never heard Albion raise his voice at Yanatha before, much less attempt to kick a door down. If nothing else, he was terrified the man's heightened emotions might spark the Alkonost again. Gyldan was in no hurry to come face to face with that behemoth again. "We'll figure this out, just give me a second."

Albion opened his mouth to reply, but someone else cut into the conversation with all the smoothness of a gentleman requesting a dance at a ball.

"Have you tried asking it *nicely?*"

Gyldan frowned. Albion frowned. The pair looked at each other, and then in unison, looked down the hall.

There, standing at the foot of the stairs and dressed in a black and white tuxedo that somehow made him look more like the man of the house than Albion, was Luca de Varis. The vampire grinned and waved up to them both.

"*Coo-ee!*" he called up to them. He began climbing the stairs, one hand out to feel along the bannister.

Albion didn't seem able to decide whether to frown or raise his eyebrows.

"Luca? How the hell did you get into my house?" he demanded. Gyldan couldn't help but feel a bit sorry for Albion. The man once had perfect control over everything in his life, and in the span of a few weeks, everything had cut its strings and ran away from him.

"I heard you shouting from outside. Not good for a man of your years to get so riled up, Albion!" Luca replied with faux kindness as he reached the upstairs landing. Then, the vampire's head twitched, his nose pointed into the air. A chortle split his sombre expression, sparking his face to life. "Oh? Your cologne is wearing off, dear heart." Luca turned towards Gyldan and pouted in disappointment, his hollow eye sockets directed slightly too high. "I almost missed you there! I *thought* I heard someone else, but it was so faint beneath Albion breathing like an elephant with cramp..."

"Hey, er... Luca, right?" Gyldan greeted him quickly, knowing Albion was in no mood for Luca's brand of humour. It had seemed impossible seconds beforehand, but Luca's grin ignited brighter at Gyldan's words.

"You remembered! How lovely," the vampire purred, clasping his hands behind his back and rocking up onto the balls of his feet. "Of course, *I* remember *you*, my Caladrius tour-guide—Gyldan! Forgive the informality, but you never told me your surname."

This proved to be the end of Albion's tether.

"Don't make me ask you again, *vampire*," Albion snarled. "How. Did you get. Into my house?"

If Luca had had eyes, Gyldan was sure he would have rolled them. The vampire let his jaw drop with disdain, his head rolling around in a display of disbelief.

"Oh, get out of the way and I'll show you." Luca flapped both hands in front of him, shooing Albion and Gyldan to the left and right respectively. "I would have thought you might have figured it out by now, Albion, given our history..."

Suddenly, he rounded on Albion, a finger pointed millimetres from his face. "Oh, and if you *think* of alerting the authorities over this home intrusion, I shall tell every journalist I know of your nightly jaunts as a maneater!"

Gyldan choked on his own spit.

"*Don't*... don't phrase it... like that..." he pleaded with Luca. "Jesus, God, don't phrase it like that..."

Luca turned to him and tilted his head in feigned confusion.

"Hm? But I know, dear heart! I can smell it on him. Those poor Daedalus employees torn up by a feral monster of a man! Word gets out, you know. It would be disastrous for your image, Albion."

"Fine, fine, just... if you can open the door, do it," Albion agreed, though his gaze sparkled with a combination of anger and curiosity.

The vampire shrugged, turning back to the door. He squatted down until he was face-to-face with the lock under the door handle, fingers crawling around the space and feeling the metal.

"*Unlock for me, if you would*," Luca said.

Just like that, the lock obeyed with a click. Giving a happy trill of approval, Luca straightened up and pulled the door handle down. The door swung open.

"What... did you just do?" Gyldan blurted out.

"*Variation*, dear heart. A terrific thing. Sometimes, it brings something good into the world. A human whose mind is sharper than the norm. A werewolf who can track even the slightest scent. For my family, it brought stronger abilities," Luca explained, and Gyldan recalled Griffin's warning about the De Varis family. "Imagine my father's despair when one of his sons not only didn't display a unique trait but couldn't even perform the normal vampire ability of thralling a creature."

Luca stepped back from the open door, smiling. "It took some time and a considerable amount of bullying by my gifted siblings, but I eventually discovered I *did* have my own variation after all. I can't thrall the living—but I *can* thrall inanimate objects. Oh, the ruckus I caused making 'haunted houses' and 'possessed dolls' in my youth!" The vampire laughed before extending out a hand to Yanatha's room and bowing low. "After you!"

Albion pushed past him to Yanatha's room, but Gyldan stalled at the door. He gave Luca a critical look. He wanted to ask him *how* he had kept his ability when his eyes had been removed, but another question weighed more heavily upon his tongue.

"That night I caught you in the lab. You said you climbed in through the window," he said. The vampire was still grinning as he shook his head.

"Nope. *You* said I climbed in through the window, darling. I just agreed with you." The vampire gave his confession easily, splaying his hands out towards Gyldan then clapping them together. "You understand, I can't have people knowing my particular ability hasn't been suppressed by our government's best efforts. I'd be imprisoned and tested on! Most unsavoury. Shall we?"

Luca gestured to the open door again and Gyldan wandered through, aware that the smiling vampire followed closely after. "I confess, I didn't come here for a courtesy call," Luca said behind him. "I was hoping to check up on my business partner."

"Business partner?" Gyldan asked. "You mean—?"

As he looked around the room, however, his question died in his throat. Gyldan thought he had witnessed horrors when he had encountered the Alkonost—how foolish he had been.

Yanatha's room was no place of rest. The walls were plastered with papers and charts, the floor a mishmash of machinery and cables. Equipment balanced precariously on every table and desk, some etched with Caladrius' logo, others with Daedalus' branding. Not even the bed was spared, with jars of gruesome liquid containing indecipherable objects floating within strewn over the bedsheets. Gyldan picked his way carefully through the room, doing his best not to stand on anything. He found himself drawn to the bed, looking down at the labels on the ghastly collection of jars.

One sample in particular caught his attention. It was labelled: '*Penelope de Varis—Homo sanguinis (ascended). Sample #47.*'

That alone was enough to draw bile burning up Gyldan's throat. But it was the sample resting next to it that turned Gyldan's knees to mush, bringing him down to the floor in sickly, cold shock.

'*Caelan Warlock—Homo lupus (standard). Sample #4.*'

Though Albion glanced in Gyldan's direction, Luca paid his collapse no heed. Instead, the vampire was bent at the hip and picking up jars from the bed. He gave them a tentative sniff, a scarred eyebrow cocking in thought.

"It's a terrible habit to bring work home with you," Luca commented, letting a glass vial roll out of his hand and back onto the bed. It bounced on the mattress and clinked against the other samples. "I have told her *countless* times to invest in a little self-care..."

This stirred much more of a reaction from Albion than Gyldan sinking to his knees had. Albion's interest shifted from the computer he had been searching through to fix upon Luca instead. But the vampire continued his rummaging and sniffing of objects in the room without acknowledging him.

"Wait," Gyldan said, finding his voice again. "I thought... I thought you said you were working with *Albion?*"

At this, Luca had the decency to look pained. He stopped his investigation and looked at Gyldan, even offering him a hand to help him back up to his feet.

"Oh, forgive me, Gyldan. I confess, I'm a tad distrusting by nature—I wasn't wholly honest with you that night we first crossed paths. Less a lie, per se, and more, *ahhhh...*"—Luca's voice stretched to a squeak as he searched for words to save face—"...a slight twisting of the truth. We have worked together in the past, but that was long ago. And I do donate heavily to the fundraiser, that much is true. But it's been a while since the money raised at that event has been landing in the right coffers, shall we say."

Gyldan was left to stew on Luca's words as Albion's tolerance for the non-human ended. In a few short strides, he had reached Luca and grabbed the vampire by the shoulder, hauling him around to stand face-to-face with him.

"What do you mean, the money's been moved?" he demanded.

Luca, perhaps because he couldn't see the patience drying up behind Albion's eyes, shrugged.

"Did you really think that many vampires and werewolves suddenly felt responsible for your family's little tragedy? Oh, do come down from that pedestal, Albion, you'll notice a little more," Luca drawled, swatting Albion's hand from his shoulder. "Your daughter has been rerouting the money for the fundraiser for years! A lovely, shiny front meant plenty of non-humans could donate to the *real* project without you getting suspicious."

"What. Project?" Albion grunted through his teeth.

"The cure, of course!"

"*I'm* working on the cure!" Albion's face was growing steadily redder as the vampire wound him up further. "Not Yanatha! Why the *hell* have you approached her about *anything?*"

Luca pushed out his bottom lip, mocking Albion's anger.

"Aw, don't get competitive now. I did so enjoy working on the mask of mirrors all those years ago, Albion. But I'm afraid Yanatha simply had a better pitch for *her* project. Daedalus had a few interesting pieces we borrowed, and Caladrius had some wonderful little breakthroughs we could take note of. But the sad fact is that our paths were going different ways, dear heart."

Gyldan got to his feet, keeping part of his attention on Luca while he stepped over the jumble of equipment in Yanatha's room. His hand trailed over some of it, brushing over Daedalus' hammer-and-forge logo.

"That's why she partnered with them. She just wanted their equipment," Gyldan muttered to himself more than anyone.

"She must have been working with them for months before the public announcement. That wasn't to announce the start of the partnership—it was the end. She's ready to test her project."

"No. She already has." Luca leant in a fraction of an inch, sniffing Albion's neck. Albion immediately slammed his hands into Luca's chest, causing the vampire to fall backwards onto the bed. Glass jars bounced off the mattress and thudded to the floor. Even fallen, Luca managed to retain his composure. He sat up, beaming. "You smell like these samples. Like her cure."

Gyldan froze.

That's how she knew, he realised, turning to Albion as the colour drained from his own face and left a sickly chill in its wake. *She knew because this is her creation.*

Albion went to speak, but Gyldan quickly stepped in.

"How is this a cure, Luca? Why would you help Yanatha create the Alkonost?"

Luca drew his legs up onto the bed, crossing them and then folding his hands neatly on his ankles.

"*Alkonost?* Is that what you've named the maneater? How quaint. Well, I suppose I ought to be frank with you. To make up for those little lies in the lab. But let me ask you something first— I had kept mine and Yanatha's business partnership hidden from you all for so long. Why do you think I would be so open about it right here, hmm?"

The vampire flashed Gyldan a fanged smile, waiting patiently for his response.

"...Because... you've fallen out?" Gyldan ventured. Luca nodded.

"Of sorts. I began to suspect Yanatha had taken our little project in a different direction than originally proposed. I agreed to help her find a cure. I even allowed her to exhume my sister's corpse as part of that process. I'm not too bitter about that part— my sister was quite terrible. Quite special among my kind, but often one finds those with higher powers tend to stumble down paths that lead to their worst selves. But I was quite looking forward to something *good* coming from Penelope for once."

Luca shifted, propping his elbows into his knees and resting his chin sullenly between his hands as he continued his tale: "I confess, I was quite jealous of Penelope. We all were, my brothers and sisters. We all had our quirks taken away, well, other than me in secret. But not Penelope. She could thrall countless people at once. But, as well as being gifted, my dear Penelope was also *arrogant*. She always had to push things a tad further than she could handle. She loved to test herself, you see. She always said if anyone tried to take her eyes, she'd thrall the whole room and have them kill each other. It was a stalemate between the government and my family, and one that got more turbulent each time my mother asked Penelope to cooperate.

"While all that rumbled on, my little sister was off testing herself. One night, she escaped her room and thralled an entire group of poor werewolves. A fragment of anger in Penelope fired out over her thralls—but a little anger to us is a spark to ignite *rage* in a werewolf. And she had seven under her command. Seven berserk werewolves dashed off, obeying Penelope's command for *anger*. They... tore apart a fellow family of vampires." Luca's voice dovetailed towards sorrow, his smile long since disappearing and revealing a glimpse of his true self.

Gyldan, meanwhile, could not speak. His mouth dried, his throat constricted, and he dared not ask the question he already knew the answer to.

Was that... Rukshana's family?

Luca sighed, straightening up and lifting his head out of his hands.

"Humans seldom realise that thralling is an ability, but it isn't *easy*," Luca explained, and Gyldan recalled Griffin's comment about how difficult it was to thrall the Alkonost. "Every emotion you have can bleed into your thrall if you're not careful. Penelope, the fine fool, saw the bloodbath of her own kind being eaten by her wolves and must have felt guilt. A brief moment where she wished to die for her sins. Her thralled werewolves heard her."

Luca turned his head towards Gyldan, waiting a moment before concluding his sorry tale with a wry smile: "Rather a dire irony, but dear Penelope was mauled to death by her own thralls. Didn't concentrate for one second and lost control of her dogs. Silly girl."

"Did... anyone survive?" Gyldan asked, though his tongue felt cumbersome in his mouth. Luca cocked his head to the side and shrugged with one shoulder.

"I suppose it's possible. Depends when exactly Penelope's conscience finally hit her," Luca replied, though a waver in his cadence told Gyldan he knew well if anyone had survived. "Quite frustrating. I had been working for months with Albion on something strong enough to curtail her powers, only for it to be rendered unnecessary. Still, I would have liked to have taken the prototype with me. My beautiful mask of mirrors."

Something clicked in Gyldan's memory.

"You were looking for the mask that night I first met you," he said, watching Luca's scarred brow wiggle up and down playfully at him. "That's why you were in the labs. You were going to take it back. Why?"

"At that point, I suspected Yanatha was not using my sister's genes towards our agreed goal anymore. The mask is my safety net against such an event. And now, given the smell of all this and how it clings to Albion, I can be sure of it."

Luca twirled a hand towards Albion. "You, all this, it all reeks of her cure, the one *I* funded. But it's obviously not what I wanted—replacing you all with monsters wasn't quite what I had in mind. I must say, I am disappointed in Yanatha. I, for one, was rather looking forward to a world without humans."

Gyldan reeled, and he could see Albion going pale.

"A world without... without *humans?*" Gyldan repeated back to the grinning vampire. "But-but the cure, the cure was to change non-humans into humans, wasn't it? I thought—you said you were looking for a *cure!*"

Luca's laugh trilled like glass shards pouring over porcelain.

"Yes! A cure for *humanity*. Humans are the disease, dear heart, isn't that clear? That was Yanatha's winning pitch! Caladrius and Daedalus were looking to cure vampires and werewolves, but Yanatha? Oh, she had bolder ambitions, particularly for a human herself. She could see the truth. Humans are the ones that need curing, boy. I came here to discuss the *interpretation* of that goal with Yanatha today. I suspect she's trying to accelerate a change in humans, to evolve your kind into something stronger than a vampire or a werewolf. That is not what we agreed. We had agreed that the cure wasn't to *better* the human race but to wipe it out in one decisive move. I would never have let her dabble with my sister's remains for anything less."

Luca's voice turned venomous then, smile thinning to become crueller and robbing the usual jovial air the vampire wore so easily. "It solves all the problems really, doesn't it? No more humans, no more eye-guards or collars, no more tragedies for humans to worry about. You said it yourself, dear heart: why *would* anyone want to be human? Yes, that did rather tickle me! Get rid of you all, that's what I say!"

Gyldan couldn't respond to this deluge of bitterness. His throat had constricted, his mouth dried, and he needed to place all of his focus on dragging air into his lungs. Luca started to get to his feet, his wicked smile still painted over his pale lips. Gyldan wanted to back away, to keep as much distance as he could between him and the vampire he now knew loathed his kind.

But he didn't have to. A hand struck out and latched onto Luca's throat, driving the stunned blond back into the wall furthest from Gyldan with a sickening slam. Luca coughed and gasped, hands clawing at Albion's wrist and arm as Albion dragged the vampire upwards. Flailing feet failed to find their grip on the floor, leaving Luca to kick out at the trembling man pinning him to the wall, his former elegance brutalised by Albion's outburst.

Guttural sounds spilt from Albion's throat, the back of his shirt tearing as his body grew. Black, ragged wings cascaded down to the floor, his silver hair dulling and darkening like ink poured upon fresh paper.

"*Not... him...!*" Albion choked out between growls as the sharp tips of horns rose around his head. "*Not... Gyldan...!*"

Chapter 16

Gyldan wasn't sure who he was trying to save at this point. The squirming vampire pinned to the wall, whose face was rapidly bruising dark red as he struggled to rake in air? The growling human turning feral before him, crushing the vampire's windpipe? Or his own conscience?

"Albion, stop! Listen to me—killing Luca won't solve anything! Let him go and we can—"

Albion's black-maned head whipped around to Gyldan then, his elongated snout wrinkling as grey lips quivered around a snarl. The rest of Gyldan's plea suffocated in his chest the moment he realised Albion wasn't listening anymore.

But the Alkonost was.

Behind the grey-skinned goliath, Luca gasped as the Alkonost's grip loosened a touch.

"*Tan-gle... him...!*" Luca coughed. At his command, the curtain ties hanging by the window spiralled out from their hooks. They snaked and wrapped around the Alkonost, coiling over his face and limbs.

The creature howled in fury, letting go of Luca and stumbling backwards. Gyldan darted to the side, narrowly avoiding being stepped on by the monster as it thrashed and ripped the curtain ties away with ease.

Luca scrambled to his feet, tripping over equipment in his hurry to leave.

"*Close! Lock!*" Luca issued his commands as he bolted out of the room. The door obediently slammed shut behind him, the lock dropping into place before Gyldan could yell out in despair.

"Luca! Don't leave me in here!" Gyldan wailed, dashing to the door and yanking on the handle in vain. His heart pounded, and his mind snatched all of his common sense away. Gyldan's fingers stumbled over the lock—for the life of him he couldn't focus long enough to undo it.

Behind him, the Alkonost's roar ripped the air asunder. It was the only warning Gyldan had to dive out of the way before the beast crashed bodily into the door in pursuit of the vampire. The wood burst apart, offering as much resistance to the Alkonost's array of horns as paper might to a sword. The monster bounded away down the stairs after Luca.

Gyldan kicked and scrambled over the littered floor, cold sweat weeping down the back of his neck.

"Shit! *Shit!*" Gyldan got up and, despite everything telling him not to, gave chase to the Alkonost. Gyldan could only hope Luca would realise what they had to do—goals be damned, they could not let Albion leave in this state.

Gyldan half-ran, half-slid down the stairs in time to see Luca yelling and running across the hall from the kitchen to the living room, his neck already stained with purple bruises. Gyldan stopped short of landing in the Alkonost's path as the beast barrelled after its prey.

"*Charge!*" Luca's shrill and desperate voice commanded. Suddenly, the kitchen chairs ran in unison across the hall before a perplexed Gyldan, an army of immaculate furniture charging dutifully at the Alkonost and smashing itself against the beast.

Legs. Chairs have... legs... Gyldan reasoned, wondering just how much Luca could ask of an inanimate object. He didn't have time to consider the details—the furniture made for poor combatants against the Alkonost. Its great clawed hands swatted them away with ease, eyes trained mercilessly on Luca as the vampire scrambled around the living room. His left sleeve was ripped to ribbons, blood dripping from the outstretched limb as he felt his way around the room, seeking out what was available to him. Luca had lost all of his graces now, panicked whimpers dripping from his lips and blond hair flopping over his scarred face.

"Luca!" Gyldan called from the doorway, risking drawing the Alkonost's attention. "Mirror on your left, sofa on your right. Table behind Albion!"

Luca found Gyldan amidst the chaos, though whether he was confused or grateful was unclear. Still, the vampire nodded, darting to his left and hauling the mirror off the wall. He cowered behind it as the Alkonost brought down its talons to cleave it and Luca in twain.

"*Reflect!*" Luca yelped from behind the large mirror. As soon as the Alkonost's claws struck the glass, the beast reeled back with a pained screech. It wasn't until it stumbled around that it became clear what the mirror had done. Four deep cuts bled bright red against its grey face as if it had been clawed apart by another Alkonost.

Luca peered out from the now-shattered mirror and sniffed. Then, he risked a smile.

"*Run*, please!" he said, though Gyldan wasn't sure who he was asking. He wasn't going to take a risk, even though the coffee table sprung to life and dashed forward, knocking the wounded Alkonost off its feet. Gyldan turned and sprinted into the kitchen, taking in the layout of the room and where everything was within the monochromatic and sleek-cut space.

Luca ran in shortly after, glass-bitten hands finding Gyldan's shoulders.

"Parley?" the vampire requested with a weak smile. Gyldan arched his neck to look behind Luca. The Alkonost was rising in the ruined living room, and if it was anything like its human counterpart, they would be answering for its wounded pride now too.

"Don't kill him," Gyldan replied, taking Luca by the hand and guiding him through the kitchen. "Usual stuff at your disposal. I... I dunno, what is the most useful object to you?"

"I-I-I'm restricted by whatever the item itself can conceivably do." Luca gave a hurried explanation, hands flapping.

"*Conceivably do?* What, like making chairs run?" Gyldan retorted, rushing through the kitchen and opening all the pearl-white cupboards and drawers, cutlery and dishes chiming.

"They have legs!" Luca replied, pulling shards of broken mirror out of the palm of one hand and licking the blood away from the wounds. "Legs are for running, my boy!"

Gyldan didn't have time to question just how fast and loose Luca's strange thralling ability allowed him to play with semantics. A crunching at the door chilled him to his core.

Dark claws hooked around the archway, cracking the wood as the Alkonost ducked its hulking mass into the room. It was still trained on Luca, having shown little to no interest in Gyldan despite their past encounters.

"H-How long does he stay like this for? Generally?" Luca squeaked, sidestepping to put Gyldan between himself and the monster, who appeared hesitant to strike with Gyldan in the way.

"Not long. We have to wear him out. We can't risk him getting into the city again." Gyldan took charge even though he felt like he was chewing on his thundering heart. "I'll get help."

"W-w-wait, don't leave me with it! Oh! Safety net!" Luca exclaimed, pulling his tuxedo jacket open and ferreting about in the inner pocket. After a second, he produced a mask, smooth and faceted with tiny mirrored panels.

The Alkonost was not about to wait for their strategizing to finish. The beast burst forward, its slobbering maw wide open—Gyldan turned and grabbed the vampire by the shoulders, shoving him towards the kitchen worktop and out of the way of the charging behemoth. Luca slammed stomach-first against the ebony-topped counter, the mask of mirrors dropping from his grip and skidding across the floor.

"If you think it'll work, use it!" Gyldan said, his own tone running higher and higher with fear as the monster tracked Luca. Gyldan ducked out of sight behind the kitchen table.

"Where is it, where is it? Ah, *cut!*" Luca yelled, followed by a screech of pain from the Alkonost. Gyldan tried to ignore it, pulling out his phone and dialling Griffin.

"Come on, pick up, pick up!" Gyldan muttered, peering out from behind the table to try and find the mask. It lay closer to the vampire than Gyldan, and he couldn't risk catching the Alkonost's attention to retrieve it. "Luca, mask is at your two o' clock, Albion's at twelve!"

The phone line connected with a fluster of movement from the other end of the call. Then, Griffin greeted him:

"Bloody hell, Gyl, is he getting his clothes tailor-made? You've been gone ages!"

"Griff, you know the way I walk home when I'm staying at a friend's house?" Gyldan hissed, rolling back to cover behind the table.

"Yeah... what's happened?"

"You know the full route?"

"It was the worst-kept secret you ever had, son."

"I need you to get here—"

As if on cue, Luca screamed and bleated: "*Burn!* Oh bollocks, that's not good... ah, Gyldan, darling? We might want to evacuate!"

The room was rapidly filling with smoke, and tears began streaming down Gyldan's face as he sank low to the ground, crawling out from behind the table.

"Gyl?" Griffin had lost his usual relaxed lilt and snapped over the speaker. "We're on our way. What is going on?"

"Albion... transformed. And there's a De Varis here."

"What? I told you—never mind, can you hide somewhere?"

"I think Luca just commanded the oven to burn."

"...Get outside. Lock the doors, try and keep—wait, *Luca?* Jesus, I'm surprised Albion hasn't eaten him already, he's hardly a fighter."

Gyldan glanced over the room, catching sight of Luca crawling under the smoke towards the hallway. He couldn't find the mask on the floor anymore and assumed the vampire had managed to retrieve it, but he wasn't feeling bold enough to try and fix it on the monster's face. Meanwhile, the Alkonost was searching through the thick black smoke, sniffing and turning wildly to try and find the vampire among the madness. It was true—somehow, the Alkonost seemed less like it was aiming to kill.

Unless...

"Gotta go. Get over here, please!" Gyldan coughed, the heat rising and clinging painfully to his flushing skin. Gyldan pocketed his phone and crawled out after Luca. The vampire was already patting along the wall to find the front door. He opened it, and much to Gyldan's surprise, turned to usher him out first.

The pair staggered out, coughing and gasping into the fresh air.

"C-*close*! Lo-*ack*! *Lock*!" Luca commanded, doubled over with his hands on his thighs. Soot and blood were stippled all over his face and suit, yet he somehow had the energy to give a cheeky grin to Gyldan despite panting. "Pity I couldn't... get the mask on him... but that was nowhere near as bad as I thought it would be..."

"Because I put him off," Gyldan snapped back, wiping sweat from his forehead and glancing at his now soot-smeared hand. The Daedalus employees, Walter, Gyldan himself. It made sense now. "The Alkonost... it follows whatever thought Albion last had before transforming. I told him killing you would solve nothing. He must have paused to consider that before the transformation finished. I just saved your life."

He does listen to me after all, a small, hopeful voice dared to mutter in the back of his heart.

Luca's mouth dropped, the tips of his fangs poking out from under pale lips. Then, he swung a hand back to the house.

"*That* was saving my life? Dear God, what kind of violent lifestyle do you consider safe, boy?"

"He was protecting me, but he wasn't trying to kill you because I asked him not to," Gyldan stood firm. "Thought you seemed the type to honour an owed debt."

Luca's face crumpled with irritation, but he was quick to relent with a sigh.

"Oh, what do you want then?" he groaned, though he kept sniffing towards the house. "Anything to put a little more distance between me and your guard-gargoyle."

"You're going to help us find Yanatha," Gyldan said, watching the windows of the house for any sign of the Alkonost. Part of him wanted to see it there to know Albion was safe. Another part hoped its shadow wasn't standing among the billowing smoke, trapped within the burning building. "And you're going to help us stop her."

"Teamwork? I shudder at the thought." Luca turned his nose up and faced the mansion again. "Can we please leave that thing in the fire?"

"No. I've phoned for help. We've subdued Albion before, and we can do it again. Should be easier this time with your *safety net*." Gyldan started hobbling around the house to peer in through the kitchen window in search of the Alkonost.

"You know what this does?" Luca asked from behind Gyldan. He didn't need to turn around to know the vampire had the mask in his hands again.

"Albion said you worked on it together. That it was a failure 'cause it turned the wearer into a vegetable."

"...More or less. A vampire and a werewolf's abilities rely on emotion at their base. I thralled every piece of mirror on this mask to reflect an emotion away."

Gyldan looked over at the vampire then, noticing the mask properly for the first time. As Luca turned it in his hands, mirrors glinted not only on the outside of the mask but the inside too. "When I saw that creature on the news, I suspected my dear sister's genetics would be involved. That I would need her unused mask to defend myself if I were to confront Yanatha about it. Still... something feels *off* about our lovely Albion."

Luca stopped feeling across the mask's mirrored surface, tilting his head towards Gyldan. "If that is what Yanatha has been working on, it doesn't seem so much as a step forward as a step to the side. I wonder... if dear Albion is merely a prototype himself." Luca lifted the mask—the prototype of the eye-guards and trap-collars—and gave it a wave to emphasise his point. Gyldan didn't rise to the bait, turning instead to look back inside the house. Something was moving in the smoke, certainly large enough to be the Alkonost. If the spreading fire concerned it, it was in no hurry to leave.

The vampire went on: "After all, he's just a feral human really. Like the rest of you, he'd tear the world apart to protect a tiny handful of people just because they're important to him personally. How selfish... how human. How *flawed*."

A voice that did not belong to Luca answered, echoing painfully in Gyldan's head:

"*Precisely...*"

From the vampire's puzzled expression, Luca had heard the strange voice too. Before Gyldan could question it, however, the world around him surged away, bleeding of colour and swirling into a grey mush without detail. Gyldan panicked, stepping forward, hands out to search for anything that could tell him where he was.

"Don't panic. Have you never been thralled before? How lucky."

Hearing the voice again, Gyldan realised it was familiar.

"...Yanatha?"

"You will have to be patient with me. I've never done this before. See what I see... join me in my memories."

The world around Gyldan began to melt and reform—buildings became walls, trees became furniture, shadows became people, all without colour.

"What are you doing? Where are we? What—" Gyldan yammered, spinning on the spot and trying to take in his shifting surroundings.

"Pity. I thought Luca would be here too. Perhaps it will take time to develop across the other species. No matter. I will show you for now. I think it's important for you to know. For you to see. My father never could... but you? You have something my father doesn't."

As Yanatha's disembodied voice spoke, one of the shadows built up to become the perfect reflection of her father. Gyldan staggered back, unable to tear himself away from the odd doppelgänger. The copy's hair was darker, his face less lined, but Gyldan recognised Albion standing before him all the same. Beside Albion, a young boy was holding a piece of paper up to the man, bouncing up and down on his feet to get Albion's attention. Behind him, a beautiful woman was sitting at a grey table, braiding the hair of a young Yanatha, who was sitting on a chair and letting her legs swing to and fro.

Gyldan realised who the young boy must be, and questions appeared when he dared to speak.

"Al? Where are we?" Gyldan asked, earning a chuckle from Yanatha.

"This isn't real. Just a puppet. We're going to put on a show for you."

The carefully crafted room shattered into utter chaos—a window to Albion's left exploded, and young Caladrius at his side was knocked forward. The doppelgänger of Albion, stunned, caught the boy mid-fall, crumpling to his knees and cradling Caladrius in his arms. Blood crept out from the huddled pair and across the colourless floor.

Gyldan stepped back as the blood oozed towards him, frantically trying to both watch and look away from the horrible scene. It was then that he spotted her—a young Yanatha's tiny figure huddled in the corner with her mother. Through the shattered window, people poured into the room, vampires and werewolves. Most went straight for Albion, tearing the bleeding boy from his arms and throwing him aside. Caladrius hit the far wall, sliding down, still moving, weeping, an arm reaching for his father. Albion scrambled towards him but was dragged back with ease by the assailants, disappearing behind a blockade of bodies. His wife darted out towards Caladrius but was shoved back by the attackers.

"*My brother was still alive*," Yanatha narrated the scene with a detached calmness that did not belong here. "*He would have survived the bullet wound... had my parents been strong enough to fight back against these non-humans. But they couldn't. Time wasted away...*"

Gyldan wanted to close his eyes, but to do so felt like it would be an insult. The attack went on, security pouring into the room, and as the seconds ticked by into minutes, Caladrius' movements slowed. Finally, just as the combined efforts of Albion's security and his own ferocity pushed the attackers to retreat, Caladrius went limp, eyes clouding and unfocused.

"*Caladrius died that day. I remember everyone being very concerned for me afterwards.*"

The scene twisted like a kaleidoscope, the pieces coming to rest in a different room. Young Yanatha was sitting on the edge of her bed next to a shellshocked Albion.

"I wish I could do something to make this right, Yan," Albion said, shoulders slumped in defeat. "I wish... I could make this better for you."

"...You could make a cure," the young girl said resolutely, not looking at her father. "I want you to cure the world, Dad. So, no one has to die like Caladrius anymore."

Albion's eyebrows raised a little in shock before a proud half-smile lightened his face.

"A cure? Wow, that's... that's pretty huge, Yanatha."

"Will you promise? Promise to cure the world so no one else dies like Caladrius."

Albion hesitated, then pulled his daughter into an embrace with one arm. He nuzzled his face down against the top of her head, but Yanatha did not even lift her arms to return the hug.

"I promise..."

"*I suppose I ought to have been clearer, in hindsight.*" The older Yanatha regarded the scene from somewhere above it all. "*My father promised me a cure. But he failed to deliver, chasing after some absurd notion of curing vampires and werewolves and turning them into something as pathetic as we are. As if that would solve anything. My brother died because none of us were strong enough. Humans make tools to progress, Gyldan, and we are long overdue making a new tool—a cure for our remaining weaknesses. It was easier to just do it myself than to try to explain to him. Still, he got to keep his promise, in a way... by being my test subject.*"

Again, the scene spiralled in and out of focus, but this time, showing snapshots of many memories Gyldan could barely keep up with. Yanatha pouring something over one of two plates before turning and setting them down on the dining room table; sprinkling something into a glass at Albion's side; pouring out medication from a tub and refilling it with different pills.

"Th-this is..." Gyldan didn't know where to look, what to do. He could only watch as the scenes continued to whirl before him.

"*Necessary,*" Yanatha concluded for him. "*Still, the recent tests prove he is a failure. A monster with no sentience. Hardly a cure for humanity. I'm not here to trade our self-awareness for brute* strength. No... I want it all, Gyldan. Luca is right—the creature Albion has become is a sidestep for humanity. But I've been working away, watching, investigating... and I have figured out the missing component."

The image before Gyldan shattered, leaving nothing but a white void all around him.

"Yanatha?"

"...It's me. I'm the ascension this cure needs. You know, I've never really felt much for anyone. Family. Friends. For a while, I thought I was broken. But I'm not. I'm just one step higher than the rest... the link between you and the next stage of our species."

"Why... why are you doing this? Why are you telling me this?" Gyldan yelled up to the white sky above.

"Because you joined Caladrius for a reason, didn't you? At some point, Gyldan, you felt it too. Something my father has never felt—a weakness for being human. A desire to change it. No, don't tell me..."

Once more, the grey stage built up before Gyldan: a home nestled near the forest, a full moon above. Sterlyn running home, fear pushing him onwards, too late, the moonlight boiled his blood, bringing rage, bringing—the werewolf.

A single lapse in judgement, a moment of carelessness... a home torn apart by a wild, silver-furred werewolf.

"No... no, you don't... you don't get to..." Gyldan put his hands over his ears, shutting his eyes against the images. "Not that!"

"You wished you were stronger that day too. I understand, Gyldan. Truly, I do. We're not so different, are we? Strange. Maybe this is empathy. Isn't that funny that I should feel that now?"

Screams echoed into the false night; his own from years ago—a silver werewolf bounding from the house and out into the forest, why had he not killed him too?

"We can be stronger, Gyldan. Equals. I will cure humanity, bring us from this disgusting larval form to something greater. Something stronger. Something perfect. Even physically weaker, look *at all we have achieved. We're destined for this. We've earned this. We've struggled and fought to stay at the top. Now... I will be the spark to ignite our final stage of—"*

Something cold pressed into Gyldan's face, and Yanatha's voice cut out sharply. So too did all of his fears, his hammering heart screeching to a halt almost painfully. A sudden, dizzying wall of calm slammed into Gyldan, and it took a moment for him to come to his senses enough to realise that he was looking out of the eyeholes of a mask...

...looking at Luca's scarred and hollowed eye sockets.

"Ah! It worked! So *that's* why Albion kept it... ah, apologies—I was stunned by the most awful headache for a moment there," Luca said, patting Gyldan on the shoulder. It wasn't reassuring. It wasn't irritating.

It wasn't anything.

"Luca?" Gyldan asked, muffled by the mask.

"I suspect this might be a tale best shared around a cup of tea. Your friends ought to be here soon. As for our dear Albion—it appears he chose to exit through a window," Luca said, turning Gyldan to face the shattered kitchen window, glass sprinkled between the blades of grass on the lawn and glittering like dew. "That I am still alive means he must have new orders. She thralled you too? Oh Lord... she's perfected her cure, hasn't she?"

Chapter 17

    If it wasn't for the mask still fastened to his face, Gyldan was sure the impromptu tea party in his living room would have been awkward. The mask of mirrors pressed cold and heavy against his skin, a suffocating sense of calm forcing its way through his mouth, his nose, his very pores. He made a weak attempt to feel anything, but the mirror's shining surface refused to let it escape, reflecting every emotion harmlessly away at all angles, scattered in silence.

    It might have been a perfect hell, standing in the middle of an emotional void. But to Gyldan, it was a lonely heaven. The last few weeks had been a painful and hellish storm. The mask's repression was a welcome alternative to crushing guilt and frenzied panic.

    For a blissful while, Gyldan felt nothing at all.

    It was no doubt why Gyldan felt comfortable enough to sit next to Luca.

Luca set his teacup down on its saucer, the delicate chiming of the porcelain crashing like a shriek in the silence. He had taken it upon himself to update the others of their encounter with the Alkonost and the need for Gyldan to be protected by the mask for now, its ability to reflect emotions working both inwardly and outwardly across its shining surfaces. But it hadn't escaped Gyldan that Luca had opted to gloss over some aspects.

He wasn't angry about that though.

He wasn't upset.

He wasn't anything.

Seraph was standing at the edge of the room, leaning her shoulder into the doorframe, arms folded across her chest.

"And why were you there?" she pressed Luca.

Luca cleared his throat, but Gyldan interjected:

"He is working with Yanatha to eradicate humans. But she took their project down another route—she isn't going to kill us all. She is going to change every human into a higher being. The Alkonost was a failed experiment," Gyldan said, his voice steady, slow, and monotonous. Luca pressed his lips tight, the slight colour he held there flushing away.

"Yes, well, *thank you* for that, dear heart," Luca huffed, waving one hand. "Yes, yes, it is as he says. But, crucially, Yanatha and I have terminated our partnership due to creative differences. I am here to help protect my fellow vampires from her madness, nothing more. Do not mistake my being here as a change of heart. I have no desire to work to save humans."

Gyldan shifted in his seat, his listless gaze wandering to the window.

"You saved me with the mask," he pointed out without malice. "You put the mask of mirrors on me to shield me from Yanatha. You saved a human."

Luca, who had lifted his teacup once again to his lips, coughed and choked. He put it back on the table and pulled a handkerchief out of his ruined tuxedo jacket, dabbing the corners of his mouth.

"Yes, well, you scratched my back, so I scratched yours. I would be more concerned about what it *means* that she could thrall you, and less about discerning my moral compass."

Rukshana had been sitting in quiet thought, a finger trailing over her lips. She pulled her hand away to answer Luca's proposed concern.

"Yanatha has perfected her cure and used it on herself."

"And gained my darling sister's all-encompassing ability to thrall. As well as, presumably, whatever it is the dogs do," Luca added with a flippant gesture towards Seraph, earning himself a sharp-toothed snarl. "I suspect the change is gradual. Right now, Yanatha's ability clearly extends to her own kind. Her attempt to thrall me at the same time did little more than give me a migraine. I imagine it will only be a matter of time, however…"

"You imagine?" Seraph's face scrunched up in disbelief and distaste. "C'mon. You *worked* with her. You didn't look at the cure once?"

Luca sighed, acting as though the question were incredibly droll.

"When you look at a liquid, can you rattle off every ingredient and effect it might have? No. I think not. I left the science to her—I was a money fund and material gatherer. Nothing more."

Unrest rolled over the group like a wave, which crashed against Gyldan's immovable heart as it reached him. He was aware of nervous looks cast his way from Rukshana, Seraph, and Griffin, but it didn't bother him. He knew it should. But it just didn't.

"Well, I'm guessing you can't make a few billion of those masks to keep us all shielded from her," Griffin said, nodding over at Gyldan. "So, we need a plan. What's she got, what have we got, and how do we fight her?"

Seraph shook her head, pushing away from her guard-stance at the door to walk into the room properly. Not once did she shift her icy focus from Luca, though the blind vampire was either unaware or unconcerned.

"Hold up. How do we trust a single word this guy says? Yanatha wouldn't have gotten this far without his gullible ass."

"And my handsome bank account, don't forget that!" Luca added with a cheeky grin. "I'm much more than a trusting soul, dear heart."

The werewolf turned to Rukshana for support.

"You get me?"

Rukshana nodded once.

"She has a point. For all we know, this is a trap. Another way for your wayward business partner to take her testing to the next level."

Luca pushed out his bottom lip, making a motion that was somewhere between a nod and a one-shouldered shrug.

"I can see why you might think that. I suppose a display of goodwill without a debt being repaid could be in order. Tell me— you both sound critical, jaded, and otherwise sceptical of authority. Are you a younger generation of non-human, perchance?"

Luca finished off his tea with one large, loud sip, ignoring Seraph's growling.

"Yeah. What of it?" she asked, though her scowl loosened just a touch.

Setting his cup aside for the last time, Luca straightened up and shuffled to the edge of his seat. He interlaced his fingers and stretched his arms out, cracking the knuckles.

"Then you will have had Caladrius-grade trap-collars and eye-guards fitted when you were children, yes? Objects are my friends, my dear. Perhaps I can help you with your little problem, and then you can help me with my larger problem, hmm?"

No one moved. No one spoke. Gyldan was left to struggle with the odd sensation that he should be shocked, excited, and yet, being completely unmoved by Luca's insinuation.

"You... you can... you can take these off?" Seraph spluttered, hooking a finger around one of the iron bands of her collar, stupefied. "Without triggering them?"

"Mm-hmm!" Luca gave an enthusiastic nod. "They are designed to be attached and to be removed so that you can replace them as you grow, are they not? So long as it is within an object's ability to do so, I can command it."

All Gyldan could think about was stampeding chairs.

Seraph, meanwhile, hesitated. She turned to Rukshana, and the pair had a wordless conversation within the span of mere moments. Then, the werewolf took a step towards Luca.

"I'll go first," she said, sitting herself down on the floor in front of him. "That way, if you do set it off... I can die knowing what kind of mess Rukshana and Griffin will make of your skeleton."

"Rude, but fair," Luca replied, shifting even further forward and hunching down to the woman sitting on the floor in front of him. He put a hand either side of the trap-collar, the silver band harmless to him. "Truth be told, I would rather deal with trap-collars. Silver isn't a worry, but on the off-chance those horrid UV emitters go off on an eye-guard, I might be reduced to a pile of dust myself!"

"Yeah, yeah, what a hero, get on with it," Seraph muttered, rolling her eyes.

The vampire tutted under his breath, but around a long-suffering drawl, he commanded the collar: "*Unfasten*, please."

In just two words, Luca achieved what the group had been fighting for for years.

The collar fell away from Seraph's neck.

Luca lifted the collar up, holding it between his finger and thumb, then dropped it unceremoniously to the carpet.

"Now then, the eye-guard. Sadly, my dear, yours won't be as effortless. I do hope you have some painkillers in the house."

Seraph paled and turned to Rukshana, but Rukshana did not seem phased. She got up from her seat and nodded to her girlfriend for them to switch around.

"What do you—?" Seraph asked, getting to her feet, one hand investigating her own collar-less throat as the other tentatively brushed Rukshana's shoulder.

Rukshana knelt down in front of Luca where Seraph had been sitting moments before.

"I understand," the vampire said. "I have had the eye-guard replaced several times growing up. It is never a pleasant sensation to have the bolts removed."

Luca splayed his fingers, feeling around the edge of Rukshana's eye-guard. In the corner of the room, Griffin silently got up and headed into the kitchen. Soon after, the sound of cupboards opening and packets rattling told them he was putting together a makeshift first aid kit.

"At least this time, I shan't be putting new bolts back in over freshly healed skin," Luca said almost kindly. "But this is certainly going to sting."

Griffin came back into the room then, carrying a few small white boxes in one hand and a glass of dark red liquid in the other. He set them down on the coffee table behind Rukshana, then sat himself back down on the sofa next to the fidgeting Seraph.

"You want me to hold your hand? Or just, I dunno, sit with you?" Seraph asked. Rukshana only shook her head in response, and Seraph's expression became pained, her want to do something to help clearly squirming under her skin.

"Go ahead, Luca," Rukshana said, closing her eyes. It didn't escape Gyldan's notice that her hands balled into fists within her lap.

Luca nodded, then said: "*Unfasten*, please."

The six steel bolts framing the eye-guard each began spinning counter-clockwise, unwinding from the bone of Rukshana's eye sockets with a dull, crunching whirl. The vampire huffed through her nose, her lips pressed together tightly, but she did not utter another sound. Even as the bolts began to drop to the floor, covered in her blood, she did not flinch.

Soon, the fastenings fell away, and the ruby lens joined the bolts on the floor by Rukshana's knees.

Rukshana opened her eyes, blinking away the rivulets of blood that trickled down from her brow and over her eyelashes, mingling with her unspilt tears. Angry bruises blotted around the slowly closing holes where the bolts had been removed.

"Seraph?" Rukshana called out, her voice a touch lighter than usual. "I'll... I'll have that hand-holding now."

***

The room had swirled and resettled around him a few times now, but Gyldan had not moved an inch from his comfortable old armchair. He had no desire to speak to anyone, though something burning in his chest forced him to at least inquire as to how Rukshana was doing.

"She'll be fine," Seraph had replied as she fidgeted in her next to the sleeping vampire laid across the sofa. Gyldan knew the barely hidden discomfort was not just her fretting for Rukshana. It was caused by him too.

He didn't mind.

Instead, Gyldan turned to Luca.

"Why don't you just do that for everyone?" Gyldan asked, pointing at the discarded trap-collar and eye-guard on the floor.

"Because there are billions of vampires and werewolves, my sweet," Luca said, as though he were explaining something dreadfully easy to someone astoundingly dull. "Assuming I did not sleep or eat again, it would take me around 400 years non-stop to remove all of the devices out there. Hardly the most efficient route. And I do so enjoy a nice drink now and then."

"...So, the release codes are still the most efficient way..." Gyldan mumbled, going back to the still waters of his mind. They had gotten so close. It felt like years had passed since he had directed Griffin and Caelan into Albion's office.

It did not seem possible that his life would settle enough to try again. That Albion would ever let someone into his office again.

"Quite. But we should take care of the more *pressing* impossible task before setting up another," Luca said.

To Gyldan's right, Griffin had perched himself on the arm of the chair, having given up his seat on the faded brown sofa to let Rukshana lie down.

"Dealing with Yanatha. So, what, do you think this cure of hers will have changed her like Albion?" Griffin asked. His hands twisted and turned around the purple silk he had removed from his face. After all, Luca couldn't see him.

Luca shrugged.

"To a more refined degree. If he is a failure, one must assume the perfected version would still see some change to her form. Abilities of all, possibly a few new ones tapped from previously locked paths of potential human ability. It's quite the conundrum. Do we wait and see what she becomes to deal with that, or attack her blind and hope we catch her before it gets worse? At the very least, she can thrall humans right now, and depending on how many she can sway, that could be quite the army."

Again, Gyldan was subject to the peculiar sensation of being aware he should be panicked, worried, concerned, yet unable to feel anything beyond sheer, glassy calm. It was as if he were watching a scene unfold before him, a movie of his life that he was floating an arm's reach away from, safe in the audience.

Griffin gave a heavy sigh to Gyldan's right, shifting on his perch.

"What about silver? UV? If she's splicin' up our DNA for her crazy experiments, is she getting our weaknesses as well as our abilities?"

Luca shook his head.

"Yanatha is obsessed with achieving perfection," the vampire explained. "It seems unlikely she would allow our imperfections to be part of her life's work. Besides, even Albion, who she deems a botched prototype, has been bounding around as an Alkonost in broad daylight."

"He wears a silver ring on his right index finger too," Gyldan commented, earning everyone's attention in one muted mumble. "Hasn't bothered him."

Opposite him, Rukshana stirred on the well-worn sofa. The leather creaked as she sat up, one hand lifting cautious fingers to dust over where the bolts had been around her eye sockets. Seraph's immediate reaction was to lean forward, a hand on Rukshana's shoulder, all focus now entirely on her.

"Hey, woah, take it easy there," Seraph said. "You just got a load of metal taken out of your face. You can have a lie down for more than ten minutes, y'know."

Rukshana twisted around to Seraph, the corner of her mouth tugging in a tired half-smile. Deep purple marks blotted her dark skin in increments around her eye sockets, framing her now-unshielded rose irises. Curiosity sparkled them, and the vampire moved a little closer to Seraph, studying her.

"How strange," Rukshana muttered, tilting her head ever so slightly. "I can... almost feel you in my head."

"Ah! That'll be your abilities," Griffin chuckled. "I guess you haven't felt your own thralling ability since you were a kid. Yeah, get used to that. You kind of have an... awareness of people around you that you can thrall. Like a weird heat-map in y'head, or pressure in the air nearby. S'why I always know where Seraph and Gyldan are, even with this on." He waved the silk eye-wrap in his hand. "Probably feel weird to start with, and it can be a nightmare in crowds. That's why a lot of vampires just stick with their own kind—our ability doesn't work on other vampires."

"My heart bleeds for you," Luca drawled, curling his lip into a sneer. "You don't know a *migraine* until you've been *me* in an IKEA..."

Rukshana turned from Seraph to Griffin and Luca in turn.

"Yes... I can't feel it with you two..." she murmured. A soft frown pulled at her brow as she looked then at Gyldan. "But I can't feel you right now either. That mask is perplexing..."

"It's just doing as I asked," Luca crowed, crossing one leg over his knee and lacing his fingers together. "Every fragment reflects emotion away, whether it is coming from the wearer or from outside. Our ability to thrall is powered by emotions, and lo, it is deflected into the aether."

The blond vampire unlaced one hand to twirl it up into the air above his head. "No harm done, though as you can see, it is hardly practical for everyday use."

"Perhaps not," Rukshana agreed, pushing up on one arm to sit up straight, still watching Gyldan as though he were an interesting museum exhibit. He didn't mind. "But then Yanatha isn't our everyday problem."

"You... wanna try and get the mask on Yanatha?" Seraph asked, getting up off the floor to sit down on the sofa next to Rukshana.

"Whatever she's done to herself, if she's using vampire and werewolf genes to do it, her abilities will stem from the same source—emotions. The mask nullifies that both ways. If we can subdue her and get the mask on her, any abilities she has taken from us will be void."

Griffin slid from his perch on the arm of Gyldan's chair and plodded over to the window, hands shoved in the pockets of his jeans. The setting sun spilt burnt-orange hues over his face, highlighting the spikes of white and grey stubble that had grown longer than usual over the course of a frantic few days.

"That's the hard part sorted," he said, turning to look up at the sky, the wrinkles on his forehead deepening. "Now the even harder part—finding the lass."

* * *

Their discussions went through the evening as rapidly as Luca went through Rukshana's favourite box of blood tea. It was around the time discussions turned to the likelihood of a vampire being able to thrall Yanatha that Gyldan had excused himself.

He had no answers, only questions. Questions he was sure his friends could not answer any sooner than Gyldan could answer theirs.

Weariness thickened his bones as he dragged himself up the stairs to his room. Every step felt like an effort, and Gyldan was mutely conscious that this was likely down to the mask. He had been running on fumes of late, and the coal providing those fumes had been a blaze of emotions and fears. Without them, Gyldan had nothing left to spur himself on.

He trudged into his room and kicked his brogues off without untying the laces. Bashing into his office chair, Gyldan lumbered over to his unmade bed, dropping into the wrinkled navy sheets without any attempt to get under the duvet first. His masked face hit a bundle of scrunched up pyjamas he had left on top of his pillow that morning. He had half a mind to just stay where he was, to lie there and listen to the rain tapping a soothing song outside his window as he drifted off.

But then again, Gyldan had his face buried in dirty laundry.

It wasn't sitting well with him.

Gyldan pushed them aside and let his head sink into the pillows. That he should smell Albion's earthy scent rise from them took him by surprise, but not nearly as much as what that familiar fragrance did to his heart.

It fluttered.

Strange, Gyldan thought to himself, letting the aroma cradle his dazed head as his heart settled to a steady beat once more. *That was almost...*

A knock behind him drew Gyldan away from his sombre thoughts. It might have alarmed him, especially as the knock was less civilised and more a frantic pounding against his window, a harsh word mumbled behind glass.

Gyldan stirred and rolled onto his side to look over at the source of the sound. It was odd to be so at ease with a situation that would normally have petrified him.

There, crouched in a precarious balancing act on the windowpane, a palm pressed against the glass, was Albion. Rain wept over his bedraggled form, darkening his silver locks and smearing them flat against his head. Droplets on the glass distorted him like a kaleidoscope, but Gyldan knew well enough that it had to be Albion.

Who else would clamber to his window? Who else could?

Gyldan got out of bed and went to the window. He hesitated, one finger coiled over the latch.

"...Gyldan, *please,*" Albion begged. "We... I..."

His voice cracked, a strain of exhaustion and confusion knocking Albion's usually dulcet tones out of tune. He let his head hang forward, palm still resting against the glass, rain dripping from his fringe. "I got it all wrong, Gyl... God, I... I didn't think... I thought I had it. But I was so far away..."

Gyldan unhooked the latch, the sound of rain sharpening and swelling into the room. The window swung open, and for the first time, Gyldan could see how unsteadily Albion was balanced, his bare toes curled to find any semblance of grip on the rain-slicked window ledge.

Gyldan stepped aside, watching as the drenched man dropped into the room with a clumsy stagger. Wet footprints stained the wooden floor like spilt paint, a trail of raindrops following Albion from outside over the windowsill. He was shirtless and shivering, arms now wrapped around his midriff. Purple and jade bruises covered his body, gathering around his joints in particular. His shoulders were a mess of welts, his upper back raw and red with freshly healed skin.

Gyldan simply pushed past him to close the window, absently straightening the photo frames on the windowsill that Albion had knocked over like a selfish cat being let back in.

"G-G-Gyl?" Albion stammered, sniffing and shaking a drop of rain from his long nose. "What... what are you wearing th-that thing for?"

"Yanatha thralled me," Gyldan explained, heading over to the wardrobe at the far side of the room. "The mask stopped her."

Without warning, Gyldan pulled out a black towel and threw it at Albion. From the indignant noise that came his way, Albion had caught it with his face. "You're dripping on the floor."

Albion began sloppily rubbing the towel over his arms, but it wasn't long before the man's knees buckled. He crumpled to the floor in a trembling heap, leaving the towel tangled under him.

"Gyl... I... I don't know what's happening... I was... at the house? With you? And-and Luca, and then... then Yanatha was there. No, no not there." Albion shook his head, his voice rising as he talked himself in tangles. "But I... I knew where she was? I could... I don't know. Sense her? But... but when I found her, she was... surprised to see me. Gyl, she, she didn't even care that I was there, she didn't care that I *knew* what she'd done. I..."

Albion looked up, his face blotched red, sparkling tears bringing life to an otherwise drained and dull complexion. "How can I fix this? How did I get it all so *wrong?*"

A thousand answers void of emotion rattled behind Gyldan's teeth, a prisoner to his manners for now.

Because you're arrogant. Because you're cruel. Because you're elitist.

Because you're you.

But while the mask of mirrors had robbed Gyldan of his emotions, it had not robbed him of who he was.

Gyldan was not arrogant. He was not cruel. He was not elitist.

He was Gyldan.

And he was better than that.

Gyldan squatted down in front of the sobbing wreck of a man, arms resting on his knees.

"Is Yanatha nearby?" he asked.

Albion shook his head.

"N-no... no, she's at the pier... warehouses there, miles away."

Gyldan nodded once, then raised his hands to his own face, the cold, fractured surface of the mask pressing sharp edges into his fingertips.

Griffin had said targets he could thrall could be sensed nearby. Gyldan could only hope Yanatha's borrowed ability followed some of the same rules. Perhaps now was as good a time as any to do a little experiment of their own.

"...Will you put the mask back on me if she thralls me?" he asked.

Albion's lips parted, a few half-formed words dancing wordlessly across cold-stained lips. But whatever he wanted to protest died there, and he nodded.

With that, Gyldan took off the mask.

Immediately, the sorry sight of a dishevelled and scared Albion shattered Gyldan's heart before it could even reform. He dropped the mask aside, hands clamping on Albion's injured shoulders. The man hissed, but he didn't flinch away.

"Albion! Are you okay? Listen, you have to help us stop her, we can try to fix everything, okay, we can do it together." Gyldan babbled out everything he hadn't realised he had wanted to say. The realisation that Albion had admitted he was wrong blessed him with hope, with a sense of victory that the man he loved was everything Gyldan had believed he was in the end.

Albion had proved Gyldan right. He *was* a good man, deep down. He *could* be made to see that—

"Stop her?" Albion frowned. "But... Gyl, she's got it *right*. I had it all wrong... so wrong. My own daughter hates me... I let her down. She wanted me to cure the world and I failed her. I... I must fix it. I must help her do what I couldn't."

Once again, Gyldan was left to freefall through blistering disappointment. He drew his hands away from Albion, a sickly wave rising in his throat.

"What?" It was the only word Gyldan could pluck from his mismatch of anger and grief.

Albion shifted to sit up, pulling away from Gyldan.

"I spent my whole life weakening people who could hurt us. You said it yourself, it wasn't fair. Hurting them to keep us all on the ground. But Yan? She could see that wasn't the problem. The problem is that we're being left behind, Gyl. She's going to let us all soar. No more eye-guards, no more trap-collars, just like you wanted, tiger! But for that to happen, for us to be safe— humans need to be stronger."

"What, like you? Albion, you can't even remember what happens when you transform. You've *killed* people," Gyldan spluttered, straightening up and stepping away. "Seriously, you want everyone to go through that?"

"You haven't *seen* her, Gyl," Albion protested, rocking back and tightening his grip around his torso. "It's not like the mess I am... it's... it's *perfect*. It solves everything... her, you, society. It fixes everything, we won't have to fear them anymore. We don't have to rely on cages. I thought you'd be happy."

"*Happy?* Albion... I was happy when I thought you had finally opened your fucking eyes! When I thought you had realised what you're doing is crazy!" Months of reserved anger frothed forth from within Gyldan and unshackled his tongue. "But no, no, of course not! You *know* Yanatha's plan is crazy. Humans aren't weaker, you're the *last* person who would accept that! We're different! We're creative and adaptive a-a-and we endure, and we build. We don't need to change who we are. We just need to remember our hearts. Jesus, God, why is it so hard to believe there has to be a better way for everyone to live together without trying to change every difference in each other? Why can't we just—?"

Gyldan's own ranting dragged him before an internal wall he wasn't ready to surmount yet. It was one he had encountered a number of times before, one that stopped him dead in his tracks.

A small part of him that knew he wasn't quite correct. That there was one person who did indeed need to change.

"I'm a monster, Gyl. A-a *failure*." Albion's sombre confession rumbled over the sharp silence that grew between them like thorns, the last word spoken as if he were unsure of the pronunciation. "I can't be saved. I just... wanted to save you. I know I didn't change the world. I changed *their* world to suit mine. But Yanatha's going build a new world. I... don't want you to be left behind."

It was almost romantic. It was almost heartfelt. It was a gesture of love delicately wrapped in barbed wire.

Gyldan turned to Albion, jolting back as he came face-to-face with the man who had evidently gotten up and closed the distance between them silently. That once-comforting, earthy scent of amber still pierced through the damp that clung to him.

"Albion," Gyldan spoke in hushed tones, splintered hope cutting his words. "I... I don't think I need you to save me. I need... *me* to do that."

To save me from you.

A sad smile mourned what was now lost between them, and a calloused hand brushed lightly against Gyldan's cheek. For a short while, the two men stood in the middle of this chessboard, meeting in the middle yet still on opposite sides. Their stalemate had gone on long enough. It was time to sweep the pieces away and end the game.

"...Can we just pretend we're still in love?" Albion asked abruptly, his speech roughened by a painful acceptance. "Just for five minutes."

Gyldan closed his eyes, a minute twist of his head bringing him a touch closer to nuzzling into Albion's hand.

He wasn't sure why he pushed himself up onto his tiptoes to capture Albion's lips in his own. But now he knew a kiss goodbye wasn't like it seemed in movies and books. The stars didn't shine brighter, the world did not right itself, and hearts did not mend.

It just hurt more.

Chapter 18

An unspoken truce honouring their time together gave Albion the chance to slip back out into the night. Gyldan allowed himself a minute to come to terms with what had happened, to try and settle his heart.

One minute, then he would go downstairs and tell everyone what he had learnt. One minute, then he would be fine.

One minute, then one of those things would become true.

Gyldan moved on basic necessity alone, a dull set of instructions forcing his limbs to shift.

Pick up the mask.
Walk out the door.
Walk down the stairs.

He was at the living room door by the time a scant few drips of colour began to return to his world. Gyldan inhaled, forcing the tightness that had wormed its way around his ribs to ease somewhat, then opened the door.

Griffin had shifted to occupy Gyldan's previous seat in his absence. Luca wasn't anywhere to be found, but the sound of over-jovial humming from the opposite door told him that the aristocrat was in the kitchen, no doubt brewing himself another drink or rummaging through Rukshana's stash of snacks.

Rukshana was kneeling by the coffee table, scribbling on a piece of paper—behind her, Seraph was sitting on the sofa, leaning so far forward to read over her girlfriend's shoulder that she was practically resting on Rukshana's back. The three in the living room acknowledged Gyldan's appearance, though none of them looked pleased.

"Dude, the mask!" Seraph yelped, flopping back onto the sofa and fixing a startled expression on Gyldan. "Woah, woah, woah, how do we tell if he's thralled?" She turned to Griffin in a half-panic, though the old vampire was already getting to his feet and heading over to Gyldan.

Gyldan held up his hands in surrender, the mirrored mask gleaming in his loose grip. He set it down on the coffee table near Rukshana's pile of papers, the mirrored surface of the mask dazzling under the electric light above.

"I'm not thralled. Remembered you saying about it feeling like a heat-map in your head for people nearby you can thrall... and Yanatha isn't nearby."

Griffin didn't reply but drew close to Gyldan and leered down. Ruby eyes met Gyldan's gaze, shifting sharply left and right, up and down, searching for signs Gyldan wasn't aware of. He stood perfectly still, wondering if that would help the other man with his investigation into his psyche. From this distance, Gyldan could make out each translucent hair on Griff's stubbled chin, the lines on his bronze skin, a tiny scar on his nose that Gyldan had never noticed before. His breath was sharp, metallic—he had drunk blood recently and it lingered.

"Aye, he's good," Griffin declared, smiling and ruffling Gyldan's hair. "And that's good to know, that her thrallin' is kinda like ours. You got that, Shana?"

"Already written it down," Rukshana muttered behind Griffin, pen scratching against the ink-crammed paper in front of her. "Distance is the same... confirmed she can thrall humans and fellow Alkonosts, unknown for werewolves... appears to be developing the ability to thrall vampires."

"A-actually, she can't thrall Al—er, the Alkonost. Or, we don't know," Gyldan interjected, his free hand gesturing to Rukshana for her attention. "Albion sensed her nearby after Luca burnt the house down. That's why he ran off to follow her. She didn't command him to come to her like we thought."

The pen was set down deliberately, carefully, and the spotlight shot to Gyldan. No one needed to ask. The question was dangling in the silence. Gyldan shifted from one foot to the other. "...Albion was at my window just now. He's... not doing good. Whatever Yanatha's experiments have done, it's messing him up. I... I let him in to talk for a second."

Seraph opened her mouth, no doubt to scorn Gyldan's softness, but Griffin swiftly interjected:

"And what did he tell you?"

"Just that. He sensed her, so he went looking for her. She was surprised, he said."

Griffin began to rub his chin, lips pursing, brows knotting. He angled himself towards Rukshana, a nod that set her off writing again.

"Interestin'... so maybe he can thrall too. Why's that just shown up now? He never tried it in the past with me or Seraph fightin' him."

"Quite obvious, dear heart!"

Luca returned from the kitchen, stirring a teaspoon held between his index finger and thumb, letting the metal trill against the china cup. "He didn't because he *couldn't*. The man's a *failed* Alkonost. Stands to reason his abilities are as botched as his beastly form is."

"But he sensed Yanatha?" Seraph said, rubbing a hand through her short blonde locks, making them stick up wilder still. "So... he can thrall humans?"

"Consider the timing, my sleuthing sidekick." Luca took the spoon out of his cup and waggled it at Seraph as though she were his student. "Albion transformed into the beast and spent a fair while chasing me around his house. Had he sensed his daughter from the start, he would have no doubt prioritised finding her over attempting to relieve me of my giblets. But, as Gyldan has said, he bolted the *moment he sensed her*—a good time after. So... what changed?"

Seraph scowled at him, though there was no anger at Luca so much as at herself. She then turned to Rukshana for answers.

Rukshana was tracing the tip of her pen around her lips, staring out into the distance. Suddenly, her focus snapped back.

"*Yanatha* did. He didn't sense her when he initially transformed because she was still human. The moment she became an Alkonost—"

"—our cuddly behemoth bounded away!" Luca grinned, twirling the spoon through his fingers in victory. "Lo, Albion never attempted to thrall anyone before now because there was no one he *could* thrall. I suspect Albion's botched ability is a reverse of the standard—his only works on his own kind. Such a mess. I suppose I ought to apologise, really."

The vampire put the spoon in his mouth, sucking the drops of cooling tea from it before adding: "No doubt the De Varis genes are to blame for that rather rubbish ability variation."

Seraph blinked, her face slacking as a thought visibly hit her.

"Wait, so... vampires sense what they can thrall. So... *you* can sense where objects are?" she asked, and Luca responded with an enthusiastic nod.

"Useful when one is blind," he added cheerily. "If it weren't for your clothes and what I assume to be bracelets or a watch on your wrist, I'd have no idea where you are."

At this, Seraph's face went pink, and she deflected back to their previous conversation.

"So, we just have to worry about Albion's claws, teeth, and full-moon-werewolf attitude, not his thralling skills?" Seraph concluded, one eyebrow arching in a show of disappointment. "Cool. Square one. Only there's *two* of them now. And we don't even know where to find them to stop them."

Despite saying this, Seraph began contemplating Gyldan with a smirk. She was followed by a less-thrilled looking Rukshana and a watchful Griffin.

Gyldan gulped, suddenly finding his socks very interesting.

"...Yeah, he let slip where Yanatha is too."

***

The roar of the motorbike tore most of Seraph's voice away from Gyldan, but he could tell from her cadence that she was asking the same question over her shoulder again.

"You sure you don't want to stay home with Luca?"

Gyldan nodded, catching the visor on his helmet against the back of Seraph's with a *click-clack*.

"I have to go with you," Gyldan shouted over the whipping wind and howling engine, the city streets blending away into neon abstract either side of them as they tore down the road towards the pier. "You might need me."

"Always need you, dude. Listen, I know he's a prime asshole but, er... I'm sorry you and Albion didn't work out." The words sounded awkward from Seraph, though the sincerity behind them made Gyldan's heart skip a beat in shock. "Don't get me wrong, I was *so pissed*. But... y'know... guess I kinda understand wanting to change someone's mind and help 'em see a new world."

"I'm sorry too." It felt all the better that he had to shout his apology to be heard, to really tear it through the air. "He hurt you guys. Falling for him was... I never expected it. I guess I'm kind of an asshole."

Seraph shook her head, pausing as they turned a corner, bike dipping low to the ground. Gyldan hugged into her back tighter, focusing on keeping his shoulders in line with the werewolf's.

"Nah man, you can't help who you fall in love with. Sometimes it's the last person you expect," Seraph said. "Their bullshit isn't a reflection on you. Who knows, in a different life, maybe all the nice things y'saw in Albion coulda made for a cool guy. Just not this one. His loss though. You're a good guy, Gyldan. Naïve. And a nerd. But good."

"...Thanks, Seraph." Gyldan was sure that she hadn't heard that. But it felt good the clear the air with her, and though he felt Seraph was being far too forgiving, Gyldan would never forget this. He made a silent note to redouble his efforts to help his friends.

Really, he already had. Despite a near-argument with Griffin before leaving for the pier, Gyldan had demanded to go with them to confront the Saint-Richters. If Luca was right, Yanatha might already be able to thrall vampires and maybe all other groups outside of her own newfound species. They were all as much at risk now as Gyldan was.

And there was only one mask of mirrors to shield them.

The mask was nestled in the khaki backpack that was bobbing on Gyldan's back as Seraph's motorbike hurtled along. Its creator had elected not to join them.

"As you well know, I'm not much of a fighter, dear heart," Luca had drawled as he settled into his comfy seat in the living room. "You cannot deny my brains have been useful, but I shall leave the upcoming fisticuffs to you. Besides—I'm only miffed Yanatha changed the goalposts of our project. I'm not about to get myself killed to help your lot. Best of luck though!"

Gyldan allowed a rare, self-assured smile to creep across his face behind the helmet. Luca had planned to simply don the mask he had worked so hard to recover and keep himself protected from Yanatha for the foreseeable, living out his lush and happy lifestyle without a care for the rest of the world.

Gyldan wondered if the vampire was throwing a tantrum right now, having realised the mask was no longer on the living room table.

* * *

The damp air carried the scent of sharp salt, burning Gyldan's nostrils as Seraph brought the motorbike to a halt at the pier's entrance. Above them, wingbeats grew to a crescendo, signalling the arrival of Griffin and Rukshana. As the pair landed, both elected to keep their wings folded neatly behind them.

Griffin made no effort to hide a disapproving look at Gyldan's presence, but he could have sworn he saw a glimmer of pride beneath the older man's displeasure.

"And y'won't just wait by the bike while we check this out?" Griffin pleaded one last time.

Gyldan lifted his leg up and over to get off the bike, fumbling to unfasten the clip at his chin.

"Nope. And you wouldn't want me to," Gyldan replied, pulling the helmet off and brushing back the wayward locks of black hair that dangled around the edges of his vision. "Exes or not, me and Albion have a connection."

Seraph made a retching noise behind him. "...*And* I might be able to use that to distract him," Gyldan continued with a pointed look at Seraph. "Slow him down. Buy us time. Who knows?"

The blonde gave him a snaggle-toothed grin.

"Gyl's gonna flutter his eyelashes at that old creep while I kick Yanatha's stuck-up ass." Seraph laughed, drawing up her arm and flexing. "Teamwork, am I right?"

"You're not kicking anyone's *ass* until we find her," Rukshana pointed out, glancing over at the warehouses that lined the industrial pier. Most were old and disused, with faded company logos scratched and sun-bleached away on their sides. Gyldan's stomach bubbled as he spotted one marked with Daedalus' logo, the memory of Walter's grim demise flashing up.

"Start with the Daedalus ones," Gyldan said, swallowing the bile down that crept up his gullet. "She was playing them for resources. If not, I know Caladrius hired a few of these a couple of years back to store the faulty E-Clips line…"

"Oh man, I was gutted that my collar change appointment didn't come up that year," Seraph noted, coming to join them after storing everything away on the bike. "One of my mates got an E-Clips collar and it *fell off*. He freaked out so bad that he actually turned himself in for a working one, the dumbass…"

"Eh well, he was lucky. That faulty mechanism had a 50-50 chance of either springing the iron band open or springing the silver band shut," Gyldan recounted, running a hand through his hair as he studied the sprawling docks. "Closest we ever came to getting shut down. People were legitimately angry, and not just werewolves. I kinda hoped that was a good sign. But people love to go back to normal almost as much as they love a dramatic shake-up from time to time."

He paused, squinting through the night at a movement nearby. A staggering, lurching shadow accompanied by the sound of bare feet across the splintered boards was coming towards them.

Before Gyldan could react, Rukshana and Griffin stepped in front of him, shielding him and blocking his view of Albion.

"That was quick," Griffin muttered despondently. "Guess he got a werewolf's nose in this deal."

Gyldan stepped to the side, watching over Rukshana's shoulder at Albion's approach. He looked even worse than when he had left Gyldan's room only a short time ago, though whether or not a transformation had torn through him again was unclear.

Night-darkened emeralds found Gyldan, a thread of crimson threatening through the whites of Albion's eyes as he pinned down his target.

"I thought it was you." Albion greeted him as though no one else was there, making Seraph huff in irritation. "Really wanted to believe it was *just* you."

"I'm not changing my mind, Al." Gyldan rejected him once more, his voice steadier than he felt. "I won't change me for you."

Albion scoffed at this, though the action appeared to drain him of whatever energy he had left, shoulders sagging.

"But you want me to," he pointed out. "You want me to change my mind about *their* kind. To let them all run free despite killing my little boy."

"That's not changing, Albion. I'm not asking you to become a forgiving person. There's nothing to forgive. They didn't kill Caladrius. No one's guilty of being the same species as a criminal, or we all would be. Me and you, are we guilty 'cause there are bad people within the human species too?"

Albion scoffed, and for a split second, his attention shifted from Gyldan's face to slightly over Gyldan's right shoulder and back.

"I'll grant you: I was wrong about humans," the man admitted, a tired arching of his eyebrow accompanied by a one-shouldered shrug. "I thought humans needed to be protected. But that wasn't it—humans need to be *perfected*. Vampires, werewolves, they just prove it—humans are a larval form. We're meant to become something new. Something *higher*."

"Oh good, he's gone completely batshit," Seraph said jauntily, cracking her knuckles. "Can I cut in on this dramatic monologue and knock your last marble out, dickhead?"

Albion's nose wrinkled in a thinly veiled response of disgust at Seraph, a lingering look on her collarless neck, but he didn't address her further. Instead, one final plea was dropped into Gyldan's hands.

"We want the same thing, Gyl. A better society for everyone. No more fighting, no more fear. This way, everyone gets to live."

Gyldan could only wait for the familiar wave of disappointment to crash over his battered soul. But this time, it didn't sweep him out to a sea of sorrow. This time, he stood his ground.

True, he wanted nothing more than to believe the illusion Albion was offering. He took a step back, distancing himself from the other man's words as they glanced off good intentions and landed in a twisted heap of cruelty. Gyldan wanted to be selfish enough to just believe Albion and rush back into the memory of their love—but he was glad he wasn't.

"I can see the good in you, Albion. I always have," Gyldan said. He shook his head. "But it's not my responsibility to prise it out of you."

The idea that he needed Gyldan for any such thing clearly sat ill with Albion. Or, perhaps it was the final rejection coupled with the sight of Gyldan's friends standing by his side that finally tipped Albion from irritation to anger, those tell-tale tremors wracking his body once more.

Griffin reacted first, lip curling above needle-like incisors.

"Oh no you don't! *Stay there!*" Griffin snarled, striding forward to bring the rapidly mutating man under his thrall. Perhaps Albion intended to throw an insult at the vampire, but all he managed was to spit teeth and blood at the other as rows of fangs barged their way through his gums, skull cracking and reforming. Griffin flinched then barked over his shoulder: "Find her! I can't buy you much time with this. Urgh! *Stay! There! You don't wanna risk hurting Gyldan.*"

Rukshana made to move forward, protesting: "But I can help—"

"Not with this you can't," Griffin grunted under the effort of thralling the Alkonost. "You've no practice in this, Rukshana. Go!"

Gyldan grabbed Rukshana by the wrist, turning her to face him before she could protest to remain with Griffin.

"Come on! I think I know where she is," he said, looking over at a warehouse behind him. Albion's gaze had faltered for but a moment, but it was enough of a tell. "She can't have finished turning, maybe we can catch her—"

"*No!*" Albion's yell was drowned under the raw tide of the Alkonost's roar taking over him. He bounded forward, breaking free of the vampire's persuasion as a new desire overrode everything else. He struck at Griffin with one mangled arm, partly his, partly the beast's. Talons ripped the vampire's shirt and chest to bloody ribbons, throwing him away. Griffin's head slammed against the ground with a sickening crack, eyelids fluttering closed. "Don't go... near her!"

"Griffin!" Rukshana pulled away from Gyldan's hand, starting towards Griffin. Seraph caught her bodily, blocking her way.

"Wait! I got an idea. But you gotta help me," Seraph said, nodding up to the cloudy night sky. "Remember our back-up plan for me coming out tonight? We need to change it up a little. I'm gonna need the extra boost."

Rukshana began to relax, nodding once at Seraph.

"But I've never..."

"You got this. Trust ya with my life!" Seraph gave Rukshana a wolfish grin, patting both hands against her shoulders. "And, y'know... Gyldan's and Griffin's and everyone else's'..."

Gyldan didn't have time to ask. Seraph rounded on Albion, who had been far too preoccupied with the painful spasms of transformation breaking and pulling at his fatigued body. His writhing performed a lurching shadow play along the pier as the pale spotlight of the moon broke from behind the clouds for the first time that night.

A full moon. With all the chaos of the previous weeks, Gyldan hadn't even thought about the ever-present danger in the sky. The simple act of tracking the cycles of the moon was rooted in his normal life, a life that seemed so far away from now.

Moonlight brushed the pier with a soft grey glow, settling over Seraph like a mantle. Blonde hair spiked up wilder, creeping down her neck and under her leather jacket. She shrugged the garment off as silver-gold fur washed over more thickly muscled limbs, a far more fluid transformation drawing over Seraph than Albion's cumbersome display.

Seraph shot her opponent a fang-filled smirk, a feral growl rumbling through her throat. "How about a rematch, asshole?"

Seraph turned to look back at Rukshana, and despite her bravado, there was a hint of fear echoing beneath the rage that radiated from her. Gyldan had never witnessed Seraph transforming under the full moon, and he had no idea what to expect. If it weren't for Seraph's trust in Rukshana, Gyldan might have run before he could find out.

But regardless of Seraph's bold display of faith, Gyldan's legs still felt like lead. Memories of wolf claws, blood, and his parents maimed bodies burst forth, but he pushed them aside. He didn't have time to confront any of that right now.

A guttural snarl announced the Alkonost. As the grey-skinned beast reared up, tattered wings shaking and horns piercing the skies, so too did the ivory-gold werewolf. Seraph rose up to meet her foe, far larger and fearsome than Gyldan had ever seen her before. She stood taller than Rukshana and Gyldan, with sharp fangs hanging over trembling black lips, golden fur wild and glinting under the moonlight. Long silver claws matched the Alkonost's own terrible ebony talons. The wolf was practically vibrating with energy, muscles quaking under her fur, waiting to chase, to hunt, to kill.

Rukshana brought a hand up to her head, stumbling back. Gyldan caught her, steadying his friend as she winced.

"Damn!" she hissed, scrunching one eye shut.

"A-are you—what are...?" Gyldan babbled, unable to turn away from Seraph despite speaking to Rukshana.

"I-I'm fine! Thralling is—new territory for me. I fear I've chosen a difficult first target..." Rukshana huffed, sweat beading across her skin as she too watched the strangely still werewolf. "Seraph! *Hold the Alkonost off! Do not attack anyone else!*"

The werewolf pounced at the Alkonost. Her teeth and claws smashed against the monster's rough hide and fearsome horns. The Alkonost roared, meeting all of Seraph's moon-boiled savagery with its own mindless violence.

As the pair of non-humans tore at each other, spit and blood splattered over the wooden boards of the pier. For the first time, the Alkonost spread its maimed wings to take flight, an impressive wingspan of leathery stone hide splaying out behind it. A single wingbeat rolled like thunder, bringing the beast skyward enough to rake clawed feet across Seraph's face.

It wasn't long before the monster crashed back down onto the pier, malformed wings flopping behind it like a cape once more. Seraph howled and swatted away at the Alkonost, momentarily blinded. Blood poured from her forehead and dripped down over her brow, staining her light fur.

"Gyldan, go!" Rukshana begged, pushing him away towards the warehouse. "Take the mask and stop her!"

"I—" Gyldan's entire body was locked simultaneously in frozen doubt and trembling fear. He didn't want to leave his friends to face this monster, yet he knew Yanatha could be so much worse. He could just about feel his feet enough to drag himself away, grabbing his rucksack and starting to move towards the warehouse Albion had looked at.

A strangled howl had Gyldan turning back so fast that he twisted his ankle, slamming to the ground halfway between the fight and the warehouse.

The Alkonost had gotten the better of Seraph, despite her moon-heightened strength. With one knee pressed down into Seraph's chest, the Alkonost clawed at the wolf's muzzle, pushing her skull into the blood-speckled boards beneath them. The monster brought its jaws down on the werewolf's exposed throat, accompanied by a wail of desperation from Rukshana for Seraph to get up, to *please* get up, to keep fighting.

Its brutal teeth never reached her flesh.

The Alkonost roared in outrage as a booted foot slammed into the side of its face, forcing it away from its would-be fatal blow. A beat of copper wings carried Griffin into the fray, stealing the Alkonost's attention.

"Waddya want, huh?" Griffin sneered, seeking a way to bring the behemoth under his thrall once again. "*Don't you just want to sleep? That transformation looked exhausting...*"

The Alkonost brushed the wounded Seraph aside, jumping up and grabbing at Griffin's ankle. It missed by millimetres, its movements sluggish and slow as it stumbled across the boardwalk.

"*Sleep,*" Griffin commanded, flying just outside the monster's reach. The creature crashed down onto all fours, struggling against a command that tapped into something so simple, so unquestionable: Albion was bone-weary and broken from the experiment breaking his body, they all knew that.

With a final rumble that could have been a threatening growl, the Alkonost fell against the sea-dampened wood.

Chapter 19

Every nerve ending sparked, demanding Gyldan address any and all immediate threats as they presented themselves. For one moment, the potential risk Yanatha posed abandoned his mind. Only Albion bombarded his thoughts.

He had nearly killed Seraph.

If Griffin hadn't gotten there in time...

If he'd been just a wingbeat slower...

Adrenaline pulsed through Gyldan, making his skin buzz with hypersensitivity. The air was too harsh, and he could feel every drop of sweat crawling under his clothes, running cold tracks down his back. Despite this, his twisted ankle became numb, refusing to hold him back in his fight to survive.

Splinters clawed at his palms as he clambered back up to his feet. Yanking his backpack open, Gyldan let the bag fall away as he grabbed the mask of mirrors from within the bundle of clothes he had wrapped the delicate artefact in. He practically landed on the slumbering Alkonost in his haste to shove the mask over its inhumane face.

He was dimly aware of someone shouting his name, but Gyldan ignored them. He couldn't risk someone dying for this, not while he had the means to prevent it.

As the mask settled on the Alkonost's face, its short snout receded almost instantly, letting the mask fit better against its skull. The beast's whole body shrank down, a muffled but human groan sounding from behind the glassy surface.

"Good thinking, son." Griffin came to land next to Gyldan, squatting down and dragging Gyldan's discarded backpack between them. "I don't think there're any fumes left in this guy to try transforming again. But we gotta move f—"

All at once, the world shattered.

Behind Gyldan, metal screamed and shrieked. He turned in time to see the doors of one of the warehouses peel and curl like a flower bursting into bloom. A blast of heat made him wince away just as Albion stirred and complained at his side. A sloppy arm swiped at the mask on his face, getting progressively more agitated as he did so.

"*Hnngh*... off..." Albion grumbled, managing to squirm and shove the mask from his face. Gyldan grabbed it, torn between the problem in front of him and the nightmare that had arrived behind him. He stole a glance back, though nothing emerged from the ruined doors of the warehouse yet.

Taking advantage of this calm before a promised storm, Gyldan attempted to slam the mask back onto Albion's face. A partly transformed arm blotched with grey skin and two talons smacked it away.

If it weren't for the fear of what was unfolding behind him, Gyldan might have been more afraid of the state Albion was in. Griffin was right—the man had no energy left at all. Anger demanded he transform, but Albion's body simply could not complete the command. One arm was a corrupted mishmash of human and Alkonost, with patches of grey hide and bloody fingernails mingling together. His left eye remained as the beast's tell-tale emerald starburst among a bed of crimson, but the other was glossy and unfocused, an emerald iris searching for answers. Tufts of ebony hair clashed with Albion's silver locks, and bloodied lips framed a chaotic array of blunt incisors and ill-fitting fangs.

"Don't..." Albion managed to cough out around his clicking jaw. One leg pushed against the ground, undeveloped talons cracking from his toenails and scraping across the wood. He achieved little more than pushing himself a few inches along, unable to even lift himself up. "She... she c'n... make us bet... better..."

It was strange to see Albion like this and not feel his heart breaking. Maybe it was because it was already broken. Maybe Gyldan was just tired of hearing Albion's blind judgement.

"I don't need to be better for you. For anyone," Gyldan said, picking the mask of mirrors back up and getting to his feet, leaving the struggling man where he was now that it was clear he couldn't harm anyone other than himself. "I just need to be better for me."

Griffin's hand clasped on Gyldan's shoulder, coaxing him away from Albion, as well as turning him to face the now-wrecked warehouse nearby.

"Here we go," the older vampire grumbled, gently pushing Gyldan behind him. "Wanted a dramatic entrance, huh?"

Off to Gyldan's right, Seraph had regained her composure, standing slightly in front of Rukshana in much the same way Griffin was shielding Gyldan. Though blood matted and tangled her fur, the werewolf was trained on the warehouse, a warning snarl to greet the creature emerging out onto the pier.

Opal-skinned fingers curled around the edge of the doorway, sharp nails clicking and clacking against the metal. A hunched humanoid uncoiled from the warehouse soon after, standing a good foot or two taller than Gyldan. More astounding than the creature's tall frame was the way its metallic skin caught the moonlight, its perfect surface swirling hues of purple and cyan. Yet all this paled in comparison to the fanfare of feathers that erupted in the creature's wake—four wings of brilliant orange and scarlet pulsed with a golden light of their own, burning like a star in the night.

"Yanatha…" Gyldan breathed, a sense of awe washing over him that he could not restrain. Panic shot through his chest then, and Gyldan nearly dropped the mask of mirrors in his haste to put it on. That same panic turned to ash the moment the old mask embraced him once again.

Yanatha finally turned to greet them, though her golden lips did not part to offer words. Her right eye opened, the socket swimming with darkness pierced with silver flecks like a tiny galaxy in its own right. Her left eye did not open, however, and it was then that Gyldan noticed that, much like Albion, Yanatha's new form granted her two extra sockets upon her forehead, though they remained closed.

The creature brushed a lock of translucent hair away from the left side of her face. Her brow creased, frustrated as she attempted to open the stubbornly closed eyelid.

"…No matter," Yanatha said to herself, content to ignore the witnesses to her rebirth. Golden wings arched upwards, and her smooth face angled towards the city skyline behind them.

In one fluid motion, Griffin whirled and snatched the mask off of Gyldan's face.

"Sorry!" he snapped, unfurling his own wings. "S'all in the eyes, kid! We have a chance!"

"What? Griff!"

Gyldan couldn't stop the vampire before he flew away, chasing after Yanatha. His heart hammered in his chest, brain whirling in search of any sign of Yanatha's thrall.

As Griffin approached Yanatha, she stopped mid-air and turned to him.

She smiled.

Her right eye opened, earning a gasp of horror from Griffin. His wings beat forward in a vain attempt to put distance between himself and the new Alkonost, but it was too late.

"*Fly back down, old man,*" Yanatha commanded, watching with a sneer as the now-thralled Griffin dropped down to the pier with a thud, persuaded to obey his natural fear of her. "Now... *why not take a walk?*" she suggested, pointing an elegant finger out to where the pier ended and dark waters began.

Griffin's limbs twitched like a puppet, guiding him away from Yanatha. He strode out across the pier, paying no mind to the rapidly shortening walkway and the approaching sea.

"Let him go!" Rukshana yelled, a blur of feathers and rage charging towards Yanatha.

For Gyldan, Yanatha was no longer his main concern. He bolted after Griffin, praying he could coax the vampire from the Alkonost's mental grip.

"Griff! Griff, stop!" Gyldan pleaded, grabbing the older man's hand and trying to pull him back. Griffin didn't acknowledge him, continuing his sombre march, fixated on the ocean awaiting him. "Griffin! Listen to me! Snap out of it! Please!"

Gyldan dug his heels in, but the vampire wrenched his arm away, leaving nothing but the damned mask in Gyldan's hand as he did so.

"No, no, Griff, stop!" Gyldan yelled, almost dropping the mask into the water as he clawed at Griffin's shirt. The mask clattered and skidded over the sea-soaked boards at their feet. "Stop!"

Griffin shoved him away one last time, knocking Gyldan with enough force to send him sprawling onto his back.

Gyldan lurched up in time to see Griffin fall from the end of the pier, the churning waters devouring the thralled vampire.

A scream curdled thick with disbelief lodged in Gyldan's throat. The world around him shuddered to a halt, leaving him trapped in this awful moment. What could he do other than stare out to where Griffin had been mere seconds before?

He can't be...
Griffin... can't be... gone.

Time and energy surged back into Gyldan's limbs. With a frantic skittering of arms and legs, he scrambled to the edge of the pier to look out for any sign of Griffin. Among the churning waves and lapping waters, not even bubbles remained of Griffin's depleting breath.

She... she's killed him.

Gyldan scanned the water below, praying he would catch a glimpse of the old vampire, anything to dive in after, some small hope.

Nothing looked back at him but the ripple-distorted reflection of his own pale face, grey eyes blending into the unforgiving and murky water.

She killed him.

The words brought with them a spark of fury, of grief, of *vengeance* that demanded Gyldan rise to his feet.

A low growl greeted him as he got up and turned to face Yanatha, at the disaster that was spiralling out before Gyldan.

Standing between him and the new Alkonost, the moon-crazed Seraph snarled at Gyldan, pacing forward.

Something primal in his blood rushed to his legs and screamed at him to run—he was her prey.

Behind the slobbering werewolf, Yanatha was watching the performance with bored regard. At her side, a glass-faced Rukshana offered no assistance to those she no longer even recognised as friends.

"I think I'm getting the hang of this," Yanatha hummed, running a pearlescent hand across Rukshana's dark hair. Then, she nodded towards Seraph. "Pity I can't thrall her kind yet... but then again, she hardly needs my order to want to kill you anyway."

Seraph's lip quivered as it curled, thick canine teeth glinting.

One foot forward.

Claws clicked against the rotten wood.

Gyldan slowly lowered himself to a crouch, keeping eye-contact with the werewolf. He pawed to the side, blindly searching for the mask, trying to ignore the tears that burnt in his throat and demanded to be spilt for Griffin.

He had one shot to best a werewolf in a fight. Somehow, Gyldan would have to wrestle the mask of mirrors on Seraph's face. His trembling arms told him exactly how fruitless this aim was.

Gyldan dared to swallow.

Like a match to a fuse, the motion sent Seraph wild—the werewolf let out a wicked roar, lunging down on all fours to rush towards her target.

On raw instinct alone, Gyldan cowered. He closed his eyes tight, arms wrapped around his head in a pitiful attempt to shield himself from the rain of claws and teeth that promised to fall, his breath stuck somewhere between his heart and his mouth.

But instead of a symphony of wolf howls and tearing flesh, Gyldan was treated to the chiming and scraping of metal, accompanied by a roaring surge of water. It wasn't until Seraph began whimpering that Gyldan dared to uncurl himself, glancing around to find where the expected painful death had gone.

A mere foot away from where Gyldan was rooted, the werewolf was caught in place too. But it wasn't fear that held her down—instead, a tangle of thick chains encrusted with barnacles and salt crystals had ensnared her, the boats around the pier rocking and swaying as their anchors were dragged from the water.

"Coo-ee!"

Gyldan's head snapped around to the source of that familiar, obnoxious, and oh-so-welcome voice. There, striding down the docks, was one Luca de Varis.

"I believe you have something of mine, dear heart." Luca smiled before his expression faltered. His whole face went slack, though something in the way his fair eyebrow twitched told Gyldan that this was not entirely Luca's doing.

Gyldan didn't have time to deal with that now. He had been bought a precious moment by Luca, and he couldn't let it go to waste. He grabbed the mask, dashed forward, and clambered up the slippery, slimy chains that bound Seraph like a monstrous marionette. The wolf snapped its jaws at Gyldan as he got close, but to no avail. He shoved the ill-fitting mask over the werewolf's snout and, as with Albion before, Seraph's skull began to shrink back. Her form shifted and dwindled as her anger died, and she slipped from the grip of the chains.

Seraph and Gyldan landed on the pier with a thud, followed by the ringing of chains dropping around them.

"What... huh...?" Seraph mumbled, an investigative hand brushing over the mask on her face. "Oh... that's... I don't know what that is."

It was strange to hear Seraph speak without a single spark in her tone, without any energy in her aura. But, as with everything caught up in the tornado of events around Gyldan, he could not pause to grieve this.

"Seraph, get yourself out of the moonlight," he ordered her, clapping a hand on her shoulder. The focus was good. Anything but remembering Griff disappearing into the dark sea. "One of the warehouses, go in there, I'm going to need the mask back."

"...Right," Seraph agreed monotonously, getting to her feet. She seemed more like a puppet now than when she had been suspended on Luca's strings. "Right."

"Not so fast..." Yanatha hissed, annoyance bubbling under her calm façade. The perfect Alkonost demanded their attention, and yet, she did not seem ready for an audience. Her jaw was locked tightly, that smug smile all but wiped from her gilded lips. One hand was balled into a fist at her side, and with a strain upon her words, she said: "Luca, be a *dear*..."

With a wave of his hand, the thralled Luca commanded every warehouse door to close and lock. Another wave brought the sea-slick chains snaking after Seraph, catching her by the ankle and dragging her back into the moonlight.

"No!"

Gyldan ran to Seraph's side, only to be blocked by Rukshana landing between him and the bound werewolf. He reeled back, fearful of what Rukshana might do under Yanatha's thrall, but she simply stood as a sentinel, observing his every move.

"Get the mask, you *idiot!*" Yanatha snapped at Luca, then rounded her full spite upon Gyldan, "and as for *you*."

Stars exploded behind Gyldan's eyes, pain shooting through his head with enough ferocity to bring him to his knees. He gasped, palms slamming into beds of splinters upon the boardwalk. Yet... he still had control of his limbs. He could still twist to see Yanatha's distorted face and Luca's twitching, jarring movements.

Perfection seemed to be missing the mark that night, and it was enough to give the broken man a reason to smirk at her.

"G-guess an imitation isn't as good as the real thing," Gyldan mocked Yanatha, a bizarre feeling of freedom blossoming in the face of defeat. "Penelope could thrall four people without *sweating* like you are…"

Yanatha didn't respond with words. Instead, the insulted Alkonost slammed another wave of command into Gyldan's head, a vengeful and petty demand for his half-thralled mind to relive *pain.*

For a blessed moment, the sea-swept pier melted away. The spiking of splinters abandoned his hands, the grief of Griffin's death froze, and the anguish of defeat became a distant echo. In their place, long-buried memories rose from under him, taking flight at Yanatha's command to make him suffer.

The memory of a werewolf crashing through the front door of Gyldan's family home. So stupid. So careless. Why had

Sterlyn risked it? He should have just stayed home. Was that too much to ask?

His mother couldn't do it. Call the authorities. What would it matter? By the time they arrived, they'd all be dead anyway.

Blood. So much of it. So much of it painting rooms that should have been the backdrop to fond childhood memories. So much of it tainting what should have been a safe haven.

White claws plated with crimson, *drip... drip...*

The gaunt, lifeless face of his mother should have frozen Gyldan to the spot, but gods, a fire burnt in every limb, primal and terrified.

He ran, he ran from it all—if he ran fast enough, if he never looked back, then maybe it had never happened at all.

Through the woods, tripping on roots, slashed by branches reaching out at all sides, snagged by thistle and nettles. Gyldan ran from the traumatic memory, air rushing into his chest, scorching his throat, mingling with the panic that throttled his lungs.

"You couldn't save them. You weren't strong enough to do anything..."

A burst of brilliant, luminescent light in front of him, promising salvation—

"Oh, poor Gyldan..." The voice from the light soothed. *"But what if they had been strong enough to protect themselves?"*

"I—" Gyldan gasped out, tears pouring down his face, legs still pushing him through the forest, away from the house, away from his parents' corpses, away from Sterlyn. "I—"

The world fell away once more, throwing Gyldan forward into another memory. He hit the reception desk of Caladrius headquarters stomach-first with such force that he gagged.

"Your dream job, was it not? To help protect humans from them. You had seen what they could do... you wanted to make it right. Once upon a time, you thought just like him," Yanatha chided, a

phantom of Albion walking past Gyldan and across to a far corridor out of sight. "*So... what changed?*"

Fingers flicked through his memories, every movement a fresh pang of pain as Gyldan hurtled through years of recollection. Caladrius headquarters fell away from him, sending him spinning through a flurry of colours and lights, sounds and voices.

"It's none of your business!" Gyldan yelled out into the void, landing on his feet on the concrete outside of the office. It took a moment and a gulp of air for him to settle and process his new surroundings.

Across the road, a commotion was brewing. Several youths—human by the absence of collars and eye-guards—were clustered around a man lying on the floor. It pulled at Gyldan's need to help, his desire to protect those who could not protect themselves.

He crossed the road, shouting at the group to leave the old man alone, exactly as he had done that day. They rounded on him, spotted the logo on his shirt, and decided against fighting. The group scattered, leaving the poor man to get to his knees, spitting blood on the pavement... fangs flashing.

Eyes hidden by purple silk, the older man turned his bruised face up to Gyldan with a grateful smile.

"Hey, er... thanks, pal," the old vampire huffed, starting to get unsteadily to his feet. He sniffed the air once, looking confused. "Human? Wow, not many would risk that. Awful kind of you."

"You're... a *vampire*," Gyldan recounted the spluttering sentiment he had said that day. "You coulda fought them off yourself! You could have... well, y'know..."

"Killed 'em?" the vampire offered, scowling. "Technically, so could you. Honestly, you lot, it's one rule for you an' one for the rest of us, eh? Is it so hard to believe not every vampire goes around killing everything weaker than them just 'cause they *can?* Do *you* go around killing people just 'cause you could?"

"W-well, no, but—"

Something about this vampire went against everything Gyldan thought he knew. He hadn't fought back. He hadn't hurt those guys, even though he very easily could have. He didn't even have an eye-guard's UV light to deter him. Yet, he had not raised a hand to his assailants.

All the stories, all the fears, they were all thrown into question so starkly that Gyldan couldn't help but think to himself—how much did he really know about non-humans? How much of this tapestry had he weaved from the bloodied threads of one awful event and decided that that was enough to judge them all on?

"Ah, whatever," the vampire sighed, looking more upset now than when he had been on the receiving end of several boots. "Shouldn't get mad at'cha. You helped me out there, so, er... right, thanks."

The vampire began to walk away, muttering something about having had his wallet stolen too as he patted his coat pockets. It compelled Gyldan to start forward.

"Wait!" he called out, earning a curious and startled look from the vampire. Gyldan wasn't sure why he had stopped the non-human there. He wanted answers, though he wasn't entirely sure what questions he ought to be asking. "I... I could... I could buy you lunch? I'm on my break anyway s-s-so... so if you... you wanted a cup of er... w-whatever vampires drink after a hard time. Vampire-tea... or... something..."

The vampire frowned at him, but it quickly broke away to a wide grin.

"Seriously? Hey, if you're offering, pal," he replied, shuffling back over and extending a hand out. "I'm Griffin. And a blood tea would certainly set me right, so I shan't say no to that!"

Gyldan reached out slowly to take the vampire's hand, but the scene was whipped away once more, sending him careering through a void again.

"*How heart-warming.*" Yanatha's words echoed all around him as he fell. "*A willingness to change your opinion. Now isn't that a rarity? Still, what did it matter in the end? You still couldn't stop him from dying either...*"

"But I... I just... I—" Gyldan stammered, unable to find his footing, unable to anchor himself, falling further and further into Yanatha's thrall. "I—"

"Hey! Get a grip, nerd!"

Bam!

Pain smashed into Gyldan's jaw, the wooden pier slamming up into his side as he brutally returned to the present day. The mask of mirrors skidded off to his left, and Gyldan blinked stars away from his vision and looked around.

Seraph was under a shadow cast by one of the warehouses, fingertips bloodied and ripped from the effort of clawing her way there while chains around her legs pulled taut, trying to drag her back into the moonlight. She was no longer wearing the mask, having clearly taken it off to hurl it at Gyldan's head.

"Seraph..." Gyldan muttered, dried tears tightening the skin on his cheeks.

"Cry later!" Seraph barked at him, the muscles in her arms quaking with effort as she fought against the chains. "This bitch ain't so perfect! She couldn't even *move* while she had you all spaced out. So, get your shit together, put the mask on, and *fight back!*"

Gyldan took a shaking, sharp breath and grabbed the mask again, facing Yanatha. She had taken flight once more, though one hand at her head gave away her struggle. She was wincing, and Luca and Rukshana barely moved, awaiting orders that Yanatha could not separate between them. Seraph was right—Yanatha's growing power was still limited, and while she had several people under her thrall, she appeared incapable of issuing simultaneous commands...

...Yet.

Even as Gyldan deduced this, above Yanatha's left brow bone, a third eye was starting to peel open.

Her power was still growing. Perfection in progress.

Another pulse of discomfort pushed through Gyldan's skull like a blunt knife, warning him of her gradually strengthening grip on his mind.

He lifted the mask to his face, cutting off Yanatha's influence.

It's all in the eyes, Gyldan recalled Griffin saying. *A third eye... a third species.*

Time was running out, but there was no way he could reach the airborne monstrosity. Such a priceless opportunity of distracted weakness and Gyldan couldn't make the most of it. This was their last chance, but what could he do? He couldn't hope to fight Yanatha on any sort of equal footing. Were humans really so weak after all?

Gyldan shook the thought from his mind.

He had to at least try.

"Gyl... *don't...*"

At long last, Albion shifted and groaned a short distance away, still caught up in his broken body's inability to find the strength to fully transform into the Alkonost or revert back to a human. "Don't... she'll... she'll kill you..."

Gyldan didn't respond, though he knew Albion was right.

He was human.

He wasn't the strongest species. Every person here could best him in a fight.

He was human. He could not fight Yanatha on her terms and hope to win.

Gyldan glanced at Rukshana, who was still standing dutifully between him and Seraphina, awaiting orders. He lowered the mask from his face, considering the hundreds of tiny Gyldan-faces staring back at him.

He was human. Humans made plans and adapted. They worked together to change the world. They faced threats bigger than themselves.

They survived.

That was where their strength lay, and it didn't have to be a bad thing.

Gyldan had to believe that.

He glanced towards the pitiful mess that was Albion, ignoring the echo of sadness in his heart. Albion, who had adapted. Albion, who had changed the world to suit him. Albion, who had faced threats wherever he saw them... and turned that strength towards such cruelty.

"Yeah, well... if you're not going to protect *everyone*, Albion—I will."

Instead of putting the mask back on, Gyldan whirled around and pressed the mask over Rukshana's face. Clarity cleared the haze from her eyes, and she staggered away from Gyldan, making a motion to pull the mask off. Gyldan caught her arms, coaxing them away from the mask. Freeing her from Yanatha's thrall would only free up space for the true Alkonost to thrall someone else instead.

The clock was ticking.

"I know it feels weird," he said, words pouring quicker than his tongue could form them. "But trust me. Listen to me. I know it doesn't feel important, but if you remember anything about any of us—get that mask on Yanatha. You're the only one who can get up there."

Overhearing Gyldan's words, Yanatha gave an inelegant grunt of irritation, her wings spreading wider, burning brighter. With Rukshana freed from her grip, Yanatha looked much less exhausted and far more enraged.

"Idiot! You insignificant, writhing little *maggot!*" she shrieked.

The full extent of her fury crashed through Gyldan's head; every hook that had been pried away from Rukshana's mind now burying into his.

Everything dulled from his senses, save for one, crystal-clear command dripping with acidic malice:

"*Go find Griffin.*"

Chapter 20

"Go find Griffin."

Of course. Why hadn't he done that already? What did any of this matter if Griffin was gone?

Gyldan walked along the pier, the sea spray sprinkling his face. The welcoming arms of perfect tranquillity awaited him. Nothing had ever made more sense to him than to fall beneath the waves and search for Griffin.

Someone shouted his name, but that didn't matter.

Someone shouted Yanatha's name.

That mattered more.

It was as if something had struck Gyldan in the head again. The man staggered to the side, the very edge of the pier pressing into the sole of his shoe, warning him of the suddenly uninviting waters below.

A gasp brought his senses back, his mind returning with a shivering snap.

Immediately, he began searching for Yanatha, expecting to see her bound by the mask of mirrors.

Instead, Gyldan was greeted by chaos—Luca had collapsed to his knees, the chains around Seraph's legs slackening enough to let her crawl into the safety of the shadows. Yanatha had Rukshana held by the throat, hoisted from the ground effortlessly. Yet she appeared to struggle to do much else other than cast a furious expression at someone standing nearby.

He had been released from her thrall, but Gyldan couldn't see how.

"Let. Me. Go," Yanatha hissed, each word clipped with effort.

Following the line of Yanatha's wrathful glower brought Gyldan to Albion. The man had finally hauled himself upright, his disarray of human and Alkonost features taking their toll on his balance.

"*Put the mask on*," Albion hissed, his voice laced with persuasive tones usually reserved for vampires. But when Yanatha didn't move, Albion grew agitated. "Dammit! *Put the mask on!*"

"How did you—? Urgh! Let. Me. Go," Yanatha repeated, her fingers tensing around Rukshana's throat. Whatever grip Albion had managed to wrangle over his daughter's mind, it was as imperfect as his transformation. The stalemate between the Saint-Richters festered, with Yanatha unable to break free of her father's thrall and Albion ill-versed in using his power.

Gyldan staggered forward like a drunkard, sloping towards Albion.

"S'gotta be something she would do. *Could* do," he spluttered, a migraine crippling his skull after so many mental assaults. "Even a small chance, deep down…"

His own words made his soul run cold as he recalled Griffin falling beneath the waves, Rukshana standing guard between Seraph and himself…

Even a small chance... but it had to be something they would do. Something they *could* do. It had to burrow deep into a person's mind and coax out those dark doubts.

Albion caught Gyldan's eye for a second, but he merely nodded in understanding.

"*Let the vampire go*," he tried, and though Yanatha's arm trembled, she did not relinquish Rukshana.

"I'll. Leave. You. Behind," Yanatha ground out, cosmic-swirled irises blazing utter contempt to her father. "Coward!"

This visibly struck Albion, though his change of expression wasn't one of hurt. It was that same slack-jawed millisecond Gyldan had often witnessed just before Albion announced a breakthrough in his work, a eureka moment in another one of his designs.

"*Fight me*," Albion spat, his shoulders hunching in preparation. "*Attack me.*"

The result was instantaneous. Yanatha dropped Rukshana and soared straight for her father, gleaming claws aiming straight for his eyes, golden lips made unbeautiful by a wicked shriek of hatred.

She slammed into Albion, sending the broken man careening across the boardwalk. An ethereal bird of prey, Yanatha circled in flight and attacked again and again, like lightning striking from stars, beautiful and terrible.

Claws cut Albion's flesh; mighty inferno-hued wingbeats broke his bones—the strength of a beast delivered upon angel-feathers.

For a moment, Gyldan couldn't see what Albion's plan had been. If this carried on, he would surely perish.

He couldn't risk waiting for Albion's eureka moment to present itself. Gyldan threw himself towards Rukshana, pulling the mask off of her. If Luca had been freed, Gyldan had to hope Rukshana would be safe without the mask.

"I'm sorry," Rukshana gasped as Gyldan drew the mask away. She reached out for the artefact. "Let me try again. I can get her this time."

Gyldan nodded, handing her the mask and helping her to her feet. Behind him, Yanatha wailed, the sound accompanied by a guttural half-roar from Albion.

Albion swung his mutated arm up and caught Yanatha by the ankle. He twisted around, yanking the perfect Alkonost from the sky to slam her into the pier next to him.

Before she could so much as gasp for air, Albion pinned her down, that same demonic arm grabbing a fistful of feathers and—

—Yanatha screamed.

The chilling sound made Gyldan's stomach clench, threatening to send bile up to his mouth.

Albion threw a torn wing of emberglow feathers to the ground a few feet from where Yanatha sobbed in agony. Golden blood caught the moonlight as it oozed from the ruined limb and spilt over the pier.

"What... kind of *failure* of a father... attacks his own daughter?" Yanatha snarled around her tears, twisting to unleash unrestrained hatred at Albion in a mere look.

The agony of his choice settled like lead behind Albion's mismatched emerald and garnet eyes. He huffed a breath through his nose, too far from relaxed to be a sigh, too hollow to be a laugh.

"The kind who's just upset that his boyfriend broke up with him and wants to prove him wrong," Albion said, though Gyldan knew the man well enough to know that that was a lie.

The once-perfect being tried to escape, a pitiful crawl that was brought to a swift end by Rukshana. She wasted no time in fixing the mask of mirrors over Yanatha's marble-carved face.

Somehow, the mask of mirrors made Yanatha look less aloof. With a strangled whimper, her whole body sagged in defeat. Her head dropped down to the boardwalk, the mirrors of the mask clicking against the wood. To Gyldan's surprise, she did not revert back to her human form, though the milky-filmed eyes that bore out from behind the mask confirmed every emotion and every power was being fractured and deflected by the device.

Albion staggered away from her, and no one moved to stop him. Instead, Luca came bumbling forward, rubbing his temples and looking as though he had been dining on lemons.

"In hindsight, I ought to have been more careful," he announced sourly, making a show of 'accidentally' catching Yanatha with his shoe as he walked by. "That she would already have developed the ability to thrall vampires in so short a time... Still, Penelope wouldn't have been impressed by that ludicrous display. But, she will only get stronger, dear heart. Ergo—"

Luca circled his wrist, and on command, the chains that had ensnared Seraph wriggled over. They bound Yanatha's hands and feet, with some even winding around her skull, keeping the mask in place.

He then rapped the tip of his right shoe against the boards near Yanatha.

"*Break*, if you would." Luca smiled, and the wood beneath Yanatha cracked and groaned.

"No, wait!" Gyldan started forward, grabbing one of the chains to stop Yanatha plunging into the freezing water.

"Oh, you can't be serious!" Luca folded his arms. "People do not change, dear heart! I would have thought your escapade with Albion might have taught you that!"

Gyldan frowned, looking down at the chained woman.

Albion had taught him a great many things. So had Luca, in a similar way. That was precisely why he wouldn't see Yanatha drown. Even after all she had done.

"The mask is on her. She's not a threat now," Gyldan countered. "Caladrius has facilities designed to hold vampires and werewolves. We can keep her there until we figure this out.

We're not killing her, Luca. We can't kill her just because she's more powerful than us. If we do..."

Gyldan looked up then, trying to find where Albion had gotten to. It was only then that he realised that the man was nowhere to be found.

*　*　*

With Yanatha restrained by both the mask and Luca's chains, Gyldan had pulled as many strings as he could to get the highest-trained authorities down to the pier to apprehend the new creature.

It was strictly confidential, Gyldan had said. By Albion's orders. This new species isn't to hit the headlines.

"*I know Albion Saint-Richter*" still held power after all. But only time would tell whether loyalty or fear would win out.

With his streak of phone calls at an end, Gyldan made his way to the end of the docks. Rukshana and Seraph were both sitting there, Seraph with her feet dangling over the side. The sun was rising, chasing away the fear of the full moon and casting a garish light on their losses.

"She deserves to die, Gyl." Seraph sniffed back tears as Gyldan approached. She rubbed her face with a tattered sleeve, hiding her broken heart. "She deserves to die for what she did to Griff."

Gyldan sat himself down next to his friends, watching the waters below.

"...Albion said the same thing about the people who killed his son," he said, his voice low and steady. "And then it spiralled out. Nothing felt like payment enough for his loss. Killing Yanatha won't bring Griff back. And it wouldn't be justice. We know that. It hurts right now... but we know that."

Seraph just sniffed again, unable or unwilling to respond when her nerves were so raw.

"We lost so much for this fight... and we're still at square one..." Rukshana said, her voice barely above a whisper as she looked out across the waves.

Footsteps sounded behind them. Gyldan turned, then immediately sprang to his feet to greet their visitor. Though he was sure Luca could sense his way around, something about an eyeless man walking down a pier set Gyldan's heart on ice. So, he looped an arm around Luca's, guiding him the rest of the way to where they were sitting.

Luca gave him an appreciative, fang-filled grin.

"Forgive me for eavesdropping, but did you lose something? I sensed something dropping into the ocean as I arrived. I did rather wonder if it was something important."

"Some*one*," Seraph gritted out between clenched teeth.

Luca's smile dropped then, and he looked decidedly uncomfortable. It was so unlike him that Gyldan couldn't help but nudge him with his elbow to snap him out of it.

"O-oh. Oh, well... I sent one of the anchor's chains after it as I arrived and hauled it out of the sea... but I left it hidden under here in case it was important and not for Yanatha's prying eyes. I do hope you have a set of dry clothes in that bag of yours," Luca said, swallowing. "Poor thing will be soaked..."

He pulled away from a stupefied Gyldan then and got to his knees next to Rukshana. With both hands grasping the pier, Luca swung his head down to address someone in the gap under the pier.

He can't possibly mean... Gyldan didn't dare hope.

"Ah yes! So sorry, dear heart! You must be frozen!" Luca called to an unseen person. He then pulled himself up, turning to Gyldan. "I can't tell, but he may be dead. Or unconscious. Would one of you kindly check?"

Gyldan dropped down so quickly that he could tell bruises would blossom on his kneecaps in the morning. Seraph had already swung under to look, a cry of joy greeting Gyldan as he hung his head upside-down to investigate the space under the pier and above the sea.

There, coiled by a chain held rigidly above the ocean at Luca's command, a soaked, shivering Griffin lay unconscious. His lips were purple, and raw patches of salt-stung skin blistered over his cheeks, but he was very much alive.

"Holy crap, you dapper son of a bitch!" Seraph exclaimed, hauling herself back up. From the sound of Luca's yelp, he had just been subjected to a werewolf-hug. From experience, such a hug was minorly less painful than a bear hug delivered authentically by a grizzly. "Bring him up, bring him up!"

The chain began to move, gently carrying the old vampire back up and over onto the pier. Gyldan straightened himself up too, crawling over to where Luca lay Griffin down. His heart pounded, swelling with joy and disbelief in equal measure.

For the first time in many months, a true, undeniable smile demanded to be shown on Gyldan's face.

* * *

"Do you need anything? Hot blood latte? Er, a nice hot meal? What about a bath? Baths solve everything, y'know."

For the seventh time that day, Seraph flittered around Griffin like a fretful hummingbird, her nerves palpable by the clenching and unclenching of her hands. Griffin's chest heaved in a silent chuckle, but he waved Seraph away.

"I'm *fine*, Seraph. Jeez, how long are y'gonna keep this up for?" he croaked.

It had been a few days since the incident at the pier, but time had done little to ease everyone's collective concern for Griffin. Sure, he seemed fine, but nearly losing him had amped up everyone's concern for his health. Gyldan smiled and went back to his phone. Griffin would have to put up with this landslide of love for a while yet.

"All right, well, just say, okay?" Seraph said, then repeated with her eyebrows arched: "Okay?"

"Okay, okay!" Griffin laughed, nodding towards the kitchen. "Why don't you ask Luca if he needs some help? Gotta admit the guy can cook, but I still get antsy at the idea of a blind guy chopping stuff..."

"He doesn't," Rukshana pointed out, flicking through a magazine from where she was curled on an armchair. "The knives do. He'll be sitting on the table sipping *my* tea while the utensils do all the work."

"Like a scene outta *Fantasia* in there," Seraph agreed, glancing over at the kitchen door.

The sounds of metal clanging and chopping boards being struck served as their only clue as to what Luca was rustling up for dinner. Not that any of them minded—Griffin was right. Luca *was* a good cook, despite naturally having no stomach for human food. He would always come up with something to suit each species' palette and appeared quite happy to do so.

Seraph's lips pursed in thought and she addressed the group again: "So, he lives here now. We're just... we're good with that?"

Griffin settled back in his chair, closing his eyes.

"Well, he did save my life."

"Oh yeah, I don't *mind*," Seraph replied, flopping down on the sofa next to Griffin. "S'just we never really discussed, he just sorta... swanned in. Besides, hasn't he got his own place? A *bigger* place than this?"

"Probably easier to keep an eye on him here. Remember, he was working with Yanatha originally. Besides, maybe he'll be useful," Gyldan offered, eyeing a notification that popped up on his phone. He scowled at it then set his phone on the table. "After all, we're kinda back at square one."

Another notification lit up his phone. Then another. And another.

Gyldan reached forward and flipped the device over so the screen was facing down against the coffee table.

"Albion?" Rukshana asked, having caught sight of Gyldan's simmering distress.

"Kinda," Gyldan replied, shifting in his seat even as his phone buzzed again. "Work. Caladrius execs have got a lot of questions, and I don't have a lot of answers for them."

"Are you going to go back to them though?" Seraph asked, crossing one leg over the other. "Like you said, we're kinda back at square one. We still haven't freed everyone from the eye-guards and trap-collars, though we freed 'em from Yanatha's impending brain-heist. And Luca would take a few hundred years to get everyone free, so that's out of the question."

"You and Rukshana are free though. So, square zero-point-five," Griffin offered unhelpfully.

His grin disappeared as Gyldan's phone buzzed loudly across the table again. "God, answer it, son. The next thing'll be them knocking on the door."

Gyldan grimaced, but he leant over and scooped his phone up. He tapped open the first of several email notifications. Then the next. Then the next. Most of the same questions, none of which he had the ability to answer yet: *where's Albion, why isn't he replying to our messages?*

He had no idea where Albion was. After the events at the pier, the man had skulked away into the shadows, and with their attention firmly on Yanatha, they had lost track of his whereabouts. Gyldan had checked in at Albion's home, though the fire-gutted mansion offered him no clues. The man had not reached out to Gyldan either, and Gyldan couldn't find it in himself to call.

Perhaps he should. Perhaps he could. But somehow, it didn't feel like the right thing to do.

He tapped open another email. This one brought him to pause, and he leant forward as he read through the message twice.

Dear Mr Crawford,

Thank you for reaching out to Mr Saint-Richter on our behalf. We are delighted that he has been able to get in touch with the board, and though we remain concerned as to his sudden absence, Mr Saint-Richter has expressed his desire to take a sabbatical this year.

Nevertheless, at Mr Saint-Richter's behest and following an extensive review and discussion with the board of directors, we are pleased to inform you that you have been promoted to the position of Acting Chief Executive Officer at Caladrius until Mr Saint-Richter returns from his agreed period of absence.

We look forward to discussing this opportunity with you further on Monday.

Kindest regards,
Miss Aurelius
On behalf of Caladrius' Board of Directors

His shock must have been obvious, as Seraph was already getting to her feet.

"Right, where is he and how hard do you want me to kick his stupid ass?" she asked, putting her hands on her hips. "Seriously, he doesn't get to keep upsetting you, Gyldan."

"H-he hasn't," Gyldan squeaked, then cleared his throat to something closer to a normal voice. "He, er... he's promoted me."

The mood in the room sharply tilted. The unsettled silence that fell over them was only broken by Luca singing in the kitchen.

"Promoted to what?" Griffin asked, though Gyldan could tell the vampire had already guessed by the look on his face.

"CEO," Gyldan murmured, holding his phone in a loose grip that saw it nearly toppling to the carpet. "A-acting CEO. Wh- while he's, er... while he's gone..."

His phone buzzed in his hand, falling between his fingers and to the floor. Gyldan scrambled to pick it back up. He flipped it over and his heart burst with ice at the sight of a text message notification.

Go on then. Show me how it's done, tiger.

* * *

It was so strange, crouching in front of the holy grail of a safe in Albion's office. In Gyldan's office. In Albion's office.

Gyldan didn't want to call it his own office.

It didn't feel like his own office.

Plus, given what he was about to do, he doubted he would have much time to settle into his new workspace anyway.

He punched in the code to the safe and was mildly surprised when the door still popped open. Albion hadn't had a chance to change it then, despite discovering Gyldan's betrayal long before now. There were a few objects inside that Gyldan didn't bother much with—he knew what he needed. A crystal-style USB stick, an old piece of kit to be sure, but Albion had guarded it with his life up until this point.

In a way, it was his life. His life's work… and how to unravel it.

Gyldan thought he would feel something when he picked the USB stick up and removed it from its years-long home. But he didn't. He didn't feel bad at all when he headed over to Albion's—*his*—desk and logged in to the Caladrius network.

He didn't feel guilty as he plugged in the USB stick and scoured through it, finding the release codes with ease. He didn't hesitate before using that very code to send out a signal through Caladrius' Registered Non-Humans Network, initiating the emergency protocol to deactivate all devices.

He didn't feel scared as he sat back in the leather computer chair and watched emails ping up on his screen, a trickle of confusion that surged into a deluge of demands. Capital letters, high-alert symbols—*breach, breach, breach!*

Gyldan smiled as news bulletins picked up the rumours far too quickly, a problem in its own right, but not a problem for Gyldan to worry about.

CALADRIUS MALFUNCTION: NETWORK GOES DOWN, GUARDS AND COLLARS OFFLINE
PANIC AS NON-HUMAN SAFETY MEASURES FAIL
CALADRIUS STOCK CRASH: VAMPIRE AND WEREWOLF THREAT RESURFACES

Gyldan allowed himself a moment to catch his breath, a surge of adrenaline as he realised the exact gravity of what he had just done.

He had plunged an unsuspecting world back into utter freedom.

With a trembling finger, Gyldan switched the computer off without opening a single email demand from furious directors and heads of department.

He straightened his tie in an effort to gather himself and headed to the door. As his hand touched the door handle, a motorbike revved outside.

Time to go.

Gyldan darted out of the office, sprinting down the hall and avoiding any and all faces that turned to him, insistent on answers. Arms reached out but he slipped away, crashing down the stairs and dodging his responsibilities all the way down.

As he reached the lobby, in his bobbing vision, he could see a pair of black-clad security guards approaching him from the front doors. Freedom abruptly looked so far away.

Then again, he could also see Rukshana and Griffin entering the building behind them.

"*Let him past*, would ya?" Griffin announced, pausing to keep the door open for Gyldan. The security guard on Gyldan's right lumbered back and stood stock-still.

"*Stand aside*," Rukshana echoed, the security guard on Gyldan's left obeying as people in the lobby shrieked. "We have to go. Now."

Gyldan burst out into the rapidly manic streets. People were rushing home, panic-paled faces blurring by Gyldan as he headed to Seraph's awaiting motorbike. Sitting astride it, the werewolf was chuckling away to herself.

"Seriously, look at the vampires and wolves, eh?" she said, nodding out to the confused non-humans in the street, watching as humans ran by them in fear despite not one of them lifting a finger. "Reckon everyone will calm down once they notice we literally just want to get on with our lives?"

"I hope so," Gyldan said, shoving his helmet on. "I don't think for one second Albion's had a change of heart, you know. He's just looking forward to saying 'I told you so' when this all goes wrong."

"Then we'll prove that asshole wrong." Seraph twisted the throttle on her bike as Griffin and Rukshana flew away either side of them. "*Again*. Hey, do you think Luca's house is nice? I'm gonna miss our old place, but a big ol' fancy house will soothe the sting."

With that, the pair tore away down the street, the madness only growing as they rode through the city. They were the most adaptable species when it came to survival, and yet, ironically, the slightest change sparked primal fear and panic among humans. At least to begin with.

Gyldan took a deep breath.

He had changed the world around him, and now he and his friends were on the run, abandoning their old home and lying low for the foreseeable future. But he had no doubt it was for the best, and one day, they would be able to enjoy the free world together.

Indeed, he had changed the world around them all. Despite everything, Gyldan believed that humans would learn to

live alongside non-humans. Once they had calmed down, they would adapt to this new change and survive. And no doubt thrive.
They were very good at that.

Fin

Acknowledgements

Firstly, I would like to thank the wonderful team at Gurt Dog Press for supporting my work and for helping me to achieve a lifelong dream.

I would like to thank Matthew, my fiancé, for putting up with my endless babbling about plot ideas, character arcs, and grammatical rules. I also thank you for taking one for the team and reading Version 1.0 of every book I've written.

To Sophie and Leeroy, who have stood by me and supported me over the years. Sometimes, you've even scraped me up off the floor, hoisted me over your shoulders, and ran with me towards victory when I struggled.

To my parents and my brothers, who showered me with endless love and support. I would not be the person I am today without you all.

To my gran, who has always believed in me. You inspire me every single day with your strength and wisdom, and I will be forever grateful.

To my grandad, who taught me to always stand up for what you believe in. You were, are, and always will be my hero.

To Si, for teaching me there are still combinations of swear words and insults yet to be discovered. Several were used in the writing process of this book, but I shall not repeat them here.

To Jenny, for devouring the first version of this book in a matter of days and encouraging me to look into getting it published.

To my Wattpad readers, without whom I would never have gotten this far. Your invaluable feedback and support on this journey will always be treasured.

To you, my current reader. Thank you for purchasing this book, and I do hope you enjoyed it as much as I enjoyed writing it (if not a little more, given the copious amounts of swearing I referred to earlier...).

About The Author

A.L. Haringrey is a British author and occasional archer. She lives with her better half and her lizard son somewhere not nearly close enough to the sea for her liking. She has a degree in English Language and currently works as a copy editor and copywriter.

Ms Haringrey loves a good fantasy book, especially when it dips its toes into the paranormal or supernatural side of things. However, having grown tired of saturated tropes—especially concerning vampires and werewolves—she decided to write her own stories. She started publishing on Wattpad and ended up winning numerous user-run awards. Her works have also been featured on some of Wattpad's ambassador profiles.

When she's not writing books, Ms Haringrey can often be found trying to get several arrows to land somewhere close to the middle of a target, drinking far too much coffee, or playing video games.

https://twitter.com/alharingrey
https://www.wattpad.com/user/alharingrey
https://www.instagram.com/a.l.haringrey/
https://www.facebook.com/alharingrey